T0106609

A Tutor's Guide to Parables Inspired by the Animal Kingdom

Charles E. Miller

iUniverse, Inc.
New York   Bloomington

A Tutor's Guide to Parables Inspired by the Animal Kingdom

iUniverse books may be ordered through booksellers or by contacting:

iUniverse
1663 Liberty Drive
Bloomington, IN 47403
www.iuniverse.com
1-800-Authors (1-800-288-4677)

ISBN: 978-1-4401-0598-2 (pbk)

Printed in the United States of America

iUniverse Rev. 12/19/2008

In Memory of My Mother, Mrs. Mabel McCall (Miller) Campbell Who Taught Kindergarden In the Los Angeles City Schools For Almost 40 Years, A Faithful Servant, A Treasure to Her Family and A True Bard of the Art of Story Telling in the Oral Tradition.

Contents

Introduction

The most ancient tradition of story telling was almost universally, amongst nomadic and barbaric tribes, oral in in manner and dramatic in content. It was only when some form of written communication became a practiced skill that pictographs and hieroglyphs began to eclipse the spoken word. Indeed the oral tradition has never completely disappeared—the popularity of gossip and newscasting is sufficient proof.

A categorical imperative resides in man's psychological and spiritual makeup which continually urges him to re-late to others of his kind what happened. Singers of ballads, the bards of poetry, campfire story-tellers, the king's raconteurs, official soothsayers and messengers of antiquity all worked within the tradition of the spoken narrative. The chief variants, setting aside the events of the narrative, were the charisma of the teller, his voice and spirit—and his oracular conscience, as it were, that insured his preservation of folk fantasy and myth in his chronicle.

I make these few remarks to preface an assumption-long held by myself and others—that the art and craft of story-telling began in the pre-dawn of civilisation in Mesopotamia—perhaps after a tiger hunt or in barbaric man's appeal to his gods of terror. Under these crude yet compelling cradle circumstances fiction inevitably mingles with fact and fantasy with reality. It was necessarily so; therefore the creatures of nature, among whom man dwelled, became both the the objects of the story and the tellers of it. Man has that strange affinity with nature that he can find in the beasts of the field, large and small, and in the fowls, birds and even insects, reflections of his own behavior.

Behavior and not conduct is the right word. In the stories of this collection much of the animal action, if not most, is underlain by ethical choices and their consequences. I think the methodology is valid both to entertain and to instruct, providing the reader will willingly suspend his disbelief and allow his imagination free play. As to the animal-man concept of affinity, it hardly need be mentioned that a powerful attraction to, and a concern and affection for—and fear of—animals is rooted in our prehistoric and primal ancestry on this planet.

The Animal, in the minds of men, is significantly re-lated to nature worship and, assuredly, to the religious e-thos of the cosmos and the human presence within it. Consider, if you will, that the monster Minotaur of Greek myth. King Minos of Thebes dedicated to the god Poseidon each year the best of the newborn bulls, but one year the king cheated on the god and he caused the king's wife to fall in love with the bull. She gave birth to the Minotaur who was half man and half animal. (See Classical Gods and Heroes, by Rhoda A. Hendricks.)

Other wierd animal-man combinations emerge in the myths of the Ancients. The Egyptian Spinx, who is part lion and part woman, posed the riddle for any suitor to the The b-ian Queen Jocasta's hand: "What is it that is of itself two-footed, three-footed, and four-footed?" Grecian sailors tell of the wooing of sailors by mermaids, causing them to wreck their vessels on rocky Mediterranean shores. The Egyptian god Ra, sun divinity with the head of a hawk and body of a man, commanded a following of worshippers. The Kachina masks of the Hopi Indians depict animals and birds within which the man-spirit lives. In Native American Religions, Sam D. Gil 1 quotes Emory Sekaquaptowa, a Hopi:

> "I am certain that the use of the mask in the kachina ceremony
> has more than an esthetic purpose. I feel that what happens
> to a man when he is a performer is that if he understands
> the essence of the k a-china, when he dons the mask he loses
> his identity and actually becomes what he is representing....
> He really doesn't perform for the third parties who form the
> audi-ence. Rather the audience becomes his personal self.
> He tries to express to himself his own conceptions about
> spiritual ideals he sees in the kachina." (p. 72)

The folk beliefs of every articulate people in the earth are the genesis of a rich legacy of the literature of animal lore. Paul Radin in The Trickster writes of the Win-. nebago Hare Cycle that Hare, a religious god-figure, be-comes sacred, empowered to control other animals. I found the dialogue to be a revelation of human insights, cultural myth, taboos, customs and animal idiosyncrasies.

In the classic book by James G. Frazer <u>The Golden Bough</u>, (Avenel Books; 1981/1890), he states that whilest Greek writers attributed to the Egyptians abhorrence of the pig, the fact is "the view that in Egypt the pig was a sacred animal is borne out by the very facts which to moderns might prove the contrry," that is, that the animal was repulsive and evil. (Ibid, Vol II, p. 53) The Omaha Indians whose totem (sacred animal or plant) is the elk believ e d that if they ate the flesh of the male elk they would break out in boils and white spots on different parts of their bodies (ibid, p. 53). "Primitive man believes that what is sacred is dangerous." writes Frazer (Ibid, Vol. ll, p. 55) To the Bechaunas tribe of South Africa, of the croca d il e clan, "the crocadile is their most sacred object; they call it their father, swear by it and celebrate it in their festivals (ibid, p. 55). Anthropormorphism is the representation by a god—in these instances the crocadile. the hare, the bull and elk—of human traits, propensities, motives and passions.

Leviticus| Chapter 16: v. 7-10 of the Old Testament, tells about the ancient Israelitic sacrifice by the Pries t Aaron in which, after the rite of atonement, the sins o f the Jews are placed upon a goat and the animal is releas e d into the desert wilderness as a sin offering to God. In the Western Himalayas a dog is intoxicated, then chased and killed to purge the village of disease for a year. Many countries possess their version of the Corn Spirit, who se exorcism or confinement preserved the crop and a people fran famine. In Germany, "The wolf sits om the last sheaf," says the ancient saying. (<u>The Golden Bough</u>, Vol II, p. 4) A hare, dog. cat. goose, cow"J (ox. bull) pig and horse are similarly represented as the "Corn Spirit." Holland. Sweden. Italy. Norway. France. Germany and Slavonic countries all cling to this superstition to a greater or lesser de g re e . These instances of "parallel invention" thread through out folk literature.

There was a sacred and transforming power in the blood of animals. Frazer tells of how Aegire. a Grecia n priestess, drank blood before she descended into her cave to prophesy; and that the South Indian devil-dancer consumed the blood of a decapitated goat so that he could become a god. "The King of Egypt seems to have shared with the sacred animals the blame for any failure of the crops." (Ibid, Vol I p. 50)

In the folklore of America, especially in Appalachia, instances of human-like animal behavior plentiful, buried a s they are in the memories of a people who have lived in the back woods since our country's beginnings. In Eliot Wigging-ton's The Foxfire Book, Vol. Ill, he tells of the goose that adopted the cow and sleeps with her in the stall. In Volume I, he passes along a mountain tail (p. 345) about a "big ol"thang that one night caught n.y aunt in the road and ch o ked her like a bear."Never did see what it was. It was a bi g thang like a bear." Fear and mystery and an inate love for telling a story come from the lips of these people in Appalachia whose imaginations are rich with tales of snakes. bears, turkey hunts, all born and embellished and invented out o f the folklore of the American wilderness. (Vol I)

D. C. Jarvis, M.D., in his popular <u>Folk Medicine</u>, (p.l7; Fawcet Crest Pub.) writes that "animal laws apply to man as well as to animals. They can teach us many valuable lessons." Examples: Animals refuse to eat when sick, creating a biochemical state which "assists in hastening recovery." Again-"The hen tucks her beak into her feathers when she sleeps so she sill breathe warm fresh air." The fox. when sleeping on top of the ground, "covers its face with its bushy tail so tha t the air it breathes will be fresh but warm." And horses stand with their heads together on a cold day, breathing in mutually warmed air. So much for man's wont to sleep with the window open for good health. One more detail is worth not in g in regards to demestication. The collecting of food and d o-mesticating of animals are found juxtaposed in time, the evidence having been dug up from around 9000 BC, in the Shanidar Cave and at the nearby site of Zawi Cemi Shanidar. (<u>Scientific Creationism</u>, by Henry M. Morris, Phd., p. 190; Creation-Life Publishers. 1974). Instances, verified parallels, ne w archaeological findings and contemporary oral myths, stories, superstitions and regional beliefs about man"s relationships to the animals have deepened profoundly the fascinating history of animal folklore.

In writing this simple collection of parables, I see the fundamental sanity of relating human actions to animal activity, a joyous, a comical, an exhuberant concept that ex tols the majesty of the Creator God and man's poor efforts to gain self-knowledge and insight through His other creatures, the animals. In these stories the parable may not always be visible, but I ask that you not belabor the parable—which is the total story rather than the particularized symbolisms, as in allegory—but rather that you enjoy one, perhaps two or three, as I have enjoyed writing them.

Tujunga Winter, 1990

Whither flies the crow to
seek its own shadow or to know
That whatever it sought man
knoweth not
Yet follows the skyprints of
the bird's wayward flight.

Crow's Gold And The Buffalo Patch

Malagre, a black crow, circled, cawing high above the shifting rise and fall of buffalo backs, snorting stones o f flesh that crawled like shadows pushed about by the pr a iri e winds. Another caawww, caawww. Malagre circled lower, coming to alight on the horn of a cow skull, the animal overtaken by disease, weakness and the snows of the severe winter before. The crow, a bird cautious by nature, eagerly tilted his head and pecking eyes to watch a particular buffalo. Malagre had long distrusted the big beasts because they left no morsel of life—or death—to feed upon. Dead lizards, pieces of a coyote 's kill, the torn shreds of ground vines and prairie seeds in hollows of soil, in spring wells, had thwarted the crow's omnivorous appetite. He would have liked to rid the prairie of the beasts. In this wicked desire he found his friend in the white man| the stranger who with his gunfire slaughtered the thundering beasts. He had brought the huge hulks down to the ground, thrashing in final moments of doom and ecstasy and blood. However. Malagre did not possess that power and he was puzzle d as to why.

He searched, a shiny object caught his eye. He waited patiently until one of the enormous bearded animals moved over a trifle, the width of a thatch. The beast was pawing, had pawed at a spot in the prairie sod for so long that the place was barren of grass. The beast, with its forehoof, scored the soil and had raked it of every blade. What the crow saw was a shiny object, not food. Like most crows, Malagre yearned to express his curiosity, and so he flew in a hop or two down to the ba 1 d spot on the ground. When it looked as if he might seize the object he did so. He hopped to a point beside the object a n d snatched it in his beak. It delighted him as a curiosity, ju st as beads, tinkling shells, nuts and berries tease the curiosity of the parrot or the ground squirrel or the marmot.

Malagre flew up into the air with a flutter and almost dropped his prize. Gathering his instincts, he flapped off in-to a distance ." to a place several miles away. A herd of cows and a train of settlers" wagons had drawn up into a circle. Malagre glided to a clumsy landing on the canvas hoops of one of the wagons, dropping the metal piece onto the floorboards, below the driver's seat. Jessica Turlock saw it fall, picked it up a n d ran to her pa with the shiny thing clenched in her small hand .

"Pa, Pa! A crow dropped this in the wagon seat," s h e said excitedly.

The father, Timothy Turlock, took the piece of metal with hardly a thought, cried "Gold! Gold! Gold!" In only minutes the entire wagon train o f settlers had gathered around him. I t was a moment of pi a y after aha r d day.

"Jessica says she saw a crow drop this."

"What is it, Timothy?"

"Gold—it's a gold piece."

"A gold piece!" men in the party echoed.

"Well, I'll be a rattailed coon!" the cook swore.

"If it ain't a piece of—yup, gold American coin," said the preacher in the party. "But what's it doing way out here on the prairie?"

"Could"ve fallen from another wagon train coming through," said one of the drovers. "They"s more than this one, you know . We ain"t the first to make the crossing."

"I know, I know. Jessica—which way did this crow come from?"

"I don't know, Pa. I didn"t see it. It just landed and dropped it. I didn't see which way it come from."

Timothy Turlock looked up into the sky. He saw o nly the hot prairie blue of the falling day. He shook his head.

"Just dumb luck—just chance." he said to others who remained around him. There was work to done by the end o f dusk—supper, the animals grassed, the guard set up. That night, however, the campfire was fueled by stories of lost gold and of treasure abandoned on the long trek westward, imaginary and real purses of coins, of gold nuggets hidden here and there along the trail by settlers who intended to come back for the m later but never would—and tales of mines discovered and mapped and lost forever.

The day dawned bright and clear, but Timothy Tur 1 oek had not forgotten. His little daughter had the sharp eye o f her mother| Jinny, she who had died one hundred and f i f t y miles back from a desperate fever. Her grave marked the mile along the trail. The gold piece lightened his burden of grief somewhat. In the back of his mind was the thought that if h e could follow the crow he might fine a cache of more gold coins that would help pay for the costs of the trip. Sometimes, venturers buried large amounts.real fortunes that he had heard stories about.

Caaawwwl Caaawww! Caaawww! He could not believe his ears when he watched a crow settle on the sideboard of t h e cook's wagon begging for handouts.

"Feed that crow, Ezra! For the sake of God's l ove l Feed it! It just might show us where more of them coins are.'

"One don't make a fortune, Timothy."

"Just do like I say, Don't cost you nothing." The crow took all the handout fragments the cook gave it and then, without any clue that it would do so, took flight in a particular direction.

"You ain"t going to follow that crow, are you, Mist e r Turlock?" the cook asked.

"Not with this wagon train ,» but if I can borry a horse, I intend doing just that. I can catch up with the party later."

Malagre did not tarry around the wagon train. He set a course directly for the site of the gold. Turlock hu r r i ed to the wagon of his neighbor and seized the reins of the horse that Stinson, the neighbor, was about to ride. Astonishme n t crossed Stinson's face. He grabbed the bridle.

"I'll bring him back, Stinson," Turlock promised."For her sake—Jinny"s sake—let me got" He mounted up, his neighbor released the bridle and he set off at a wild gallop in the direction of the crow's flight. His hat flew down about his shoulders, the mane of the big roan flew in the wind as Turlock poured the fury of his steed and his own ambition out in-. to the open prairie. The settlers watched him go, followed him with their eyes in quizzical wonder and astonishment"

"He' s sure set out for that crow—the Way the cr o w flies."

"I guess he thinks there's more gold out there on that prairie," a friend of Turlock"s spoke up. "Never was one for holding back much."

"I 'spect so—anyways, he's gone," said Missus Stin-son. In a short time the rider and his horse had vanished over a rise in the ground and was lost in the gathering thunderstorm clouds.

"We better get a hustle on," Stinson said ruefully.

"What about little Jessica, Jim?"

"Let her ride with us."

Stinson put the two oxen into their harness, drew the wagon around, and tied the reins of Turlock's animals to the tailboard of his own wagon. "Your Pa was in a pretty big hurry this morning so I figure we'll have go to to find him."

"He gave me the gold coin." said the girl.

"You hang onto it—hang onto it, child," said Missus Stinson.

"We'll find my Pa, won't we?"

"I sho uld hope so, dear," said Missus Stinson. "Now you just get up here in our wagon and ride with us until w e do." The little girl dutifully climbed up the wagon seat, with a boost from the husband and stood for a moment or two watch-ing in the direction where her father had vanished.

The crew flew on, the settler astride his roan in pursuit. Malagre would lead the man directly to the exact patch of bare ground, several miles away. When he arrived over a rise in the horizon, there stretched out before his amazed eyes was the milling, restless herd of thousands of buffalo. Malagre flew to the very beast that had pawed the coin from its resting place in the ground. The black bird alighted on t h e same derelict skull it had first perched upon to watch t he great beast's efforts. Seeing the crow alight, Turlockreine d up at once. He noticed the bare patch of ground, dismounted immediately and ran over to the spot. He kicked at the sod, dug it with the heel of one boot, searched around frantically for a tool to dig with and then, realizing that he had brought his gun with him, he blew a hole in the earth with his Winchester. The sound frightened the big animals and sent some of those nearby into a run. The drooping, bearded head of a-nother mammoth beast nearby, picking up the electricity in the air on its horns, a purple aura, pawed the ground nearby bu t hardly moved. In vengeful anger, as if the beast had cheated him, Turlock put a bullet into its head and it dropped in its tracks.

Thunder now rumbled close by and a bolt of light n ing, jagged, purple and ominous, flasned across the darkening skies. He looked for his horse, but the roan had bolted at the first sound of his rifle and stood off a ways, terrified by the flashing heavens. Turlock stood alone on the prairie, beside the dead buffalo.

One of the beasts broke from the herd and came charging at him. He fired at it but heard only the click of the pin. Another with its head down ran ominously close to him. He swu n g the stock of his rifle at its flanks and broke the gun s t oc k . The buffalo herd—not easily frightened like a remuda of w i Id horses—now began to panic. Then the stampede was on. The herd mass came toward him their hooves rumbling and churning up the dust as they broke up the sod and sent tufts, dirt, grit, fine sand and prairie grass flying into the air. They charged a t him with breakneck speed. Turlock tried to run behind the fallen buffalo, but the great shaggy beast, now inert in death, gave him no protection from the onslaught of hooves. for they ran very close around their fallen kind. A horn caught Turlock i n his clothing and, like a drawn slingshot. flung him into t h e thundering mass of animals. Malagre. the outcast, the evil power, had caawwwd, caawwwd and flown away, gone to his own home.

The crazed buffalo herd, by the thousands, ran toward the wagon train, drawn up into a column but not yet closed up and presenting its oblique side to the onrushing beasts. The crazed herd ran toward the settlers, who had not fully stowed their belongings. Fathers grabbed their children and threw them into the wagon beds—and none too soon as the wild-eyed animals» o n their mouths froth and in their haste an implacable power. ran through the camp. Members of the party scattered where they stood and got into their wagons. The frightened beasts trampled whatever lay on the ground. mangling domestic animals, a few goats, one ox that found itself in the path of the stampede, and a family dog. Close to one thousand passed before their sta r-tied eyes and frozen faces. the wagons gently rocking as t h e beasts thundered by and around the immobilized prairie wagon s" Then, they were gone—beyond, as the rain began to pelt the canvas coverings. The wagon-master, finding little to keep them there, snapped his whip and sang out with the cry—"Wagons-for'd-d-d-d!"

"Is my Pa going to come back?" little Jessica asked Missus Stinson.

"Hard tellin., child," Timothy said. "Your Pa wanted that gold in the worst way. It just may be he—found it—h i s own way."

A look from his wife told him he had not answered the girl's question. "He means—your Pa was—lost out there o n the prairie because he "couldnH give up what he wanted morc'n anything else in the world." She clasped the little girl to her breast and wept. B i g tears welled up in Jessica's eyes. Th e wagon train—as providence would have it—passed not too fa r from where Turlock had fallen under the pulverizing hooves. The sharp eyes of one of the men of the party saw his remains. and while the train paused for a few minutes several of the trave 1-ers, Stinson included, went out to bury in a trailside grave what was left of Timothy Turlock. They kept the girl in the wagon to spare her the sight. The preacher read a psalm, said a prayer—and then the settlers moved on, in the arms of t h e Stinson woman their newly acquired little adoptive daughter.

> A herd of animals will stampede in terror, out of the reach of death and danger. Exhausted, their terror dissipates as their energies subside, though the cause may continue—as bolts of lightning. One may conclude from this that terror is a rudimentary construct of biological nature that is guided by an insepa r-able logic of cause and effect. It has to be a behavior learned b y species training and reinforced by the principle of shared behavior. Thoughit appears mindless to us, the internal logic of terror among members of herds in the wi1d guarantees their survival.

The Rainbow Walker

A highflying bald eagle, glancing, circled the campsight of the lonely camper, his tent staked down beside the quiet waters of the American River in California. The sound of freshets of water dashing and burbling over the stones filled t he twilight for the man. He happened to look skyward. Seeing the bald eagle he ran for his binoculars. He watched it as it cir-cled down lower and lower, intending. he thought, to settle in the top of a nearby snag. That is exactly what the great bird did. Then the man's glasses revealed a strange phenomenon.Clamped in the sharp curve of the eagle's beak ... and difficult t o hold by a tool designed for ripping and tearing—the man thought he saw a hard object that was not a fish or anything that r e-sembled food. The eagle boldly glided down to alight on a nearby manzanita bush, moving its strong wings with a fanning sound to find repose. To the astonishment of the man the bird then flew off as if frightened by a sudden movement of the hand. The bird performed a flyby and dropped a coin close to the camper"s feet.

"I'll be dashed.' the man said.

"Cut you in on something real nice," the eagle said. The man was dumbfounded by the words the eagle spoke, even more by the bird's reasoning intelligence and the articulation. "C u t you in on something real nice" the eagle said again. It occurred to the man that parrots talk—why not an eagle?

"What?' the man said, daring to sound crazy, doubting the sanity of what he was participating in

"The rainbow—gold—the ransom of lives." The eagle alighted again in the manzanita bush.

"Come on with you I don't believe that old pot-of-gold story. That's only so much malarkey!"

"What you believe is not the heart of the matter, shooter."

"I believe what I see and what I know," said the man.

"Do you believe in mystery, in fantasy. in things gone but not forgotten, in broken promises and ugly visions—in just about everything where you— have worked your will?"

"What are you getting at, eagle? I have to build a campfire. It is going to be a cold night."

"You will not need a campfire," said the eagle. The man grew irritated; he wanted to throw a rock at the eagle just to see it take off. The bird excited his imagination.

"You trouble me."

"Gold will redeem you from the shadows of your trou-ble. You have a conscience, I see."

"I hope so." said the man.

"I am glad of that. Listen. Listen to the eagle" s voice. I know where the pot of gold sits."

"Again that same old dilapidated myth. Go away—if that is why you came to agitate me."

"Not the only reason—not the only reason," said the eagle.

"You are pretty clever."

"Cunning. I have to catch my prey—outwit it. And you? Cruel. Cruelty is not cunning. But then it o f ten works in catching—food."

"What works is good/" said the man.

"Most of the time—until failure sets in. What then? What then? Rotting flesh in the wilderness for the buzzards." A long silence followed. "If you will work. exert a little energy, I can find you a remedy and adrug that will always work."

"Utopian—meadow muffins!"

"It will replace your time and conserve your thermal dynamics—"

"That is your gigue, Baldy."

"And—make your enemies look sick."

"Wait! Before you go on any further—why did you drop this coin in at ray feet?"

"It is one of a great many—in the trove up there. in the cache of gold up there."

"Come on—come on," the man said in a mocking voice.

"You do not believe me. That is evident," said the eagle. "Yet—do you not see that rainbow across there—on the other side of the clearing? Where does it end?"

"On the top of that tall cedar snag."

"Good eyesight| shooter! That is right. It rests on the broken end of the snag where—a promise ends and begins."

"Now you puzzle me and I am in no mood for ridd 1 es. I need to build a fire."

"The exercise will do you good. Remember—cruel one that the price of gold is no longer thirty-five dollars an ounce either."

"I doubt all that you are saying," said the man.

"Doubt is your wisdom, bitterness is your worrawoo d, regret is your night's repose and love for others is y ou r scorn."

"You donU lift my spirits a bit, eagle."

"I did not come for that. I came to invite you t o share with me in—the flight of the eagle."

"Come on now, eagle."

"You scoff at the good things of life because that is your style."

"I am just realistic."

"Scornful, embittered—but a good marksman. I have friends who can prove that." The eagle fluttered and with impatience shifted his talons on the branch. "Do I have to fly away in disappointment?"

"You want me to thank you for this coin. Why did you not build it into your nest?"

"Ignorant fellowj This is not the season for building nests. Look up there. Do you see that golden urn. Use your glass eyes. It is filled to the brim with many o f these—tokens."

"I will not go out of my mind to prove you are wrong."

"The climb is easy. Short, broken limbs will provide pegs for your feet and hands. The branches are not far from the ground. You can see a great picture of the countryside from the top of that snag. I promise that you will find gold—many pieces—just like the one I dropped on the ground"

"I will have to exert myself to climb up there and that is painful."

"It is only a short climb and then you are there. What do you say? Come ahead. Leave your gun there, inside your tent and try me—try the climb. You can lose on 1 y your energy and your sweat. It will be good for you. I t is easy and—why struggle? Take it easy. You have ende d the struggles of creatures for so many years. They wil 1 admire you for sharing with them some of their wisdom."

"That—tree?" the man asked.

"That tree," the eagle replied.

The man"s gun leaned against a tree stump, in the e-vent that game should suddenly appear in the clearing. He put the firearm inside his tent. He then walked over to the decaying tree and, throwing his arms and legs around it, h e began t o climb. The ascent was hard and laborious for h e had to hug the tree and scoot upwards, as he had when he was a boy. All the time the eagle hopped upon one branch and then the next above it. A cawing sort of scream, reserved for the nestlings| drew the man upward, higher and higher. The air was cool and rainwashed. The climb proceded without any impediments so that in due course the man drew himself up among the shattered splinters at the top.

"There. I told you there was no pot of gold!" he said.

"But there is, there is/" the eagle cried, "buried i n the heart of the old dead tree. Lift up your eyes. What do you see?"

"Just a rainbow."

"Just—a rainbow?" While the man rested cradled within the crumbling crown, feeling v e ry foolish for allow ing himself to be talked into such an adventure, he heard strange sounds at the base of the tree. He looked down, and to his utter amazement he saw, prowling restlessly about, two huge black bears—and there stood several deer. motionless e x-cept for their gaze upward. One was a doe out of hunting season. A flurry of jackrabbits covered the open ground, alo ng with a cluster of squirrels—and a perfect replica of th a t moose he recalled having shot in the north woods.

"I see you recognize them—your friends. You shot the moose just last summer. Its head hangs over your m a ntle. A real treasure—the rabbits? Target practice. You sold one of the bears to pay for your gun—and your girlfriend got the other. You were a hero in her eyes."

"How—but why—?"

"They are here to—applaud you—if they could. But since they are poor walking, ambling, scampering creat u r e s, they do not possess your hands— only paws—for clapping. They are your—admirers," said the eagle.

"Come on now, eagle. This is some sort of trick."

"They have come to watch you start off—go—cli m b-walk."

"I don't know what you mean. Besides. I need a good look through my binoculars at the landscape. I climbed up here for that—a good look around."

"Take a good look then over your shoulder. What do you see?"

"That silly rainbow everybody talks about. Ought I to see anything else?"

"No, not actually—but you will see it for a long time?"

"You don.t make sense, eagle."

"You will walk back and forth over the arch of the rainbow for the remainder of your days and the rest of your life—forever."

"My life—forever? I don't understand you. These animals—"

"They would not take your life—unless you try to go down. They hunt for food. You hunt for the pleasure of killing them. That is wicked."

"Say, what is this? Are you a wizard or a magic i an or some—reincarnated witch doctor?

"You can never go down again, shooter. They will attack you and devour you."

"With love, I suppose. You canU keep me up here any—longer." The man began to descend. As he did so he heard the bears clawing wildly on the dry wood at the base of the old tree. The small animals ran around in a frenzy and the moose gave out with a bellowing horn call.

"You see—they will kill you—but while you remain up here they will fear and admire you. After all is tha t not what you have wanted all the time?"

"No, it is not what I wanted! Wait—if I get m y gun—"

"You will kill them. That is your purpose for the gun—to kill for the love of killing—and that is evil."

The man looked down and then at the rainbow, stretching in colors arrayed over the late afternoon sky.

"I will die."

"Our God will protect you—wicked one. Dominion over life was yours, but you mistook the intention of the Creator. Dominion means care, not extermination." The man sat and pondered the eagle's words for the longest time. "S o—why do you not arise. You are getting cold just s i tting there, and begin your—journey?"

The man slowly stood, his legs unsteady, atop the tall snag. Shaking and with painful caution, he stepped out into the brisk air of the afternoon and began his end less journey across the rainbow. It was his condemnation that he should, for eternity, have to walk back and forth over the spectral arch in penitence for his mindless slaughter of the animals—they who continued to watch him with upturned eyes at the foot of the great snag.

"The arch has good footing," said the eagle. "You will not need to eat or sleep along the way. You will feel no pangs for the things of this life."

The man began his centuries-old pacing over the rainbow. The eagle flew away into the falling sun to settle a-top its own snag, 'distant from the man's gun. The animals remained transfixed while they watched the shooter g o forward upon his crossing the bridge and turn into a speck in the luminous grey sky. Far off, a wolf howled in it s loneliness. and in its instinct for death.

The High-class,
Low-brow Elephant

It has rained and rained and then rained some more. Mud like black lava clung to my legs and sucked at m y big flat feet. It clogged the forest trails where I walked and tarred my trunk, thick and sticky. Of course, an elephant may seem to make small talk out of mud, but not me. The mud squished and sucked and gurgled when I walked.

I worked in the mossy, deep woods of Ceylon—teakwood, some purplewood—pulling those hugs logs after the cutters felled them. Work, work, work. But then, Thimbal, my driver, was kind to me and almost never layed the lash to my thick, wrinkled hide. I weighed a considerable tonnage, and I was against running through the woods. Thimbal called me <u>Plod</u>, short for Plodamaranath" Strange name. Ex otic name. The only thing exotic about me is my A-flat trumpet. Ahhh, eeeehooooooooweeee!

I was pulling this heavy log one day and Thim b a 1 leaned down from the top of my head and whispered into m y big, flappy ear. "Put it over there—on top of the others"

I saw the pile off to my right and so, wrapping my powerful trunk around that particular log I swung the end into position and pulled it with my leather head harness and chains to the mounting pile. Thimbal unhooked me and I lifted that boggy. watersoaked, sapfilled teak log to the top of the stack. Pretty shaky and as slick as elephant grease. Those logs were still wet and the forest moss was like hark. slime between them.

We then turned and plodded back into the cuttings again where some men were chopping away with their ax e s. It was hot. Rain and heat made the mosquitoes explode into the air. They stung the insides of my delicate ears. I flapped them to keep cool—like big fans, and plod, plod we went into the dripping dark to fetch out another log.

We had not gone two hundred meters when I h e a rd the most awful crash and rumble and splintering sound-caaarunnnnch! What a sound! Then—the trumpet sere a m of an injured brother and the shriek of a man crushed beneath the logs. It was all over. That high stack of teak logs had rolled and crushed the legs of one of my brothers. The tumbling cut trees had killed a driver. Bio od mixed with mud that morning. It was horrible. a brutal accident in the woods. Then there followed the wild, excited shrieks and shouts, the clank and clatter of harness chains as <u>Josephus</u>, my younger kind, dragged the logs free and to one side. The driver was a skinny, little fellow in a loin cloth and turban whom others called Nirvo.He was as dead as a buried rock. Some of the workers pointed their bony fingers and angry eyes at me as the cause of the accident. My brothers flashed their trunks and trumpeted at me in disapproval of my very presence in their midst.

I heard Thimbal arguing. "He is a good elephant. but he does not think for himself."

"He is dangerous around here, Sahib." said th e other voice. Men were prying the killed driver from b e-tween the logs and wrapping him in a sheet.

"I will not get rid of him no matter what you say. It is my fault."

"He is wild. He is untamed. He does not obey commands."

"I do obey commands./" I thought, but I was tired of work in the woods.

"<u>Plod</u> must go!" said the strange voice.

"Perhaps he needs more—leisure time away fro m pulling logs for good behavior. The Sultan? A zoo in a foreign country?"

I sucked up a trunkful of muddy water and dou s e d Thimbal with it to show him my love for him. I also tugged at my chains to show him that I still wanted to e s-cape from this drudgery.

"I cannot find so intelligent an elephant to work here in the woods. "Thimbal said.

"We can get along without ill-tempered elephants.The gods have cursed his brain. Buddha has deprived him of the wisdom of the elephant. And we have many hectares to e u t still. Even now the axemen have caused us to fall behind.In another month the creek will rise so that we can get the logs down to the river. We must work faster, and this is very big work. But Plod—he is too untamed, too stubborn."

"Will you not give him one more chance,"' Thimbal pled.

"Well—perhaps. See what you can do with this. I n side the forest about one thousand meters the rains and the animals have dug a deep swamp hole.

Seepage keeps it boggy. A man could easily disappear from sight if he stepped into it—and we cannot afford to lose any of our laborers. It has to be filled with dirt. Take <u>Plod</u> and fasten the spike. heads to the ends of a cut teak log and drag dirt to fill in the swamp."

"Yes, master. We shall do it today." Thimbal was talking to the overseer. We set off again and soon reac hed the place of work. He hooked my chains to a log, dim be d astride my knob of a head, and I began to drag dirt and loose rocks from the forest floor into the pit. It was a very deep hole, and it took many trips with that drag to gather the dirt and stuff to fill it. In fact the day was stretched thin by the sun, and then it got dark like a gemstone at night, dark early in the Ceylon woods.

We were making sure progress, clank and rattle, a jab from Sahib Thimbal now and then. I was not looking when—<u>kap-loosh</u>!—I slipped and both of my hind feet dropped down into the oozy bottom of the swamp hole. Thimbal flicked his switch on my flank and across my back, but I just could not get my hind feet up onto solid ground. Then, pretty soon, as the bank crumbled away my two front feet slipped on the rainslick sides of the hole and they also went down in, deep. <u>Burble</u>, <u>burble</u>. I gave out with an A-flat blast on my trumpet. All I really needed now was for me to fall over and I was gone. I would not be able to arise. Imagine—tons o f real live elephant stuck in a forest mudhole. <u>Plod</u>. I put Thimbal on the embankment with my trunk. He scratched his turbaned head and muttered strange words.

"You stay put and I will go for help. He left o n the run. Meantime I could feel myself sinking deeper a n d deeper into the bottomless pit. Thimbal soon returned with the overseer.

"This is the last slop. the very last slop for <u>Plod</u>." he said. The McCaw bird screeched and the monkeys fled into the treetops at the sound of his voice. It was frightening.

"Won't you give him another chance?" Thimbal begged.

"Never! He has had his last chance . even if al l of Ceylon turns to sand. Pack up your trunk—<u>Plod's</u> rations of fodder and two worn blankets. I am selling his services to the Sultan."

"Oh, no, no I" Thimbal cried. "Then my gentle, old <u>Plod</u> will have to wear all those stupid bangles and a chair on top of his back and blankets in the heat—and rings fro ra his ears—and colored pads and blinders and all that jewelry stuff. He will not look like an elephant any longer but only—a thing."

I sighed with a weariness in my plight. I would have to part from *my* forest mates. They would grieve forme. I sucked up some thick mud and blew it over the head and into the eyes of that overseer. I covered his turban with goop and his face with forest mire.

"You will learn some manners from the Sultan." he said in anger.

"I know about obedience," I said.

"He knows about obedience." the overseer said

"His body language tells you that he obeys commands," my driver replied. "Is that not enough?"

"The Sultan will teach you not to complain so much."

That was a shock, since I do not recall doing much complaining—ever. Orders were orders. Thimbal packed the gear, I hoisted it up onto my back and four others of us slogged off through the quagmire and forest to Timbucktoo and to the palace of the Sultan. Once there, I overheard gossip about how his new concubines needed some sort of transpor t to get them about on the streets. Walking was not good e-nough for them. It happened that I was chosen *one* of the five living jitnies. Thimbal Satara came with me, ray Groom, they called him.

A month broke us into the palace ways—like the circus ring my forest mates used to talk about. The air w as always perfumed with burning incense and all around me I saw dazzle, glitter, reds and blacks and golds and I heard the weird sounds of horns and bangles and the jangle of c o p p er bongs and nut shells. I walked in some parades. I was outfitted mighty prettily, washed down every day beside the riv-er. Slaves doused me with buckets of water and naturally I turned my own hose on myself to cool of by. Mine was a life of luxury and Thimbal almost had nothing at all to do w ith me any more. It was a different life, what with the rich Sultan and the elephants all gussied up while we walked an d cavorted around the city, showing folks in the streets how rich our boss was.

Then one da?" my stubborn streak got the best of me, when a handler told me to roll over because he wanted t o scrub my other side with that thick, big brush made of thistles; they scratched even my thick black hide.

"Roll over, you lug dumbo!" he shouted at me. With a piece of chain he struck me across the flanks. I wanted to crush him and scrunch him like a miserable little sa t in pillow. But Thimbal, who had seen it all, came running up. There was a fight between Thimbal and nay enemy. Thimbal won but from then on the parade master put me at the end of t h e parade column. Words soon got around about ray bad temper "I had my flareups. A squeel and a trumpet and an inner explosion.

Why, the handler asked, did I not enjoy the p a l a ce fodder? Was it too delicate—like yams and peanut wine, like cedar-bark soup and orchid petals? The poisonous grass they fed me gave me the bloatations and made my insides rumble.Bar the rest of the day, when I refused to eat their palace slops; I had to stand around and look nice and gentle and tame and happy behind a fence strung with pearls. What a putrid fraud I was! What a boret

The whole scene was an upchuck mess. I am a wild animal meant for the forests of Ceylon.

I could not stand things any longer. I went into rebellion mood and threw some bales of hot pepper stuff a t my handlers. I ripped up their corral of skinny tree trunks-stickwood splinters. I blew t unksfull of water at them and trumpeted at the top of my fine lungs. I was a bad one, all right, and then and there I guessed the retaliation by t h e royal Sultan. He wanted to get rid of me and send me back to the woods.

Poor Thimbal—he wept against my hide and I flapped my big ears. His happy life had turned into a real tragedy.

"We have to go back/' he said to me between sobs one night. "Back to that nasty woods boss."

I communicated to him that he ought to let me handle matters this time. Work, work, work—that is what I wanted.

"You will not complain about the work this time—by deliberately falling into a mud hole?" He lifted my blind-ers; elephants were not supposed to see the maidens of the harem—only the Sultan's eyes, fed on their beauty. I communicated to Thimbal that he could ride with me whenever he wanted to—he always did anyway—and he could sleep on m y straw and share my fruit and nuts and other dainties of the woods—forever and ever.

He said that I was such a big, old hunker of a kind elephant; that he, himself, had helped to bring this trouble upon me and others by his harsh demands for obedience.

"Nonsense!' I thought. After all. he had not cut off my tusks and he had not chained my legs to keep me from running away.

"We shall go tomorrow, back into the woods of Ceylon."

I was ready on short notice. A day and a half later I and Thimbal hove into the woodcutters" camp. Let roe tell you there was real rejoicing amongst the bothers. The fact is they were so glad in their grieving—they had wilted a—way i n months of sorrow—and they were so all-fire joyf u l to see me that they threw a big party of baked bananas cooked over a dung fire for flavor. A real woodsy sort of welcome back.

"And I am here again to tell you that—well, let-<u>Plod</u> speak for himself, "Thimbal said.

So I communicated that I would never, ever a gai n say another bad word about work, because what was not wo r k was the pits—turning us into dainty, sickening, pamp e r e d beasts of burden. And that described my place in the palace of the Sultan. My elephant brothers ought to feel glad over their plain food and their simple life in the woods out there.

"No more chafing about drudgery?"

"Never again," I squeeled to Thimbal. "And I will watch out for all the mud holes."

"You will obey—always? You will not cause t r ou-ble in the camp?" I swung my trunk in a slow arc for "yes", and I spewed clear water over Thimbal. He liked the spray job and so he smiled happily.

"Good—then we are home at last—life on its own terms." he whispered to me over the top of my big ear. All my brothers at the homecoming feed gorged like gluttons on the roasted bananas as a token of their esteem and love for me, Plod, and for my driver Thimbal.

> Why should the dumb creatures that man trains accept hi s caring, his caressing when down through unrecorded history there was always prim a 1 estrangement between man and beast? What is the explanation for the simultaneous attraction and repulsion whe n the utilitarian competiti o n for food and survival is satisfied? Does the curiosity of an animal in the wild towa r d man furnish a bridge for rudimentary co-adaptation? If so, then the utilitarianism o f evolutionary theory lacks a singular dimension—prim a 1 curiosity.

Amongst The Pharaoh's Edibles

Chatter is my name. I come from a long line of herbivorous. grain-eating grasshoppers—locusts to be exact.My legs are made of spring steel and ball joints. I am slender and spiney. I can fold my legs for a leap from a crouch. We are strange, green hopping noisy wing-chatterers" Our wings rattle when we huddle together for a meal. They are as thin as a maiden's whsiper but as strong as papyrus reeds and in fli gh t we are something awsome. My eyes are as big as buttons and my nibblers as neat as garden clippers. We are all pretty much made of the same stuff—see-through green, high-strung busy-bodies. And we work at eating.

One day I flew belly down from this date palm. The desert dates were still hard and I had taken scarcely a nibble. In my descent I fell upon a Turtle Plant, a plant that turns its belly upwards when the sun gets hot.

I said to him, "Upside down one."

"Are you talking to me?"

"I am not talking to those Tiger Lillies over there." I had not heard them give off with a roar all morniag.

"What do you want?" Turtle Plant asked.

"I got a proposition to put to you."

"What is it?"

"I have been told to look in on the Pharaoh at his palace and I have other things to do. I was wondering if you would stand in for me."

"But I am only a weed in the Pharoah's garden, . said the Turtle Plant. A fresh flow of tears dimpled the hot desert sand.

"Then I will cast my spell upon you and give you legs."

"Legs! Legs!" A grasshopper has a heart, but is is hard to see under all that green schmutz. Now Turtle Plant no longer had to stand rooted in the garden of the Pharao h but he might go whereever he wanted.

"Why do you do this for me?" he asked.

"With ray special magical powers I wish to help others."

"Your magical powers?"

"They are mine. Watch." I leaped over to a prya-canth bush and destroyed a leaf in an instant. I leapt hard again, my springsteel legs and oiled ball joints lofting me into the same date palm. "Hey, Turtle Plant 1 I'm up here!"

I heard a voice emanate from the hollow shade cast by the palm. It possessed the brightness of sunlit sand in a mirage; it cast billows of blue smoke down around me a n d the Turtle Plant. "Chatter! Who gave you the powe r t o transform a plant into an animal?"

"Nobody," Great Thunder."

"Exactly. You got it right that time." The thunderous voice in the desert spun dust into my two thousand eyes. "You are arrogant, grasshopper. You deserve punishment."

"I am a free locust. My legs are like springst eel and ray joints are well-oiled and my wings fly like the gentle promise of a maiden."

"I have heard all of that bragging before. You are still an insect. But you have stepped out of line."

"Sorry."

"That is not enough—to say you are "sorry'."

"Turtle Plant"

"Listen up! You are not as free as you think you are. I made you—you will obey me."

I hopped into a nearby agapanthus plant. "It is hot out here in the Egyptian desert."

"You possess the gift of chatter in your wings—a matter of rhythm when numbers of you get together. The Pharaoh has one weakness—he loves the sound of rhythmic chatter produced by millions of your kind . grasshoppers shimmering, whirring, shaking. tearing. thrashing—"

"He does?"

"That sound turns his harm to running and squeeliug with fright. The very sight of his wives fleeing thus is as sweet to him as a thousand agapanthus blossoms or Nile lillies. He comes down to the water just to listen to your mu-sic."

"He does?"

"He does. The Thunder Voice had no sooner uttered these words than the Pharaoh appeared dressed in his helmet of g old, blue beads festooned around his naked chest, about his waist the royal blue, gold and black loin cloth. He scuffed his Egyptian sandals on the stone steps. He stood in one of the porticos, his gaze out across the desert toward the pyramids.

"I have to get rid of that Moses!" he muttered wearily into the evening breeze. "That insolent Jew wants to control myself and all of Egypt. By the gods he would convert ray palace staff to his religion if he had his way."

From royal lips he spun threads of crafty bronze lies. He waved one arm like the jib of a Nile sloop, mighty and u n-yielding. Removing his helmet of solid gold, he sipped wine from a goatskin handed to him by a black slave. "I will get rid o f him and yet—I need his followers for slaves. They are craftsmen in the building of monuments—and 1 have one or two pyra-mi ds I .i. to finish .But—they shall have no more straw for their bricks while keeping to their quotas. I shall measure their god by the sun's shadow."

While the Pharaah stood there making these pronouncements and dizzy with wine and power, mirroring the sun into the ea v e of his mind by day, one of his spouses came flying up to him. She was a sumptuous maiden whose voice conveyed the soft buzz of the mud hornet. "Oh, wise Master— wise Master—do not listen t o that insolent brickmaker Moses."

"I did not intend doing so."

"See how the statues out there gaze with adoring eyes at you. their wings motionless out of reverence for your r o y al divinity?."

"Yes—I do believe "I see those—adoring eyes."

"Quaff another drought 0, Master for you are great and powerful."

"I know that. I know that—and—Moses? He has his God."

"Papyrus juice," the Pharaoh"s harem wife explained."His God is nothing compared to you."

"That is true. That is true—although he does not believe it is so." She threw her arms around her Sire's neck like a string of hammered gold beads. My grasshopper vision of 2000-2000 took in the entire scene.

"Down to the smallest grain of sand, you are the sole proprietor, owner, manager and bossman—of all the mysteries of the Nile.

"What ought I to do?" he asked his wife. Plainly ther e was a number eight tattooed under one arm.

"Harden your heart against those swarms of Jews. Do not let one of them escape from their overseers—or let death b e his penalty for the offense against you, 0, Great Pharaoh."

"I find pleasure in your words, *my* concubine."

"They intend to make off with your wisdom trinkets and your magic bracelets."

"That Moses needs one hundred lashes to quiet his rebellious spirit."

"Take care, Sire, that such a drastic measure does not inflame the Jewish masses. Though some would stay, others are already in a passion to revolt. As you well know, they dwelt here in Egypt for almost four hundred hears—no small time."

"At what a cost—slave labor dearly bought!"

"Our crops are to be havested soon, And the A ssy-rians watch us with hot. covetous eyes."

"You are a woman of fine spirit and intelligence my plaything."

"A half a million starvlings is many. Sire."

"They are a drain on my gold and my palace garrison soldiers—but—I have come to depend upon these—Jews.'

This scene I watched with my 2000-2000 vision. in living color. It gave me a rhythm to go to the Phara oh's with song and dance—cousin cricket on the strings."

"Chatter!—where are you? Chatter! Chatter."This time the Thunder Voice came from a huge stone urn stan d ing in a portico of the palace. The Pharaoh and his wife number eight had beat it up the steps to the inside where they could joy it up together. I flew-lept to the rim of the urn and peer e d inside. Empty.

"Chatter!"

"I hear you. Great Thunder.

"Gather all your clan together. I have a s trategy for you."

"Snap, snap, snap. What is the plan?"

"Take all your friends and relatives and go i n t o the palace of the Pharaoh and—dine at leisure. No i t em on the menu is too costly."

"The Pharaoh calls himself god. He is—"

"A fool. Chatter."

"He is about to be squashed like a pomegranate under a chariot wheel."

"You are a very perceptive grasshopper. He thinks my people belong to him. They are mine. my children. I am God."

The Thunder Voice flashed fire from the urn and smoke changed into a cloud of gold dust. The heat was something awsome. That urn of stone burned clear down to th e floor of the palace.

"I hear why the Pharaoh rants and raves. What have I got to do?"

"Fly into the palace and commence to nibble o n the furniture upholstery. Take your best appetite. Inspect every room. invade all rooms. Leave no closet untouched. Everywhere you go, you gnaw, chew, spit, nibble, grind, c oug h and swallow. Understand?"

"A diet fit for a king. I.d say."

"Chew on the drapes and on the table cloths. You fray the rugs with your sharp cutters. You make the bed of the Pharaoh green, a covering of live insects. Send his ladies screaming and make the eyes of the eunuchs big with terror. DonH forget to taste the table foods—fingerlicking goo d some of them—and sample the fruit, grain, the cook's bakery cakes and breads. The wallpaper?. cloth, but tasty. Sample the wardrobe—lay off the beads; they will give you indigestion. Leather work is smart—the Egyptians oil it with sheep oil. And try a gnaw or two of the taper wax. Stay clear o f the wine. You will only drown,"

"Sounds pretty tasty to me. Highclass dining!"

"I knew you would understand."

"ArenH some of these things—poisonous?"

"Do as I tell you. Go into the royal pantry and re-. fresh yourselves on the Pharaoh's dainties. Fly clear of his pools or you will fall into them and, again, drown. The same goes for his win. skins—which he keeps unstoppered for his own emergency use."

"I hear you, Great Thunder."

"Make havoc. Life will be short for some of you. You will become casualties—but it is a noble campaign. Is the plan clear?"

"Will I survive?"

"You disobeyed me in your actions with the T u r tie Plant. Now you must suffer the consequences for your—wicked magico You now have lost your freedom to fly high in the sky. Henceforth, as punishment, you must be content to lea p about and soar close to the ground. That is forever y o ur fate ."

"Just—land for a good chew and back—high altitude stuff is out?"

"You got it right, grasshopper.'Now when night comes, you will make a lovely snapping rhythm for the Pharaoh just to torment him. That will be his concert of the winds—th e song of the pyramids. His dancing girls will scream w i th fright and send wild echoes throughout the royal palace. Those sounds together with the stench of death from your kind by the billions will get the Pharaoh to vomit up his pride.

I chirped to all my friends and kin-hoppers. Like ripples on a pond. ray summons rolled throughout the oasis and over the hot eastern sands, through the shimmering heat waves and up into the constellations. It was a buzzing, thrumming, whirring sound—our wings clacking and chattering. A strong wind from the east brought in new detachments. While I stood on the topmost date of a palm, inspecting the troops. I s a w that we had plenty of grasshopper power to do the job. I sounded the cry of battle;

"SnapI Snap! Whirrrrr! Snap!."

The thrilling call to "formation" rang out as we marshalled our strength.

Then: "To the Pharaoh's palace and gluttony or-death!" I shouted.

"To the Pharaoh"s palace and—gluttony or—death! "rang the echo from b i llions of grasshopper throats.

Before I could say "mandible" a strong wind from the east. a thermal, sprang up anew and we were winging our way to the palace of the Pharaoh.

I cannot describe the scene of pandemonium, of s h eer delirium and confusion. that broke out when we flew in througb the portico doors, through open windows, through the parlor. the pool area, the quarters of royalty, his harem and his eunuchs. I followed the battle plan to the letter.

The Pharaoh was enjoying his daily bath in sfiake oil when we showed up. He flipped out of that tub like a si ick melon seed, grabbed a towel and went running down the corridor like a raving maniac. He almost slipped and fell over my comrades a couple of times. We flew hither and thither, w e flew yon and beyond. We gorged ourselves-oh, how we ate! until our flat bellies turned round and the stench of excrescence grew. This was our glorious time of orgy and affluence. And we stayed on, the rooms of the royal residence a whirring mystery of sound and jiffy-eating satisfaction.

That first night I assembled a small company of good friends and we tuned up our wings and legs for a concert-like the drums in a band. We made rhythm for the Pharaoh. How we made rhythm! A small country-cousin cricket section, lying idle in the cracks of the stone floors, came out to join with us in musical masterworks of sound. There hasn't ever been anything like it in the world since.

The Pharaoh did not enjoy us one bit. He stuffed ragweed into his ears and buried himself under a pile of quilts. He gave orders for his sweepers to appear meantime—aimosta hundred in all—Assyrian black men with papyrus leaves i n their hands. They commenced to sweeping our troopers into piles and creating more stink. Yet there was almost too many of us. The palace guards then came with their burning oil torches. They caught some of us unaware—more by ace i dent. They sizzled grievously. But there were so many in our bat-talions that we surrounded the flames of the torches as i f they were not lit and burning. We actually put out the flames by sheer numbers, like a glove drawn over the torch. A horible sacrifice!

We covered the window openings so that the rooms were like night inside. We crackled, landed, hopped and buzzed all over the Pharaoh's dinner table, his plates of gold, the fruit, cooked dishes and linens. Good-? Let me tell you "belch, belch. He had just set the dinner for his guests an d his harem favorites, including concubine number eight. And we made the table crawl, I can tell you. Soup of hippo fat, cucumbers and frogs weren't bad, and the bowls of grapes, pom-egranites and dates were not too bad either. Ours was a mission of consumption. We gorged, we feasted, we rambled and slithered in the slops of pure joy. We chopped and g u l p ed and tasted and compared.

At last the Pharaoh came out from under his stack of quilts, and was he ever raving mad! "Moses! Moses!" h e screamed. The renegade was nowhere to be found. He calle d his servant—I was right there in the room with the Pharaoh—"Go and fetch that blackguard renegade, Noses. He is down at the brickyard. You tell him that he can start out tomorrow morning—if only he will wave his magic staff over these swarms of insects and get them out of here. They are a plague""

The messenger carried the word to Moses. He a p-peared before the Pharaoh the next night. "You are a hard man, '"the Jew said to his Egyptian master. "But do you think you are going to get rid of my people and the gr a ss-hoppers in one sweep?"

"Just get those filthy insects out of here. I know you are the cause. They have already eaten up my most expensive table linens, my priceless curtains and the silks of my beds—to say nothing of my irreplaceable wardrobe and ceremonial garb."

"What will you—give me in exchange for my ridding you of this plague of pests?"

"You may go—and take your people, the Jews, with you only remove this—this hideous infestation from my palace and my land."

"Are you saying that I and my people can depart forever? His chosen ones."

"And take your insects with youI At once! or by the eye of Osiris I will—"

"All right, all right," Moses said. "And let this be the last time we try to bargain—ever. May we neve r suffer here again. As God wills, let it be so," said Moses.

The Pharaoh. in his majestic frustration over the plague of grasshoppers, began to pitch vases across the room, rolling huge urns with mighty heaves onto the floor, and dashing madly thr ough a half dozen of his loyal eunuchs. There was no atopping his wicked anger. He diced up my comrades where they made the stone floor come alive with th e ir presence. He was surly and quite out of his mind.

Moses seized a torch from one of the palace guards—who trembled at the sight of the Pharaoh out of control-and he burned his robe in front of their big, white eyes in their brickburnt faces. I lost a few of my relatives. Moses singed his hair. He looked up at the palace walls. His eyes grew big like stones of grey marble as he raised the m in prayer. After speaking with Thunder Voice, who cracked a rumble of thunder at the close of their little chat, Moses flung the guard"s torch into the desert sands where i t it was extinguished next to the great statue of Ptolemy I, the warrior king. The brickmaker Moses then said to him-. self:

"My God, My God—protect us, guide us, feed u &" He went down on his knees. This pleased the Pharaoh b e-cause he thought the poor brickmaker prisoner was worsh i piping him. When Moses had finished talking, he stood, wiped the grit from his knees, and he said to the Pharaoh," God will not let you escape from His punishment, no matter what you do to my people."

"If you do not exodus from this palace and from the land of Egypt, I will order my chariot drivers to harness up their horses. I will put my bowmen and spear car. riers on wheels, and they will attack and wipe out the whole lot of you sunworshippers, you ungrateful slaves, your wearisome sheep. Then there will really be blood on the land."

"We possess no personal goods of worth, Sire-we have nothing to pack up."

"Then go! Go! Go! GO!" screamed the Pharaoh, going into another of his jumping and pacing moods, his fierce eyes flashing before thousands of my grasshopper troops"Moses went out of the palace and turned in the direction of the brickyard, down by the Nile River.

The Thunder Voice spoke to me from behind the wall that separated the Pharaoh's garden from his palace rooms" .to not look for me, for I am the God of the heavens and the earth."

I hear you clearly," I said. I thought that now maybe I ought to follow orders without whining. Wa s this not the Campaign of Consumption and were not the Regimental Hoppers still under my command?

"Return—fly back to your oasis, Chatter. I a m finished with you, but keep on making your lovely chat ter rhythms. Fly low for your food and for your—protection.

The Thunder Voice sucked up its thunder like a vacuum whirlwind and went flashing and smacking like a thousand cedar boughs, turbulent and shrieking, into the distance. I commanded all the troops within the sound of my chatter to assemble on the palace walls. The walls were black wi th our moving shapes. Some were standing in a double layer—since there was no more room. In a loud and clear voice, I chattered, "Retr-eatl Back to the oasis. Eastward, ho!" A strong wind from the west arose and lifted us on its its wings. Some stayed on to watch the sun go down, yet we had all cleared the palace precinct by the close of twilight except for those who were slain. crushed, obliterated, smeared and otherwise disarranged in battle.

Loyalty is a scrunch we prize highly in our colony of grasshoppers" And I can say it proved to be our salvatt i on this time. We all took it on the hopper, as it were, for the sake of loyalty—and obedience to Thunder Voice. The whole campaign was a mighty strange event in anybody's papyrus book. Come to your own conclusions about the cost of obedience.

Let me just say that palace carpet does not taste a s good as new grain in the wheat fields. It tastes more li k e weak lentil soup. Have you ever smelled wet dog fur? Exactly the sarae,

Is the sharing of the environment always mutually symbi otic between nan and the animals? If so why? Man derives food and covering, but what does his presence signify to the animals but danger and extinction? Or is there a design flaw somewhere that allows the significance of man to the animals to be conditional and not abso-lute? And is that a flaw? M y own understanding is that the symbiosis, where operative, precludes mutual adaptability, though cooperation nay be evident. The coyote is a good example of this phenomenon. H e never adapts to nan but nerely cooperates, going here, retreating there but renaining forever wild. So long as the instinct remains uppermost the craving of the animal can be manipulated; but that is not adaptation. Perhaps this is a statement of the obvious.

Command Performance

A dozen charioteers belonging to Caesar's assault troops clustered, down at Thyestra Creek. Their servants, bondsmen, shield bearers and drivers were washing off blood from the battle against the Truscans, a massacre that took place in the hills above Corinth. Among the assemblage was I, a horse called <u>Spitfire</u>, Caesar's personal war steed and intimate—friend.

I paw the ground and snort" I am getting ahead of my story. The battle that glorious day raged with fur y, heat and cries of agony from men and animals. Shouts o f pain and the wild whinnies of stricken and smitten horses rent the air. We struck the Truscans with full savagery. swords, spears and knives flailing the air and severing life with a bloody vengeance.

My master Caesar swung his sword with a hand skillfull and courageous before my delicate nose. I frothed from the strain of hauling that heavy wooden chariot over rocky ground. I felt the wind of Caesar's sword as it swooshed past ray head. A body fell to the ground between my hooves. Smoke palled *over* the skies—pitch flung in great canni s-ters by the enemy. The same burning pitch hurled over the city's walls had fired a breastworks Caesar had constructed for a long seige.

I claimed—before my kind—experience as a battle horse. I held my ground. though pieces of the pitch stung me like arrows. I rattled my traces. Again I pawed the ground to show ray impatience. Silver flashes from enemy helmets pierced the smoke, mingled with the plumes of Caesar" s troops" Enemy swords shredded Caesar's red and orange ban. ners while spears thrust through bodies of men and horses in cries of pity and agony. Standing in the field of battle was an awsome experience.

I felt the reins suddenly jerk up my head. The bit cut into my mouth and tongue. I felt the reins draw and swung the creaking chariot around. The reins were held b y the hands of a stranger or an enemy. Where was my mas ter, Caesar? I could not hear his voice above the roar and th e din and the clanging of swords upon shields. I obeyed the pull of the reins. Then I knew the cause for my wonder. Cae-sar had attacked and struck off the arm of the invader of his chariot.

"Spitfire!" Caesar cried. "Spitfire—hold! Hold! "—a command I knew at once. I turned my head. There stood the great man bleeding from a ghastly wound to his shoulder; beside the chariot lay the lifeless form of the pirate.

"To the palace! To the palace!" Caesar commanded-an ancient Greek refuge at a distance from the city. As I drew the chariot around the din all but ceased at once. That was strange. The savage enemy, Truscan rebels, was retreating over the rocky hills, routed by noble Caesar's fin est soldiers. I moved toward a small gully. Beyond lay the pal-act, some two leagues distant. I was glad to depart from the stench and cries of death. Moving slowly because of the agony of toy master's wound, we reached the palace after contingents of the main guard and combat detachments had r "-turned. Not long thereafter is where I now am—while the shieldbearers and servants wash off Caesar's chariot. lam content to watch.

I tell you these events to show why I am sad and why I weep, as horses sometimes do. Caesar has picked ano t he r to take my place, to fill my traces. He had told me that I am too old to respond to commands and that I have forgoten most of my training as a two-year old. I ought t o be turned out to pasture.

What a wicked thing is this—to be turned out without any real reason for doing so! I can smell battle from afar. I paw the ground witii impatience. I am heedless o f danger. Smells of the pitch and broken ground and blood rise up to ray nostrils and I am inflamed. I plunge xnto the battle, fearless beyond any doubt. I am loyal to my master. We are as one. I snort, fling up my muzzle into the wind and run without fear into the thick of the fray.

But Caesar, when he announced his plan to get rid of me, did not hear my cry. He only fed me an Armenian apple and patted ray flanks and scratched me behind the ears—a thing I enjoy enormously. These are the barest greetings—and after nearly twenty years in battles with his standing on the boards of his chariot! Even the shafts of the chariot are shaped to my withers and flanks. H h a t truly is my chariot.

"Must I go| 0 Master?" I pleaded with him.

"It is so, Spitfire. I hate to lose you but—perhaps in a few more years, a few more battles you will understand."

"Yes, Master." Not my battles, I am certain. Does he think I am an empty-headed filly?

"You must train a younger horse to take your place. If you can do this I shall keep you on active status as a palace—soldier. If you cannot—"He snapped his fingers. "White clover and the finest care."

"I can, I can!" I whinnie d with the eagerness o f a colt.

"Then tomorrow morning you will start to train ray new steed—<u>Dagger</u>. Ah, such an animal—powerful with eyes that flash fire."

"<u>Dagger</u>—that is good—if you always know wher e the point is," I answered with no small envy.

"I am glad that you approve. Then—in the morning. But first, take my chariot down to the creek fora cleansing. Sapho, my shieldbearer., will drive. He knows the way." As if I did not!

"Pull hard—over the rocks!" I snorted to <u>Dagger</u>. I was working him on the obstacle course for palace horses. "Don't be so lazy when the ground is smooth. Run! Fill your mane with the wind and your nostrils with smoke." "You drive me hard, <u>Spitfire</u>." "Just plain 'Spit'. Let's try that again." Colored silver and blue bunting rippled in t h e fresh morning air. It draped the corral walls. Some o f Caesar's concubines came out to watch me train <u>Dagger</u>. His shieldbearer, Sapho, stood nearby to seize my bridle. though that would not be necessary. Don't drive me. I am competent for the task. I thought.

"How should I go when the trail ends? Do I take my own way or wait for instructions?"

"Always wait for instructions—until you have learned the wishes of mighty Caesar. Instinct will h e 1 p you—if you've got any." My unruly temper again. "After all, when you pull Caesar's chariot that is no small matter. It will take you most of your life to learn. Now-shieldbearer—"I said with an impatient whinny but one Sapho grasped—"drop the shaft. There. That is right. Now the shaft is broken. How do you manage. <u>Dagger</u>? You can no longer pull the chariot"

"I don't know how, 'Spit". I have only one purpose."

"Two. You have two purposes. Now your Master can leap upon your back and astride your foaming flanks. You become a horse of the cavalry . Easy."

"Maybe for you who has served Caesar for a 1 m o st twenty years "but for me—"

I looked at this poor specimen of equine coura g e and sighed and sadly shook my head. Caesar will surely be killed if he depends on <u>Dagger"s</u> fearlessness.

"That will be all for today/" I said. Sapho le d <u>Dagger</u> back to his stall. In the morning I would report the results of my tutoring to the great master soldier, he who had conquered most of the known world. What pre stige! To be his chariot horse, his personal and favorite mount! This dolt of a beast did not appear to understand tha t greatness is to be chosen by Caesar.

"Yes, O, Master," I said to Caesar as he watched the stable boy burnish my white coat, polish my hooves. clean their frogs, tie my mane and tail into Circassia *u* knots"He, that <u>Dagger</u>, is impossible to train. He lacks stamina. He lacks imagination. He lacks—shall I say it? W raw courage."

"I quite understand. <u>Omnia equinus non sunt Spit-fire</u>.

"Thank you, O, Master. Truly all horses are not <u>Spitfire</u>."

"<u>Ergo</u>—out to pasture you go. <u>Dagger</u> will pick up enough Latin to get by on."

"But. Sire."

"Do you dare to argue with me?"

"But, Sire."

"Ought I to turn you into glue and have your sk i n mounted for my museum?"

"I could be a—walking horse."

"Starting now. Boy—take my horse out of the barn to the barley-grain pasture. This animal has dared to defy me."

"But, Sire," I Kept protesting. "Just one more battle"

The great Caesar paused, reflected, and on the following day he came out to the barn with a smile on his rugged face. "Just one more battle then. <u>Sumraa es bonum</u>."All is well, though he would probably endure rid i cu l e and humiliation for my sake, I could no longer jump a six-foot barrier.

That battle came. We were preparing to combat the Patrae of the north in what was to prove the most exhausting engagement of my lifetime. Smoke dyed red by blood and burning, fiery arrows filled the afternoon sky. It dr i f t ed like dripping tentacles of smoldering grass smoke over the canopy of trees, infiltrated the combatants locked in their frenzied combat, hand to hand, sword to sword. I smelled the acrid tar smoke and felt the ground tremble beneath my hooves from the assaulting hordes of soldiers and the corpses that I stepped upon. Cries of the wounded shrieked into my ears. The sun grew intensely hot, I foamed at the mouth, I lathered my withers. Someone cut my traces but I stood nearby to the Master's chariot.

"<u>Spitfire</u> I" I heard the shout from afar. I turne d my head aside to see and found my Master clawing at one o f the wheels of his chariot. He was cut deeply on one side. At that instant I felt the sharp sting of an arrow as it entered my neck below my mane. What a dreadful and piercing pain i t was!

"<u>Spitfire</u>!" my Master shouted again. "Come herr-r-e!"

My agony crept like a slow poison of fire into m y veins. I snorted and backed the heavy chariot into positi o n so that Caesar could climb aboard.

"To the rear!" he shouted.

"But, Sire—one of the traces is cut."

"Then drag the cursed car by its leather—pull to one side only, you stupid beast I"

Such a command I had never received. It could be done only by the stoutest mule. I was not a mule. I was a pedigreed horse. Still, a command is a command and X had to obey. A thrown rock catapaulted from the enemy lines and whish e d with a puff of wind past my nose. The stench of death clasped all around me. The smoke thickened and choked my nostrils. I found it hard to see. My eyes ran like a brook.

To the rear I moved. upon command. As I with drew, letting the chariot roll down a grassy slope strewn wit h the dead and dying, I heard my Master moan. I had go t t e n within hailing distance of our camp when the *reBerve* mace bearers and cadres of bowmen emerged in droves from a line of trees. They surrounded my Master with their deadly and skillful fire as soldiers lifted my Master from the floor of the chariot. They carried him to a place of safety, yet weak as he was he gave an oder.

"Spitfire! Extra grain for tonight."

It began to be plain that I had performed some heroic deed by rescuing my Master from the heat and din of the bat. tie. He brought up his armor bearer, standard bearere, trump-eteers and guardsmen three days thence, when the engagement was ended. And with a great fuss he hobbled, wrapped in linen, as he led me to a greensward—down between the rows o f celebrants to a gleaming golden chariot at the end, on a stoneway to the south and sanctuary.

"The groomsmen and bucklers will harness Spitfire to the chariot—it is a gift from an old friend to his noble mount. How do you like it, Spitfire?"

"I like it well enough," I snorted.

"It is yours."

"Mine?"

"You seen not to be satisfied. Have I done something wrong? Does its gold leaf offend you? Perhaps it i s too—dainty."

"I thought that battle would be my last."

"Come now. You did not want to be put out to pas . ture. The best way to prove you are good for another twenty years is to get in, take a course around the green. See how you like your new chariot." I whinnied. I saw tears in Caesar's eyes.

"But. Sire—"

"I have changed my mind about retiring you."You weep crocodile tears. I looked forward—"Oh, loyal but ungrateful horseI" In a spit of a n-ger Caesar ordered the groomsmen and bucklers to unlock the traces. "Yes, I do love my animal—<u>Spitfire</u>. (really one of his kind." Again he wept. "Then you shall continue w i t h the training of <u>Dagger</u>."

"That I will gladly do," I snorted and flung my head high as I whinnied approval. I had cut a swathe betw e e n doubt and self-realization. The very field where I had rescued Caesar would be my pasture.

> Animals do respond to human emotions if in no other way than to show curiosity o v er tears, timidity before anger, friskines sat a playful spirit, sorrow at a master's death.

Handouts Are A Trap

Handouts! I nerer want to hear that word again. Handouts almost killed me and almost crippled a pal of mine. You see| it was like this: we got so used to hanging around the campgrounds that we just naturally thought they belonged i n out baliwick, our stomping ground, our den area. Pick i n gs were easy. The two-legged Critters appeared to like us and—for all we took from them we got so as we liked them—most of them. Then we began to relax our guard. You know, d r op into the old defense posture and come up with a snarl to the face, a left claw to the air. I can't begin to tell you how many tents we robbed, knocked over just like that. So m e pretty good chow, bear in mind. Ho, ho!

By the way, my name is Igmar Bitten and I run aroun d loosely with my pal Fiddlesticks. I call him that because he almost got clobbered one day when he saw this camper Critter fiddling with two sticks trying to start a fire. The Cri tter never got his fire built but he was so mad he came at my p a l with a piece of lumber and a wild bellow, then jumped in his car and drove away. Scared, I reckon. Old Fiddlesticks i s the curious sort—he just sniffed the air and went on wi t h his pilfering.

Me—? I amble here and I amble there. I sniff and poke and whine and grunt and taste all those good smells i n the air—bacon, sugar, fish. I am making myself hungry just thinking about camper food. Convenient grub, ma!

Let me tell you about knocking over this here tent. Some Critter fellow pitched his tent right in the middle of our hunting grounds—which is from the upper side of Sage Mountain down to Grizzly Creek where the berries and fish drip with deliciousness. Not a big territory but ours by right of smell and treebark clawings—and the squatting years.

I said to Fiddlesticks, "Let's us go and uncork one on that skinny dumpling."

"Whatchamean, Igmar," I am the northern type; so If-mar is my name.

"I mean, this here dude drops his tent and gear right in the middle of berry season. So we got to go through him to get down to the creek."

"Took lots of nerve," Fiddlesticks said.

"Stupidity is what it took. Listen. He is a sc i en-tist or maybe a berry picker . and he leaves his blue tent without a guard dog. There is lots of sugar inside. Swee t stuff. What do you say?"

"I don't know, Igmar. If the forester rides through here we could be in deep trouble."

"Are you afraid of that dude—his gun, his rifle?"

"Not him. I fear becoming marked for life."

"By him—by that forester?" I exploded.

"Have you never heard about being painted yellow o r white or red so settlers can identify you when they see you?"

"When your hair falls out it's all over," I said.

"Stained—for life!"

"You are talking nonsense this morning, Fiddlesticks. I'm clawing for things that really count. SugarI Think of that! Why, that Critter has got candy, honeyed oats, chewy junk. I can smell it. Sugar for his tea and—toothpas t e. That»s got real down-home flavor. And he likes—get this-he likes to bake cakes. He has baked two already—j i f fy cakes, moon cakes that smell like tree heaven."

"Go on with you, Igmar. You've got a fixation o n food."

"Well. now| haven't all bears got fixations. I mean, after all. how do you—they expect us to survive—by counting mud balls and never getting hungry?"

"They don't—expect us to survive. We are on their dangerous list. Bears have got no use—to Critters. W e don't belong," said Fiddlesticks.

"What do you say? That city cracker's tent—tomor-row—forenoon. He's gone—scientizing the woods then."

"A hold-up?"

"A robbery," Igmar said. "That's more like it"Right then and there I, Igmar, began to sharpen my claws on a tall sugar pine.

"I'm just afraid of that forester, not the camper Critter, Igmar—the forester, the ranger."

"I will go find me another partner—one with fat guts."

"Wait! Wait just a minute!" Fiddlesticks began t o tie and untie his rug lashings and then—he gave in to t h e chance to pick up some easy sugar. "I will go, but if we get caught and marked for life, I will never forgive you."

"Trust roe, Fiddlesticks. Neither one of us is going to get hurt. Tomorrow night, the Critter comes clomping in late, wheezing and dead. He crawls out of his den late. We hit the tentden in the afternoon. We rip his pretty cloth and enter through the back. One slitttt! Just like that, his sacred hibernating place is layed wide open. I step inside. The joint has no inner wall. No alarm system. He carries a Critter talk-box for noise. I hand the swag out to you and you drop it reverentially on the ground. When I am finished. w e run with the stuff back behind the cedartrees, a trailway. We head for the creek bank and hide the junk in the bracken ferns.

"You make everything sound so easy, Igmar."

"Planning. Planning is the secret, Fiddlesticks."

I guess I overestimated my accomplice—he seemed s o ready and so happy with the plan of robbery, so committed to the philosophy of clever stealing and so zealous to make the victim suffer. I knew that I had made a mistake when he came up to me about an hour before startup time and he said, "Igmar, I cannot do this.'

"You—cannot—do this!' I was flabbergasted throughout my fur, as any enterprizing bear with guts and growl would be. What a change of heart! "And what has caused this flip-flop to come about, may I make so bold as to enquire?"I asked.

"The victim does not carry a gun."

"The victim does not—carry a gun? Victim! Vic tim! Come now. Fiddlesticks, Don't put me on. Don't pull my hind leg. I.ra too wary for that. I"m not ready for the taxiderm-ist yet. And since when have you been concerned and worried about a—victim not having a gun?"

"Since—well., ever since I learned that stealing i s wrong."

"Wrong is it! You idiot. We bears steal all the time. Or haven't you been around. dropshot?"

"That's right. But that's exactly why we make such a bad example to our victims. We got wooly odor and bad tee t h halitoses—that's how popular we are.'

"Critters don't expect us to be perfect, "I said.

"No, but they do expect us to use good judgement, Igmar. It just don't make sense for us to rob this good man simply be. cause he stakes down his dumb tent in our hunting grounds."

"I see. You believe that, don't you?'

"I do/" said Fiddlesticks.

"Then this is not a matter of sugar. It's a matter o f viewpoint?"

"Why are you so desperate to plan out every step i f viewpoint is not a big thing? Why not go crashing into the tent any time?" Fiddlesticks was persuasive.

"As you well know, some bears do just that." Silence. "Look, you dumb smughug, you son of a porkrind, I'm not g o-ing to stand here all day arguing while you change your fur from cinnamon to white" Are you with me or not?"

"Not."

"Okay, gruhnnnnunnnnnnt, then you are out. Slop, slop," I said. It hurt me. It hurt me a whole lot that one of my best pals should back out on me, waffle on me, renig on m e at the sweetest job of the year, a clawmark cinch to pull off. I went ahead and did my thing anyway. I tore up that Cr i t-ter's blueskin tent, I scrambled his junk food, ri pped op e n his boxes and chests, rummaged in his bags, chewed and grunted and slashed his secret hiding places, made a hugp mess of his den comfortso Then I left and watched from the bracken that night. What a poor slob he turned out to bet A cracker with one thumb in his jam jar and his head in his wine bottle. Scientist, my hind paw! But he did not move his tent—if one can imagine such a thing. Insipid arrogance I

Then, like a shaft of sunlight onto the forest fl oo r, I saw what I must do. I had to get a second opinion.I would go to the forester's parrot … he kept a green parrot i n his shack to make company for him. Parrots talk like Critte rs. They are smart. I would explain the matter to the green pa r-rot. I hurried to the forester's little shack.in the woods and bobbed a glance inside.

"Look, bird," I said to the Me Caw through the forester's open window. Our scheduled day for the robbers was long gone. Yes, I had ripped off the camper Critter, but now I wante d advice. "Look, parrot, I got a problem."

"Bear up. Bear up. Cawww—cack, cack, cack."

"Eat a nut and listen up, bird. There's a camper dude has pitched his tent right in the middle of our hunting grounds. I mean, smack-dab in the middle. I took him to the cleaners but he stays on. He is an eyesore. I have to walk through his campsite to get to the creek for fishing."

"Caw, caw. I have heard. I have heard."

"Do you think it is safe for us. We are only bears.We can get into a mess of trouble."

"Mess is yours. Mess is yours. Ranger is on the prowl. Get shot. Get shot. Get shot. Poison is a cawk, a cawk—a cawk, whistlewhewwhoooo, cawk. Possibility."

"I don't squawk about your cawk, parrot."

"Sweet poison flare candles. Poison for his bugs, his bugs, bugs, bugs."

"Don't he burn them, every one of them?"

"Cawk, eawk, bugs—action. Action. Shoot the Critter, shoot the Critter, cawk!"

"You got it, Petre," I said to the forester's parrot. Smart bird. "You crack a nut and tell the forester."

"My job, my job—wise, wise, Polly wise, Cawkl"

"Tell him to dig that lump out of the woods or w e will feed on his goodies from toothpaste to oatmeal."

"Gawk, cawk—rrrrrrrrhhhhhhhhh."

"I thought you'd understand."

I hate to think that things worked out so bearishly clean but they did. The forester translated the word from his green parrot. He must've warned the Critter camp er, a piece of ranger advice, because that silly, sugar-c o a ted two-legged Critter packed up his gear. The very next morning that splash-in-the-mud hit the trail.

But that was not the end of the story by a long spit. My old pal, at least I thought he was my pal—Fiddlesticks—almost same as a den mother to me—well, he got two of his chums together and they grumbled up to me that very night while I was munching and grubbing buried in the Grizzly Creek blackberry vines.

"What's doing, Fiddlesticks? Killjoy. Wet rug. You" re that all right. Your tastebuds are in your ears, wet rug."

"Igraar, we are not pleased with your behavior a s bears go around here."

"So, okay. How do they go—garbage can to garbage can. So what? I do my thing."

"You are a bad influence."

"Why? Because I needed some help the other day in robbing a Critter's tent? You fellows rob and steal all the time."

"We knock over the garbage pails on Snow Flats Camp grounds—public property—and that's all we do."

"Slop, slop. Grummmmidgeons, I tell you. You could do more."

"But we don"to That's the point. So we are telling you to roll up your bear rug and get out of here. We do not want our cubs picking up any bad habits. We try to get along with the campers, and you know that."

"Just let me say one thing," I said.

"What's that?" They moaned and grunted together.

"I don't like your visit one claw mark. I stand up to you." Squeeel, grunt and swoosh. "Hear that sou n d? Death in the air."

"We make our rounds in the early morning-noisy can lids and all. While you "destroy, any time your slobbering jaws wants to.

"Hard words, big fellows. When you scrubs go back to scrunching and munching on berries and blowing red juice through your sniveling noses—when you go back to catching mudsuckers in the creek, you just let me know."

"We feed our hungry cubs."

"You feed your big, hungry mouths and fatter guts. Just look at you." They looked around and down at their fatness. "See. You just let roe know, and then I'll come and join you—maybe."

"You are sad."

"You are hypocrite bears. You pretend to be honorable in food huntingi but your ways are the ways of die-honor."

"Ho, ho hoooo," they hooted and rumbled, their o-pen jaws dripping pig laughter.

"Whether or not it is true, cones to the sane thing,"said I, Igmar| the magnificent. "I don't mind fish and berries, but you will starve if the forester ever takes them garbage pails away from you."

"We'll see| we'll see, we'll see," they choursed.

"Handouts are a trap—a trap—a bear trap. They will kill you with kindnesso Bear poison. You are pets of the camper Critters and do not know it . wild pets.So long—chumps."

"We will survive and grow fat, fat, fat."

However, I, Igmar Bitten, headed up the canyon by gum, and hoped I did not run into that stupid camper Cri t ter again—and have to go back on my word. What a bear says ought to be taken seriously. If I say, I am done, I am done. If I am hungry, I am hungry. I will make out on my own ". and have for a long, long time.

> If the capacity for primal acceptance of man's presence by animals in the wild is nascent, then it cannot have evolved but already existed, But that acceptance, wild and primitive though it is invades the relationship o f man-animal contacts that have always been fundamentally hostile. Does the manipulation of animal instincts disprove the possibility of a nasc en t primordial harmony?

The Bird Of Mercy

"Wrong word for a right bird. That is all I can say,"cawed the raven whom birds of his feather called <u>Ravel</u>, "I as\ as any fowl can see, a little off course. I don't know why-cawwww, cawwww—I was beating the hot air for the town dump and fishhead beaches along the Galilee shores. But-here I am, circling above the Israel wilderness, the hills brow n on one side and spring, sunny grass on the other.

Ravel settled into a sway landing atop a twig in the Holm tree. As he did so he saw a whirlegew of dust, a small cyclone, spin crystals, grey angel down and glassy sand specks into the air. It grew black. It flashed like blinding sun inside the whirling ball. It came rushing on like a summer's night of warm air. Clumps of brush and polished desert sand glimmered in its light across the wasteland.

"Nice to take a rest," Ravel said, and he cawed to see what he could stir up from the lizard's shade of brush clumps. Nothing. Lizards and beetles in the pinch of desperation-grapes and figs always a real possibility outside Israeli t e villages. He was hungry"

"You got spare time on your ". in your feathers, I see that," sounded a flinty voice that chewed words for grit.

"Water is a good ways away. I was flying there-to the Galilee Sea."

"Not yet—not yet, Ravel," said the voice.from th e whirlwind.

"What do you mean? Who are you?" The air was as still as death, except for the whirling spin of wind cast up by the cyclone Spirit.

"I am the owner. I created these desert hills. I fashioned you, black feathers, noisy caw and greedy appetite!"

"Pshawwww, cawwwww, cawwwww."

"That is a fact. I want you to go on a mission of mercy for me, raven."

"Mission of mercy?"

"This time I want you—take along a few of your fellows—to feed another life besides your own."

"You know how I don't like riddles. That is why I fly straight—like a crow.'

"You are a raven, Ravel. You must airlift food to a stsrving prophet."

"Ruffle my feathers. Cawwww, cawwww, cawwwi"

A titilating breeze came up from off the distant Galilee Sea. It quavered the twig of the Holm tree where Ravel perched. The urgency came into his silly head from out o f the whirling wind. It must have. He felt so depressed that he flew out of the tree with a snap of his wings. He gathered three of his kind to him. They agreed that circumstances had gotten real tough of late—not much dead flesh a-round, no insects to speak of, no berries in season. T he grapes were green and the figs had died from an unseasonal frost. The king was dead, the jesters rode in the sadd 1 e, the land"s plenty of grain seed was either dried up or i n the barns of her enemies. Things were in a terrible a nd calamitous state. The four ravens agreed that maybe it would be better to end the struggle right here. They formed a suicide pact among themselves. They would end the ravens" unraveled life of ravenous unfulfilled desires—voice fro m the cyclone or not. Ravel urged the birds on. The voice of command was only an illusion., an hallucination.

They began to fly higher and higher, until the a i r turned thin and they could hardly breathe.

"What do you say, fellow ravens of bleak and b lack feather? Shall we end it all now? The God of the Judeans, the Israelits, the Egyptians, Syrians and Babylonians a n d all those other folk and countrymen will be fit to be tie d when He finds that his mercy-slaves have killed themse 1 v e s in a death pact."

"Spoken with good voice—cawwww, cawwww—Ravel. W e do this out of protest."

"Protest against discriminatory laws because our feathers are black. He does not say a word to the eagle or to the turkey buzzard—only us ravens."

"We shall make martyrs of ourselves," was the sentiment they all voiced. "Cawwwww! Cawwwwwwl Caawwww! Cawwww!"

"Then let us go—earthward—kamakazee—plummet into the ground to show God he does not trifle with ravens."

The four birds topped off their high altitude cli m b$ they were at about 11,000 feet. They could see clear aero s s the landscape to the Egyptian desert. The air was thin and hard to breathe. Then they started their plunge into the roc k pile of the Gerizim foothills—downward. earthward the four martyrs dove. They hummed with beating feathers like thundering combat birds, in formation for their suicide pact with death.

But the cyclone voice, which was that of God of gods, meant business with Ravel. He sent a contrary thermal current of air, an upsweep of hot radiation against those fallin g birds. He split them apart} feathers and all went fly in g. Ravel was stripped away from his comrades in death. He l o st them. And he ended his flight, not in a shower of blood and gore and feathers against the target rocks but in a sheepherd-er's wheat patch. Nice and easy, the thermal throttled down his dive and he found himself browsing among tall, sweet stalks of Samarian wheatheads.

"Mercy. Mercy, me!" cried Ravel the raven.

"That is just what you get—unearned rescue-which you do not deserve. Mercy," said the very voice of God. "Now will you hear me?"

"Considering this—fate, I suppose so—but I cling to my right to rebel."

"Your right I From whom! Where!" The voice fixed the challenger on the thorn of his ignorance.

"Do you see that wilderness north of where you are feasting on sheepherder's wheatheads? He makes his bread from the grain."

"I cannot see a thing there is so much dust in my eyes/'

"Here. Let me cleanse away that dust. I will be you r servant this time." A huge swoosh of water came from somewhere—the sheepherder"s wife had thrown out a pan of slops. They cleansed Ravel's stinging eyesight and gave him a nibble or two of food.

"Thank you, Big Voice," said the raven.

"I have plenty more gracious treats in store for you if you obey me." The whirlwind settled into the molten brown, glazed sands beneath the wheat stalks.

"Fly up to that dead Tamarisk tree. I want to g e t a good look at you. I want to see if you are truly capable o f following orders." Ravel did as he was commanded. The sand settled. Ravel twisted his head and looked northward.

"You are sure there is a north out here?"

"Don't be ridiculous. Check your compass, bold bird," said the voice. "I gave you a compass. You forgotl Don" t tell me!" Ravel stuck his beak under one wing, found a vermin, wiped slops from his eyes and glanced at his side-mounted compass.

"Sure is north all right, where I am pointed."

"Good. Now here is what I want you to do."

"Alone—but God of the Egyptian. Syrian. Judean, Israelite gods—I"

"There is enough of them to make up a funeral proces-sion. I am the one true God. Alone it is—for now. I give you the orders. You follow them.

Trust me. Out there 1 i es stretched out flat on the sands like a shadow a friend of mine—under a Tamarisk tree and near to a brook by the Jordan and starving—a Prophet. His name is Elijah. He is very tire d, . having journeyed many miles. Lest he die, he needs food for strength."

"Elijah?"

"You got it, bird. I am sending *my* Prophet to Zare-phath. He performed a finish job on all those swaggering and arrogant all-weather seers of Baal. He showed that pagan derelict who had the real fire power. Now Elijah needs food. He is feeling low. Are you ready?"

"But why do you tell me his troubles?"

"Foolish bird! I have an errand of mercy for you."

"Caawwwwww! Caawwww!

"I want you to fetch up some fig cakes for him." R a-vel almost fell out of the Tamarisk tree. He had hardly eaten himself for two days and sharing vittles with a dying man, staggering weak with hunger who would eat a raven for break fast if he could catch it—!

"Food supplies, commander—?"

"That sheepherder's wagon right there I landed you beside—just seize the two cakes. They are stuck together .-Outside on the ledge where the wife sets them to cool—take them. Three degrees east of compass north, allow for win d s and drift and you will be there by sundown. Others will join you to assist."

"Cawwwww—you are a planner, arenH you?"

"I planned the entire universe."

"Stuff!"

"You don't have to believe me, Noisy Bird. Take a few beakfulls for your own craw, raven. That will turn you into black iron."

Ravel was a fast bird on the wing. His feathers split the air as he flew along, one of the cakes clasped in his small talons. Behind him flew two other ravens, each with a fragment of the other cake in his talons. Ravel's gl os s y wingtops took on the yellowbright shine of the morning su n. He had found the cakes without any difficulty—and he had his helpers. As he flapped along it came to him that God was good for His word. He steered his course by the Command er's compass setting.

He flew and he flew and he flew on beyond. A tail—wind came up that pushed him along, winging into the afternoon. Then—there it was! He cawwwed, cawwwwed. Five thousand feet below him on the wilderness flatlands he spotted with a gimlet eye what appeared to be a corpse. It was stretched out in the heat-shimmering haze of brown. Ravel circled down to get a closer view of the mirage, and what he saw turned out to be a man asleep on the barren gro u nd. It was a fiercely hot day. Ravel allowed, so hot that i f that corpse were not dead now it might be in another hour or two. Tomorrow he would be nothing but white bones.

Water? Where was water beside the brook, but it was dried up. There was no considering that for the moment. He buzzed the corpse—while his assistants settled down nearby. Ravel saw the body move. He saw it stir. He heard a muffled moan. He came to a swooping landing on the topmost twig of a dead Holm tree. The branch swayed under the weight of himself and the fig cakes in his beak. The bluegrey bark ran down like dried honey into the sands, near to where the man lay. The sky was so blue it was almost bitter and biting to Ravel's black tongue. Molten blue sun harrows combed across the landscape. The sun stood down in the west, hot like the poke hole of a bread oven, fiery, sc o r chin g and almost rumbling fiery. But the man appeared to sleep on, Then the whirlwind spiraled, twisted like a carpenter's auger screw into the desert and scribed a path on the sand a-round the man.

"This is my Prophet, Elijah. Cakes, Elihah. Awaken and eat. Drop the food by his head, ravens. All the birds obeyed the command. "Smell the fresh-baked fig cakes, Elijah, ' the whirlwind voice thundered. "You, bird—"

"I am mad with thirst and hunger, God. I ca nn o t endure. I am twistyfigget in my mind and feathered out all over the world. I sing this song to please the sand lizards and my water-mirrored self. Screeeech, cawwwww!" The raven called Ravel flew up and away in a circle. He did not appear to listen. He was out of his mind from the heat and his hunger and his thirst. "I cannot—obey!"

"Obey me I Power is yours."

"I will fly to Egypt and beg at the cook's ledge. I and my dead suicide kind—"

"Settle down again, Ravel."

"I am a buzzard. Where is the corpse? Oh, t h e re is the corpse. Then— upp, uppp on eagle.s wings. I fly backwards, a black eagle. Isn't that ripe for the corpse?"

"Come down again, Ravel. Take strength. Eat. Eat."

"Cawwww, cawwwww." The raven did so with great agitation and fluttering of his wings.

"Now you are black iron, black iron, Ravel."

"I cannot last forever," the raven said. "Cawww.Caww. Cawwww."

"You stick around until my Prophet servant gets bac k on his feet."

"Good-bye, never do well—never do well—it is I, the raven." Ravel flew off toward some nearby rocks.

"What are you doing here, bird?" Elijah called out.

"We brought food for you, Elijah—fig cakes."

"Praise to the living God," Elijah moaned. Ravel wa s out of earshot. He took a little rest in the shade of t he rocks, but they were scorching hot. He smelled burning feathers, his feet blazed on the broiling stones and he got one wing caught between the jagged rocks when he hurried to fly out.

"Oh, corps man. I am trapped. I got my wing caugh t in the cracks of these stones."

"Look down, bird. What do you see," said the whirlwind voice.

"A melon cactus growing from the rocks."

"Peck into the skin of one. Go ahead. It wonH poi-son you. Then we will worry about your snared wing."

Ravel broke into the melon fruit and drew up s w e e t water. "I quench my thirst," said the raven.

"You go to that dying man over there and you lead him to here. Now. Your wing is free. Fly away, bird."

Ravel did as the Commander said this time, since h e could easily have died from heat prostration in among the rocks. "Cawwww, cawww, cawww," he called and flew back and forth to lead Elijah to sips of water.

"What is your name. bird?"

"Ravel. I am Ravel, the raven."

"And I am Elijah, the Prophet. Since I am going north to Jerico I have hills to climb. This food will give m e strength, Ravel. Thanks be to God— and to you. And I will taste of the water."

"You better drink it, Prophet. while it is there. I t will keep you out of the grave."

"Tell me who sent you. Yes. I know—it was ny God. For only He knows the path and dangers of my journey."

"Are you strong enough for the trip, Elijah?" t h e voice from the whirlwind asked.

"After this last figcake—"The prophet consumed completely the second cake. "Tell me—what made you so sure you would find me, Ravel?"

"I read my side-mount compass and took a reading f r om God."

"You are some bird. I'll say."

"A flyover and a food drop—that's all. You got work to do, why are you sitting in the rocks? That mel o n is as dry as a gourd now."

"True, God does not abide much tarrying."

Elijah stood up, a little shaky, fixed his turb a n on his head against the baking sun. He brushed the sand from his tunic and shook out his black beard.

"I see you are freshened up and ready to go," Ravel said. He flew up into the Tamarisk branches.

"Just one more thing—a compass heading t o war d Jerico."

"You perch!" came the command as the whirlwind spraqg up anew and inscribed a trail upon the sand to the north east.

"Thanks for everything. Ravel, the raven."

Already the big black bird was in the sky with his fellows and turning into specks upon the blue glazed t i le of the Israelite heavens. Kneeling, Elijah gave thanks to God and then set off upon the trail in the sand.

> Utility is the basic premise of evolution—competition for food and survival. But if this u-tility is all that matters in the animal"s life, why do the other imponderables even exist in e-mergent behavior, such as trainability, submergence of instinct, affectionate attraction, denial of offspring, etc.?

Amidst The Sea Caves I Swam

Silver water chips slid down my back. I swam down in-. to deep waters where crags rose up and seaweed floated li ke black curtains, hung from the bottom of the sea floor. And I parted it as I swam. Then, upward to the surface where I blew out my hot breath and rolled like an abandoned log.I squeeled to fix my friend's location. Foam washed around and ove r my barnacles. A voice as big as the sky shook the sea brine a-round me with vibrations, like a swarm of darting anchovies.

"Barney! Barney I"

"Squeeellllll—gruuuuuunnnnnnnt1" I sounded.

"This is your spirit fish, Big Roar. I have a special task for you, great fish of the deeps."'

"Keep the harpooners off my back. I got no harpoon insurance"

"They will not harm you. I have a journey, a mi ssion for you. I shall demand a promise."

"The sea caves are my rest, the shimmering, sparkling plankton is my food."

"I have a command for you."

"Run me aground, would you?"

"You do that without my help—twice already in the Azores."

"A churning boat got my sound waves all screwed up."

"No excuses, Barney."

"No concessions either," I said. I swam away from the voice of Big Roar. "What good are you, Big Roar, when they are slicing me up for the blubber cookers?" I rose up to the surface and blew out my hot, steamy breath in exasperation.

"You pick up your watertaxi fare in the Aegean Sea and you take him away from Tarsish, in the direction of Nineveh. Drop him off on the beaches west of Antioch."

"Gerrruhhhhnnnnnnnt, squeeeeeeeelllllllll. Oil for their lamps and bone for their sea chests."

"You are a sperm whale—good for your oil—and for my purposes."

"I will get sick and die. What good am I then?"

"Do you try to fool God? You have not had a s i ck day in your life."

I swam in a circle. A school of albacore fli ckered by, tickled me. The deep was murky, the way lonely and vast. I idled my fins. "Who is this windjammer you want me to transport?"

"A Prophet named Jonah. You will pick him up in the waters east of Greece, in the north Great Sea. I will bring a storm upon the ship and the sailors will pitch him overboard."

"I have got to find this fishhead in a storm?"

"You are a very disagreeable whale."

"You will have to repair one of my dorsal rudders."

"What is the matter with it?"

"Jammed, it feels like. And my starboard tail fluke
is bent all out of shape. A tugboat ran into me back i n
Moon Bay."

"A tugboat—in Moon Bay. You're sure?"

"I got to carry my fare in these boney teeth?"

"In your big belly, Leviathan. In your big belly "he will ride in comfort. Off the port of Joppa comes t h e giant gale that blows the ship seaward and to the west. The sailors cannot beach her. They draw straws. Jonah, who is sacked out down in the hold, draws the short one, gets the blame for the storm, takes the guilt anger on his own. They heave the baggage overboard—along with everything else. And there is where you swallow him."

"He a—convict or something?"

"A runaway prophet servant."

"He'll be a corpse when I find him. Do you expect that sailor to breathe with me?"

"Blow hard, take a snort of air and down you go-he breathes your air."

"I won't touch this garbage without a plankton feast."

"Obey me!"

"Not one of ray kind can do what you ask me to do. We baleen whales are just a bunch of sea-straining, plankton-guzzling experts on matters of food. Look at me."

"I am. I made you, and you are ready. Barney."

"Sure—disjointed dorsal fin. crippled starboard fluke, threat of harpooners and—a journey of five hundred miles without food. What do you think I am?"

"A whale, I am your Creator. I shaped you to be sleek and competent and gliding and efficient in the water. Your tail flukes thrash the sea like a palm tree in a storm. You smite the billows of foam with your huge chest when you breech. Great showers of spray reach the heavens like an ocean in birth pangs. Your spouting is like the flourishing of the myrtle tree. Even the sea birds come to rest on your back, and to taste the froth of your rolling and churning like fruit that glistens where it falls."

"You flatter me," I said.

"I will bestow upon you unbelievable power—power to make the journey. Three days in your belly. You breathe for him."

"My barnacles itch something horrible. I have this back pain when I bend over double, and my vision seems t o be fading. I got some real things the matter with me."

"I am tired of arguing with you, Barney. I could beach you right now if I chose to—raise up an island under you and thrust you into the sky on its rocks."

"My doctor would not recommend this whole thing-swallow a sailor I"

"I am your great Physician!" the voice roared and surrounded me in a shell of heavy tar sand as a trap for a time. "I am the Creator and you are my creation." The ocean depths turned into a whirling maelstrom and sucked me down a thousand feet, round and round. whirling. panicked by the contrary current and dizzy. Jelly fish and stingrays and jillions o f swimming sea life tumbled and spun and vanished, going dow n through the black tunnel of angry water.

"Stop! Stop. I want to get off!" I cried.

"Now you understand my power—and that I am de adly serious about this whole matter."

"I see but I do not understand."

The Big Roar's voice sounded as flinty as a coral reef under the sea spray. "This mission is my will."

"What did you say this sailor's name is?"

"Jonah-he is a prophet and a fugitive on his way to Spain. He will be turned about and go to Nineveh in Baby 1 on to preach."

"He will poison my system. I will be out there all a-lone in the Great Sea with no way to get in contact with my own kind. Whale doctors are shore people. I may get sick and die."

"You love your waterbed too much. Pick Jonah up west of Cyprus at thirty-five degrees north latitude and thi r t y degrees east longitude. Set your compass. Drop him off o n any beach north of Avad and south of Tarsus."

"Then what—?" Silence only filled in around m e, like a growing deafness. I swam to the waters west of Cyprus, in the north of the Great Sea and idled around waiting for the Joppa ship—and the great storm. Feed was good, the water warm, salutary for a whale. I saw this phosphorescence in the stirredup brine over my head, a flashing of pur pie froth through the sea storm, the wake of a vessel—and a slender stick of bubbles and sail cloth plunged into the murky turbulenceo I swam up close, opened my big mouth a nd then—"Oh, God! Oh, God!" I heard the cry of a dying man in a sea cave.

"Jonah of Joppa. I presume. Down the hatch, Prophet."

"I am he."

"You got the fare for this trip?" I asked.

"Cuff it," he said. He was mad and scared. Put him on credit? We were off to a splended start.

"Do you see those big waves up there. If you don't get smart and give me a straight answer I will spew you out."

"Why am I in here. I thought I was drowned."

"You are headed toward Nineveh."

"I am not! Let me out! It was Him sent you to do this. You are a wicked, blasphemous whale, I want nothing to do with Nineveh."

"My gullet is slicker than whale grease, so don't get frisky, sailor. You are not getting out unless I stand o n my head, and that is not likely."

"I am in prison. The best thing for me to do is start praying. "0, God, save me, save me. I am in the brig like a stinking barroom brawler. I been thrown overboard fro m the ship and pitched into this smelly whale's stomach."

"You will prophesy in obedience to me, Jonah," said a voice from the confines of my stomach.

"Since we are both unhappy about this whole thing, "I said, "why don. t I cut the trip short and drop you off some ... place in France—maybe the Riviera—have yourself a g o o d time—play with the pretty girls—draw straws. You like to gamble. Said so yourself."

"Plenty of wicked gusto down there all right, but you got me wrong, whale."

"He won.t ever find you there."

"Who?"

"You know who—God. Not in a jillion years. If yo u should change your mind, here is my number—Baleen one through nine hundred—and we can go from there—our own little agreement."

"I thought you said I must not get frisky."

"You give me indigestion, prophet. But you tickle me."

"I will not allow this cunning and deceit." The Big Roar put a drag on my flukes. He rolled me over like a ba r rel of rum. He gave me the h ickups. "You will m a ke no more compromises 1"

"Sorry, Lord," the prophet burped.

"Once a preacher, always a preacher," said the Big Roar.

"What is that—some kind of a fish—a preacher?"

"He tries to convince people they are wicked a nd then hangs around for the results."

"Like baiting a hook?" I asked. This was interes-ting.

"Right—sort of like that. They are dead when G o d gets into action. But I can just as easily preach in Tar-shish. You can swim there and I'll get out."

"Jonah—Jonah! Are you listening to me?" came the voice of Big Roar. "If you disobey me this time I will bind up your spirit in the rags of poverty. I will cur s e you with the dregs of bad company and poor circumstances.I will give you woes that you cannot shake off. Your hands will turn to putty— useless even for working ropes and doing sailor's chores. Your face will turn to paste so that none will see you for Jonah, the man and the Prophet. Your appetite will fail and you will shrink but you will reject good food. I will bring sleepless nights upon you so that you will fall over as if dead and faint from fatigue."

"All that upon me, O God?"

"All that." Silence from Big Roar.

"Look at the blowing manes of them green horses, "Jonah echoed aloud. "And the scudding water like ten thousand stones flung into the ocean. It is not like I planned this whole thing, "Jonah grumbled. "The swabs on that cargo ship figured the gods were angry with them—I a d-mitted Jehovah's involvement—now they bow down to Him. Some good come from the storm. I suspect."

"What's the trouble back there?" I asked. Now and then I gave my sailor fare a swish of water. "Stay u p close to my teeth if you want to watch what's going on."

"Can't you operate this tub any better?"

"You are fussy. You're getting a fre ride, sailoxv"

On the next morning I felt Jonah rummaging arou n d in my belly. "There is no galley down there, sailor."

"No steak and onions. How about some minnows?"

"We are blasting through a school of them right now."

"I'll give them a try." Off and on we talked. The entire second day went like this. The storm raged above.I heard the booming of the giant waves through my sonophonic ears. The stirred-up tides and currents rolled me with rub' bery ease. The blackness looked even blacker. I saw small golden fish like weaver's shuttles dart under me, a b i g fish like a sky kite curve around, his feelers flash i n g blue sparks. I ran through a swarm of jelly fish, like coral light, transparent and beautiful patterns, glowing red lines like the veins of a leaf of seaweed put to fire. It was all gorgeous even to my whale eyes. I love my home in the sea.

"There is a lampreyf" Jonah shouted, up close to my teeth whilest he held his breath, He saw the glowing blue-brown snake that squirmed through the milkfroth of sea water. Rocks fell from above, but they were phosphore s-cences splashing into the surface of the sea. Their light was dazzling to my blurry sight. The burning light was like the flames of a burning ship I once saw go down to the bottom. Jonah just sat and marveled, then ran back into my belly for another gulp of air.

"We are not there just yet," I said. "I hate to tell you this, but you are really beginning to give me acid in-digestion. And I got no sick policy to cover the heaves-especially the prophet heaves." Then I dove.

"What are you doing?" Jonah cried out.

"I am diving. What's it feel like?"

"Like you are diving. My ears hurt. Re me mber-whale, don't try to run up the fare—because I got no money. Them swabs emptied my pockets when they pitched m e overboard ."

Then Big Roar cut in. "You are anxious for what you do not need, Jonah"

"And me—?"

"You are the kind that belongs to the deeps. That is sufficient. Tarsus is approaching. You will be close to the drop-off point. Check your compass setting, Barney."

"I've done that—right on course. I will dro p Mm off in fifteen fathoms."

"You will vomit him up on the beach. My pro p h e t tastes like junk food and, true, he is not digestible.Bu t if you disobey me, whale, I will leave you to rot on the sand so that the children will laugh at you and old men will poke and prod your rotting carcass."

"There is a forest of seaweed up ahead, Big Roar."

"You let me handle that one, Leviathan."

"Burp, burp. One, two three—upl One, two, three and whisssshhhhhh! Out you go, sailorg" I squeeled with immense relief. "Tell your sailor friends to put away their harpoons}" I tried to shout after him, but he was gone, swimming into the pounding storm breakers with powerful, courageous strokes.

"You make such a fuss of foam and waves, Barney," said Big Roar.

"You know how much I like compromise."

"I know—don't tell me. Reverse rudder one hun d r e d and eighty degrees and you will find plankton sufficient for a feast. There's nothing wrong with you a little real food won't cure. Your starboard fluke works again, your dor sal fin is no longer disjointed and bent out of shape, your back pain is gone. I have removed the itch of your barnacles and deterred the harpoon from your back. I do work with my crea—tures sometimes. no matter how obstinate they are. Out and over—Big Roar."

> Man seeks beyond utilitarian "meaning" to find spiritu a
> 1 significance in the animal kingdom, and therefore h e
> embues animals with his own spirituality. pagan to be sure
> but nontheless ace ept-able to his primitive imagination.
> This animal "so u1" allows him to co-exist in harmony with
> the animals.

The Big Shot And The Insect

The renegade bear browsed and srauzzled and dripped through the brambled berries. Tree nuts were scarce these miles from his scratching forest and good fishing lay on the other side of the mountain. In a fight he had s c ar-red one eye and lost a patch of hair on his head, Klaus was a fighting bear—and always a hungry bear.

He also liked to climb. On the way up a tall pine one day he had gained a friend, a bark beetle whose sharp pincers pierced the bark of the tall sugarpine. His carved and chewed hole gave him access to the sweet, succulent juices of the cambrium flow of the tree. Klaus and Grumb 1 e s, affiliates, shared the same pine bark.

"Where are you going, big shot/' the beetle asked Klaus one day.

"To the top.". The bear was unaware that the be e t 1 e had watched him sharpen his claws on the trunk of the tree bark at the bottom.

"So—to the top. It's sweeter inside the bark," said the beetle.

"You silly insect. I smell a honey hive up there. Also, I like to sway and look out over the forest."

"One tree at a time, I always say."

"Me too. But I am a nature lover—the snowy peaka, the creek. I can s e e it through the pine needles when I'm swinging and swaying to the music of the wind. Ahhhhhhh."

"That's the whole trouble with you—too romantic. Now take me."

"You got no sense. Look at the woodpecker. Does he kill trees?" the bear enquired,

"They" re almost dead when he chops his hole," the beetle replied.

Klaus ignored the logic of the insect and found t he hive buzzing. He pricked some stingers into his muzzle but chewed the thick wax and sweet treacle with delight. He then clambered down, jumped over fallen limbs and rotting stumps. He located the loggers from their smell and noise and soon came to the edge of the forest where he stood watching t h em.

"What now?" he heard the bark beetle say to iiim.

"How did you get here?" The beetle did not reply. "Erop dead, you silly insect. Can't you see I've got work to do?"

"Okay, big time—but let me warn you. Them"s the Enemy.'

"Why are you hanging around then. bark beetle?"

"Grumbles. I caught a ride on your coat on the wa y down. Too far to fly. Tschew, tschew, tschew." The beetl e flew down upon a fresh, newcut log.

"Smoke gets to me," the beetle said.

"Noise scares me," said the black bear.

"What are you doing?" the beetle asked as Klaus smeared some fresh mud on his face.

"Terror—the mud, my scars, my huge bulk—that's my way. Put the fright of the tree gods in them,"

"I'll just come along and observe."

"Go back to your tunnels/" Klaus snapped. He loped up to the lumberjack and growled. "Enemy food "greelicious!"

"Bear! Lookout the bear!" the enemy screamed. Klaus would block their way into the woods, scare the Enemy t o a halt. Those black trees were his home. The Enemy just stared.

"May I make a suggestion?" said the insect.

"I will do things my way," said the renegade nam e d Klaus.

"There is only one of you. There're ten million o f roe."

Klaus began sharpening his claws on the bark of a felled cedar. "I need more—realism. I am not as romantic a s you suppose," said the bear. "Then I can scare the Enemy into running." He reached down to where a meadow spring trickled water into the grass and this time smeared huge gobs o f mud on his coat. He smashed a little chipmunk who sat nearby and smeared its blood around his eyes.

"Do you think I am hideous enough now?" he asked th e insect.

"I can take you or leave you," said the insect.

"Well, I am going to save my territory from death,"said Klaus. A growl of determination came up from his belly into his throat. He meant his threat.

He pretended to flee from the lumberjack Enemy. They left no trees to rot. They chopped big spaces where only the birds settled. What a disasterl On the fringe of the woods Klaus waited.

"They will come down any minute now," said the beetle.

"Are you still with me? You stupid insect!"

"Look, big time. I got ways you wouldn't dream of."

"This is my fight, bark beetle."

"I just thought I'd let you know."

Here they came. yellow monsters crushing down little trees. They puffed black smoke like burning mesquite into the air. Their noise screamed like bear demons in Klau s. fragile ears. The Enemy came down out of the woods withbup-ning fire in their mouths. Their strange claws were magi c "They severed a limb from the trunk. They ripped open atree from its nest in the ground and it toppled—carrrumpph! The bark glowed red. The forest floor thundered, the ne e d l e s scattered like the wind scatt e rs the rain when it falls. Then the Enemy became like big, black ants that crawled i n among the limbs and chopped up the flattened tr e e. It was horrible!

"Let me call my clansmen/" said the bark beetle."Take a little longer— but you keep your trees and we raise u p the next generation. Under the bark. Marvelous tunnels. Oh, sweet and succulent and juicyI"

"Look. you silly insect. Before you go into ecstacies of joy let me remind you that the Enemy has two weapons:fire and poison air."

"Sprays! I know all about them. Lost three milli on clansmen in a colony up the creek. Horrible death. Tsch ew, tschew, tschew."

"What are you doing?"

"Spitting out wood pulp. My code word."

The racket went on. The bear and the beetle continued to observe helplessly. Then, Klaus was gone—up the tree a-bove the Enemy lumberjacks. They had stopped to fix their magic weapons. He watched them blow fire out of their nuzzles and then he pushed a loose limb off its resting pla c e up in the tree. It clattered and cracked through the foli—age to the floor and thumped close to the Enemy. They sea t-tered. Too late. They turned their small smoking muz z1e s up toward him. He hid behind the tree trunk.

"Hey, big time. Ira witcha. Titter, titter.chewitt!"The insect made curious noises.where he perched on the limb next to the bear's face. He cleaned the sticky gumbo from his nippers. "A bear's life, ain.t it?"

"You got to follow me around all the time?"

"Vacation.," said the insect.

"You take this confrontation with the Enemy awful casual, black bug," said Klaus.

"There's a whole juicy forest out there waiting fir me."

The monster of the Enemy came growling and clanking up the mountainside. Klaus let out a weird scream, a sound like his prehistoric forebearers used to make. Territorial—a warning. The Enemy was a superstitiou s bunch. They all peered into the woods. Klaus shrieked again, making the sound echo deep among the sorest shadows.

"I am at rage. I am hurt. I am dying. Death o f a black bear."

"Oh, come on now," said Grumbles. "You got a long ways to go. Keep up the old incisors."

The enemy grabbed their shiny, cutting weap o n s of magic.

"I got nothing you want," the bear growled b e-tween his teeth.

"Same," said the insect. "And I surely don't want to be as clever as you are, big time."

"Let's get rid of the weeds and keep the forest," Klaus said.

"Oh, yeah, ha, yah, yah, tschew, tschew," the beetle replied.

"First—grub, food." The bear scrambled down the tall sugar pine and dropped into the midst of the Enemy. They scattered with wild death-spirit shrieks. Klaus broke open their nutpails with slashing paws and d e-voured the fish sandwiches and sweet stuff, the apple s and candy. He slobbered over the fragrant taste of everything. The beetle looked on with condescension and smiles. He agitated his nippers—and dreamed of cambrium juice. Filled, the bear sat down to rest. The Enemy did not return at once.

"Simple, simple, simple, simple," the beetle said in agitation, and as he did so his friends began to gather. "Infest the woods. That is the only way. We will make new homes for us in his trash of broken limbs and chopped-up wood."

That weird cry again sprang from the dripping muzzle of the bear. Grumbles heard its echoes like a message passed along. The cry rose up, a river of protest, from the throat of the beast and the primitive mind o f survival. Then—silence in the woods except for t h e scolding blue jays and squirrel chatter. A woodpe c k e r rattled away somewhere deep and up high but invisible.In due time, out of the forest depths five or six mammotb, grown black bears lumbered, heads waving, sniffing the Enemy and giving cries of greeting to their brother Klaus.

The beetles began to chew and gnaw and era c k le and buzz. Their numbers gathered like dark clouds.

"Follow me! Into the Enemy camp!" Klaus commanded.

"You got rights/" the beetle chirped. "Slash, cut, bang, knock, growl! You are wizards. You got power. Yo u got ancient roots. You got beauty."

"Forward, beasts of courage!" shouted Klaus.

"Got to see this," the insect said, and again he hopped a ride in Klaus's heavy fur coat. The monsters of the Enemy were pitching trees into the air. The whining of their engines of death vibrated the skies and strange shouts cam e from their fire mouths.

"I have left orders—"

"What?" Klaus shouted.

"Orders!" Klaus shook his head in the deafening noise. The insect flew up on its glossy wings and landed in the bear's ear. "We will infest the woods and the piles of slashings and the injured ones and the dying and weak. W e are too many for the Enemy.

Klaus gave out with a small cry from his panti n g, slobbering muzzle. "Terror is our weapon. They cannot pos-sibly shoot all of us."

While the Enemy jabbered) Klaus picked up a pine cone and flipped it into the fireface of the Enemy and knoc k ed out his fire. Crazy Enemy! They started to fight among themselves. One lumberjack chopped off the beard of the other. Another pinned a boot heel of a companion to the log he sat on. Then they began to club each other. Dust and noise rose up, cries of the wounded, blood ran, weapons flashed in the sun. Klaus raided another food cache nearby. An adze dug into the ground near him, a single axe split three lo g s with a blow. Several of the Enemy looked dead. Here and thexe a lumberjack gripped his limb to stop the blood.

"Attack! Attack!" cried Klaus to his bear kinsmen. The Enemy who could scrambled for the yellow school bus, others for the cab of the truck. The bears emptied the loading platform. The swarms of bark beetled arrived in full force, turning the skies black and falling into the tree tops like shattered pinecones and hail and pinyon nuts.

"Looks like we did it this time, good buddy," said the bark beetle.

"Yup, sure do," said the bear, "for a time. Your clansmen—?"

"Tunneling for the juices of the gods, the tree gods. Your woods—our woods."

The entire operation shut down for the day

News Item:

> MERE DE WOODS, Ca.—Fire broke out in the Klamath National Forest last night, in a remote area leased by the Chancellor Logging Company. The US Forestry Service contained the fire after it burned over more than 500 acres. It is believed to have started from careless logging p r a c-tices and was touched off in the vicinity of the company's operation. T h e cause, however, is still under investigation.

> For centuries men have made the survival of wildlife a matter for either God or Ownership to decide "Only when the State has become the Protector has the question of survival been totally ignored. For what belongs to all belongs to no single person and so, therefore) irresponsible "management" has assumed the role of keeper. Now that most of modern civilized society presumes to have put God in His place, the human spoilers are free to destroy and to conquer at will, without either foresight or conscience., And those who dare t o privately protect their preserves have fallen into disesteem. The trade-offs are visible for the continued propagation of certain species. Man has it within his power either to honor or to discard them.

Magnificent Observation

There is an old saying among mountain folks: "If the smoke drifts with the wind, it's a following fire," M y name is Cracker, and I happen to know the veracity of this adage. You see, I am a crow that got himself involved with an obnoxious, stubborn, independent, block-headed, wind-sniffing mountain ram one day. And I will never forget it. The truth of this old folk saying came out clear and hon-est in my dealings with Ironhead, the ram.

Ironhead was oldest of the cliffhanging rams. H e had earned great respect from his flock. It was said—I heard it from Caw-Caw, the itinerant raven—that Ironhea d could walk a ledge so narrow a crow could not perch on it! Feather that out. And he also could scamper up a nea r 1 y vertical slope as fast as the eagle flies into a cloud.Iron-head could swim like a beaver—was shot at by a bunch of wildeyed hunters one day, who almost felled him, but b e-cause he could swim so fast he beat the buckshot across the river to the other side. Once. this twist-headed mounta i n sheep confronted a lion-He so surprised the beast with his booming bleat that the lion moseyed out of the cave and left it. Just the mention of—strange happenings brings me back to my subject, me and Ironhead.

The first time I met him I said, "Ironhead, you have browsed on this rock weed way up here for some time. Isn" t there more pasturage below, cool water, shade and all?"

"Look ahead.' he said. "Smell what's way off at a distance."

"I can see way off into the distance, but I don't see any danger.'

"You got good eyes, but my nose is better at smelling out danger than your eyes are at seeing it."

"Is that so? Do you want to place a wager?"I said.

"Mountain sheep don't take chances. That is why we are alive today, why we mounted up into the rocky cliffs above. We all left the wolves and hunters in the valley below."

"You are kind of proud of that, aren't you?"

"Sure, Did you ever watch the way I look off at a distance? Proud, seeing, sniffing, my nostrils acquiverfcr the scent of danger," said the ram.

"Some day that confidence is going to get you i n to trouble, Ironhead."

"Go caw, caw one for me, Crow."

"Cracker's my name."

"Go find you a sick turtle dove to show off to, Cracker ₀ I am the mighty mountain ram, Ironhead."

"Maybe your brains are all outside. Feather that one out"

Ironhead was getting his water heated up. I could see that. "Give me a test. I mock at trouble, the tel 1-er of bad and good fortunes because of my keen sense o f smell. I am a predictor of wolves, lions, jackals and all other enemies of the flock. I live in these crags. I know who my killers are."

"Do you see that circle of ants down there—mi1 es away?" I asked.

"Those are not ants. They are shooters."

"See that they are up to."

"They are dancing around a fire," said Ironhead.

"That is right. Caw, caw. To eat you."

"Crap! I will fly down there and bring back a piece of their pride from their banner HUNTERS ANONYMOUS. Th e n you will believe."

"Bring me back some hairs from the coat of a k i lied brother."

"As good as done." I flew down on a straight glide path. I settled on a pyramid of stacked guns. I plucked some hairs from the flanks of a dead ram and flew back t o the ledge among the crags. The round trip did not take me long."

"I'll be stoned!" said Ironhead. "You got me th at time."

"Sure—but then again, I had a purpose. You and me have got to work together."

"I don't underFtand," said the ram.

"I cannot see them because my eyesight sees only greys. But you can see them as red, ripe, delicious. Let us hunt together."

"Now there is a wild march hare of a thought."

"Don't you tell no member of your herd, Ironhead, or the friendship is off,"

"Forget the lizards and the locusts and the dusty trail. We're going down to where there's water and berries."

"That's great! I am all for it," said the ram.

"The low altitude won't affect your breathing any, will it?" I enquired.

"Not at all."

So. down we went. I, Cracker, circling while Iron-head leaped and jumped and frisked gracefully among t he rocks—until we reached the creekside. It was going on summertime and the berries were sure to be plentiful. I cawed ravenously. Ironhead would follow me. I circled. The ram looked up, saw me and corrected the dire c t i o n in which he was running.

"This way, Ironhead," I called from the sky. "Over here. I see many berries." And it was so, I and the ram stopped for almost half a day and gorged ourselves. What a feast! What a team of food hunters! With mutual promises to meet early the next morning at Finger Rock, w e parted for the night.

Deep into the blackness and starry night heavens, an awsome sound broke out, but not until morning did I discover the cause. Two cinnamon bears, their paw prints in the deep sand of the creek, had attacked Ironhead and he had barely escaped with his life. He had run up into the high rocks again.

After a long search I found my berrying friend.

"Come on down again. Let us ignore those beasts. Let us find some succulent, juicy berries to feast on."

"Not me. I'm staying up here"

"Then I will go alone," I said to Ironhead."Feather that one out." I took off. "Follow me," I called from the sky. "Follow me to the berry patch!" I little e x-pected that mountain sheep to do anything but pant in the hot rocks and watch me. But here he came. Down, down, down and down. Once again we were among the briars along the creek.

"There's some good ones," I sang out with a <u>Caw</u>!

"They are sour," said Ironhead.

"Let me direct your eyes then to that briar pat c h on the knoll."

"Lovely," said the ram.

"Shall we enter therein and feast our bellies on the fruit of the season?"

"Don't go high-falutin" on me, crow. After all, you are just a crow and I am a ram."

"Enter," I said, and Ironhead did, pushing his way into the thicket for the innermost ripe, red luscious berries. It was a challenge all right. "Oh, I see some more!"

"Where?"

"Right over there, across the small ravine."

"But I cannot get out—these confounded brambles pick and pluck at my coat."

"See them. Smell them. I can see them quite clearly"""

"They are gray and dead ripe," said the ram.

"They are red and black and filled with juice," I said.

"I am caught ..."

"Then—I think I shall go enjoy them—alone. There really is not enough food to go around."

"You tricked me. You tricked me. You tricked m e! "said the ram.

I listened to that simpering voice as the ram th r u s t himself further into the briars by bucking and leaping.Every new struggle further ensnared him. I saw a tall man with a graying beard and dark, fiery eyes, holding a small boy b y the hand. They were coming up the mountain. The boy carried wood on his back. I circled overhead in a hoi ding pattern.

"Here is where I think we can build an altar. What do you say to that, boy?" the man asked.

"That is fine. I am glad to carry the wood. I hope you have the coals."

"I have the coals." The tall man's lined face glistened with sweat in the hot noon sun. "Here is where it i s to be then." They cleared away brush and gathered stones and began to build for themselves an altar.

"You are cruel," cried Ironhead.

"I must be clever to survive," I cawed down to t h e ram.

The man gave the boy a kiss and bound his hands b e-hind him. "What are you going to do?" the boy asked.

"I obey the commands of the God of the heavens," said the man. I circled the place where the man and the boy had stopped—and where poor Ironhead struggled and fought t o get free from the dense, long thorns of the briars. For want of food the man is about to kill the boy. This is a detestable thing to see, I thought. Have I no way to stop this?

As the man raised his arm, in his hand I saw the blad e of a knife flash; but then, coming from under the ground a voice told him to stop and look up. Hesaw my trapped and caught and entangled berrying friend, Ironhead.

"Look! A ram is caught in the thicket 1" the b o y cried.

"We will sacrifice the ram," the man said.

"You treacherous bird!" the ram shouted up at me.

"You will never learn to keep to your own terrain, Iron-head. You and your kind always wander into the camp of the enemy."

"I trusted you."

"You cannot trust any beast or bird who is as clever as I am|" I said, and I <u>cawed</u>, <u>cawed</u>, <u>cawed</u>! "Feather that one out!"

Ironhead backed up, bucked into the thorns, yet they only bit deeper into his wool and held him fast. "Wait un-til fall, Ironhead. I get all! Caw! Caw!"

"This is a miracle," said the loan to the boy.

"Find your own berries, high roller!" I cried down into the brush as I observed the ram's terror. The ma n walked into the thicket. He raised his hand again. I saw the flash of the knife and knew that my competitor for food was done in.

"I will feast on the berries—alone, Ironhead. You believed a lie. Now you must die, Gawwww! Cawwww! Cawwww!"After these parting words I flew away—toward the creek a-gain to satisfy my hunger.

> In the wild animal's primal acceptance of man's presence in its domain, that accord is e i t her nascent or else it did not evolve but was "i replanted." as it were at the genesis of life. A basic hostility between nan and beast has always existed and been evident. Therefore, how c an one explain that capacity of the animal to be trained, making its performance sore urgent than rewards of food? Is the animal's fear the only answer? Or does its primal acceptance show a subtle and mysterious affinity remaining yet to be probed? Many of the explanations for unusual behavior in animals appear to be simplistic.

Pig For Company

Few pigs possessed the perspicacity of Simeon, the Big One, yet he saw no reason for folks to laugh at pig behavior simply because he liked mud and slops, had no religion, and hated good manners. But then that is the way with the whole world nowadays" Mud and slops and crude manners. Simeon was also a pig of some fame and reputation. He belonged to a herd t h at fed on the hillsides above the Galilean Sea. He kept him s elf nicely fat on roots and gopher burrows and wild grain and turnip roots. He was. as all the swine knew, a good digger, root-er whose wet, broad nose was joined to an uncommonly strong mind.

Word went out over all the land by way of swineh er d rumblings that the Man in the Cave was on the search for a pet. a cave pet, one like their kind and drawn from noble pig stock, who could keep the cave dweller company. Since he was a ma n of violence. of broken shackles and twisted chains, crying out to the heavens because of his loneliness, he layed only a few demands upon competitors: any pig. who might easily become a hog in the master's service, had to be gentle in disposition, willing to train at breaking the house and dwelling amid the comparative luxury of the hillside cave, where at this Cave Dweller hung his fur.

No sooner had Simeon announced his apllication for the position, wallowing in a dust pit to cleanse his bristles, than a competitor pig, approximately a hog named Asparagus, put in his bid. Asparagus had earned his name by his practiced a-bility to smell and root out field wild asparagus, no sma 1 1 feat when a hog's blunt nose was detached from root intelligence. He also had his following and, like all pigs of character, his pride turned wrongside out.

"I am going to become the Wild Man's companion/' A s-paragas sad to Simeon.

"No, I am. I have the qualities the Wild Man looks for."

"But I have the capacity to be trained. You lack even—basic politeness," said Asparagus with a loud snort.

A third swineherd member., a dark pig, joined t h ei r small group of two to solicit the Wild Man's love and companionship. He was a mottled pig. All herd swine called him Dynasty when, in fact. he resembled a leper pig rather than a creature with noble markings. He preferred the name of Hogarth! the Hog. but accepted "Hogarth." A strange threesome, these hogs. when on a bright and sunny day they oinked at the entrance to the Wild Man's cave and, rolling on the ground in the muck, begged an audience with him.

Hogarth spoke. "We have come to apply for the position of companion to yourself in this glorious cave."

"Come in. Come in, and rest yourselves in my cordial mud bath. Slop and wallow and splash as you will. Each o f you has the same mission in mind?" the village Terror asked.

"We do. We do. We do," they chorused.

"But you do not know what it is I need. Company her e in this lovely, lonely booming cave is just the start. Hear how your voices echo?"

"Oinkalooooo."

"Oinkalooooo."

"Oinkalooooo," each said in turn. The sound of their hog voices, like tinkling fragments of exotic nose-blow ing sound, echoed back into the far reaches of darkness.

"I shall give each of you a test to see if you are qualified or not." The Wild One clattered lengths of broken chain over the rocks as be shifted about. With his tongue he cleansed scabrous places on his wrists and ankles ru b b ed raw by iron shackles. "My keepers—"he screamed and howled into the cavernous depths of the cave. "The villagers call me mad. They say I am a visionary—actually—a seer i n to the future. At one time I worked for the government of Caesar but they exiled me for having too many visions."

"I am terribly sorry, Wild Han. My name is SiPeon."

"Let me peer into your hog skull. The Mad One rap-ped a bony finger on Simeon"s skull. "You despise the caresses of politicians, you surround yourself with the wealth of dir t, with the enticements of manufactured love and joy and ga i e t y and frivolity."

"You have deep insight into my—pig"s makeup."

"Yet your hide is tough enough to resist—temptations?"

"I—oink—think so, Wild One."

"Can you count to four?"

"I have never tried."

"When you do, I will send you off into the firepat c h where you'll find the Fagots of Fagdom have cooked all your meals for you. No longer raw roots, uncooked field hens and the like. Deck your purse ears with delectable and titillating diatribes. Go and visit the Den of Zen where you shall enjoy philosoph i c peri shine nt forever, a state of inner sanctif ication and moti o n-less life suspension—a hog dreamer, a pig of circumstance and prehensile meditation." The Wild One grunted.

"You are mad," said Simeon, the pig.

"Do you doubt it now? You will find this kingdom of dross and fatuous fornication at the far end of my—cave." A wierd laugh broke from the mossy mouth of the Cave Man, the dwe l le r among unimaginable sacrististies stuffed with doubt and trivia l quests. "Go-o-o-o-o—"the echo reverberated down through the cave of recorded time—cold, bizarre, echoing in among the sensate, quiescent obsidion rocks of the Wild One"s dwelling place. "And you—?"

"I am Asparagas," said the nippy, little, frisky, trivet of a pig.

"That is your name, Little One?"

"It is, it is."

"I measure your stress by my rock-o-stress meter. You must be able to bear up under stress—like the rocks in this here cave."

"I shall—oink—try. I—oink—shall try."

"Try! Try! I will not hear of it. You mist succeed!"

"Feed me columbine slops and purple tips and I shall."

"Furth-errr-mor-eee, a thin veneer of smoke haze sepa—rates you from your hill dwellers—rabble!—a kaleidoscop i c tumble of spirit shapes gathered from poisonous roots and dotting condiments of wood and trees. Do you comprehend the mag i c of it all?"

"I do, I do. I am to periginate, to spin and cavort like a goat until I gather speed, and then I shall sail off in-to space ."

"You have hit it! A hog with a pig"s imagination," said the Wild One. "Your only sacrifice is to—loyalty—to me, the Madcap of the Caves."

"I will try, Mad One."

"Try! Try! I will not hear of it! You must succeed! And what is your name, bagatells of the slop trough?"

"My name is—Hogarth, the Hog."

"How clever l You worked your name into a patrimony. I love, I adore clever hogs. They are so—masculine."

"You will never find me wanting in attention to your needs/" said Hogarth.

"Do you climb upon walls?"

"Do I climb upon walls."

"That is what I said. Are you deaf? Climb up a n d across the roof of my cave."

"That is impossible."

"Think of levity, of levitation, of wicked designs, of unearthly ruminations—haaaaa, haaaaa." That wierd laughter again rose from the Mad (toe in phosphorescent green. "Rum innate upon the ceiling. attain self-mastery, crawl upon the slimy rocks like the bats of agitation, who will keep you company"

"You are hideous."

"Do you doubt now that I am mad. Do it and see for yourself."

Strophic music with a crippled beat, thrummed on dinosaur guts, filled the black putrescence of cave space. "I ruminate, I reflect, I concentrate. I meditate—"Hogarth began to rise as if from a pot of steam, to gurgle with the sounds of shouts from the crevasse between the floor rocks, as the throbbing beat of the rock music quenched his ears and sight and mesmerized his sense of this presence. He felt humanoid again.

"New life—ruminate, and it is yours." said the seer. He waved his bamaloo stick three times in the silky. bland cave air and a frosty trickle of spring water formed upon th e floor from which emerged an assortment of snails. guatiposes, festaroons and maggots. "These are your imaginings. What i & prettier?" the Mad One laughed.

"I did not apply for the job of companion to be—i n-suited."

"Chase these quarries, these tiny life fragments, these inedible quadraloons of crestamontemania."

"You puzzle me, Wild One."

"You amuse me, Hogarth, the Hog. You are a replica of man's—have you never heard of him?—of man's deepest longings outside of Saturnalia. the sky gleam."

"I can barely see them as it is."

"Sorry for the poor light in here," said the seer."You will adjust if you become—mine. Now-go, go seek your brother in the darkness—down there, through the cave trough of mud and danger and moaning winds." Hogarth set off. "Why do you hang around, Asparagus? Go with him, and while I confine you to the pennin of trumpernity as I make my decision, you can find choice morsel of delectable gratification in my-prepared darkness."

"You are mad—mad—mad." The voice of Asparagus only turned into brittle glisterlings, like frog wings and snake scales iced by the wand of demon demonology. He set out into the further darkness while the Mad (tee stood tremulous amid his brassy-colored smoke puffs, drew in deep breaths that hung lite shreds of half-digested dross upon his lips.

The Mad One came out from his cave to consider his applicants, rare specimen flockings upon the night of the cave. O, gesticulations of infernal paradise! Soon thereat, upo n the road to the village, he met up with a strange and unmitigated man, before whom he fell down upon scrofulous knees. The bearded Giant swacked the stones of the road into the heavens" They became daytime stars. "You have come out to dig up the wild potatoes?" asked the Giant, kicking aside the chain leng-ths of the beast, aroused faintly by the clank of the leg irons. "Well—is your hearing dilapidated?"

"Sometimes—I come out—partially and albeit whenever the circumstances confess of confabulation with con je c-ture."

"You speak in riddles, Mad One," said the Giant. "Here. Let me touch you."

"Stay away! Get away from me. I have a rumination to finish. I am about to chose a house pet for my cave—one of three hogs who came to me this morning."

"Quaint. How quaintt"

"Yes, I thought so," said the Mad One.

The hogs on the hillside kept a derelect eye upon th e visitors to their root kingdom and their swale of inedible legumes. Nearby to the men on the road the hogs tore up t h e ground with snortings and rooting, honking omnivorously as if in quest of life, not juicy succulents. A thousand swine- or thereabouts-tossed wet dirt over their eyes and heads i n playtime abandonment. Pigs seldom do that.

"I am a wierd one for keeping my eyes open—to daylight."

"Luminiscence if my name," said the bearded one.

While the Wild One and the traveler stood conversing, the herdsman sat a ways off, atop a rocky outcropping, drum-ming with a beat—on his drum of an inflated sheep's belly-a beat that fractured the stones and rumbled the earth, terrorizing the termitic squigglies of worm life and rat caperchance. The hogs dug and dug and a pony dog. yapping with fre n z i e d and pontifical forensic declamations snapped at the heels of the swine. They all dreampt of what the three candidates for the Cave companionship wanted—golden troughs where slops were eternal and never empty at hand and there was a choice between old bread, rotten meat and vinegar gruel. Choice cam e hard to the hogs. They were a finicky lot—would never touch cranberries or any bitter herbs or condiments of rotting wood that cause a sneeze—or bitters and old wine, or wormy corn" Nice eaters, they were—trichinosis was one of their real hangups | coning from a bad diet. May the Giant favor the hogs i n the darkness of the cave—sacrificial pigs of circumstances an d pragmatic circumlocutions. Yet—they, the petitioners, made out and were doing so on this day after the laurel Application For Employment was heard.

That Cave One, half-naked, his sin bones shining in the sun, his sackcloth torn and shredded and filthy, charged t he swine on the hillside. He carried a jug in his hand—he was drunk on cheap wine—and he blew into the top of the jug. I t gave out with a deep tone of sentient noise and ambience of gentle, fluted musicality. Evidently the herdsman liked it, for he raised his jug again to the skies and blew so so hard that his face shimmered in its profuse pinkness and his ears grew tra ns-lucent with redhot heat and his eyes rolled back into his head like stones of black pitch. He was a devotee of sound, that one, decibelic and embecilic sound.

Worms emerged from their ventricular holes—like beetle caverns in tree bark—out of the ground, mealy worms, long and yellow with teeth in their jaws like small snakes. Only, they were no bigger round than a tree twig with moss skin, and th e y attacked all the hogs—all of them, and they bored theraselv e s into the hog's hide, but most of the swine kept right on root- ing and digging. The man on the first jug, the Cave Dwe Her, ran up to the Giant and gave him a hug, like two compatriots without rotting limbs and purulent speech of rotting noise. The lapping of water in the wind waves striking the rocky shore be l o w the cliff infiltrated like a lulling sound the herd of rooters and diggers. Pretty soon the hogs began to bump into other hogs and the herdsman sent his bounding quadraped in amongst them t o whip up their frenzy for the slop trough. Glutted, they were slacking off.

The swineherd began to count them with his patroona stidt while the Mad One watched nearby and sat upon a round rock. H e picked up the abandoned belly drum and frocked the cloven hooves with his diactinic drum beats that shook rocks down upon the hillside and annointed the blue lake with a wither and lather of whitecaps. It was as splendrous a sight as ever those swi n e saw, regaled to perdition. He and his yapping quadraped counted all.

"Three is missing."

"In my cave yonder," said the Mad One between beats. "I need a pig for company" Three have applied—Simeon, Asparagus, and Hogarth."

"Three are missing."

"I will return them to you, their skins inside and their sausages inside out."

"You are so funny," said the herdsman to the Mad *One.* "Hem will you know if one of them is your right choice?"

"Easy—the hog that sits upright upon the cireurnstanc e of ethicality and paternalistically ejecting."

"You make sense," said the swineherd.

"Course I do. But look—there go the lot of them." The entire hillside of at least a thousand swine threw then-selves over the cliff and onto the butchering rocks and water below. Faint, distant words floated up like ethereal music to the ears of the swineherdt "Last one in has got to pay the herdsman's wages."

"Strange pigs, even stranger grunts of words," h e said

"What did we do to deserve thisssss?" went the headlong squeel of final dejecturement, the perfect picture o f death and obloquy and eclipse of intelligence. The last hog dove over in a glissade of squeels.

"Bring the three to me," said the swineherd.

"Peace be upon you. Wild One," said the Giant and he touched the shaggy head of the Mad Man. "Go and bring them out from your cave, Not one of them shall be yours to keep."

A loud, anguished cry cascaded from the lips of the Mad One. "I intend to keep them all-with me."

"At your peril," said the Giant. "At your peril."lte Giant departed, and the herdsman, boiling with rash anger and hostility toward the visitor, went on his way. toward the village and the owner of the swine. The Mad One ascended the hillside to his cave. there to settle upon one of the hogs as a choice for his companion. But when he arrived, he foun d all three, not asleep but dead in the poison trough at th e cave entrance. In the jaws of one was a stone that flamed with blue incadescence, the rhomboid darkness of snake land carried up for a souvenir to duty. Thrust into the stomach of the second, who claimed Asparagus as his name, was a silvery lancet that glimmered in the pale sundown light. His hide, his innards were half carved but bloodless and dea th had hazed over his eyes. The third, Hogarth, had grown hu-man ears, and fingers adorned his hooves on the front feet, toes on the rear, and he seemed to fit the contours of the rocks as if he sprang therefrom. On his face black lace covered his eyes, his snout a mask of rosy reasoning, a de-ception that appeared to pulse though life was gone. The Mad One picked up a saber tooth from the floor of his cave and began to pick his teeth. Once rid of the demons, death would still be his companion—unless . maybe he ought to go and enquire of the Giant, who appeared s o cool about the whole scene, as if he comprehended.

The Donkey & The Camel Who Couldn't

"It is stupid to think that a camel like myself cannot walk through a gate to the city without hunkering down on his knee pads like a carpet layer. But that's the swagger of gossip among some pot merchants these days. I t old <u>Tarsus</u>, my donkey acquaintance at gate life, about the drift of this prejudice. <u>Tarsus</u> just brayed through his u g ly teeth—what else? He said it was all in the minds of t h e timid pleasers of Caesar who come into Jerusalem from Cairo, Athens, Jopa and other such places.

Then the notion that I am too big for the gate g e ts mixed in with needles and tent-makers and rich merchants and folks who count.

"It's all confusion to me," I said.

"The whole thing is without any taste. No delicacy like you got plenty of," said the donkey.

"At least Matthew, the money-changer and tax collector over there appreciates you." <u>Tarsus</u> showed me his stiff upper lip. "But that gate ruffian, my own master, Pfleugelschmaltzen, spreading it around that I'm humpbacked and overweight—that's what scruffs my shag."

"Can't say I blame you," said <u>Tarsus</u>" "I su ppo s e my own ugly smile does get in the way of friendship a t times."

"I'll tell you what," I said, "Lets us try t o change our public image—just for kicks, just for the riot."

"Like how?"

I jangled my neck bells, shifted from one foot t o the other in the shade of the city wall. Pfleugelschmalt-zen was off dickering with the money-changer, Mat. N o w was our chance to plan.

Tarsus spoke first. "The thing that has happened is that gate is filled up with sand blown in from the desert—four hundred years of sand storms. I'll just bet mybx&y that gate's actually lower by ten feet."

"I never thought about that. You"re a pretty smart donkey."

"I just watched that German-Arab dummy upside your hump whip you with his rope line. I seen you sera pe on through—and how hard it was to keep your temper. You r honky bellowing was sure called for."

"I do, I do have a cussed time hanging onto m y temper. Bit him one time, I got to tell you."

"Bad scene," said Tarsus. "But you got one hump only. What if you had two?"

"Twice as bad-tempered, I guess."

"Your knee pads are made for hot desert sands—not for bowing down to no rug merchant." Tarsus brayed, looked around. "Listen close. There under the turban, ju s t inside the gate—my master in his stall scooping up gold for Caesar. Well, Mat has got a broken-down chariot-one wheel missing—took it in for security on a Roman deb t last year—he keeps it over by the Three Rocks Camel Bar. Why don't we drag it over here and block this gate?"

"You out of your bridle, ol Tarsus?"

"Block the gate in the middle of the night so's to stop the merchant caravans coming through." I balke d, naturally. Tarsus saw this. "Donkeys got strategy minds, camels got shuffle, grunt and push minds."

"You're so simple," I bellowed. "Then what?"

"The Sanhedrin finds the gate blocked up, no traffic, blackbearded Mat gets his money purse in a sling-his wheels block the way. They say, 'Move that u nholy chariot. Casey has him thrown into jail, fines him,"

"Casey?"

"Caesar, Dullrock!"

"Taxes and profits stop. The Sanhedrin is alarmed-

"Whoa—whoa! You think all this is going to happen, just like that?"

"Naturally. Traffic backs up—peddlars. rug merchants, herdsmen, wine and incense vendors—the usual crowd that rattles through the gate. Mat's a Jew. Sanhedrin is riled up by now, steps in, offers a slogan to Casey: A TALL GATE FOR TALL MERCHANTS."

"You're pulling ray fetters."

"No. I aint, Dullrock."

"Won't do any good. When the keeper locks the big gat e at night, the small one has got a soldier in it. We got to get around him. No. I don't trust no one."

"Go ahead then. Nastylip. Hunker down on your kne d pads every time you enter Jerusalem. Let your pots scrape through the gate and your rugs jam against the stones. I was just trying to help you out."

"Scruff my fuzz. Pfleugelschmaltzen always has to unload me, it's true— unlashes the ropes and drops all that junk to the ground."

"Right there at the gate. I know that. You see what I mean? What does he care? No, you follow ray instructions. Get Chalice, the blind war horse, to drag blackbeard's broken chariot into the gate."

"All those folks coming down from the hills to buy new cloaks, pots and lanterns and sweetsraelling incense and perfumes and Baal toys—and then can't get in! Thunder and lightning!"

"Now you're getting the idea, Sugarlump. Remember-I.m doing this for you."

"I'll remember."

On the following morning a representative from the Jerusalem City Planning Commission showed up. I was tied up. I'll get to that.

"Heard you're not happy with our gate. Too small." h e said to be hard and ugly.

"Way too small! I'm a registered camel. Name's S u-garlump."

"I see. I see. Tough to get through, huh. Gate's a-about seven. nine." That's all he said. Just walked away.

"What you do about my plan?" Tarsus asked me.

"I said I told Chalice vhen he come by here pulling a load of barley. And I said Chalice said he'd haul out that broken-down chariot when the sun went down."

"You give him—?"

"A lick of salt and some vegies from the marketplace."

"Good for you, Rubberlip. Oh, you're a sly, old beasty, you are. Good job, Lump!. Good job!"

Tarsus left with Mat for other parts in the city. As usual, that night the outer gate was closed and locked. No guard at the small entrance. Strange. And my master had gone—probably to the Three Rocks Camel Bar and got tankad up. Along about dusk here came Chalice—poor thing." dragging blackbeard Mat's broken-down chariot. The blind *horse* dropped the shafts right smack in the middle of the gate-opening. He bumped into the stonework, crashed into one of the empty vendor stalls and had a mangy dog nip at bis hind legs. But he did his job. A faithful one.

Now if that donkey friend of mine was right we ha d only to let the guards find the chariot. They had records to show it belonged to the Jew Mat. He gets a fine of one hundred denarii and jail. But he goes bail and pays the Jerusalem Department of Public Works to enlarge the ga t e, Money does it eve ry time.

Pfleugelschmaltzen came by later on and moved me-he was so pie-eyed he didn't see what had happened. He found a rest for me at City Camel Stalls—and was I glad to get rid of mangy dogs. dust and fliesI

"I'm going to have trouble with that gate," he mum-bled and fell over into the dirt. Strong stuff at T h e Three Rocks! He picked himself up. "I got to unload you ev-ery time—nasty beast. Vy can't you—hie—be smaller?" I screamed and flung up my head—high. Scruff m y fuzz! Not once did I ever knock over a vegie stand-not onceI He led me away.

Next trip out, Mat's broken-down chariot was gone. Pfleugelschmaltzen curried the sand and flees out of m y scrubby hair, lifted my upper lip to check my teeth, fed me some barley and water and we left. We walked by black-bearded Mat at the collections table by the gate, but h e paid us no mind. Outside the Jerusalem wall we travel ed along the blistering road to Joppa, in a fog of dust throw-ed up by passing Roman chariots. Sweaty! Ruts in the road—lots of them. In the town of Joppa by the sea Pfleugel-smaltzen broke my back with junk, and we started home. to the walled city. From a ways out, the white pray e r-towers rise up through the shimmering sand. The sun was a hot ball. As the city got closer it began to get on m y nerves. the banging of pots and bells and tinwork. Thes e junk sounds showered into the desert air.

We halted at the gate, outside the wall, same as always. I watched this Arab drive his donkey into the gateway with curses, and he just almost—well. hardly got through with a high stake of clay pots and bullrish backets.

Through the gatewell I heard <u>Tarsus</u> bray. "Where do you think you're going?"

"Through that gate, donkey!"

"Not now you" re not. See all that commotion there?"Sure enough, there was a crowd, some slave, dark skins, Roman soldiers, loin cloths and turbans and Mat standing eyeball to eyeball with an official, I guess, from the Jerusalem Department of Public Works. My master Pfleugelsch-maltzen beat me with his rope whip. I honked in my m o st pitiable way, hissed and curled up my fat lip. At whi c h time he began to unload my sore back. He beat me to m y knees with his fat hand. My neck bells fell into the sand. Master Pfleugelschmaltzen dropped off a sack of cocoanuts. My feet were sure blisteredo He slid tapestries off m y hump and banged the copper pots to the ground—realex-pense goods.

"Whoa, whoa!" called out a slave parked at the out er gate stoneSo

"I am coming on through. I am Pfleugelschmaltzen, a trader, well-known in Jerusalem."

"I do not care who you are," the slave replied. A city official walked through the gate to discover the cause of the rancor and stoppage. The slave said to him:"Thi s here trader says he is a big fellow and has to get through the gate—tonight."

"Can"t you see?" said the angry official. "We are deepening the gate. It will take us another week for road repairs."

"Another week!" my master shouted.

"Go around then to the Fish Gate," said the official.

"I cannot waito I roust come through. My rugs will fade in the hot sun. Thieves will steal my pots and m y tapestries. I have no food for myself or straw for my poor camel here "He at last gave me some consideration.

"Thoughtful fellow." I snickered.

"You did not tell me the gate was so small." said Pfleugelschmaltzen to the official.

"You did not ask me. You are grossly overloaded with junk. You will have to remain outside the city.

"But why?" Then—"No, I will not! <u>Tarsus</u> danced around on the street, before the gate.

"You see," said the donkey.

"See what?" I asked. "It is almost night and now I shall have to spend it outside the wall.

"No. you will not. Come. Walk around your master's junk." I did so. "And bring what you carry."

"Come back here! My camel! He is walking away!Come back. come back!" Pfleugelschmaltzen shouted.

"We are not going far," said the donkey. "Here he is, master." he said to Mat, swarmed upon by angry mercha n ts and officials of the city.

"That camel there. You—you onery, flatfooted, nasty, stubborn, surly beast—You could not get your master through the Jerusalem gate. And I cannot collect my tariff for t h e Roman government. It is all your fault. You ought to kneel. But no—you are a proud camel. Strike him! Strike h i ml"said blackbearded Mat to several slaves, who began to wh i p my scrubby hide with reed switches"

"How do you like being in debt to the tax-collector and to Caesar?"' my donkey friend asked through his braying laughter. "Now you must pay your master"s gate and tariff tax."

"I think you are having fun with me."

"The Jew controls the gate—for Caesar."

"Go get your master!" Mat shouted over the din File will load up your back." Already Pfleugelschmaltzen had order e d slaves to carry his junk through the gate and he repacked m y load—pots to the front of my hump, rugs on top, clay lanterns and co coanuts behind, brass bells around my neck.

"Now to Mark Schrubber's straw loft!" Pfleugelschmaltzen muttered, and we left the action at the gate behind.

"Curry down this fine animal," he ordered the gr oo m s at the stables. By now 1 had decided to bolt. Tarsus was nowhere around to stop me. I ambled across the city and headed through the Dung Gate for the outer desert. Worst of all calamities, a Roman soldier caught my halter rope and tied me on behind his chariot. He then had the brass to run his horses at a gallop until I lost my wind and my tongue h u ng out—all the time my master's junk rattling, banging, ring-ing through the streets and folks laughing at me …

Pfleugelschmaltzen rewarded the soldier with a g ol d coin—there was only one camel barn in Jerusalem. My master bribed me with some desert figs. That night passed withou t any bad marvels, however, in the morning, when my master u n-loaded me in the marketplace, I saw a new sign over the gate that read: "CLEARANCE—18 METERS".

"Frosty"Grotius, a Centurion and captain of the Jerusalem storm troopers garrison, saw me stop at the gate. I guess I was his target. He recognized me at once. He was Caesar's man.

"Hey, you! Junk carrier!" he called to Pfleugelschmaltzen, "sell your fine camel there."

"No, he is a very fine camel and I shall keep him."

"Too bad. I need a leader to carry troop baggage."

"I need my poor Sugarlump or I will starve."

"I will give you gold and wine for him."

"He is too valuable for me to lose or give up. This haggling over my carcass was hard and ugly. I sa w the gold and the wine change hands—but I am only a h umble camel

"Your fine camel is the reason Caesar—hail, Caesar!-got the gate height changed, and a new Gate Height Code enacted. Now you will no longer have to unload him or suffer him to cut his hide in a low gate."

"I will never enter Jerusalem again!" I snarled in a last bid for independence.

"I am your master now," said the Centurion, "so dont raise your voice at me." He struck me with his hand, and I snarled, giving him my grungiest upper lip. Fift e e n meters is still a bit low.

"You can't win for losing," said a familiar voic e. It belonged to Tarsus.

"Fat lot of good your scheme did. I still got t o kneel, gate or no gate."

"You are being your old nasty self, I see," the donkey said. "You still got your pride and those lovely eyelashes o You wanted an easy gate—and an easy life. You got them both, Lump."

"At least I do not make up the rules as I go along-like some donkeys I know do,"

"You are just bitter, Sugarlump. See you around."He sauntered off. My new master led me by the halter rope-to his garrison stable where I met all the horses. As I passed by the gate for a last look, Pfleugelschmaltzen sat propped up against the wall, laughing himself to death.

> Any man who abuses an animal violates God.s authority over the animals.

Quarry On The Run

He liked to run with the pack, yet his tongue rolling and his frothy jaws agape he liked running alone . Smirky was a wild jackal, a fearless hunter whose powerful shoulders and the smirk on his muzzle set him apart when he trotted in the lead of his hunting mates.

This bone-crusher mingled, touched noses and, gather-ing to his kind, went out on a hunt one day with his confreres in death. An ancient precursor to the dog, he now and again stopped at a rock, a bush or tangle of weeds t o sniff, leave the odor of his presence and the boundary o f his territory, trotting off again with his mates. As the dawn sun slowly rose and the dew evaporated from the lotus petals of the cactus flower, Smirky's instinct informed him that today was to be his day.

He was the swiftest member of the pack. He howle d with a thrilling glissando of sound. The hills and the morning sky often echoed to his notes. He barked almost never, yelped with great gusto. And most of all, his jaws watering, his eyes intent and ears lain back he crun ched the bones of his kill and seized the best morsel for his hungry stomach with a consuming relish.

This day he had gone without food for three suns. He was ravenous. He grinned—or so man would assume—while he ran with slack jaws across the open grasslands. His comrades had flushed a quarry, a fawn mule deer. They had i t on the run. Instinct informed Smirky the deer could not last long. He knew the limits of his own stamina and cunn in gi They were equal to the hunt. Smirky claimed little pres-tige in the canine world, however, he was at bottom a vain creature of the wild and almost too independent for his own good. Friends envied the tawny tufts in his coat, his full brush of a tail, his high, muscular shoulders that stood him above the rest of the pack. His white teeth sparkled w i th kill saliva, sharp daggers of hard agate rock, capable o f severing sinew and joint. Smirky grinned at almost everything his brothers did. It was so dumb the way they hunt e d often without any exhausting chase.-wasting the day light and often the night, sleeping until hunger prodded them t o their paws again. What a drag! he thought. Life to him was a bag of mouth-watering bones to be grappled and seize d by cunning.

On this one day he felt especially superior to his mates of the pack. He schemed to emulate the fawn with camouflage, lying still in wait, only to pounce upon any gam e that wandered by mistake through the grass. Prodigal in its excesses and violence, nature had also taught him patience. He was a proud jackal, a better hunter than any of the other jackals who ran with him this morning. He would crouch like a lion in the tall grass and leap upon the back of his quarry when it met its fate.

He settled into some concealing clumps of grass. H e waited for the pack to drive the kill his way. He would take what then really belonged to him. He lay there for so long that heat waves rose from his fur and the very rocks turned painfully hot under his pads. Maybe he had made a mistake in strategy; the pack was not chasing a fawn. Presently. h e heard thrashing through the dry grass. The pack came upon him.

"I'm resting. Can't you see? I am waiting for the deer to dash this way. You can see for yourselves I am camouflaged."

"It is you who are dumb, brother," said a particularly offensive female. "Now that we know where you lie, we wi 1 1 chase the deer in the opposite direction."

"You get up and run with us," said Gordy, the Dog. His sharp words were an insult, for he was part shepherd. "You run with us or we will drop you from the pack like poisoned bait."

"You are deceiving yourself," said the bitch. They howled. They knew what Smirky was up to. By nature he wa s a lazy jackal. They were not to be put off the scent by his lion-in-wait excuse. They ringed around him. He had to o-bey Gordy and the pack. He got up to run.

However, since he figured that he was smarter than they he would strike a small bargain with them. He yearned to seize the leader-post of the pack.

"If I run ahead and bring down the kill—perhaps the fawn you now chase, and if I share its sweet delicious meat with you, can I be leader of the pack?"

"No, no, no!" the other jackals cried. They stood panting in the ground heating of the sun, beneath a shade tree, ready to set off again. "Gordy is good to us. We cannot betray him," said the pack runt. "But you run on ahead, Smirky. You are lazy. You need the exercise and the advantage more than we do." The slops and the licking of chops and the sniffings and growls followed "signs of acquiescence to the runt's insult.

The pack's refusal to give in to him stung Smirky. Their silent jeers made him mad. He suddenly leapt tip from his crouch in the grass and lost them over the crest of a small hill. He quickly found the fresh trail o f the fawn. Its scats were recent.

In seconds he smelled out his prey, then he saw it. It was a maturing baby deer, with spots still in its coat, a yearling. Chasing it, he brought it to the ground. As is the way in the animal kingdom, he kill e d the deer for his first meat in days. But then he decided that he should retaliate against the taunts of his jackal brothers. It was best that he outsmart them, and so he began to drag the still-warm carcass off to a fox den he had seen.

The bitch fox was nearby. She said to the jackal, "Where are you going with BO much food?"

"I am going to hide it from my friends-to give them a lesson they won't forget. They do not respect me. They do not honor me. I am the fastest runner in the pack. I have the most intelligence. See my beauty?"

"Ah, I well understand," said the fox. "I too a m chased because hunters and their dreadful horses disdain me. And—I appreciate beauty—my red coat is very lovely, don't you think?"

"I do, I do," said Smirky.

"But—let me take a look at you. Then maybe I can get more perspective on your—difficulties."

Smirky was surprised and he felt flattered by this adulation—truly the fox was a good judge of beauty and merit—and thus he did as the fox suggested. Smirk y walked off a few strides, turned about in a neat little pivot on his hind legs and smiled again, when the fox said from a distance:

"Look into the sun. It will make your eyes shine as if you are in love, so you can meet your love with tender eyes when she comes with the pack."

He remembered her taunt but forgot it in the fox" s praise, and so he did as the fox told him to do. He liked the fox's idea. He liked the fox's kind of approach. He liked the fox.s style. At this moment the fox simply pulled the dead fawn into its den and closed in the gro u n d behind it.

Smirky turned around. He could not find the fox anywhere. It had disappeared. Worst of all calamiti es, the larder also had vanished and the pack would soon b e upon him. They would want to know where their food was. As sure as sundown, here raced the jackal pack around a rocky outcropping and breathlessly up to him.

Gordy confronted him. "Ah, ha, you greedy jackal! You have eaten our dinner for us. I see the blood i n your jaws. You will let us suffer in our hunger." Yelps and howls raised Smirky's hackles. "We will punish you for this," said the pack leader"

The jackal pack drew a ring around Smirky. They waited for their leader's signal to attack—a deep-throated growl. Each was allowed to bite the wrongdoer a t least one time. Gordy sounded his growl and they charged in, not a single one going for the throat of the miser e-ant but all inflicting their sentence upon the dishonorable one.

They bit and bit until Smirky was bloodied from tail to chest by the chop. chop. snapping of their sharp incisor teeth. As soon as he dared to turn his back upon them. he lit out for the high rocks and soon was out of sight.

"Stay!" cried the pack leader. They obeyed Gordy's command. "Let him go. He will starve. He is so smart. He does not need the advice or help of others of his kind. He is independent. He is better than we are. That is why he smirks. That was why he always smirked when he hunted with us." The pack sniffed and whined in agreement.

Smirky| the proud jackal. was never seen in t h e territory again. alive. His brothers found his care as *a* hanging on the barbed wire fence of a farmhouse, not far from where the fox had stolen the fawn. His confreres at once knew that Smirky had thought himself more c u n n in g than the farmer. He had gotten into the pasture and the farmer had shot him dead. a victim of his dumb pride.

No Matter How Small

Wilson was a field mouse of uncommonly good judgement. His disposition was also cheerful. That proved to be a good thing in painful, traumatic circumstances that befell the mouse community in the village of Peanut. Some four thousand of his fellow mice lived in and around the houses, barns and rocks of the village, but most of t h e mouse population dwelt in the fields that surrounded this village of about five hundred souls. Wilson had set u p house in a splended field of weeds, two old automobiles rusting away, some large boulders and the usual bro ken bits of glass, wire, rotting fences and castaway furniture. There a cogent mouse like himself could exist through fifteen generations, give or take a few, and live quite comfortably without fear of eviction or extermination.The field was airy and cheerful and, of course, Wilson—something of a rebel—shared the accouterments, the comforts and amenities of the field with almost a hundred other s like himself, all of life one grand gnaw and nibble. They lived in ground holes, scampered between the stuffing of the sofa and the wild grain that had sprouted up throu g h the truck fenders and pieces of corrugated rusting ti n. Life was—heavenly.

One day, unannounced. there came a crashing and a squeeky, metalic rattle—a horrifying noise, a rumbleaid clatter such as shook Wilson and his compatriots from their ground holes. Little beady black eyes scanned the landscape from passageway openings" Wilson ran to t h e top of the overstuffed sofa.

"I do not believe it," he muttered in mouse squeeks twitching his whiskers. Black smoke clouded his visi on. "What on earth is going on?"

The monster was shoving mountains of dirt to one side. It was ." it was churning heartlessly over the holes and tunnels of the entire mouse community. This threatening, ghastly machine, belching black smoke and fright-ening all by its suit of yellow armor, was breaking into their peace, challenging their life style. Without any warning or invitation, it was clearing their field o f rubble that had provided such a splended refuge over the years.

"Disaster," cried Wilson, "is upon us1Hark!Squeek! Chitter! Squeek! Do not delay. Gather your little mouseens and scurry, scamper, run for your dear lives toward the village above the field!"

There ensued a great commotion. From his command position atop the sofa back, Wilson watched his friends"flight, their escape into the future, their nar r o w squeeks, their harrowing race for safety. It thri lied his mousey nature, and it it terrorized him. In a day that monster would turn over the entire field. It woul d push the junk into one corner and clear the lando

"We field mice do not have a beggar's chance,"Wilson squeeked aloud, alarm, tender, whiskery sympa thy and understanding hypnotizing him to his post atop th e brocade seat back. Like the route of a valiant army. it was.

"Mme. Julian, take your little ones—now—whi l e the monster is on the other side of the field."' He rapped on mouse holes, awakening the sleepy, the indolent) the unaware to the danger.

"What is happening. Wilson? Why are you so e x-cited?"

"Come look!" She peeked out of her hole. "In hours it will all be over for you, for me,"

"Oh, dear, oh, dear. I must flee."

"This minute. Sir—Tiny Whitecheeks," W i Iso n called down into a neighboring hole.

"Yaahhhhsssss, what is it? I am still asleep."

"You will not be asleep for long. You will be dead, if you do not move," Wilson warned. "The cat is coming."

"Cat—cat! Ohmygosh! Where?"

"There!" Tiny poked his head into the clear morning air. "Ohmygosh! What a huge catl No whiskersf"

"It eats mice when it finds them—one gulp."

"Oh, preserve me, preserve me!"

"FleeI Run for your life then, Whitecheeks." And so another tenant of the field raced to safety to spare his own life.

"Miss Terrycloth!"

"Oh, hello, Wilson. Won't you come in? I'm j u st having breakfast of some grain I plucked from an old a u to tire growing inside."

"No time for breakfast—get your grain bag and run—the cat is on the loose""

"Cat! Catl Where? Oh, I hate catsl They're so nosey."

"There—!"

"No feet—Wil-san, you charming fellow, you are trying to flirt with rae,"

"Flirt I Joyous Terry cloth, you must run and save your life. Soon this entire field will lie in ruins. They are destroying our tunnels. We are being driven out, like outcasts, unwanted creatures."

"Oh, you are right. I see it. I see it. Oh, I am so blind sometimesI"

"Flee!"

"Squeek—oh, I could mash your little pink paws. You are my hero. Good-bye, sweet home." With those endearing and sad words, Wilson watched his good friend Joyous Te r-rycloth run for her life. He must continue to play fireman, and so he ran from tunnel to tunnel, awakening those who had not heard the monster sounds. All morning Wil s on sque ekcd hole to hole in those parts of the field the machine had not combed and leveled. In the middle of the a f-ternoon, his heroic job was done. He had saved many lives. Only the mortality figures gathered by Blackie, the mouse undertaker, would reveal the death toll.

This—this wholesale rape of mousetown was a s can-dal. It was an outrage, a wicked act, a crime, a heart-less thrust at the life of Wilson"s little community o f mice. As soon as he was sure there was nothing more that he could do he went to Albercrombe.s garage. He drew a sheet of paper from an old rolltop desk inside and c o influenced to compose a letter in mouse script to the ma y o r of the village.

> "Dear Deidrich Kleinschmidt, Mayor of Peanut:" He paused, dipped his whiskers in a bottle of laundry bluing. "As you wel 1 know, you and your monster have driven me and my loved ones and friends from our homes in the vacant field. This heartless act, this deed that ought to outrage all sensible mice, took place without a hint of a warning. You are the Mayor of Peanut. Then why, in the name of the Grannery, did you even try such a thing without at lea s t giving us a chance to get out from u n d er the crushing feet of that cat? I deroan d an explanation) if not an apology. 1 await your answer. Send it to Albercrombe"s garage. Signed| under-Citizen Wilson de Re-marque, the Courageous Mouse."

Wilson held an improptu town meeting with his fe 1-low field mice. "Good friends/" he said from the gat e post down by the abandoned farm. His friends had gathered, by their squeeks and squeals, in the tall gr a s s grown up around the fence gate. "I have written to the mayor of the village. I await some sort of apology,"

"You ain't going to get it, Wilson," said Elmer Threeclaws.

"Why not? He damages us, all of us."

"He's stubborn. You got to put some pressure o n him."

"I'll see him in a overstuffed sofa first/" Wilson retorted with indignity.

"You may do that, too. He's got people behind him. We got the villagers over us. Makes a difference."

"Well, I just want you good mice to know we're together in this. We will not let the trap snap. No trap snap for us." The defiant words thrilled his lis t e ner mice. "I am working on the matter. I have written t o Major Kleinschmidt. I should hear from him in a few days. Meantime, this old farm ought to give us affordable housing for the destitute. Be of good cheer, brother mice. We often overcome the world."

The crowd scattered with a rustling of the g r as s to places they had already selected for temporary hou sing. In just three days, Wilson was sitting on the roll-top desk, pondering his own fate, when a letter was slipped under the garage door. He scampered down and slit it open with his incisors.

Cynthia—Wilson knew she was the mayor's almond-eyed feline secretary—had transcribed the return message. It read in part: "Sorry, Mouse Wilson, but the old housing had to go to make way for the new."

He would not recant his attitude—this—this mayor Kleinschmidt. Supposing he made a shambles of the Mayor's house. There would come justice and retribution, all right. Surely this reply looked like a stubborn re je c-tion of his appeal to justice and human compassion for mice.

"We are not rats. We are mice. We do not consort with that wild, wicked class of brigands and buccaneers aid rogues," Wilson cried aloud within the raustiness of Alber-crombe's garage. His agile mind and twitching nose whiskers searched for some solution that would bring justice to the mouse community. There was only one way—open confrontation.

"I shall not forewarn the mayor of the villagers just as they did not forewarn us. We shall invade the village of Peanut—an army of field mice on the march t o bring justice to their kind. Citizens of mousedom!" rang the silvery voice of Wilson from his accustomed gatepost .

"Hear, hear! Tweek, tweek, tweek! We hear you I"

"We are on the march—the disenfranchized ones, all those without a voice, the evicted, the homeless ones. W e march tail to tail, paw to paw—to the village of Peanut. Are you with me?"

"We are! We are!"

"We shall demonstrate to the villagers that they must share their pantries, their kitchens, their domiciles with us."

"We"re behind you, Wilson."

"All the way?"

"Yahhh, yahhh—tweek. We got only our tails to lose."

"Let your noses define the boundaries of your invasion. I cannot do that for you. But do a thorough job of occupationo Do you hear me?"

"We hear you—loud and clear, Wilson de Remarque, the Courageous One."

"Then—every mouse to his post," Wilsom comman d e d as his words sent a thrill through the mice crowded in the tall grass. Almost as one body, they moved up toward the village of Peanut. Within hours, the screams of women, the curses of the villagers were showing that the inva si o n was proving a success. And, of course, not all mice on the move had come up from the field. The village had its contingent of several thousand well-concealed, indigenous and native mice secure in broom closets. attics and basements. They welcomed the invaders, housed and fed them with unabashed tenderness, whiskers touching in amity. There i n, within the households of the five-hundred strategy plots, the campaigns of invasion and forages about for food be-gan and did not slacken. The villagers could not believe that such an event was happening in their Peanut.

As in every war, the enemy has his weapons, too"Within two days and less, the villagers had shown that brooms and traps were not effective. They brough in chemicals to kill off the invaders. This was a horrible thing to do. Wilson watched the death throes of numerous of his friends by this wicked practice of chemical warfare. When they fumigated a cellar, sometimes a window was open, a crack in the basement wall, a hole in the brickwork that thwarted suffocation. Other times, the result was total annihilation. The war raged back and forth for weeks. The stench of mouse death was everywhere. Chemical haze filled the streets. Finally, realizing that this sort of extermination could not go on forever. Wilson thought the best policy would be to sue for peace.

Carefully. a piece of white sheeting between his teeth| Wilson walked with his truce flag into Mayor Kleinschmidt's office.

"You! You vicious little creature!" he shouted.

"I come with—peace in mind, good Mayor." Feline, his secretary, sat back smiling in her smug way.

"Peace! Peace! Peace? When for almost three weeks you and your grisly hordes have practically taken over the village."

"But—remember. dear Mayor. your big cat drove us out of the field, destroyed our homes, killed off many of us. We feel that our cause is just."

"We are people. We are more important than you."

"Perhaps," said Wilson with great calm, "but w e are living creatures."

"Too bad about that. You should all be dead."

"Tsk, tsk—such a bad attitude. I fear I cannot sue for peace. It is premature."

"All of you mice are premature—fifteen at a time—every ninety days."

"That is nature, sir. Nature." For the first time in a month Wilson de Remarque smiled at his—tormentor. "But—I am forgetting my mission—peace, Mayor Klein-schmidt."

The mayor grumbled, mumbled, muttered and rumbled. He tweeked his beard, pulled on his moustaches, glanc e d at the feline and then down at the Courageous One again.

"All right. What are your terms?"

"An immediate end to chemical warfare, Mayor i in exchange for suitable housing for my mouse community."

"Not in our houses, you wicked little varmints."

"Only in a manner of speaking."

"What do you mean by that?" the mayor asked.

"We prefer the fields to your houses—actually."

"Very well. We will end the chemical warfare-Mouse Wilson if—if, I say, you and yours will take up your abode in the village church."

"Village church! But surely—"

"You find a way. That's your problem. You foun d a way to occupy that field and—take over this village. Now you find a way to inhabit the church—amicably. You will find plenty of old hymnals in the basement to gnaw on temporarily. You'll find plenty to chew on—piety, repu-tat ions, old sermons, unforgiven skeletons, envy, anger and backbiting—packaged and broken promises. Taste the wil d grain and flowers between the tombstones. And there is ample sanctuary space out under the cemetery oak trees for your tunnels."

"I think I am beginning to see the picture—a kind of mouse reservation."

"Sort of—confine your activities to the church ya rd, and to the attic. Stay out of the bellfry."

"Those are the only terms in the peace agreement?"Wi 1-son queried.

"One more."

"And that—?"

"You mice must abstain from any free and open exercis e in the fields, passageways and streets of the village of Peanut and, instead, you must take your daily constitutionals in the tall wooden clocks that stand in the hallways of many o f the villagers."

"Tall clocks? Grandfather clocks?"

"Yes. I have, in recognition of this change, compose d a little ditty—.Dickery, dickery dock, the mouse ran up the clock. The clock struck—"

"Stop! StopI This is madness. You want to make u s prisoners of the clock works, the pendulum, the gong—in order to—mark off the hours?"

"Take your choice, Wilson. Of course, there"re too many of you for this one simple task. Yet it is a noble one ... "and you may arrange the shifts in any way that suits you. It is an honorable task—to run up and down the clock. And you do—have the right to be seen in public."

"I am—stunned—stunned. I shall have to discuss—"

"Our warfare of fumigation will continue," the may o r threatened.

"I—Wilson de Remarque, the Courageous Mouse—surrender. Tweek, tweek." Tears filled his eyes.

"Remember. To you will go the credit for founding the Church Mice Movement. It is a distinguished calling to be a clock mouse, Courageous de Remarque," the mayor finished. H e waltzed from the room with the Feline on his arm. Wilson dejectedly left the room. The terms of the surrender went into effect almost immediately and so the role of the clock mice and the presence of church mice in churches—throughout the world—remain a blazing piece of golden cheeze in the hi stay of mousedom.

The Prophet's Rebuke

In the land of the Euphrates River valley I lived, munched upon stingy handsfull of wheat, endured the rancid smells of old hay and the wrath of a beggar of a man called by the people a prophet "Prophet, mywitless bray! He could not tell a windstorm from a nightmare. It is true that we shared the roof, but sometimes when he was not making prophesies and not causing me pain with t h at whip of his and his stinging angry words, he locked u p my pride in the basket of his stupid divinations. Obsessed he was and accursed, I think, but then who am I but a lowly donkey to say? Offspring of a wild burro and a mare. He took out his anger for the day's cheat on me. My master sold water to the poor in leather jugs thrown over my back, at the same time that he conjured wicked omens. The wall between me and him in our Bethlehem house was marked by his greasy knuckles and chipped by his a n gry stick.

On the day during which the following events h ap-pened, I was in a fair mood and on the nearby road to Jerusalem. I was ready; Baalim—I got to say this—kept roe in good flesh though he was stingy with the barley. This day the people's prophet was in a rotten, morose, su 1 1 en temper. He had a small journey to make to reach the marketplace in Jerusalem, where he intended to sell water to vendors there. He had ridden me to the town well and 1 got loaded. Maybe the sun blazed him that day for he was crazy with the whip.

"Water! Water 1 Water I" he cried out as we journeyed through the city streets. He led me by the halter rope, w e stopped. He sold the water, he put the gold into his pocket. We ambled on. In this way we squeezed the life out of the day.

"My, my, isn't he a good looking beast!" said the old woman who sold him a red squash, which he put under ray nose to sniff.

"He is all I got," said Baalim, the lie coming out black and hot and twisted. He would replace me with his gold if he could. He stopped to munch with the potter, t o turn over a fine rug, to bicker about the price of s o m e smelly dried chad "» and to buy the squash.

Right now the Israelites were on war terms with King Balak, and I heard my master talking about the battles t o come. It seems that Balak wanted Baalim to spread fear a-broad and to intimidate the Jews by his prophesies. T he king wanted nothing more than for them to surrender to him. Yet he knew they thought Baalim was God's prophet. Strange things were going on there. The King's troops were just waiting to slaughter the strong men of Israel. When h e sent his reps to Baalim to get a favorable reply from the big-time prophet, he also tried to get the water vendor to come over to his side and join him. The reps hung aroun d for their answer.

"Come with us," I heard them say.

"I have got to consult with God first," my master replied, which I knew was a lie because I knew he did not e-ver do that" Like I say, we shared the same roof. No sir, Baalim was greedy for power. Especially as an ass I had no doubt about that. He tied me up to a rock gate outside a house in Jerusalem. The jugs were empty. We had just come back from the marketplace. when King Balak"s men got o f f their camels and propositioned my master. £ heard it all.

"What thinkest thou of the coming war?" they asked him.

"War—?"

"The Caananites against the Jews."

"Hasn't taken place yet," said Baalim.

"And it won't." they said. "We are your armed defense and support—providing you come with us, cross ov e r the river and talk to King Balak"s military leaders."

"I am here in the eity to sell water, not make war."

"You have got to tell them to give up, that God cannot help them now. King Balak says that it is too late."

"Too late for God"s hand to move?"

"The Jews worship foreign idols. He is angry. That is why. I have heard the Jews talking." said one of the reps.

"Yes, your life is at stake, sir," said another.

"Give me time to consult with my bones." my master replied.

"What conceit—always bragging about his divinations and announcing his wisdom!" said one of the emissaries. It was like snatching food from famished mouths to refuse t o help the king. The faces of his emissary reps were dusty white paste-masks of disappointment. Baalim went in si de the house and returned with two large leg bones of anass and a wild ox, bleached and olcLHe rubbed them together. H e looked up at the empty sky and said aloud, like a mourner wailing over a dead man, "0, God of the universe. deliver to me Thy will and Thy benediction of blessing." Snap, cradi dry lightning and distant thunder but nothing more. H e dropped those bones from his hands like burning fagots.

"Stick around. By morning, I shall give you my answer," my master said.

"Fair enough. There is an inn up the street."

"Come. Stay at my house. I will sleep with my animal here."

"We cannot impose upon you. King Balak would not be pleased if he knew." a rep advised.

The four of them walked up the street of the cit y, leading their camels. Inside his house Baalim let loos e one of his wild, wicked temper fluries against the furniture and pots, throwing and kicking things about in his wrath. He was a violent man—as I have cause to know, but like I say—a prophet of God.

On the following day he fed me a handful of barl ey, and the last of some palm shoots with stale water to wash down the mess. From his own pantry he also fed me le f t-over wheat cakes that were as hard as baked mud. He threw a blanket over my back. The emissaries had gathered their camels together and so we set out in caravan on our journey to the Israelites' military encampment"Baalinj had d e—cided, I guess, that it was prudent to inform the Jews o f the king's thoughts. I, myself, knew that God was against this whole idea of going to the Israelites. How do I know that? Up ahead and hardly outside the wall of Jerusalem. there stood a giant of a man with a sword in his hand, astride the road and ready to *sever* the head of any who might challenge him. Mercy! What a mountain of a man! He waved that sword. It spat fire from its edges. The giant's eyes burned like whitehot coals and his head was like frozen snow on the rooftop. His hands were like ten plows all bound together and his body—three cedar trunks le a n i n g against each other wouldn't match him. I heard that sword swoosh through the air. It raised a breeze and sent a shiver down my bony back. I, naturally, trotted off into a nearby field. Tufts of dry grass enticed me. Baalim kicked and spurred and goaded me with his whip and his curses to get back on the road. I saw then that the giant with the sword had gone. But I have to tell you that I wanted to turn around and go home to Jerusalem. especially after meet ing up with that giant and his flaming sword.in the middle o f the road.

The emissary camels were faster. yet I did not hurry. I moseyed along the trail. We came to a place where t h e grape-grower had built himself a rock wall and a tower as a protection against thieves. There the trail narrowed a—gainst the wall on one side; the other side dropped off into a deep ravine.

I moved in against that wall, fearing the dropoff. when I heard Baalim my master break loose aga i n with his unholy shouts and curses, his angry lashes against my hide and his bloody threats.

"I am going to convert you into a donkey wine skin when I get back, you cursed animal."

I could only listen and feel the stings of his whip and do nothing. "Heee, hawww!" I brayed.

"You will pay. You have injured my foot by scrapin g it against the stones of that wall." How could I do that unless he had reined me over there? I had no cause to injure my master 's foot. More delay. Baalim beat me many times across my back with his whip and spurred me with his sharp. rough sandals. My flanks were getting tender from his kicking. This entire journey so far was a misery trip. The drivers on the camels were looking back. trying to see what was holding up the caravan. But camels sure do kno w how to keep their footing on a narrow trail and. bes id es, their masters rode above the stones of that wall.

Whupp! Whupp! Baalim commenced to beating me aga i n and cursing. I am a humble beast, yet he beat me just the same. We went on a ways to where the trail narrowed, where it passed between two cliffs. I feared slipping. My master beat me with blows and wild oaths as if ready to kill me, almost. it appeared. Insolent fellow! I felt the hea t coming from the rocks; it warmed my usually placid temper.

"Sir. why do you beat me?" Enough was enough."I have done everything you wanted. I am your faithful donkey. I give you comfort. I give you a ride. I cost you only a drachma a month for barley. I do not run away. Yet you beat me without mercy."

Baalim was so astonished he threw his stick beside the road. "I am beating you because you turn aside for grass. You hurt ray foot. Now you balk at going on."

"You beat your animal because you are angry," said a voice from the heat waves of the hot rocks. "You have disobeyed your God."

"My God said, 'Go!'"

"I also said—do not say more than I have told you to say."

"When I reach the Jews" encampment I will speak in obedience."

"You will not be rewarded for doing wrong, when you did not reward your animal for doing right."

"You—you speak as an angel."

"Of the Lord—and your ass saw me when you d id not. That is why he turned aside." Baalim slid off m y back and bowed down to the ground and the angel said, "I am but the Lord's messenger. You will finish your mission as I have instructed you."

"Yes, my Lord, I will obey you." From that time on my master did not lay a stroke upon my back. Of that I am glad. I put all this down in the history of one donkey.s life. "I shall return to Jerusalem—and let my animal roam forever in the valley to the east."

"I do not accept your poor penance. God will deal with you. Your pride is your sin, for you know that it is the eternal God who has given you these things. You proudly reject His will."

"I will go back," my master said.

"No, stay and go on, but say only what I tell you.".

I can state that I was down on my own knees at this point, so that Baalim's feet touched the ground.I thought he was going to lay the rod against my ribs again. H e only looked at me and asked, "How does it occur that you speak Hebrew?"

"The Creator God gave that power to me," I said.

"I shall go on, since this bright voice wants m e to continue my journey."

By this time the four fellows on their camels were quite out of sight. The dust of the road had set tied. The caravan had emerged from the small and narrow c a n-yon.

We reached the encampment of the Jews at sundow n. I saw strings of smoke coming up from beyond the ri v er where the Israelite warriers were tented. Baalim spoke to the camel drivers. "Those are my people. Your King Balak will not slaughter them, for our God is with us."

"The kind desires only peace," said one of the e—messaries. from the back of his camel.

"Let us go then. I will build two altars, one for a ram and another for a bull, to make a sacrifice of thanksgiving."

That ended the journey. God is a wonderful God, and 1 guess if He wants to make a donkey like rays elf talk, he certainly can. Never underestimate the power of Holy God.

> Though animals to not speak in the human sense, it is a well-known and accepted fact that they comm u n i cate vo-cally. The substance of their communication is responsive reaction based on instinct rather than on conceptualization. Petting, feeding, caring for is the bridge that link s the two sorts of communication between animal and hu-man.

Quaint Subterranean Visit

My guide paused, as a creature shaped like an hourglass, slender of body, possessing a big head visibly filled with sand| removed a police whistle from his coat pock-. et and blew on it. White smoke and vermillion light rose from the sound. In the Cavern of Lost Legislation, he had summoned the workers to their tasks. Laborers at Failure, they scrambled about in the murky tunnel. I noted that they were dressed in tall hats and frayed coats, in tattered shoes and dirty, bearded faces.

"These folk are—?"

"The outcast Trucklers to special interests from far above ground. They have supported sterile legislation."

"Condemned?"

"Exactly. I refer you to the Semantics Room, later. But watch this."

Gnomes from the limbo my guide referred to rumbled in on their iron wheels and cushioned on pink satin to watch the nightly display.

"They do not seem interested in work," I remarked.

"Work? Perish the thought. Work is even a waste of futility," my guide said, and I was truly astonished a t the reasoning. "Buttt—we do have our shows here. Over there—"

Behind a wall of clear, solid crystal stones I saw a covey of stick figures fashioned from brass and wood.

"Those workers are the Laborers at Failure and behind those crystal walls they are employing their tale n ts in the Degeneracy Room. Observe, please."

These somewhat humanoid figures appeared to bend o-ver a pit of mud and—scooping up gobs, they surely took delight in flinging it into their own faces. They bespattered the walls of the crystal room. As I watched. a tall fellow, one of them, attired in what looked like a diver's suit lit a candle and the figures stared at the flame in astonishment. As he cast the light about the room they danced crazily to the music of "Fantasie," in triple time.

"What is all that about?" I asked, my eyes finally having adjusted to the dim subterranean light.

"Nightly, we conduct this test—it is only a test-to see if these creatures, the Laborers at Failure, accept the light or not, they are so accustomed to the darkness "Their hero—you see him—?"

"Him?"

"Their spokesman. He has won their trust but not that of the Senators above the ground "» only of these denizens of darkness, lobbyists who don't give a damn for anything but themselves. They shun the light of politic law."

"Politic law? I confess my ignorance."

"Just. fair. wise."

"I see. Yet—how absurdl How strange!"

"I thought you would be amazed. Degeneracy at its finest. <u>Wonderous</u> is the word. We are in the Cavern o f Lost Legislation, you know."

"That fellow with the whistle."

"He is called 'The Mask'"Watch. He blows again. "There issued another blast from the sound of colors. "Now—take care where you walk. At your feet—"

Below my shoetops I saw a most amazing sight.

"Those are the Beetle Spirits."

"Beetle Spirits?"

"Yes. It is they who keep trying to promote le g is-lation that will expunge all original environment."

"Wilderness, you mean?"

"Sometimes. That particular Beetle Spirit is a dominion expert. God said man should—"

"I am familiar with what God said," I interrupted.

"Good. Watch them as they roll their dung balls—this is the most sacred part of the entire tunnel system. That one there, the big beetle with the shiny back and the retractable feelers—does he ride a horse? No, he motors. And that one there with spots in his black back—he calls his dung ball The Quality of Life. Imag i n e that! See how he rolls it up the slight incline and i t returns to him unchanged."'

"Quality of Life? What is that?" I enquired. "He does not look capable of knowing."

"Precisely—because he—it—has not learned how to separate dirt from purity. He simply rolls his d u ng up and back again."

"Preposterous!" I exclaimed.

"That enormous one—there! He rolls the huge dung ball called National Debt Reduction.' My guide consumed a full three minutes to discharge his laughter.

"Why do they waste their time in this manner?" I askedc

"They do not know what they do—only what they dream of. Dominion utopia all over again, friend. Every age has its significances, its manner of demonstration. its characteristic idiom of expression."

"And these are the practitioners of failure."

"Laborers, sir," my guide responded. There-that glossy specimen with the broken leg—he desires to regulate all of life by means of the laboratory. An omnibuds-man of Science."

"I must say he has aspirations I will never u n der» stando"

"Plus insights you will never fathom."

"Sir! Sir!" I heard a harsh, shocking voice brea k into my reflections. A frocked clergyman grabbed my guide and almost tore off his satin collar in exasperation.

"What is the matte r, clergyman?"

"I am here—to be comforted. I had to confess."

"You have come to the right Cavern but to the wro n g room. You need to kneel in the chamber of Semantics, not here."

"I". so sorry. Those! Those! THOSE!" the clergyman screamed in terror. "Little creatures. They"re bee-lies! What are they doing down there on the ground?"

"As I have just explained to my visitor, they are dung beetles. It is in the spirit of frustration that they roll dung balls up the incline, only to have them roll back without effect."

"Oh, if we only had had some of those beetles i n our collection plates to return our money to us in the same way! Is that not a waste of time what they do?"

"Sir, not in the least. You need to have your faith sucked dry of hope in order to achieve purity of belief-your Utopia of failure."

"I have tried that."

"Good. Then you qualify. Down here, where we are bathed in the philosophical music of <u>Amazing Trace</u>—by which the world mocks us—time is nothing and effort-justified effort without achievement—is everything."

"That sounds a trifle futile to me," the clergym an said."

"It is, it is."

"May I give some advice?" the clergyman asked.

"Why, yes, of course. We have no qualms against bad advice," said my guide.

"Make these Beetles of Senatorial Frustration into a glorious activist campaign committee so that with sh e er gold—and that alone—they can accomplish more than persuasion or integrity ever could—more than rolling dung balls up and down ever can."

"Sir. You do not understand, being a man of the cloth. Down here, those—I call them unelected manipulators-down here they go through a transmogrification in order to conform to the tradition of getting nothing done. The Altar-ian Chambers do not miss their zealotry. They are away from their posts while they are in the flesh—and confidentially, I have to tell you, there are Senators am o ng them also. They continue to labor on issues of frustr a-tion and failure. Tireless, futile, adamant, don't you think?" my guide queried the clergyman.

"Yes, yes—your testament of failure overwhelms me." He departed.

"All their effort is not worth the trouble?" I asked.

"Trouble? Trouble on the floor, unending clash es, filibustering, unpopular comments and outcries of injustice? What is the use? To the musical corridor of Ever-lasting Trace—the hue and cry of others who know. A n d so—"My guide shook out a large tarpaulin and shed his tears.

"Then these Beetle Spirits are not converted?"

"Not in the religious sense, no. Furthermore, logic has lost the battle up there. But take these beetles I have just pointed out—there. See how they crawl, feelers agitating, legs scurrying, dung balls rolling awkwardly—heavy frustration is truly heavy for them. Jus t think. What a waste of time it would be to have them walk without ceasing to their Chamber of Congressmen—to have these—unelected manipulators always clinging to the Senators" coattails like a lot of ragamuffin children."

"Sir, they do so anyway. Are not the mudslingers we watched—are they not considered official helpers?"

"I told you once, those stick figures are Trucklers to these . these I"—here an expression of loathing appeared on my guide's face—"trucklers to the Beetles of Frustration."

"Truly they make a team—the selected and their in-sect companions."

"You comprehend,"' my guide said. "The money gotten unlawfully for the warchests of the Senators—there is n o question of that down here."

"Then all the Gnome laborers at Failure and the Trucklers I saw—as you so quaintly put it—are in fact actua l prisoners?"

"If you wish to put it that way." said my guide.

"Do the Truckler Spirits of the Congress ever go back? Resume their places on the chamber floor? After all, they cannot remain away for too long or they will be missed."

"Missed! Missed?" My guide laughed. Billows of acrid black smoke choked the air momentarily, like that emitte d by burning tar. "We have an answer for—missed."

"What is that, 0 Guide?"

"These clever beetles—let me make it clear—repre-sent specificity of particular proposals. The Beetles are themselves the spirits of transmogrified promoters, the true pests of frustration. And believe me, we have lots of them on the premises. The place crawls with frustration."

"They are permanent—but don't they ever get tired-the Beetles, I mean?"

"Never. They are tireless—like the Gnomes and t he Truckler stick figures."

"What if we could fumigate and destroy them all?"

"Frustration is indestructable—the Fourth Law of Human Dynamics," said my guide.

"Except, I suppose, when a good law passes in the Legislature."

"When that happens, the appropriate dung ball is r e-moved and thrown into the pit and the Beetle given another."

"Sounds pretty complicated to me," I said.

"It isn't." He pulled a scroll from 4 quiver and read the names of certain Beetles: "Scrandon, Samarish, Ptablon, good names, all. Now pick up a beetle in the palm of your hand."

I revolted at the thought. I shivered. I could not see the sides of the Cavern momentarily. Smoke filled the cracks in the walls like burning red rock. I heard the a-gony of creature man when he tries to scale a wall by his fingertips. My guide picked up one of the beetles for m e. He began to caress and to address the insect.

"Oh, black beetle, ancient insect, bringer of dea th through frustration, enigma of hope—"

"Hold on there a minute," I said. "Beetles don"t talk or understand us folks."

"Sir, your familiarity offends the insect mind. Yet this one does, granted intelligence under the porcelain eye of Osiris. Its mind is undeveloped by the ult im a te pragmatism of evolution."'

"I see," I reflected. "I think this whole cavern is weird. Everything's weird."

"What is the essence of your frustration, 0 Beetle?"

"I represent Senator Osmarkian from Tavilala State, and we are—I am hoping a bill to prohibit noise will fail."

"Oh, Beetle, what blocks passage of this bill?' m y guide asked.

"Makers of machinery, car makers, cataleptic music at three hundred decibels. Just all sorts of junk sound. Ear-splitting mute music lies in the future. No hearing, no speech. One thing will raise the level of ear-deafening noise."

"And that—"

"Nasty pictures—to explain the noise. I shall be employed forever."

"How far away is the end, 0 gracious beetle?"

The insect wiggled its antennae, paused and with low sobs replied, "Not too far and yet so far, closer than you suppose but more distant than you imagine."

"See there," my guide said, "you want a diplomatic answer, there it is. Samarish is happy. His happiness is his frustration."

"I think I have had enough of this whole scene," I complained.

"You have yet to see the best part," my guide said. "Just step this way. Er—watch it you don't trample on the Senatorial Beetles of Frustration."

"I'll watch my step. I am a private citizen, not a journalist, you know."

"Here. Hold this candle. Now what does it become? It glows, it bursts into magnetic rays that burn with a pearl and agate and blue turquoise effulgence. This array of light is fully within your control, but upon one condition," said my guide.

"What is that? And what is the meaning of this strange light?"

"The flame is the illumination of enlightenment, of supreme intelligence, which you possess so long as you hold the candle. Now walk slowly forward. What do y o u see?"

"I—I—"

"Exactly. You see—you are the porcelain eye o f Osiris, and this is the pit of consternation and frustration, the resting place of bills blocked in the halls of the lawyers."

"I know that. Why do you show me all these things?"

"So that when you return you will comprehend wha t the Senators face. The Beetles of Frustrated Spirits, the Candle of de-enlightenment, the pyrotechnics of dis-esteem, the cant of judicial de-publication, and—the whimsy o f de-inf ormation."

"Hatched from addled legal minds with the phrase "Strike that!" I offered.

"Brilliant I"

"Sounds all so negative to me," I said.

"Indeed, it is. Now let us leave the Beetles a nd return to the floor of the Chamber.

We did and promptly, when ray eyes had adjusted to the blinding light I perceived what I had not observed before—a caucus on the floor of a kind like the corner country-store talk session.

"You have had your sight restored," said my guide. "You perhaps thought that Senatorial frustration had condemned the Senatorial spirit and his bill to eternal death and silence. But not so, for with you has come a breath, a putrid and stale air, to be sure, from the subterranean chamers and tunnels of darkness. not light. Yet on your face there radiates the truth."

"I had not thought to go through such an ordeal."

"You wanted to know the meaning of the Cavern of Lost Legislation, of the Gnomes, the Trucklers and the dung Beetles of Frustration. Well, there it is: death and negativism and frustration."

"I shall look heavenward with delight and not int o the pit with sorrow. I shall cling to success and n o t to failure. I"

"Thou seest well," said my guide. With a loud, screechr y sound and smells from the Cavern, he was caught up in a canopy of blue haze, vanishing like a faded photograph i c image before my very eyes.

"The visitors gallery is upstairs," I heard a voice say to me, as I turned to find one of the Chamber guard s pointing to the door I was to go through.

Dangerous Rebellion

For the life of me I cannot understand why most of my kind do not show the true grit of independence, the stuff of daring-do that took my forebearers up into t h e high ridges. Sure, I am a sheep and we got a stinki n g reputation for always following. Pick up the baaa, baaa, follow the smells of wet wool and you know what, ke e p your head low and humble, hunker along, be always hungry nothing new, exciting, challenging. Always the same o Id nibble, nibble, nibble. Like an eating machine-then end up being chopped five ways into legs, ribs, brisket and Lord knows what else. Stew, mutton stew. India n stuff, sheepherder's meals. Paaah! It's enough to disgust even a goat.

What is it ails us? We are cowards. all of us. That's the truth of the matter. We run from thunder, from our own shadows, from gusts of wind, a tumbleweed plant. We run from the hiss of wind faeries and the snap of m u d clobbers. We cower when the ice rain stings our n oses. or when the bleatings of the sheep spirits rise thr ou gh the warming grass mists. No mortal man, no wildling animal or beast knows these things, but sheep do. They are all around. Harry, the coyote, spends an entire day i n sharpening his teeth on grimstone. So does the gray wolf slice his voice to trick the innocents. He trims his coat on a harum-scarum plant and makes out he is one of us. Small wonder we grow shy and panic at trifling shimmers and w o rs-can curleyblows. They are frightening! But that we must remain this way—forever. To that I say, "Sheep plop!"

One day I realized, by the actions of old Shaman, the Indian terrier with white stuff down his back, that my kind want to bleat and follow the stinking, mud-squishing hee l s of the mob ahead—rather than go independent. Security-it's that simple. Mob mind, gehmeinschaft security, herd instinct. Call it whatever one wants. And since cows are independent, cowpunchers naturally hold us in contempt. T o them we are grass-destroying nothings and—always—we are noted in Holy Scripture as placid followers.

But I sure don't feel that way. A follower? Me? W e are lumped together like biscuit dough with no distinctions, no individuals, all in the name of cudding safe and sound in the bosom of a crookstaff shepherd. Paaahhhl It's e-nough to disgust even a goat!

Listen to this! Shaman said to me one day, late i n the afternoon when the sun was settling, "Look, Curley, i f you want to settle down into some of the finest grass and water you ever wrapped your tongue around, why—when the flock Splits on the other side of that rise, you head for them rocks at the foot of the mountains."

"Baaaaa. Are you leading me on or something be c a use if you are I've got a big surprise in store for you, frisky dog."

Shaman barked, nipped at my feet, but he did not fool me one bit.

"Then stay with the bunch!" he burbled over his loll-ing tongue.

I said, "You think I'm dumb or something? I'm going to prove to you just how smart I am—and independent."

"Like how?"

"I intend to bust up this bunch of slow-witted crazies. That's step number one. Then I am going to do my own lead-ing. We are going—me and my gang .t we are going over t o those rocks and hide until that bent-handled, misguided, un-derpaid, fluteplaying, outfoxed, grumbling sheepherder comes and finds us."

"You got a mighty big vocabulary for a ordinary sheep."

"I am not ordinary, just falsified and insulted by ba d press. That little hide-and-seek will show Maelstrom, the herder, what's the right persiflection and consternation towards us sheep."

"I get you—in pieces, but I get you," Shaman said. "You are going to do all that?"

"Flat out promise—to show that herder I can think independent from the flock. Suddenly the grass turned all purple and flinty, the skies splintered into cloud rays, dust riz up from nearby hills and stung our noses with gust s of hot and shadowy sand. Shaman's voice faded, bubb l ed through like pond gas. shrill, warning barks that echoed death from among the high rocks. We sheep catch these scents and sounds.

"You will find out that there is more to leadingg." The voice was lost then trailed away. "—than beingg a rebel. You have not got a cause, Curleyyyyyyy." I shivered at the moan of Shaman"s voice and he nowhere around.

"I will do what I intend to do," I said.

"Don't, don't, Curleyyyy. Come back herel" But I did not hear his words of warning. I had it all. I was off and running, passionate for fr e e dom.

"Baaaaa!" I bleated in a dying voice, and I charged down through the middle of the flock. They split as nicely as a cedar log. Some went right and some went left. I saw scuds of water, tufts of wool, clods of turf fly e "» verywhere. "Baaaaaa!" I bleated again and again. I bumped and banged blackies and stubborn breakaways out toward the rocks. The rocks rose high. Threats of howls and bobbing and dancing shap. s riz up "» screams of wolf cries long ago returned. Bloody water ran down the cracks and sandstone faces of the rocks, but I was set. Maelstrom could tootle loud and long. He would never come look i ng for us in the bad-sheep lands.

About half the bunch, the flock—around two hundred—followed me. And I can tell any I was—burp, burp, gesticulated by the scene, goaded by my belly.

"Come back herel Sheep 1 Sheep! Come back here." That polite bag of bones shouldn't nevertve come out of his herder's wagon this morning. We were getting lost just nice. My rebellion was working,

Cud-chewing clods grumbled and mumbled, che win g grass a day old. They stumbled and bleated—sere lining crazies. They jumped, ran, leaped about. They babbled-slush, slush, chew, chew—burp—all sorts of queer noises among them.

As if in desperation we drove toward the blackening rocks, rocks covered with remembered sheep killings and the blood and sounds of returned wolf cries. Weirdl The rocks were getting bigger and shadowing black with dust the mists from the hillsides. The crushed grass and our sweaty bodies, the press and churning and tear of them.b squeezed the last of the day into strips of pale yello w light that reached through the boulders. Crows above and way off cawed through the sounds we were making. Sham a n was nowhere in sight. He must have split. Gone. Dumb dog.

"Curley! Curley! Is that bloody honest you?"

I looked up in among the rocks and there he was. He was laughing, his tongue hung out with its frosty, hot drip, eyeing all the lambs. It was my old arch eie my, Dagzun, the wolf.

"What are you doing way up here? Brought me some good sweet-meat eating, I see."

"I haven't brought you a thing, Dagzun, that yo u won't try to dig out for yourself."

"Now there is one smart sheep." He was pant ing.

"You"re the cause of a lot of hungry days, Curley," the wolf said.

"I wouldn't care if you starved to death, Dagzu n .

Your taste is all in your jottings on the rocks. Under stand me?"

"Sniveler! But put your little ones in my dish and they are real tasty. Oh, but you wouldn't agree."

"Of course I would. Chop, chop."

"Is that any way to talk to an old friend?" Dagzun asked.

"You are no friend of mine. We lost some newcomers to you."

"Delicious morsels."

"Wild-eyed scavenger."

"Hungry is all. There is more than one wolf around here.'

"Walking stomachs"

"You ought not to talk," said the wolf.

"You must have a rock hole somewhere nearby."

"Don't get nosey."

"If I had my way all wolves would be exterminated from the face of the earth."

"There you go—more of your extremist garbage! I thought for a minute you were starting to show a little independence of mind and action. But, ho, hum. I guess I was wrong."

"I am independent, only you don't notice.'

"How careless of me—not to notice, I mean."

"I am in charge here now—just me."

"Really—1 You in charge? Howhowhowhow," laughed Dagzun. "Why you are nothing but an obseqious, fawning, imitative follower."

"I am not. Watch." I moved in close to Dagzun s o that he could see the flash and gleam of independence in my eyes.

"I like your spirit, Curley, ol' boy. Got real spirit, real spirit, I'll say."

"Thanks, Wolf Dagzun, and there's more where that came from."

"Come here just a minute. Let me test you. L e t me see just how independent you actually are. Come on. Come on."

"I know you. You're trying to get me to come in close so that you can snap your jaws at me and grab me."

"Whatever put that little thought into your mind?"

"You did, Dagzun. But—just to show you."I glided in close. My dainty feet—messengers of freedom-crushed the new clover. The sweet smells of the twilight floated over the hot rocks when-SNAP! I heard the dash of those powerful incisor teeth and fangs close 1i ke a trap of steel" I looked up and there sat my enemy Dag-zun with tufts of my wool caught between his teeth. 0 n his face showed a look of dismay.

"You see there. I knew all along that's what you were after," I said. "Why, I.d be airlifted off right this minute into the high ridges if you had caught me."

"Why, whatever put that thought into your head?"

"You did. Dagzun—but I'm sporty. You see this mob? They are my followers up here—every smelly, bleating, munching one of them."

"They look happy."

"They are in dreamland. No shepherd to holler at them. No stupid cur to nip at their heels. Sweet peace. Get the picture?"

"I do. And I know you also like to gambol about. I have watched you many a day with my head on my paws. Besides| I am on a hunger strike right now."

"You! A hunger strike!"

"That's right."

"Well then. I'll tell you what I will do—just to show you I'm fair about the matter—that I'm indepe n-dent and—"

"You have got grit, real courage there, Curley."

"You come down from that rock and sit here nearby, and I will nibble grass along real close to you. We ca n live alongside us, can't we."

"Real friendly like/" said Dagzun. "Gooperativ e living. I like the idea. Sounds great—full of hope and anticipation for a good, good. good tomorrow." I saw the wolf lick his chops.

"Just my line of reasoning, Dagzun," I said.

"It's a deal. But—"The wolf scratched his head with one hind leg. "What will that prove?"

"That you got real control down inside, self-control."

"All wolves have got deep-down control—excepting one or two I know personally."

"Well, you have either got it or you don't."

"I've got it."

"You got it, that's for sure, even if you—can't tell so yourself." I mewed.

"I'll tell right soon if my control is turned on,"''said Dagzun.

"I got grit. You control yourself and I'll put on a little demonstration of courage."

"Sayyyy—now that's a real fine plan. That calls for my best howl."

"Don't, tfolf. You will scare all the Innocents."

"Sorry." Dagzun jumped down from his rocky perch and in a nimblesecond—a very short piece of time—he was sitting among the clover. I ambled in close to him. I bleated one time real long, my mouth flung wide s o that my wisdom teeth showed—and my croppecsstained b y grass. Then I dropped my incisors to crop some especially luscious tufts of clover, when SNAP!—the cla sh of bare white teeth again, and the powerful jaws of Dagzun held in merciless grip for his supper one fine, fat sheep.

The rest of the flock fled in all directions, excited into panic and terror. The loud blast of Maelstrom's horn sounded across the darkening hillsides and in amongst the rocks. However, this time Cur ley did not respond. He had proved he had grit and independence and that it was tiresome always to follow. He had scorned security. He had ignored the laws of the wild. Yet he had shown his foolish believers, now being gathered by Shaman and the herder, that it was safer sometim e s not to be too rebellious and independent. There were always dangers in that direction. Here came Sha man, barking furiously. Dagzun had hiked into the h i g h er rocks with his fat meal between his powerful jaws. That night the herder called Maelstrom counted one less for his flock when he penned them up. Curley had had a choice in following the lead sheep. Now he had to follow the gray, hungry wolf; forever. This closing was writ by one of his faithful admirers.

Dog's Day In Court

I am a house dog. Folks look at me say I am pampered. But I will tell you a story that just might change their minds. Sure, I go to the dog groomers—The Blue Room—once a week. Sure, I use special perfume called "Cat's Fur" my boss likes the groomer to douse me with. Sure, my paw nails are painted red and my curly coat i s done up in bows—top of my head, my tail and sometime s my dainty forelegs. So—?"

I sleep between clean sheets embroidered with m y name "Foo Foo" every night. My mistress sets a place at the dinner table for me, a posh cushion, a special h i gb chair, an embroidered napkin and, best of all, a non-»kid meal bowl divided for briskets, mush and lap-dog soup. Great! She loves it. I thrive on it. Attention and customized meals.

The boss is a lonely gal and so I enjoy the run of the house. "Oh, I love your little voice," she once told me. Sure I tinkle a little bell under my chin and never go further than the dahlia bed out back. All these details are true, but don't you dare to make fun of me until I am finished telling you this scarry story.

Maybe you think my manicure, my trimcut and stylized grooming) my perfume are not important. Listen.Whe n my mistress sent a taxi to pick me up one afternoon, you will begin to understand. He probably was a good felliow; I heard his name called "Jacques" over the taxicab radio. All what I'm about to tell you actually happened. He wa s a good cabbie but a little dense and did not understa n d my sensitive nature.

"Where's the dog?" he bellowed at the door to T h e Blue Room groomers.

"Dog! Dog?" I growled.

He came in, grabbed me like a bundle of old ne ws-papers, opened his cab door and dropped me onto the front se ato Then he came around to his side and tied the end of my leash to his steering-wheel column so that I would be forced to sit in the front seato And off we go.

Of course all that was protocol to me, demeaning because I was forced to sit, but do you know I had the te-merity and the guts to jump over the back of the f r ont seat. I had no sooner dropped over than I hanged myself. Yes, hanged myself. I simply swung, struggled, squirmed, coughed and wheezed in my rhinestone collar. I cou 1 d not draw a pinch of air. Jacques swung the taxi into the curb. He reached over the seatback, grabbed the scru f f of my neck and hauled me out of the claws of immin e n t death. A thrilling rescue if ever I saw onel He then tied a bow in my leash that scratched any thoughts of instant freedom.

I intended to make something—a legal issue, a cause of action—out of Jacques' gross negligence. When he dropped me off and handed me to my mistress, m a d e change, collected his fare and sped away like a rascal-cheap at the price against my life, I told my mistress, Sophie, what had happened. I confessed to her my narr o w escape from hanging.

She almost died of fright. "Do you mean that terrible cab driver almost let you—Oh, dear me, where is my handkerchief?—he almost let yo u hang yourself over the back seat?

"Yap, yap, yap!" I affirmed to her.

"Oh, goodness me! Oh, how frightening! Little you. My poor little Foo Foo. That nasty man almost killed you. Oh, my pet, my darling, my snoogums."

"Yap, yap," I made it clear I thought we ought te take this whole matter to court to see if we couldn't extract a little change out of deep pockets, the cab com-pany. I won't mention that ding-aling's name. I kno w that outfit has plenty of fat bones and the sweet sine 11 of gnawing justice came to my quivering nose. Ours was a clear case of negligence. I felt the bruises under my collar—my dear mistress looked for them. I felt that the case was justified.

"My poor little Foo Foo," she kept sighing. "T fa at heathen almost killed you. That big, nasty cab driver almost put you in a little casket." With those words. she again broke out into wild and uncontrollable sobs of pi ty. I felt so good over the attention I almost forgot myself.

"Yap, yap," I affirmed. I wagged the ball of my tail. I made it clear that his intentions were not worth a bur-ied stick. What really mattered was that numbskull.s feeling that his driving was more important than me and look what happened!

"Yap, yap."

"Yes, yes, yes—you are absolutely right, Foo Foo.Oh, you are the smartest dog in the world. I shall reward you with—here."Whiss! whiss! I received a nice blast or two of my favorite "Cat's Fur Parfum." See how nice it is all round to be equal to the human animal? And, Oh. dog! dog! have I ever got the support. I sigh.

My mistress, she called her lawyer} I say "our "b e-cause I felt so possessive about the fellow, since he was going to rush to my defense against that big brute of an aggressor.

He came over to my house one night, and I spent a real enjoyable hour or two, in his lap and nosing about his papers of decomposition and other legal matters. Oh, we had great fun!

"He's such a good doggie, my Foo Foo. He would never hurt anyone, and he loves to play. He loves life. Stand up, Foo Foo." I did, to show that I was still all in one piece and consternated human talk with the best of my breed. My mistress gave me a cultured bone, just right for my deli ... cate taste buds. They shook hands and drank some stuf f, and I got a petting and the night was done ...

It was set up that we would go to court ove r an attempted dog-hanging— which was actually a murder rap for that cabbie Jacques. If that gate-hinged, shank-boned, straw-stuffed, pie-eyed congestion of silence and noise—a per- feet dolt—had not shortened my leash or had at least le t me run free inside his taxicab, all this would not have happened. But then—alas! Yap, yap, yap! It did and so I am stuck with this messy court case. No pun intended ...

My case was scheduled for small-claims—<u>small</u>: I took it to mean to refer to my size. I weigh only ab o u t four pounds, you see. And our lawyer, he would have t o stay outside the courtoom or chew on his bone—a spare rib. Yap, yap. Panting. The dog fight was between me with m y mistress and that big oaf of a cab driver. Remember. H e almost tried to hang me out to dry over the back of h i s seat. Personally, I'm a real scrapper when it makes good sense to go into dog-fight position. None of this instinct crap for me.

The day came fast enough, gray and chilly. Mistres s Sophie put on my plaid coat. She combed my fur, retied my bows| gave me a couple of sweet blasts of "Cat's Fur Par . fum." We arrived. She bundled me under her arm and we entered the courtroom. There—there dressed like an undertaker was him—the cab driver. Trying to impress the judge, I surmised. Things from then on moved along smartly.

"Case number 34689—Plaintiff Sophie Esmeraldo and-her ward Foo Foo—Foo Foo?—against Jacques Sweeney, driver for the Debauch Cab Company." German outfit. My mistress put me down on the polished table at the front, just under the n o se of the judge. The Defendant oaf stepped up to the table opposite mine.

"State your case, Plaintiff." So my boss proceed e d to tell the commissioner what had happened, according to my own story. And—the Oaf gave his side. naturally—sa i d the whole s c ene was an accident and that he meant simply to keep me up close to where he could watch me. What a p i d-dly bunch of nonsense! I thought. "Fine. fine. Yap. yap, yap!"

"Please control the plaintiff," said the judge t o Sophie.

"Fine. Watch me when he ought to watch himself." M y mistress read my thoughts.

"Your honor, that, that awful man standing there ought to watch his driving."

"What has that to do with the circumstances complained of?"

"He almost smashed up the cab trying to rescue my little Foo Foo. Not heroic in the least. He ought to have sto pped in the road, right then and there."

"Block traffic?"

"What's more important, Your Honor—the life of my precious Foo Foo—or a little traffic jam? Now he is trying to rescue himself."

"But Mister Sweeney.s actions—where they intentional? I mean, did he intentionally try to inflict pain and suffering upon Foo Foo? Let the defendant answer that, i f you will, Miss Esmeraldo."

That big clod shuffled his feet. "Nothing was intentional, Your Honor. 1 did not try to hang this woman's dog. I like dogs."

A lie, I thought.

"I like her."

A fraud, I guessed.

"I am a careful driver."

Yap, yap. It sure did not seem like it at the time.

"I wanted to keep the mutt—"

Mutt!

"—on a short leash,"

Hangman's noose is a better description.

"And so, just naturally, the dog wanted to get into the back seat to explore my cab. Then it happened.

What a piddly bunch of nonsense!

"The dog hanged himse If over the back of the seat?"the judge asked. "Because of the—short leash?"

"That's right, Your Honor," said my boss. "My poor little Foo Foo would have been dead—dead! Doesn't any. body understand—dead!"

I lay down on the table at the command and my mistress scratched me on my stomach.

"I think what we have here is a case of three, maybe

four, centripetals of confounding negligence and an assur-
ity of exasperated confabulation."

"What does that mean, Your Honor?" my mistress askedo

"Doggone it—harumph—no pun intended. The little critter ought to
stay put. If it's so intelligent, you ought to give it instructions to mind when
going t o and fro from the dog groomers."

"It!" my boss exploded.

"A dog, madam, is an it. Take my word for it."

"But, Your Honor, my Foo Foo almost was killed."

"You, sir. You do not keep cages or kennels in your cab as a regular
protection?"

"No, sir, I do not. I—the only remedy is a short chain or leash."

"And you, ma'm, could you not have supplied the cab driver with a—
small cage for the trip?" the judge asked my mistress.

"Oh, my darling—in prison. I would never do such a thisng."

"You, sir—you, as a cab driver, your connextio wifti the mutation known
as a dog, a strange combination—perhaps lively and pretty—is at best
minimal?"

"Beg your pardon, Your Honor?" the cabbie asked.

"I mean, you are ignorant of poodles as a breed."

"Yes, sir." The judge looked as if he tapped his forehead.

"Then those terrible words—I hate to say them-instinct missing—is bred
out of them. That applies i n this case."

"Sir, you dare slander my Foo Foo." She came to my rescue all right

"No harm done, Miss Esmeraldo. I was just reflec-ting upon the general
state of dogs these days. Why, madam, they don't know an enemy from a
friend or a stranger from a close relative." I could not believe my ears. What
a piddly lot of stuff!

"I am going to report you to-"she started to say and then burst into tears,
which always makes me feel tender.

"Try the local pound. Miss Esmeraldo. One dolla r fine for you, sir, for
messing up my day. And after this-"The judge pulled a small piece of string
from one pocket—"This is a short leash, madam. If the cab driver had tied
your little friend by a length such as this, you might, you just might have
had cause for complaint. Case dismissed." "Yap, yap," I complained. I could
hardly wait to g e t my gorgeous lips around that fake shank bone at home.
The cabbie put on his cap and pounded out of the room.

I tell you, life can be awfully exciting at tim es when your neck and a
dollar are at stake, Awsome!

Golden Fields—Forever

A bald eagle settled in the top of sycamore tree one day while a coyote panted, half asleep, in the warm shade below. His belly was fullo A lamb's skin and the sundered remains lay a short distance away.

"Listen, wise guy," said the eagle. "That f a rm-er has been potshooting at me and you've been getting by with murder."

"Got to eat, you know."

"I took a pellet in my wing feathers the other day» Do you have to make raids on the local pasture? Can't you find enough varmints in the hills?"

"Got to make a living, you know." The eagle flew off in exasperation and returned. He was a high-strung raptor.

"You never play at hoops or ball. Work, work, work."

"That's just my nature." said the coyote.

"I could make work like puppy play for you-show you a pasture where you can go and kill and eat and gorge and eat some more and fill your dog belly with the best."

"What are you talking about? I can do that right here."

"You have no imagination. I soar high. I see lots of things you miss, Mister Mangy. Golden Fields."

"It's spring. That's why I am mangy. Say, where are these ". Golden Fields you're talking about?"

"A distance away—out of gunshot range for me an d for you. You don't want to be killed, do you? And me? I flew over enemy territory the other day—Why tell you the scarry details? *My* spirit said, 'Go. Search fcr other visions to feed your hunger ... So—I am here."

"Why are you telling me all this if you don't plan to stick around here?"

"Word travels fast in this high country. If you kill many more sheep every bald eagle from here to the eagles. Final Roost will die. Survival is why I t ell you"

The coyote arose, stretched, yawned, went over an d sniffed the carcass of the lamb, most of which he ha d already consumed. He turned away.

"Golden Fields—?"

"Exactly. I have pinpointed them with my sh a r p eye."

"I hope you know what you" re talking about. Besides, I could get shot myself some dark night."

"Especially since they know you"re hanging around." The eagle lifted off, flapped its heavy wings, dropped into the shade then soared into the sky again.

"You're too fast for me!" the coyote cried. The eagle soared, circled in the airy silence. Then an a-mazing thing happened. The Spirit of the Eagle has the power to change the landscape. It is a supernatural power, power from the Eagle God. The hills shifted like roiling water, the valley became a ridge dotted with trees, and the distant peaks fell from sight like a sinking ship. As the coyote loped along, the grassland had turned into a lake,

It must be that lamb he ate, the coyote thought as he ran patiently keeping the eagle in his vision. T h e trail circled some rocks, was lost at the base of a bi g cliff and resumed again through a narrow slit in t h e rocks. The coyote was eager to see these golden fields. Food without work! FantastisticI

The landscape continued to shift so that now the ridge lay in a deep ravine and the lake rose up to b e-come a snowcapped craig of grey granite. The hills turned as if on slick stones, like a cattle gate. W h a t faced south now faced north. The?and rose higher and higher.

"Come, come! You are doing the right thing," sang the bewitching call of the circling eagle. The big bird had become a phantom. The coyote panted harder and harder as the way grew steeper.

"You fool me. You trick me," said the coyote.

"Why would I do that? I told you we will both be safe when we reach the Golden Fields. Remember? Food without the hunter's gun."

"And no work."

"And no work."

"But the way the land keeps changing—like in a maze—?"

"That is in your vision, coyote. Your mind plays tricks on you."

The hills began to slope, grass grew, the gully disappeared again, a wide gulf of a canyon lay ahead, Then, the skies darkened, the moon rose and the coyote sat down to catch his breath.

"Do not stop. The night will pass away." Just as the eagle said that, the sun rose and pushed the moon down to bathe the night sun. Trees took the place o f dense chaparral, then thick, brambly underbrush, so thick with thorns that the coyote got caught on them.

"What is the matter, coyote?"

"These cursed brambles."

"Life is filled with struggle, coyote. Do you wish to be saved from the hunter's gun?"

"Yes, yes—but those golden fields. You promised."

"They lie just a short ways ahead. Keep up your courage," said the eagle. The coyote broke free from the thicket whereupon, but a few miles further on, the cle a n sheer edge of a precipice appeared. When the coyote a rrived at the dropoff, he looked down below. His eyes now wet with tears roamed over the great landscape. He saw more sheep than he had ever beheld before, more than his clever imagination could envision.

"Are they not glorious, lovely to behold, fill e d with promises of joy and-». food?"

"Surely there must be a hunter somewhere around."

"Only one, the Spirit God that remakes the m ou n-tains and the plains and the rivers and the dry gulches."

"How do I get down there?"

"If you think long and hard you will make your way down. Meditate—food, love, joy, paradise without e f-fort and no hunters. See how freely I fly, without e—ver a cautious eye toward a farmhouse. There is no house down there."

"But why are they there—and so many of them?"

"Foolish coyotel Go. There is what the e a gle.s Spirit God has promised you. I speak for the Eagle Spirit, the Great One who has changed the mountains for m e and brought you here."

"I shall find a way down." The coyote peered over the edge of the precipice. "CouldnH be much of a drop," he thought. Small ridges—but then he was no mountain goat. "I think I'll just—chance it."

"You will never regret the day, "said the Eagle Spirit. "I will—fly down and—see how you are getting along. Come. Come." The eagle's soft, friendly voice indisposed the impatient coyote to remain any longer o n the rim of the precipice, and so he leaped. Of course, he was soon among the lambs, there to stay always, beyond the range of the hunter's gun.

"Bad choice," said the eagle and flew into the molten, distant skies, while the lambs cropped as close a s they dared to the well-fed carcass of their enemy pred a-tor.

Captain Kidd and His Billy Goat

Captain Kidd, among honest men's enemies on the high seas, was a fierce-looking pirate who sailed many years ago. He wore a patch over one eye, lost in a rapier duel. A dee p scar traced down one side of his face, put there by the flashing sword of a rival buccaneer when they fought on the decks of a French ship for the wealth of jewels and gold and rich silks and spices in the hold. Both pirate sh i ps claimed the French vessel at the same time and had fough t until the oaken decks were slick with blood and bodies lay strewn everywhere. Piracy on the high seas was a capital crime punishable by hanging, but Capt, Kidd knew no law but his own. He was also missing a finger severed by the fuse of an iro n cannon below decks. He was crafty, courageous, and an expert swordsman—and his heart was as black as his moustaches.

On the day this story begins, a stiff breeze from off the whitecaps caught his satin coat and baggy pantaloons"The black-flagged vessel <u>Mirage</u> rolled on the billows, that clapped with thunder beneath the ship's bowsprit and her ster n quarters. Up the the wheelhouse her helmsman held her steady on course, north by northwest toward the Caribbean. The huge expanses of patched canvas snapped above the captain's head and tugged at the singing sheets that held them taut. The <u>Mirage</u> rolled, then slid into the valley between two waves as high as green mountains. Every nail and pe g in the wooden vessel creaked. Every rope drew as tight a s bowstrings. Ahead of the buccaneer ran a Portugese merchantman. Captain Kidd planned to slide in alongside and b o a rd her and, by force of pistols and sword, take her rich treasures for himself and his crew. She had picked up rum i n Haiti. Through agents, he would later market his plunder at Liverpool and Cadiz, as salvage from sinking vessels of commerce.

One weakness, apart from strong grog, rum from th e Caribbean, was his affection for a goat that he kept t e th-ered in his cabin when battle raged. Captain Kidd would chat ter to his goat for hours when he was alone. And the goat appeared to know when its master was getting ready to go into battle.

"Heee, hhhhh, heeeee," whinnied the goat.

"Hoo, ho, ho, hoi" chuckled Kidd. On this day h e scratched his billy goat behind its ear, grabbed his cutlass and leaped up the companionway to the after deck t o supervise the "hooking"—when the grappling hooks and ropes should draw the two ships in against one another whereupon they remain tied until the capture is complete and one o r the other is victorious.

A cannon fired in the distance. Capt. Kidd saw the white puff of smoke come from the square canon port of t h e Portevedra. He scanned her to determine her guns and i f possible her crew. Some merchantmen reduced their crews in order to take on more cargo. She was a Portuguese ship returning probably from Malasia, around the Horn, bound for the Liverpool black markets and then home to Lisbon. All of these observations and calculations went through the shrewd mind of Captain Kidd.

A rich haul, he thought, as he closed his telescop e with a snap and returned it to the deckhouse cannister. H e would ignore the warning shot.

"All hands on deck!" he roared. Pell mell, scrambling over one another to reach a swordsman.s advantage, the ragged crew, some of them half drunk, appeared from below the decks of the Mirage .

"A Portugee merchant!" the captain shouted over the rush and crash of the troubled seas through the pinrail.

"Starboard! Side! Look ye sharp, mates I" He was mistaken about the quarry's guns for when she presented her full broadside to the Mirage, at least a dozen three-pounders assaulted the pirateer from her ports. The deception was cunning—a merchantman outfitted into a man-of-war.

"Man-of-war!" Capt. Kidd boomed in a voice like a hawser rope, "Your stations!" he commanded. Some, clad in native moccasins, others in boots, and still others their feet bare skittered up the ratlines to the rope ladders aloft. It would be a bloody, perilous, ha r d-fought battle, Kidd not reckoned.

Others of the crew sought high places on the fore—and quarter-decks. Still others stood at ready bes i d e the belaying pins on the rails, their knives clenched in their teeth. The cannoneers took up positions b e h i n d their iron pieces on the deck below. All of the ere w were ready for combat, their swords in hand, their cutlass e s newly sharpened, several with French rapiers. Not a man stood by who was not eager and ready for the for-ay.

"Mirage drew alongside the Portevedra and too k a trememdous cannonade of broadsides that knocked out the deck canon at once and killed two of the four ere w s below decks. Captain Kidd's pirates flung their grappling hooks and hauled the two ships together, so clo se that even the man-of-war's cannons were useless without self-inflieting damage.

"Take all or none, mates!" shouted Kidd. The pirates swarmed over the side of the captive vessel. The clashing of steel, the ringing of swords, rapiers and the groans of the slain and wounded rose into the after … noon sky. Flame and dense smoke came the roar of the <u>Pontevegra's</u> deck cannons. which raked the foredeck o f the <u>Mirage</u> andwutilated the pirates who stood in the way of the fusillade. So great was the din, the smoke, the tangle of severed sheets across the deck of th<u>e P o r te-vedra</u> that visibility diminished. Still, the hand-t o-hand combat raged on, amidst cries of agony, the deck planking slickened by blood of both pirates and Port u-guese sailors.

At some point in the melee that was hard to fi x, the fighting slacked off. Captain Kidd forced his captives, together with remaining members of his own pirate crew, to go below and fetch up casks of rum from t h e hold. After almost three hours of unabated hand-to-hand combat, Capt. Kidd had at last subdued the <u>Portev edra</u> and now it was time to celebrate. Some of his most valiant buccaneers lay dead o n the deck.

After the first trick of grog, the seamen of both vessels carried up immense bales of ornate and expensive silks, Middle-Eastern brocades, tapestries, loom fabrics. Captain Kidd, himself, slung over his shoulders two giant caldron pots of jewels and behind him his pirates appeared with heavy baskets filled to their brims with gold pieces of incalculable worth. These trinkets, this gold, he and his crew transferred over to his cabin on the <u>Mirage</u>. He would sort them out there and distribute them among his ship's crew as swag from the capture and as rewards f o r their fighting services.

All this while the goat named Satan, having somehow escaped from the captain's cabin, kept in the background, . It had scurried about, jumped up on the ventillator above deck, dodged the swordsmen and dashed between their le g s to keep from being struck by swords and belaying pins.

However, once back in his cabin Captain Kidd noticed that his goat was missing. He had by now recovered his calm after the fray. He called to Satan. The goa t dutifully ambled into the cabin and nuzzled the bloodi e d hand of the pirate captain. With his heavy palm, tou g h as leather, he leaned down and stroked the goat's ringlet coat.

"Here, here. This one is for you to chew on." Into the opened mouth of his pet goat, held aloft by its chin whiskers, Captain Kidd dropped a large ruby almost the size of a big strawberry. Satan swallowed it with a gulp} it made a lump first in his neck and then in his stomach "The captain roared with laughter, causing his mates . t o grin and the cabin tinware to vibrate. He heard his crew up on deck chanting "¥o, ho, ho—fifteen men on a dead man's chest} Yo, ho, ho—and a bottle of rum.'"He broke out a bottle of captured rum and drank deep. He got drunker and drunker and drunker. Soon he could hardly sit u p in his chair.

"We are honest thieves, are we not, Satan?" t h e captain grunted. He stroked the head of his pet. Through the ha ze of his mind and eyes there came the rush of a new danger and calamity—fighting among the men on de c k over the booty.

"Go get'm, you son of satan!" Captain Kidd bellowed and untied his goat. In its desire for freedom it rushed up on deck where its greatest peril lay. The drunk e n buccaneers had begun to stab and fight—more dead sai l—ors. Then, out of anger at Captain Kidd, a seaman ran the goat through with his rapier and wiped it clean. The captain never knew all of this until the bloody and lifeless body of his billy goat was flung down the ladder before the door to his cabin. Coming out, he saw that hi s precious animal was slain. He went into a rage. He dashed topside at once and accosted the sailor, one of his o wn crew, who wielded a rapier and still held it in his hand.

"You have killed my goat, you beast—and its stomach is slit!"

"You hide things from us, Captain Kidd/" retorted one of the buccaneers| his last words. The enfuriated captain skewered the man's guts on his short sword"

"Where is the ruby?" he demanded, his mouth frothing in his rage. The pirates kept silent. The enormous jewe l was nowhere to be found, either aboard the ship or on the persons of its crew. Like an avenging messenger from hell, Captain Kidd, with the help of his First Mate and his Chief Cannoneer, put the others of the crew in irons lest t h e purloined ruby turn up and be disposed of. Yet it never was

Topside, Kidd, his First Mate and Chief of the Cannons cut loose the <u>Portevedra</u> from the <u>Mirage</u>. When she had drifted out a distance. he aimed his remaining cannon at her waterline and fired five rounds in quick succession. The <u>Portevedra</u> began sinking rapidly. He had put out no life boats for survivors.

Captain Kidd watched for a time and then went below. He took down his log book from a shelf and wrote t h e s e words:: "Friendly ship sunk in gale. All lives lost. Rescued—one goat. Murdered by fiends. Managed to salvage part of cargo."

When the <u>Montevedra</u> rolled and started below, with a great sigh of escaping air, he thought that he heard the distinct whinny of his Satan. Captain Kidd puzzled be h ind his black moustaches: How did they—anyone—know abo u t the ruby Satan had swallowed? Found out—but how?

He fell to floor, drunk and slept for three days while his First Mate ran the undermanned ship with its par ti a l crew of battered and maimed buccaneers.

The Outrageous Owl And The Taunting Pussycat

Some folks consider the owl to be a very wise bird. I am not going to dispute that notion, since it is true. I like to be thought of as smart and sure of myself—and swift" Just for instance, when I looked at Gaugaun, the calico, with my big yellow eyes, I did not blink. And he, poor thing, guessed simply that I did not want to miss what he was up to. Would I miss the doings of that mangy, tree-climbing, weed-crawling alley tramp? Not me, not me.

The fact of the matter is, I stare a lot. I do.It's not polite one bit, but I can hardly see in the daylight. I'm so used to night life and night flights. Actually, I am more of a blind owl than a smart one. In the daytime.

Naturally I would never tell Gaugaun that. We are friendly enemies. We work the same territory. Me? The barn is my haunt and roost. He knows, that cat, that my horns may be feathers but that I can cut the throat of a mouse with one slash.

Let me tell you a little story that will exp lain what I mean by "friendly enemies." I was sitting up high in an oak one night and this despicable wretch of a pussycat tramp wandered by. "Where are you going, kitty cat?" I asked with vinegar in my voice.

"I am going a-hunting for the big ones you c a n ' t catch."

"Zat so?" 1 said. "I can catch anything with a tail and four feet that you can."

"Then what are yo u doing way up there in that tree hiding in the leaves?"

"I am watching, that's what. You scare all the game away by walking around in the grass like you do."

"Come over to my barn. I will show you what r e al juicy pickings are."

"Insolent., whining fleebag!" I said.

"Whistlehooting fowl," this vagabond insults.

This sort of barrage of acrimonious slander w a s common to our relationship. We set off together. I fle w up to the rafters in the barn and waited for Gaugaun, the "vag," to show up. This, in fact, was my home hunti n g grounds. The pussycat did not know that. Anyway. whe n he showed up I laid it on again. "Why are you perambulating around. Vag. You're not trying to scare up a meal, are you?"

"There are rats in here—big ones."

"Is that for real—or just a suspicion, daint y-paws?" That independent, sneaky cheater was so dumb h e wouldn't know a raw fish if it swam in on a rainstorm.I'm onto him. What he really wants is for me to help h i m hunt wild game. I flew down once, buzzed him, and glided up to my roost again. "Tell you what, Flim-flam, you meow with seersucker night vision, you trembling apostrophe in your master's obituary-"

"You have got a wild lip today, Ole."

"If I see a rat first, I'll hoot. If you see something move, you meow. First one to pounce upon it gets first-choice of the flesh."

"Finders keepers," said the cat.

"I can taste the delicious things to come," I said. I knew what that pussy cat was up to. because fce wi&re-and had been for a long time—rivals in the same territory. He would not surrender, so much as a wild spit t o me or to any other hunter hereabouts. His mo uthwas too big for his stomach and he was scared of fighting, that cat.

I executed a wheelie umbrage in the barn—that is a complete circle in the dark, coming back to the starting point. "Did you see that?" I called down to Gaugaun.

"What?"

"That rat! It ran right across your path. Looked you in the eye—and you didn't see it? How are we going to hunt together, Puddlepaws?"

"I tell you honest—Ole. I didn't see it."

"Then you've got buttons for eyes."

"There's no sense in getting all upset, "said Gau-gauru

"LookJ Lqok there! There goes another one»"I said with a great horned scream.

"Where? I swear by the garbage of the saints I didn't see it."

"You lazy bag of furlice. It ran around to your tail and even pulled ito"

"I didn't feel a thing. I did not feel any r at pull my tail!"

"It did or I'm not a great horned owl. Hold itright there, you slick-asgrease fake, you stalking gate squeek, you privet-hedge habitue!"

"What is it now?"

"Didn't you see that? That lizard scared up by your noise. It moved right smack dab under your paws. You ' re supposed to meow."

"I swear I did not see a thing," swore the cat.

"You have got poor night vision, pussycat."

"My vision is as good as yours. You see that hole there? Now watch." The cat gave a little whine, scuffed some straw with its paw, and a small mousehead appe ared through a Knothole at the bottom of a board in the barn wallo The cat made a wide pass with one paw, expecti n g to snag the creature with its sharp claws. He missed.

"You are really a pitiable thing, pussycat. My estimate of your hunting expertise is even lower than when we first teamed up." I saw that the cat was getting madder and madder. I hoped to work that furlined meow into a fury so that we would never be rivals again—in my territory. "Hooooooott!" There it was. I spiraled down to the ground and snared a field mouse and lifted it, squeel-ing, up to the rafters.

"You didn't hoot first like you promised," the cat said.

"I did. You were not listening."

"I was rubbing my fur against a post."

"You dumb backpeddler, you mealymouthed simpleton, you padfooted skid-on-a-crack, I got no more use for you. Why don't you get lost—or tend to business?"

"I'm cautious."

"You are lazy. Well, the mouse is mine now. I couldn't let it get away." As soon as I had finished m y barn meal I watched the cat pretend that he was slee ping. He all at once gave a big "Meow!" as if he had spotted a rat twice his size. Bold in his tracks and staring and frozen in its tracks, Gaugaun, the pussycat, just sat there and confronted the little besst, his tail acquiver, licking his chops. A gorgeous feast! I remarked to myself"

"Pounce!" I cried from the rafters. "Why you dimwit!""I screamed down at him. But the cat and the rat remain e d perfectly still, facing each other

A still, small voice inside me kept saying. "Go first, go first!" I did not want to be greedy. What a kill! m y instincts urged me. Go down there and snatch that rat from under the cat's nose—would serve him right.

"Go ahead, pussycat! Practice your best pounce. Hooooooottooo!" Gaugaun was still frozen—as was that big barn rat. I'm thinking I may be a little greedy—so why do I wait any longer? I swooped down and grabbed up t h i s monster mouse—rat is *the* word. Gosh, it was heavy and did not feel like it had fur on it. It sure had a slick coat. It squeeked one squeek, and then it was dead. I flew u p onto a rafter and put the rat under my talons and ripped at it.

"The trouble with you, big fowl, is you've got no sense of smell," said the cat from the floor of the barn.

"Mine is just as good as yours," I grawked back.

"Don't get heartburn!" the cat warned. And then I knew why the cat howled with such great glee. I had captured a large rubber rat the cat had warehoused. I dropped the ribber thing to the ground.

"Your pride's got a hole in it somewhere—where your humility ought to be. Wise old owl! Rubbish!"

"You are too cunning for words," I screeched down at him. "You tricked me4"

"That's your trouble, fat bird. You got more hind-sight than foresight."

"I will show you how to hunt from now on," I screamed in barnyard rage. "And I hope you starve, you clumsy night-walker, you congestive pig of the garbage pail, you ""

"Say on, fat bird. We're done." The cat se re nely walked out of the barn into the moonlight. I perched a n d ruffled my feathers, totally put down by the entire episode. As an owl I would never trust a cat again.

Weasel, The Night Weaver And His Clutch

"Well, I'll be hornswoggled!" the farmer exclaimed when he saw what his chickens had done to the weasel.

Most folks think chickens are pretty dumb, like turkeys, but there was a fellow down in Buford County who owned a house full of hens that would not take "Chicken, die!" for an answer from any weasel worth the name of "weasel." This farmer learned a thing or two from his hens, too, The matter alluded to refers to a bloody murder case—which could be r e-constructed and was, in fact, reenacted every time somebody tied into a drumstick coming from that henhouse.

It seems that this weasel, "The Night Weaver"'he was called by All the local clucks, had made it a regular habit to visit this particular henhouse. He had gotten away with several of the less alert hens, particularly when they were roosting with their eyes closed. The Night Weaver was fast acquiring a reputation for being furtive and deadly, leaving the same clue always—the dropped pieces of grain beneath the feeding trough—before he performed his dastardly deed. Hen feed spilled on the boards and the blood and feathers on t h e henhouse floor always announced his presence. The roostin g board was never safe so long as The Night Weaver prowled the countryside.

There was, however, an uncommonly smart hen among th e lot of them. For the sake of annonymity, one may call her Clarita, or little caller. She had followed the details o f the grisly murders in "The Local Discratch," put out on butcher' paper by the Roosters" Editorial Board. "The Local Dis-cratch" seemed to delight in wallowing in the gore of fine details—like how many feathers were left behind, whether o r not the weasel had decapitated her, were her guts spilled o n the henhouse floor and such matters as good taste forbids u s to mention. It appeared that the farmer had always lo c k e d the door to his henhouse and always the weasel, The Night Weaver, found a way to get inside and to the sleeping hens.

Clarita had a sharp mind, sharper than her bill and twice as sharp as her claws. She knew what most of the other hens did not—that The Night Weaver was a very vain wea sel» It made him feel powerful to kill a young friar—that word has no religious meaning. It made him feel wild and untamed to take a chicken's life. Worst of all, it was evident that The Night Weaver wore a mask of black around his eyes, whi c h he stripped off before attacking so that the hen could s e e how beautiful was the weasel who was about to take her to her death. The whole scene was p itiless and gruesome. But accounts by the hens attacked and escaped have confirmed that this is the way The Night Weaver went about his horrible act.

She, Clarita, would confront this masked killer on his next raid and tell him exactly what she thought of him.—and then present to him her plan. She did not have long to wait. When the last cow had tankled past on her way to the barn and the wheezing sound of the old water pump, drawing night water for the family, had ceased, indeed, when the last of t h e crows had cawed overhead as was their way in the early ev e n-ing, this monster of predatory skill, this sleuth of sanguine portent and conniving connoisseurship slid through the tall grass. Clarita saw it wave, the stalks parted, and there peered two black eyes like berries from the brake of gras s.

The farmer had locked the henhouse door. Clarita waited, all acquiver, to find out how the slender, furry monster gained his usual entrance past the heavy mesh scree n-ing. At last she had it—through a break in the wire beneath one of the hatching shelves. How clever! How absolute ly cunning! Clarita hopped down from her perch while the other hens settled, with clucking and ruffling of fea-thers into their night's rest.

"So! You have come again at last!" said Clarita to the face and figure of the ravishing Night Weaver.

"Oh, my dearest hen, there you are. I was just waiting for you," said the weasel.

"For me to come out and romp and hop with you?"

"No, no, my dearest hen, golden voice of the hutch, the perfect beauty for my taste."

"Yes, I suppose so," said Clarita. "For your taste this time, but next time?"

"There shall never be another time," said the weasel.

"You have hit the yoke two times in a row, Mi s t er Weaselo"

"Permit me—"

"Stay back, you—you graceful creature," said the hen both warning and flattering the weasel. "I shall never have enough of you."

"But I shall have all of you if I ever catch you."

"That's what frightens me," said the hen. "But come—let us cluck together. Let us compare our-experiences our wants. Let us settle upon some reasonable thing.

After all, you will continue to rob the hen house, and I

will continue to escape and to warn others."

"You are determined."

"I haven"t made the skillet yet. Mister Weasel." "Robelard—Rob, for short."

"Suits you just fine," the hen said to the weasel."I have a plan that will allow me to get a good night's sleep which I have not had in months since yo u have been a—round. And you can always be sure you will catch some fat nice capon for your meal."

"Your logic interests me," said the weasel to the hen. "I must apologize for breaking into your night 's rest. I—actually I thought I was quieter than that."

"A cow with bells on her hooves could not have made more noise when you came—assaulted."

"So sorry, Miss Chick."

"Clarita, the Watchful One."

"What is your plan?" the weasel asked.

"You are such a gorgeous beast I hardly know how to present it. I am overcome with jealousy at the very thoutht of a rival hen."

"Come, come. I plan to eat my game, not make love to her."

"Oh, I'm sure you could do that, too. But then—I am straying." Clarita paused at the screen before the weasel had gained entry. "Not tonight but tomorrow night, I shall have your—dish—ready."

"Dish—ready? I do not know what you mean, dearest hen."

"Come up through the hole in the screen."

"How did you know?"

"Do not interrupt, Robe lard. Slide in through the hole and drop below us to the ground. Crouching in the hen house but not on the roost, with her feathers over her eyes and her head hidden you will find your morsel for t h e night."

"What is the price of this intriguing offer, my dearest Clarita?"

"That you never eat me—never try to catch and kill me—ever."

"In exchange for—?"

"A night of fun without noise—a plump friar every night. What do you say?"

"Your bribe is hard to refuse, my hen."

"Don't even think about it. Just do it and you will find that matters go smoothly—smooth and sensuous 1i ke your lovely brown body."

"Thank you, dearest hen." The weasel paused. "W ell then I shall give it a try, but if you are deceiving me-"

"Could I ever deceive someone I—well, forgive m e my passion—someone I could easily be swallowed up by in love?"

"I did not come by my lovely name for nothing," said the weasel. "Tomorrow night then?"

"Tomorrow night—and lay off the grain trough. It's a bad clue/" said the hen and plucked the wire screen t o indicate the intensity of her desire.

As soon as the weasel had d e parted through the tall grass, the plucky little hen addressed her hutchmates."Now listen to me, you dumb clucks, you're so independent—just like chickens—that I don't know if we can get this one to work. But let's give it a try."

"Don't bother us. We are about to roost.The day is over."

"I'm telling yo u, you know we have lost three of our kinsmen this past egging time. We have got to put a sto p to it—the killings, the night raids—restore safety to out hutch."

"Ho, hum," yawned a tired cluck. "And how—?"

"Work together. Quiet. We sit here tomorrow night, not a sound. Every cluck perches with her head under her wing. Get it? The weasel enters—we can hear him rattle the screen. He comes down through that hole in the screen. He is on the floor. I am the attractive ba i t "When he reaches the water trough, you—all of you, jump him and put out his eyes. You scratch and claw and go for his throat—and he is dead. You follow me?" The h e ns thought a moment, and after voicing some objections they agreed to throw in with Clarita just to keep her quiet"

The next night came on. Robelard, the weasel, approached as planned. He wove his way up to the screen.He slid through the hole in the mesh and gained the floor of the hen hutch. He looked around with his beady eyes and then he made a run for Clarita. She flew up into the air so that he missed her throat. That was the signal for the advance guard of twenty-five hens. They flew down in an attack of rabid clucking, squawking and wild fla p-ping of their wings. They pecked out the eyes of the weasel who, himself, screeched in agony and tried to m a k e for the break in the wire mesh. The hens blocked his way. They threw him over onto his back and clawed and pecked at his soft underbelly. The turbulent commotion went on, a furious whirlwind of noise and dust and manure and feathers. The weasel called Robelard, now blind. staggered a-round on the floor of the hutch. A second cadre flew down from their roost bearing sticks and bits of glass and began to rend the weasel from one end to the other. It took them a good while, but they accomplished the death of the sensual weasel, the feared Night Weaver, Rob the lovely.

Up in the farmhouse the noise had aroused the farmer from his sleep. He emerged from his house and ran down to the hen hutch with his shotgun in hand. He poked his light into the interior of the hutch where he obviously expected to confront a trapped varmint. He uttered a howl of surprise when he looked inside.

"Well. I'll be hornswoggled!" he swore when he saw the remains of the weasel. Quickly and quietly the hens were returning to their roost for the night. On the floor of the hutch, amid blood and feathers and bits of stone, sticks and glass—the hens' weapons of war—he saw the lifeless body of the arrogant weaselo He opened the door reached inside, took the weasel by his tail and flung him far into the cornfield.

Clarita clucked her signal of contentment to her hutchmates. "The Local Discratch" would have a real story now.

The Flexible Coils Of Choice

I do not know where the report ever leaked out, the insinuation that I once walked about and now, because o f my involvement with Eve, I must crawl. Poor girl. Actual. ly I felt sorry for her. I mean, she didn't have the gumption to keep clear of that apple tree, the Kumstrata-chka tree, in the Garden of Eden—and she couldn't close her ears to my pitch.

Why do I rehash all those old things. like shed skins of ugly words—sweet soothing words to my ears? You know how a woman likes to blame herself for failures i n human relationships. and I go along with that predisposition. I like to recycle old doubts. Doubt is one of my strongest aphrodisiacs.

As I scribble with my tail in the sand, squirm m y twirly writings. image pictures where I crawl about, I simply want to cough up my rejection—total, digested, an d squeezed of life—my rejection of this nonsense about previous snaky footfalls. Utter garbage! That I ever walked about instead of crawling as I do upon my bellyi Of course I am satan. The Mighty One can put me anyplace. But a walking snake? Come on now. That mocks God and I join in the laughter.

Let me glide a little closer to the subject. Doc-trine. That is a rooted belief whose plant gives out di f-ferent flowers, some poisonous. I love doctrine, a salubrious means for destroying true worship of Him. Personally, the dogmas of doctrine provide me with copious possibilities for addling the brains of believers, bringing them to their senses so that they bolt from the faith. Div i de the smug animals, like I did Adam and Eve, so damned coz y and self-satisfied.

But I am getting ahead of my story. My punishme n t for my garden persuasion was to crawl, crawl. crawl. Le t me tell you that that is not the worst fate to come out of Eden. Crawling. It provides privacy, security, a vantage point from the ground up. And I have my camouflage. Religionists have their stuff and status to hide behind. I know. Modestly, I help in the provision thereof. I have my pasttimes, also—like soul rolling. Ever see that one? I take a religionist's soul in my teeth and I go rolling down the hill. Exciting fun that really grabs the soul. I tell you, I am no bore.

It was I, little old me, the Great One accused o f causing Eve to fall. Take the word <u>fall</u>. She never really actually fell. She rose up, like all my human animals will do. On two legs and a pot of wisdom. She had the power to chose; I just happened to be a good salesman. I don't believe in all that obedience gobble-de-goop. That's where I am. Obedience is a sacrifice. Why? Why sacrifice yourself? That is suicide and even He condemns that. God and I are cohorts on that one. Perfect} total free-dom is my pitch. Naturally my freedom leaves no room fo r that obsolete notion of conscience. None whatsoever. But let me go on.

I will relate to you how the myth sprang up, how circumstances contrived to destroy my credibility because o f this cursed presupposition that I ever walked. Since I crawl I can slither up into trees. wrap my cold, muscular, gaudy coils around snits like that Eve—and Adam. Move in close on feet? I—well, I would stumble, fall flat on my kadish, break a tooth maybe. Therefore, since I left no footprints in the Garden, heel marks in the spring rain mud of Eden, I should like to know why I am so often maligned. I have thought a great deal about that. I can find nothing more absurd than a snake walking around—upright, like a vulture on a carcass, or a—human animal. Yea, verily, mind-boggling. I may be a viper but I am not stupid.

On this particular day I had slithered into a nearby Frumpy tree, a palm with a shaggy trunk, monkey-arm branches and thorns in the bark. The tree tops danced in the wind, and sweet smells of Eden perfumed the air like incense. Dew loaded with grassvvine and jewels that I love to rattle covered the ground like folds of green silk. It was lovely"jsmell-ed lovely and drugged my filmy eyes to sleep.

There he was—Adam, mulching and crunching out in his garden, very sure of his happiness. I detest that vapid state of mind. Sure, the Mighty One gave him a garden, yet he does not know a stick in the mud from a radish. He is there, whistling! Listen! Are you with me? Whistling!—the sound of his cursed contentment with Him. It pierces my ears, makes my belly rumble, shrieks me out of my sanity. He was whistling—"0, God of the Heavens, I prune for Thee.' Absolutel y turgid rhyme scheme. Words and music? I salt my flesh with notes like his.

Put to sleep that night, he was and—kazamm, kazoo and the hullaballoo! and he has got himself a mate. Differe n t from himself yet another one of His playthings. Invented, I suppose, to help Adam get along in his garden.

It"s one of the most idiotic arrangements I ever saw, and I've been trying to change it ever since. It did not make sense then and doesn't now. Oh, I know all about this multiplication crap, but there are other ways. Adam and his Eve—they were natural enemies. I could see that right away. Of course I did not say anything then and there. I and Adam were on good speaking terms, and we still rap when we can get together on my terms. Curse me, I thought to instill some sense into his Eve. She began to dance and prance when she saw Adam.She ran and hid from him—games, you know. "Tee, hee, hee, A d am, what's on your mind, Adam?" She still has not found the answer to that one "entirely. And he is still looking for the real her. That's my very own arrangement—domestic concealment, which enrichens the relationship with great new e m options of anger, fear, anxiety, hatred, arrogance and yearning. Marvelous, just marvelousl

Soon after he got his—toy, I caught Adam mumbling to himself. "Tree, apple, bush, rock, dirt, leaves, fruit, deer, elk, bird, air, water—"

"What on earth are you doing, Adam?"

"I'm giving names to all the stuff around here. I just can't tell Eve I dug up a worm beside the thingumajig."

"Makes sense. Let me ask you something. Is all this stuff yours?"

"God has said so."

"Do not—do not say that name—evert The High t y One, the Great One, yes, but God—? I shall glide away t o the Euphrates and never visit your garde n again."

"Sorry, satan."

"That's better. You know that we are friends."

"You have not discombabulated me yet, so I guess it' s true."

"You believe that there is a—Diety—excuse the expression, a God, who made all these things, the fruit trees, bushes, the spuds in the earth—to grow? Yams and berries and figs and the honey from that big oak over there?"

"I sure do, snake.'

"You got any proof?"

"No, I sure don't, snake""

"You"re crazy—deluded, fantacizing, unreal."

"I have faith, snake."

I knew there was a whole lot more to the scene than what had just transpired. For right then a voice came through the trees. It crackled like boulders splitting and rumbling down a canyon. It veined the skies with a powdered haze of agate and saphire flame, and the sun scorched the palm fronds and seemed to suck up ground moisture into its cooling furnace of smoke and noise, "I am the God who creat e d these wonders of nature."

"I do not doubt it. I cannot doubt it at all," said Adam.

"Snake, are you putting evil doubt into the mind of my man-creature, Adam?"

"No, O Great One. I was simply clearing up some perplexities and perturbations in my own mind."

"Perplexities? You had bette r stop because if you keep this up you are going to wind up in a heap of trouble."

"What do you want me to do?"

"I want you to go back and lie under that rock of pink granite. You may presume you glide with mystery, but you reek with pride, Snake," said God.

"I have a logical mind—the fangs of reason are m y venemous bite."

"I gave you wisdom and understanding. Do you abus e them again?"

"I shall hold my tongue—for the time being. Maybe I ought to go back to the sea where I came from."

"You did not come from the sea. You are not a fish, or an amphibian sea monster. You are but a plain, ordinary, presumptuous snake."

"Do I not have the wicked mind and soul of your devil-angel? I can go—"

"Whenever and wherever I permit you to go."

All the rocks shook together like nuts in a bowl, The trees waved like bowing Eve maidens and a gloom of sunshadow sent ice on the wind through Eden. "You were a.decei ver from the start. Your music crumbled, shattered like froze n skies and embalmed racket—screeching out death and hatred. The cold, sinuous, winding snake is your proper shape, for m and abode."

"I accept what you give me."

"You are no orphan, Snake. You are an original—equal to the cattle and to the beasts in the field.'

"Must I bow with coiled rapaciousness before your generous—offer and—glide?"

"Glide, as on ice, like an otter on a cake of snow, or like starling birds that skim the land or the heron that glides on wings through the river dusk. Glide—"

I was left to presuppose that Adam and I were friendly enemies, one of my most us e ful tools later on for extrac-ting the religionist believer from the tar bog of his infernal faith and saving his life for himself"

All went along well enough for a time in Eden. Then it came to me that God had warned Eve—I heard the matter for myself—He told her, "Do not dare to eat any fruit off that Kumstratachka tree in the middle of the Garden—or you will surely die."

His voice spoke like thorns into blue, crystal night skies, piercing, hurting with clarity. But reason it out. Why would He create her only to kill her? Was He sad and unhappy? Was she a defective product of Adam"s rib?

Yaaaahh! I know now that is how He performed His magic. The warning did not make any sense to me. He said. in essence, that H e would stomp out all communication between herself and H i m. Not just table talk, either. He did.

"You will positively die," He said to Eve.

"That vengeful| indifferent Jailor is not going to kill you, Eve. You are a sweet, gentle, beauteous. kindly a n d earth-digging lady of the Garden. You will cause the sun to set and the moon to rise throughout history."

"Who are you?" she asked.

"Allow me to introduce myself. I am—Snake. Have you never seen my glide?"

"Never."

"My round, sinuous, voluptuous, muscular form?"

"Never."

"My pity upon thee, my child. I am all that and much. much more. Did—I am modest to speak His name. but did-God tell you that you would positively die if you are fruit from the Kumstratachka tree?"

"He did—positively."

"The clown, the ogre, a tryant. He expects you to weed and snip and clip and never even—nibble from the Kumstratachka tree?"

"He does. What are weeds?"

"What a pity, Eve! Oh, I know your name. I lear ne d it from your Adam. He told me. He is very proud of you, you know."

"I certainly hope so. He is the best thing that ever happened to me. I want him to share everything that I have."

I chuckle. "Now be at peace. sweetest Eve. I am sure that he will delight to do just that." Monstrous, this Great One—to create a creature only to destroy her. I shall get her to blot Him out of her mind as the only remedy.

"But that tree, snake. Why must I just watch it grow and bear fruit and never satisfy my hunger. God said to me I would then know about good and evil."

"Stuff! I can give you that. That simply me a n s God approves of some things and disapproves of others-like eating from the Kumstratachka tree. It's all in the mind—good and bad. Adjust your mind—a little this way, a little that way, and what He calls evil is nothing but a bad dream, a poor vision, a wrong way of looking at life. See what I mean?"

"Do you think Adam would—would be proud of m e if I took just one little nibble and then—told him?"

"Oh, I'm sure he would swell up with pride to know that his very own mate had scaled the wall between ignorance and knowledge. That is what it all amounts to."

"Knowledge and ignorance?"

"Infinite knowledge—and I possess detailed plans for some—regione. The Great One wants to be the sole retainer, the only vessel to hold all knowledge. Selfish, I call it. Not wanting to share His knowledge with you."

"You know, snake. I'm beginning to think you are right."

"Of course I am. Right as rain. God is sel f ish, egotistical, pious, unhappy and possessive with his own creations—and terribly out of joint with the universe."

"You may be right. Oh—there is Adam."

"Hide first. Over there, by the Kumstratachka tree and why not smell the fruit? It is fresh." She went over to where this sickeningly lovely tree stood.

"Good, snake! Really sweet smelling."

"Go ahead and try some. There's one—just within reach. You don't even have to pick it."

"I will. I will."

"Poor thing." She picked the Kumstratachka fruit, yellow and red and with the most beaitiful markings o f cream running through its skin. She bit.

"Hmmmmmm!"

I could see she loved it so. A great icy wind flooded the Garden, shaking all the trees and bowing the grasses. but not one of the fruit whe re Eve stood fe 1 1 to the ground.

"Good, huh?"

"Oh, yes, Snake!"

"Why don't you call Adam and make this a twosome?"

"A what?"

"A sharing party—to give you a sense of u n ity, security and worship."

"Adam! Adam!" she called out. "He is too beautiful to approach."

"You are his mate. He will come. He is off somewhere in the Garden, naming stuff."

"Is that you, my beloved, who called?"

"It is, dearest plum of my eye, the rose of my body, the jewels of dew on our love bed. Over here."

And so this worthless animal came over to where his mate stood and she said to him, "This is such good fruit, Adam. Try this one. I have bitten into it already."

He bit, chewed, filled his cheeks with the meat o f the Kumstratachka tree. He swallowed hard and tried another bite. The two of these despicable snits stood t h e re in the shade of that tree consuming—must I say it? the forbidden fruit. Icy winds again flooded through the Garden, this time bearing stinging sleet that tormented their bare flesh and lay like drops of wild honey upon t he grounde

The voice of the Great One—I knew He would put in his finger—came like a thousand booming wings, fanning the air with a great rushing sound as of white water, beat-ing amongst the leaves, the skies of crimson clouds giving utterance to anger.

"Where are you, Adam?"

"Here, under the Kumstratachka tree with Eve. But I think we ought to go."

"I forbade you, Eve, to taste of that fruit."

"I couldn't help it."

"You could—but you did not. Your pride stripped you of your reason. And, Adam, you tasted with her."

"I know it, I admit it. I confess it fully."

"It is too late," said the Great One.

"We disobeyed. We ought to go and hide, I think."

"Here. Put on these rags—skins—to hide your nakedness."

"CanH I apologize, say I'm sorry?" Adam asked.

"We are no longer on speaking terms, Adam. Eve will give birth to twin sons, Cain and Abel. Murder a nd deceit and wickedness will now belong to all humans who follow you—and to you, also, Snake."

"What'd I have to do with all this?" I queried Him.

"A pleading of innocence will get you nowhere, Snake. You are the Temptor. You want them to worship each other instead of me."

"I and my cohorts know you exist, God."

"You do not worship me. Instead you summoned them to disobedience. They have surrendered to you."

"Can't blame me for wanting my fair share of power."

"Leave the Garden, Adam and Eve. I will placeanangel with a flaming sword to guard the entrance—the place where you lost your innocence. Never return—ever-ever-ever. You are accursed by me, Snake. No longer shall you glade but you shall crawl, writhe, wriggle, squirm. Eve shall know only agony in childbirth as a token of her wrong and disobedience. Go—at once! At least do this thing right!" the voice of the Mighty One commanded.

Thus they fled, leaving me alone in the dead o f night. I snaked out past the guardian angel, into the thorn bushes and the sharp rocks and the hot and d u sty places. Adam and Eve set up house many leagues distant. I was there to welcome them into their new way of life.

I used to glide verywhere, like a shadow upon th e water, like a shot arrow lost in the grass. I also ate of the fruit, though my usual fare is rodents and field mice, My shape was long and slender and I moved like a needle thrust through fabric. My voice was like a song-bird's that pierces the branches of the fig tree, like the fragrance of a spring morning that filtered, noise— lessly through the Garden. I had status among the other animals, the cattle, bears, wolves and lions and t h e great beasts of the uplands. They respected me—unt i l that great temptation. Now I am nothing, yet I am everything to Adam's offspring.

The Case Of The Turnkey Monkey

I was almost too happy, deliriously happy, manificently, chatteringly happy, so that that the tre e branches seemed to swing up to within my reach—oh, progressive reach! As you can tell, I have gone to the laboratory and I am well versed in the constabulatories of mankind, who hunt me and my confreres for the purposes of their i na ne experiments—and me being just a short toss away fro m their own kind at that.

But I must tell you about an experience of mine tha t taught me to think of others, not to be mindlessly happy but to consider the welfare of my fellow monkeys as well. I wanted to do something I could feel proud of—a n ob le sacrifice.

You see, I knew that tiger catchers roamed through the rain forest where I swing and chatter and make love and hunt for food—a place I love and cherish. These wild ones, fierce invaders with their baited trap-boxes are two-footed creatures who walk always on the ground. They look a lot like us, but they are smoothskinned and babble and could not swing through the trees if you put them i n a banana grove. They lack tails, a thing I always marveled at and tried to find some reason for.

With their cork hats and their guns in hand, le a d-ing black loadbearers like a column of ants, they came into my jungle one day. I overheard one babble to h i s friend.

"Do you hear how they scream and chatter? Warnings-. spiritual stuff. They are signaling to their tribe that we are clos eby. They are curious, but they fear us o"

"Then we shall have to use cunning to catch us our tiger."

"Cunning! The monkeys will see that. No higher intelligence."

"I see."

"You will."

Of course we do not scold our walking human broth-ers. That is nonsense! We simply warn our blood-brother humans of the presence of the tiger. Now it just s o happened one day that Joaquim, the Tiger, walked noncha-lantly past—and beneath—our monkey enclave. When this happened all the black porters scattered, the white hairless monkeys went to their tree perches and, my other brothers" monkey blood rising to the occasion, we put up a horrendous squeeling and chatt ering of fear and warning. Joaquim stood there o n the trail, motionless e x-cept for the switching of his tail and drooling from his moutho He was on the prowl and hungry and desperate for a meal.

I said to Joaquim, whom I recognized by his stripes, "You look so calm and at home out here."

"I am at home. This is my pantry."

"I know you are a tiger and all that sort of rot,"I said, "but would you mind laying your selfish meat-hu n t-ing aside for us poor monkeys when you are crossing through our territory?

"What is that! Your territory is it? I have a hard day some days just making my whiskers meet, much less finding a good meal on the road." Just as he said that he fell into a pit below the trail—kerthunk! A lot of jabbering and shouts and scurring about and the porte r s, by means of their ropes like vines and their stick s like limbs raised poor Joaquim to the surface and set him down beside the pit. What a pity! Through the bedlam I ras able to catch the tiger"s ear. If yo u sho uld ever want to catch a tiger's ear, it is best that he be caged.

"Mister Joaquim, as you know we Rhesus monkeys almost never bother you. We announce your coming so that we can get out of your way. We alert you to game near by when we give out with our hyper-attenuated screeches of chromatic aberration—words I learned in the Laboratory, old fellow. Naturally, I do not expect you to und e r-stand them. The very trees tremble, as you well know."I demonstrate d. "Like this—" I screamed for the tig e r to show him that I understood his present predicament and need.

"I see you have an ego problem. "said the tiger.

"Hold on there, Joaquim," I said. "I am a reject from The Laboratory, and so I have felt the prick of real trouble in my life."

"I hope so. But—as you can see—I need hel p . After all, I am now caged. Who knows but what you will be in a cage like mine tomorrow?"

"I shall have to watch myself—keep my paws out of empty gourds filled with nuts and goodies."

"Could you—would you steal the keys from the bossman?" the tiger asked.

"Keys—?"

"To this prison box I am in."

"You are a crazy tiger, Joaquim. How can I steal such a thing—from him with a gun? And—keys? Wha t are they?"

"You are Laboratory trained and do not know what a key and lock are? I will show you. The keys to my prison box hang around the neck of the bossman—s h i ny little sqwidgets, like tree stars."

"You are thinking only about Joaquin, the TJL ger, when you ask me to do this. The white beast carries a gun and he will shoot me."

"Tonight, he will bathe in the creek. I have seen him. Go snag the keys with your little paws from his skins on the embankment and bring them to me. I wi 1 1 show you how to open my prison cage."

"What will you give me in return?" I asked.

"My pawprint of promise that I shall never again hunt in your territory."

"Then I will not delay."

"You must not fail." said the tiger

Joaquin probably figured he had found a con s t a nt source of food in the hunters—I know for a fact that we monkeys are a lot of hair and not much meat down t o the bone. But a hungry tiger is lean and mighty whe n his stomach guides him. I know Joaquin preferred bigger game than us yet I gave into him.

"Tonight when the white animal comes up out of the water. that is your chance. He will spend much time i n hunting for his keys. He will fumble for his gun.I shall pounce upon him in my best style," the tiger said.

It was no trouble to fit the key into the cage lock—we monkeys are the cleverest of creatures and our hands work like the white animal's fingers. In a matter of minutes I had freed poor Joaquim from his prison cage.

"Swing high, swing low!" I screamed gleefully. "M a y the High Priest of the Enigmatic Tail reward me!"

"Joaquim grinned. "What will these hunters say when they find the cage empty tomorrow?"

"Naturally, I was thinking only of you," I said. "I only wanted to do a good deed for another kingdom c r ea-ture."

"See how the tiger drools," my friends all said."He is ready to pounce upon us for his next meal. Let u s flee."

"Oh, no. He will not do such a thing as that," I reassured them in my firmest and best monkey dialect."H e wants the hunter down at the creek for his dinner. I ha ve his paw print on thato"

My argument was of no use; it had only put one o f my friends off-guard where he propped himself against a purplewood tree. He was quite stoned o n peace food, the nuts in the gourd placed by other hunters, monkey hunters, in the high branches of a tall tree. Joaquim walked up to the dazed monkey, stiff from drugs, sniffed him, sex z ed him amidst great screams from us and carried the poor creature off into the dense jungle brush.

"Come back! Come back! Come back!" I cried after Joaquin. My screams of protestation, my wild ejacula—tions of horror, my primal bedlam of dissent did not help one miniscule bark moss. I had liberated an enemy, the tiger, only to watch him drag a colonial away in helpless anguish and gobble him up as a secret delicacy.

The whole monkey gang then swooped down upon me and began to rap m. with angry words. "Do you not understand what survival means here in the forest? Do we have t o draw pictures for you on the ground? Must we hang the carcasses of the deceased from every dead tree in t h e woods? Is our worth only—only as useful as bark rus t? We have to think about each other, not about what we would or would not like to do."

"Yes, but I—"

"But you—you did not think, Rhesus. Now did you?"

"I wanted only to liberate Joaquim."

"A tiger! A tiger! A tiger!" the conclave screamed. "How could you! At least he might have gone to the white creature .s nirvana and crunched on short ribs the rest of his life.

"Our own brother is gone for good. He is gone. That is plain to us Rhesus monkeys. Because you—to gai n credit with the High Priest of the Enigmatic Tail, did this!" Their voiced oozed acid.

"I understand now," I chattered. "I was not so wise."

"No, you were not. But since you believe in fair play, now that the tiger has enjoyed his dinner and you your pawprint promise from him, what do you say if we take from you something in return for your brother's life—your own freedom?"

"My life?"

"Your freedom and, yes—your jungle life, wise Rhesus"

With these words the gang shoved me inside the emp t y cage and slammed down the door and threw the key into t he brush beside the trail.

"What do you say to that, martyr?"

"Any monkey who lays down his life for another monkey is a noble monkey." I cried. The gang laughed and laugh ed until the trees shook down leaves and Joaquim growled a drunken growl at a distance. "You do not give up your li f e for a banana, for a bunch of leaves, for a free swing on the top branch of the tallest tree. It is good to sacrifice but think clearly, wise Rhesus—the cause must be worth the life—must be worth it—must be worth it, Tiger Monkey."

They laughed and laughed. Their warning echoed into the dripping, dark green jungle, joined by the wild cry o f the Scot McCaw Parrot, the scream of doom for me. The entire colony then departed, swinging through the top branches, and I was left a prisoner, left to reflect upon the stupidity of my actions. I had lost a colonial friend—and my own freedom—because I thought I was being a noble monkey. Pride is almost always a trap.

Snakeflames And The Death Of The Firestick

Most hunters get ecstatic with hot-gun fever when they catch me scampering across the needles of the autumn forest. The trees are my friends, and I leap into the coat of bark closeby, flying like a bat and disappearing like a flame in the wind, around to the back side. Hunters who do not come into my domain often think that I am inside the tree, or that I have dropped into a hole in the ground. They are almost blind—which makes them dangerous to themselves, me and other wildlife. I am a cautious forest creature. Nature gave me much great caution, y et I hear hunters brag between themselves about hitting one of my cousins in the eye at ninety feet. How absurd!"Crr-rrrp, crrrrrp, crrrrrp." They are not so careful t o measure their gun aim as I am.

Let me sclamber up to the touchable pine needles-a thing that shows the basic difference between my cautious eyes and the hunter's blind ecstasy. There is much difference. Then you will see fear and danger like myself.

I was minding my life's business of eating to s u rvive. I was chewing seeds from a heavy pinecone and spitting out the wood. I was scattering pulp from the leav e s all over the ground when a thunder gun, close to my e a r, chipped a piece of bark from a cedar. My eyes l o o k e d into the sun and then into the shade. There stood a hu g e two-legged creature holding a shiny . bright gun the size of a water pipe. It gleamed like frost in the sunlight. I watched him steady the bore of this fir e snake at me. I scratched up the nearest tree. Great smoke and thunder and flame filled the empty forest silence. He was a cra zy one. He missed me. I circled the tree. Whammm—bangg! The flame leapt at me like a snake 's tongue. quick and evil. He missed again. I rose into the sky, crossed tree limbs to other trees, and stopped and thought.

Why not tie his hands and feet with a clever tri c k? But I did not descend until the sun pierced the pine seedlings. I knew he did not see the sun going down red.I hid in an old log and scolded the leaves to rattle. The two-legged creature saw me and spat out his flame. I poked my head through a thicket and chrrrppppett shrilly. Another invisible rock plucked off twigs over my head. I ran up a naked pine to the first limb. found a pine cone heavy with juice and chewed it to fall. It hit the foot of the two-legged creature. I ran. He shot into the sky and wounded the sun and the quiet stars, but he hit only the silence.

The man creature with his firesnake was blind and yet he did not stop. He showed up like an enemy, at the worst time in the morning. Whammmm! Baannnggg! He stood like a rock. I crossed a bridge above the ferns and water and whistling grassed and scolded from the shadows. Flame a-gain flickered out. I threaded my way to a tuft of gras s behind him, brushed dirt from my eyes. He lowered his firesnake and threw flame at me but missed me. The game then got old. Why not get Redcap, the woodpecker, into the sport? He was hammering away at the top of a tall tree. He hid strange magic in the holes he bored.

"Say, Red, you know that two-legged animal keeps banging away and can't hit the sound if it was made of wood?".

Ratttittaty, rap, tap, rattattetty, rap, tap. I sure do."

"Hammering on hard wood. I see."

"Whatt? Ears are ringing." said the woodpecker.

"That hunter's got a size nine brain in a number two hat that's making my life one big rockpile. I cannot gather food any more—scares me to pieces."

"Ratttittytatttatt. Whatcha want, Scampershadow?"

"Help. He throws flame at me just to hear the noise. One of these days he's going to scatter your feathers for the ants."

"He wants to wear you on his belt."

"Your life is in danger, Hammerhead."

"I'm not good eating like you are. Soak you in brine would mellow you. What's on your squirreley mind, Pitty-patter?"

"Drop an acorn on his head. I'll run up his leg for kicks."

"Here he comes. I'm a butterfly," said the redcrested woodpecker. "See. I can fly on my back, roll with the wind, come right side up."

"You are a silly bird. Don't you know I'm out here for practice?" said the two-legged creature. He whamm i e d his firestick in four directions, bit off a plug of tobacco for a chew, sprinkled some canteen water on his head-for it was a warm day—and sat down to ruminate. Hammerhead, he also set down on some pine needles in front of Fireir o n Big Noise. I watched from a scatter of twigs.

"Hang your big noise on a branch," said the woodpecker. "You shoot at any animal with wings and four legs."

"I test my aim. New firestick. Cost much."

"Why do you come out here when there's no hunting. You never seen the signs?"

"It's a open season—"

"On squirrels and woodpeckers is it open?" Firestick Big Noise got uneasy in the grass. He pulled his flapbind-ers down over his ears, slid the night things down over bis eyes to hide from the sun.

"What's all this got to do with me?"

"Just close your eyes. You will find out." Hammerhead flew over to where I crouched, my nose acquiver. "You got any friends? This is the time."

"Whatchu mean?"

"The head of Big Noise will look good on a tree trunk. He needs to look big. That's why he owns his big firestick. Good noise to him but it kills the sky. I will change into a bear. You see that big dead limb hanging up there in the sky? I will drop it on him."

"You can't do that. You are only a bird."

Hammerhead flew up to a big tree limb and in a cloud of bark dust and needles changed into a black bear. "Loo k out, Scattershadow!" Hammerhead called down. He shoved a big dead limb off the other limb so that it crashed closeby to the two-legged creature with the firestick, who sat with his eyes closed. He woke up all at once and picked up his thunderstick and fired up at the black bear.

"I am invisible, "said the bear. He clawed down the bark out of sight. "Keep shooting," the bear wheezed.

The two-legged creature walked around the tree. Snake flames lept from his thunderstick. Then the flame stopped and so he stopped.

"Kill me, Thunderman, I will turn into a woodpecker when I am dead."

"Dumb. silly bird! It flew away."

"Look behind you. Look to your right and to your left. This is where we live. Two more black bears glided on silent paws into the clearing where Thundernoise sto o d with his firestick in his hands. The two-legged creature laughed hard. He began to shoot like crazy with mag i c courage. He flamed out at leaves, at branches that moved, at red sunshine on the pinewood bark, at the shimmering of the light in the ne e dleso His firestick spit flames a t a dead treestump, but it did not move—and at a r o tti n g powder log. But I was gone from that log. His flames attacked a fence post by the road. He scattered his shadow from the ground and then picked pin e cones from a branch over his head. Wild, wild! He did not shoot hisself i n the foot—I saw this bloody firebite one time.

"I need more fire!" He searched in his bag and did not find his fire. The black bears attacked Big Noise and got his blood. He lay on the ground without any life, like a rug. Pine needles buried his firestick.

"You see what power we have," said Hammerhead. Bears do not always stick together as black bears. Look up here. Here!" In a cloud of bark dust and pine needles, one o f the bears was gone.

"Up here, up here! Rattattatytat!" echoed Red Top. He clung to the silver bark of a white fir. "Here is th e face of Big Noise—this knothole where the limb broke off!"

I looked at the ground where Big Noise had gone. There was not even any blood there. The knot burl in the tree looked just like the hunter. "It was all an accident, rat-ttattetytat," rapped the woodpecker bird and flew into a tangle of pine tops.

I looked around and the other bears were gone. I t was all so crazy, what I saw. But I could hunt for ripe pine cones again and not worry about Big Noise and hi s firestick—not this time anyway. I ran up the tree trunk and peered in at the knot hole. There was no man-creature in there. There was just a face.

Wagner, The Braggart Cat

Down under—that is, down under the East River bridge there lived a sire cat. He was king of the rat catchers, for he caught not only his quota to keep himself and hi s friends alive. He also bagged enough to beat the local ga m e laws. Under the bridge, no cat was allowed to catch a n d kill more than two fat rats in excess of daily rations. "Tawney," neutered male, patrolled the down-under area nightly. Great fights erupted, but the illegal catch was always summarily dropped into the river as a lesson to all.

Now Mister Wagner, or Snutu as he was more informally known to others beneath the piers, was accustomed to awaken every morring to the clopple of horses" hooves o n the boards above his head, and the grinding sound of wheels as they rolled across the rover to the other side. He had fixed for himself a fine home out of tin pie-pans, some corrugated sheets, an old cellar door, three fine packing crates and a tangle of packing excelsior.

This was the home of Snub on the day when he met Scar-face Wildpacker, king of the East Side and a most ferocious fighter—no claws barred. They met, it is said, by day but in truth it was by night—they met when smoke began to rise from the dump and when Snub and Scarface got into an argument as to whom the remnants of a bag of old sandwiches belonged.

Rats that night were scarce. These two fearless scrappers had stumbled upon the discarded bag of sandwiches, tossed over the bridge railing, and they immediately began their quarrel. Snug, or Mister Wagner, was the braggart and thi s trait got him into deep trouble at once. He called Scarface witless and cowardly. He claimed his bravado was the ma t c h of any old alley cat's. Calling Scarface "old" was not exactly the climax of wisdom, Snug reflected, but what are you going to do with a bully who meows every time some sc o o c h touches his turf? Anyway, this obscene quarrel between Snub and

159

Scarface arose from angry growls. threats of omino u s whining, sinister spits and furry barrages of claws, i n to loud screams of hurt. Their quarrel woke up the night watchman of the road gate below the bridge piers. A te ne m e nt dweller flung an old pipe elbow at them from a fourth storey window and clobbered a tin sheet with the sound of thunder. Then—here came an old shoe. The combattants took their entanglement across the alley. There Snub knew he had witnesses, favorable cat friends, with keen logic and feli n e judgement. The battle and chase went up a nearby fire e s-cape, telegraphing the ominous and life-threatening nature of the combat.

When neighbors of Snub and Scarface could stand the angry, abusive howling no longer, in the moonlight on the fire escape, they gathered in a conclave amid broken bottles an d alley weeds. From the gloom numerous cats suddenly emerged to hear the jist of the scrap.

Now Snub was proposing some pretty scarry tests o f nerve to Scarface, the old battler, the victor of many a garbage-can rhubarb. Snub said, "I hear tell you"re the best fence-walker around these parts, Mister Scarface"

"What's that to you, Big Time," Scarface replied.

"Bravo! Bravo!" the conclave howled.

"Fences! You're ridiculous!" said Scarface. "I left fence-walking behind in my kitten days. I climb only the highest bridge girders."

"Bravo!" rose the howls from the other cats who has gathered there in the moonlight, beneath the dead elm tree.

The human enemy had had their sleep shattered by all the racket. They contirued to rain a steady fire of soap, shoes, chunks of coal and empty bottles upon the cat congress. The conclave moved on down the alley to the darkened warehouse platform. The combattants continued their bragging on the dock.

"Ikilled more big—and I mean bigt—rats in one day than you could fish out in a month of howling at rat digs," Snub bragged.

"Fishheads! It ain't rats make me ripe for a fight. It's a mangy-looking, string-haired specimen of catdom such as yourself," said Scarf ace.

"Why you—!" They whined their exchange of insuits.

"Just how long can you sleep in a ice box with out freezing?" Snub was bold to ask.

"Forever," said Scarf ace. "I"ve tippled sour milk with the mightiest of the big ones—from out of that jungle over yonder."

"My—oh, dear, you tell him," came the backup cries of Scarface's friends. The jungle was the slum alleyw a y two blocks distant. Hunting in the alley garbage cans was so good the whole of catdom called the place The Jungle.

"I say—hear me out, all of you," said Scar face, making his pitch to reason. "I've walked the deep carpets of penthouse corridors. I've feasted from the garbage pits of the finest restaurants in this city. The tenderest of mistresses have stroked me and the finest cops scr a tched m y ears."

"My, ain't you big though."

"You're just jealous," said Scarface.

"I brag, but you—swagger, loud mouth. You think your fur don't smell like cat." He put bite and innuendo into his voice. Let me tell you, I have sat on top of a telephone pole for three days without food or water. What d o you think of that. I ain't no whiner either," Snub finished.

"Yeah—they had to put up a tall ladder and r e s c ue you, too."

"I've hunted with the best and fought with the t ough-est," said Snub.

"And you—a—gentleman." There was acid in Sc a r-face.s scoffing voice. All the other cats set up a howling as lights went on in the buildings nearby. There broke out sounds of gunfire. "Ohmygosh!" they all thought as one, and they scattered in the direction of the jungle. There Snub and the other cats could bathe in the delicious smells of the garbage and the rattle of a stray dog and that exciting sound of 1it t le pink feet scurring over the stones from the blackness of a junk pile—the rat on the prowl.

The combattants" noise, growls and anger had provoked the cat congress to suggest an end to the scrap, by contest and trial.

A congress member spoke up: "Let him who can wal k across the clothesline of Maggie O'Hara win the Tunatin A-ward for stout courage and cat skill."

"What do you say to that?" Snub asked,

"Go for it, Big Time," said Scarface.

"I can trot between fire escapes and pick up the laundry on the way," Mister Wagner bragged. He glanced up a t the O'Hara clothes line where it crossed the alleyway some forty feet above the asphalt. Imminent death. He knew he was no aerialist, but he was game to try. The fire escape was lined with anxious, peering cat faces.

Scarface sent up Tufts, a mangy brown and grey of no social importance, to see that the line would be secure and to ascertain if the bra and two towels on the line would present any sort of formidable obstacle. Snub disappeared mo—mentarily, slipped in through O'Hara's window to whe r e she slept on the sufa. He purred.

"Oh, nice kitty. Come to visit me, How thought f u 1 of youo And what is your name? You must be an Irish cat."

"Do you hear sounds of the cats out there on your fire escape?"

"I thought I heard mewing in my sleep, kitty."

"They want to kill me ..."

"Kill you!" said O'Hara. "Well, I won't let them." She arose from her sofa, took a nip of wine and came to the window. "Oh, bygor, there they be—a whole heavenfull o f 'm."

"They are going to make me—walk the—walk the clo-thes line."

"But—you can't You'll fall. You'll be killed, kit-ty."

"You can help me, lady."

"Poor kitty, how can I help you? You wou like a sa u-cer of milk?"

"Scarface is out to watch me plunge to my death-just to prove he's got more cat guts than I have."

"Poor darling. I won't let him get away with it."She withdrew her head. "What shall I do?"

"I shall go first. The night is dark. Take in you r laundry. When the moon goes behind a cloud, I shall hop into your clothespin bag." She drew in the clothes line.

.Now ride across? Oh, you are a clever cat!"

The cat congress was getting impatient for the show to start. A short howl called the contestants to the fire escape, Scarface across the alley and Snub on the O'H a r a side. Siggy, a small white who clung to everything fema l e in catdom plunked the line to sound the opening.

"Are you ready, kitty?" said O'Hara.

"Yes, I am ready." The moon darkened. shadows ago t black. "Hop in, kitty. The clothespin bag. There. You will come back and see me." She laughed and laughed.

"Every night. dear lady." said Snub, and he dropped into the bottom of the bag as O"Hara, with a loud sque a k» ing of the wheels, began to haul him across the alley r a-vine to the other side. The congress put up a sere a ming howl.

"Unfair! Unfair—the ride across!"

"The only rule is to cross on the rope," shouted Snub as he soon completed his ride and stood on the iron railing to confront his antagonist, Scarface. "Your turn, Mister Scarface." "Okay, Big Time, I'll get into the bag, too." "WonH do you any good. The lady won't help you." Scarface, sensing defeat, got in the bag anyway, but realizing it was not going to move, clambered out. He put his shaky feet upon the sagging line. He made his way slowly out on the line} it swayed in the moonlight. "Oooh, ah-hhhl" sighed the cat congress as their eyes glowed in the darkness. Scarface was obviously frightened to death . His friends followed his every paw step$_0$ He slipped, gr ab-bed the line—ten feet out. He hung there for a desperate moment—wild and frantic howls coming from his tor t u red guts. And then, when he could hold on no longer, he let go. He struck the alleyway, forty feet below, and was stunned as his friends gathered around him. He was dying-tough, a real battler, but stupified, his reason, his judgement dulled by his bravado. Snub, Mister Wagner, was conceited but far too clever to be trapped by any such swagger. And so there, in a pool of blood, the two cats parted, one i n death, the other in life. And the cat congress spread the news from alleyway to alleyway that bravado without goo d judgement can be a curse.

Dig The Snake And The Rabbit

"You think you're pretty smart, don't you?" said the snake to the rabbit, "taking on that poor tortoise to the finish line in an unequal race that was a very unequal race. You deserved to lose it."

"Tireing—just to watch him crawl along."

"So you had to sit down on the job."

"You don'-t hear me bragging, do you?"

"You need somebody to do you in—really bring you *a*-round to your smarts, rabbit.

"Hare."

"Rabbit sounds better—and cooks better."

"Now you're getting disgusting—and familiar with me."

"Tell you what. I'll take you on in a contest you won't win "» ever/" said the snake.

"You can't tell me anything I don't know already."'

At this sudden arrogance by the rabbit, a lapse in knowledge rather than a collapse of humility, the snake coiled itself up and struck at a hollow reed as a means of getting rid of its fury, for it certainly did not fear the rabbit. They eyeballed each other for a long time, the snake flicking its tongue to sense the rabbit's composure and the creature of flying fur sniveling with its little pink nose. They were a pair.

"Let's go then, Slinky," said the rabbit. "Whateha want to do?"'

"Dig a hole I "shouted the snake in its wrath.

"Dig a hole!" taunted the rabbit with icy sarcasm. "Just like you to want to get lost—hide your guilt .Insufferable cold-blooded reptile!"

"I see you have a burrow of sorts—and a pretty shabby scatter—not what I'd call Continental"'

"Speak for yourself, snake, oversized worm!

"Worm!" screamed the snake in outrage.

"What I said—worm. You don't cut the dirt with me, Slinky. No, you take over abandoned gopher holes."

"Condemned holes—always!" The snake stretche d itself out upon the ground. "I'll show you, rabbit!"

"Hare."

"You dig and I'll dig and we'll see who comes ou t the other side of the world first."

"Suits me just fine. Where'll we start?" the rabbit asked.

"Right here—where it's soft and sandy."

Before the words of the viper could float into the sky—like poisonous pollen cast from the snake's amber, green, brown and red scales—the rabbit had begun t o dig. It pitched spits of loamy dirt out between its rear legs like a dog pawing and scraping into the earth t o hide a bone. The snake simply squiggled and squirmed and in due course only the tip of its tail and then, nothing, like it had sucked in the sand around itself as it we n t down into the earth. This promised to be a furious race.

The god of chance then took over, since there was no communication between them, their tunnels were so far apart. Down past the Quagtree Community of big-headed dead and the squiggleys of squirreldom, who had ravished the earth's kind spirits and doomed themselves. Down through the layers of Scofflatch Quiseritans, stellarsages of long ago who had sought their god in rock let ... tuce and the wisdom of mahem on upper earth.Down through the Cantellation sphere, that hung ball-like on distillate threads of contumely reports between nations and swung to and fro to warn Daflie People against lies, and to conjure Manifried Souls of harm from falling upward into embers from the sunheart. These strange circumambiencies, each refulgent with splendor, confronted the rabbit and the snake. On they dug, the gods of Justruttence and Cassirai-norean prudence scanning their labors.

"Do you wish to call an end to the race?" Dyeyesi u s asked, he who was the God of Chance.

"No, no, no!" screamed the snake in shrill hisses. "Neverl" shouted the rabbit in falsetto. "Then dig on. I shall see that Lumivian, Goddess o f Light and Aertrifolian, God of Thunder, War and Freedom t o Breathe accompany your efforts""

On they dug. But, instead of its getting hotter, a s scientists have said it is, molten, fiery, beyond the capacity of flesh to endure, the center of the world revolve d dizzily, flashing lightning in greens and taupe. Like a glove turned inside out, the brilliant emissions revealed the otherworld of Wisdentry

Trimatchelechtedy—of the science of conversion of thought into dewdrops, iron and lovely music. Only, this music was so melodic it strained the ears of rabbit to hear it and sent shivers down the cold scales of the snake. Like a torture, song enveloped them which, by its magnitude, its purity of notes, its v i-brations converted them into incandescent figures, like wandering ghosts.

Still they dug on, these Catellated Middle World ghosts, the rabbit and the snake, vieing to dig through t o the opposite surface of the planet earth. They saw p s y-chedelic light and heard Quisserian voices lamenting the wrongs of mortals, damning God for existing and loving and creating and ruling.

"Have we reached hell?" snake asked Dyeyesius, God of Chanceo

"Not yet—not yet" but keep on trying."

"Have we found the Middle World?" the rabbit queried.

"Somewhat. But only a hare's breadth of it," the god informed it.

"Then I shall dig on," said the rabbit.

"And I will wiggle on through the smoke and brassy sounds and sickening sulphurous sweetness of time."

On the two of them dug—but a force seized the rabbit by its small tail and flung it into a void of ice chips, Stygian music, great throbbing drum sounds and dea fening screaming voices.

"You are arrived—on the other side of the world, timid squeek of fright. You, also, snake, viper of fear a nd deceit, you have arrived. And—I am the judge of your victory, your loss."

"Do in the rabbit first," said the snake. "He i s just a crumby braggart."

"But you inject your poison into the truth—to make it death within life, corruption within the right ways."

The snake demurred, tried to plead his side but the God of Chance was unmoved. So, too, did the rabbit disavow its conceit and arrogance, though Dyeyesius gave i t credit for timidity required for it to survive on the Upper Crust.

"Your fates are fixed, sealed, denizens," said Dyeyesius. "You are both losers. "You perverted your quintessential abilities in order to sustain Mamabopolies of Tri-umeation, the spirits of dominion and deceit above all others."

"But I—"the rabbit began.

"Silence!"

"But I—"said the snake.

"Silence!" roared the god, putting both creatures into a sodden matuskan, a two-wheeled cart-like conveyance, drawn by a Quivarian Steed of Thunder. "Now you shall lose—for evermore!" entoned the God of Chance. "Eve r-more! Do you hear me?" He snapped a bolt of lightning and the cart, bearing its two occupants, lurched forward. Within the space of microseconds, it had vanished into the dust of scintillation and vapors, the atmosphere of Maluska s, the sparkling filtration of luminous pollen scattered and bestowed by tongues of flame from below the essential vision—from space, mankind would say. They were gone, the rabbit and the snake, losers, distillate phantoms of weaving, quavering, moiling, boiling spirits of purgation, envy and distrusto No man ought to follow them further but, instead, ought to turn back to his elemental assigned sphere where there exist life and love.

The Eagle And The Wild Dog

A high sun glints like frost after a storm on the eagle's spread wings. Neither man nor animal can hide from her. Her small eyes are like black pellets. They magnify the brush and search out the flickering movements of the grey lizard. She does not hear the wind since the sky is her home. Her feathers ruffle on the air currents. Her pin feathers on her wings agitate as she balances her fragile bones.

She sees the wild dog below and swoops down close. Her shadow, bold and dark, crosses the mountain brush like a silent thermal. The wild dog, a feral beast, turns a jaundiced eye skyward and continues chewing on the rabbit that he has caught and killed.

With a wise boldness the eagle falls in close, flicks out her piercing talons. seizes a piece of the rabbit flesh. The dog snaps his teeth viciously, the eagle drops her morsel. She is hungry. The dog appears sated and sleek and well-fed. The eagle alights on a manzanita branch.

"Why do you come down into my killing field?" the dog asks. "I have prepared this meal for myself."

"Do you not see with your blind eyes? I have two chicks I must feed."

"You are so high up on the cliff that I cannot see. So maybe I ought to share this meal with you?"

"Very decent. wild dog. Very decent of you."

"But I cannot do it. It is against my nature to share anything. I will fight my friends for this small rabb i t here under my bloody paws," says the dog and he growls low in his throat.

"I see that."

"Then fly away."

"There is enough there for both of us." The dog keeps on ripping and crunching. "Suppose we go hunting together. I will circle high in the sky and you lope along the ground. When I see good game, I will signal you by rocking my wingsJ"

"I can find my own food."

"Yes—but this rabbit you have killed there—it is only one. And there are thousands running about throu g h this chaparral. Think about that!"

"Thousands?" says the dog. His mouth begins t o w a-ter at the thought of so many rabbits at one time ready to be killed and eaten. While he is thinking about the e a-gle's words, the bird takes flight again. She does not return until the next day, late in the afternoon. The dog, now contented from his meal of the jackrabbit, lies half-a-sleep under a shading boulder.

"Well? What do you say, brother dog? Is it a deal? "the eagle asks from above his head where she perches on a rock.

The wild dog raises his muzzle and gives one sle e py bark. "I guess it is so—but if you try to cheat me—!" the dog warns.

"How can I cheat you? You will kill the fresh me a t or not, as I find it for you."

"That is true. Then let us get started."

The wild dog arises, yawns and stretches while the eagle takes flight again. It is not long before she spots another rabbit. As soon as she screams and signals brother dog of the presence of the jack, the pursuit begins. The dog tires out before the eagle does, but not before the rabbit hss found cover and sits panting in terror for its lif e.

"Where did the rabbit go?" the dog asks.

"My eyes are better at hunting than your nose is"Look there—just down over those rocks, you will find it exhausted. You can break its neck easily. We will share i t together."

"Where? Where?"

"Those shining rocks! Look at me and follow where I fly. Keep your eyes on me. There—I"

"The wild dog does not follow the scent but only the soaring flight of the eagle. He runs on and runs on u n-til, careless of his path and his eyes ever skyward, h e runs over the cliff and dashes himself to death on the jag-ged rocks below. His brains stain the rocks to this day. The natives say that the sign for greed is written in the blood of the wild dog who did not have the wisdom of the eagle.

The eagle seizes the panting rabbit, meantime, where it sits just inside the ring of shade from a buck thorn bush. The great bird makes off with the doomed creature clasped in its talons. Because of its blind greed the dog consented to use the eagle to kill fresh meat for itself and brought about its own destruction.

> Do not the Scripturessay that God hath implanted into every wild beast the fear of man? There is that, however, which can be tamed but only when the animal's fear for its life or the threat to its food supp 1 y is removed. What then i s the nature of this mut u al affinity that remains?

One Proud Bear And The Hollow Log

It began to get to the fox that the black bear who occupied his territory in the mountains always seemed to go around without and fearful pawfalls or turns of the head. The bear acted as if he owned the whole world and challenged all creatures to evict him, especially hated man. Brother fox, shy but clever, had to scurry around the rocks, hide behind old tree stumps, secret his private life and small cache of rodent food in the concealment of burn-out trees and old logs. He always had t o be on the alert for the enemy" This single fact of life irritated Brother Fox immensely. It gave him indige s—tion, and he was losing sleep wondering what the bear possessed that he lacked—courage, imagination, d ili-gence? One day he at last got up the boldness to ask Pokahunk Bear what was the cause for his careless walk ing about"

"You ask me that question, Brother Fox—and you are supposed to be the bright moon up here. Well, let me tell you something—my strength protects me better than yo u r wisdom""

"My intelligence makes he clever, if that is what you mean."

"Clever—intelligence—wise—whatever you call it. It cannot do the job of driving off the enemy."

"I am smart and that is enough."

"You are just jealous of my great strength."

"I am not either." said the Fox." Just to prove it, I will admire some of your great feats of strength."

At this prodding the bear huffed and puffed and felt very good for doing so. "I will do whatever you say—and you will see. My immense strength is better than your cleverness."

"Very well then, Pokahunk Bear—let me see you pu s h that huge rock down the mountainside."

The fox perched atop a large boulder that hung precariously at the edge of the ravine … The bear put his shoulder to the raw granite and heaved with all his furr y might. The boulder gave way, rolled ever so slightly, then plummeted down the precipitous slope into the ravine below … It bounded and rolled with a mighty thunder of echo sound and the crashing and splintering of the chaparral and small trees.

Brother Fox stood on his hind legs and clapped h is forepaws he was so pleased to see the bear's performance.

"My compliments to you, Pokahunk."

"Did I not tell you? Didn't I? Sure I did. I told you I could push that rock off the edge. You cannot d o that with intelligence. Got to have the old muscle in the shoulders."

"That is so. If you had to go and hide, you could drop a whole mountain on the enemy instead—just by pushing rocks over the cliff edges.

"You got it right that time, Brother."

"But yet—hmmmm. He regarded the bear closely-but at a distance. "I, myself. have seen you wade out into that ferocious river and catch yourself a mouthful of fish."

"I done that, too."

"Mightier than the river, I would say. How far t o you think you can wade—across to the other side?"

"I don't know unless I try."

"Let's do it together," encouraged Brother Fox.The two of them went down to the river, where the water churned white with angry foam and the roar deafened the ears and split the dead trees with its hard, chattering sound.

"The river" motioned the fox.

"What—?" said the bear.

"Go across—if you dare to. I will have to wait un-till the end of summer—when the water is low."

"I cannot—it is too wild."

"You are afraid. Me? I am clever. I shall simply—wait."

This comparison piqued the bear's pride. He wade d out into the water farther and farther, until he began t o have to swim. Yet swim he did, being carried by the swift current some yards downstream. He clambered out, shook the water from his coat and slowly made his way back upstr e am. He tried to shout to the fox but the roar of the rap ids drowned out his voice. He plunged into the water from the apposite bank, upstream, and returned, swimming with powerful pawstrikes in mid-current. He reached the embankment where the fox stood laughing until his sides achedo

"What is so funny, little red nit? I did what you asked me to do,"

"What a performance! That is why I laugh."

"Am I not mightier than the river?"

"You are, without a doubt," the fox replied but curbed his laughter. "Yet. in your mighty strength you cannot withstand the hunter's power and bullets."

"I can so. You see this?" The bear stood up his full seven feet, bared his fangs, his slimy, snarling, angry teeth in the direction of the fox. "That stops all bullets, b e-cause the hunters run the other way."

"Now I am impresed," said the fox.

"Besides, I will show you something else that you cannot doo I am stronge I am alive. You are weak. You find safety in your brains." The bear grunted out a bellowing peal of laughter.

"At least I have managed to avoid being caught and eaten by you."

The bear seemed not to hear. "See!" he cried, from a place ten feet off the ground. He had already begun t o climb a tall sugar pine. "Betcha canU do this."

"Who wants to?" said the fox.

The bear Pokahunk climbed up to the first big branch. "Lookout below!" He began to pitch pinecomes down to the ground below, narrowly missing Brother Fox with se v e r a 1. He leaned back with one arm and a paw on the tree trunk, and he taunted the fox who stood below, warily watching the bear.

"Okay, okay. Come on down. I believe you," said the fox. The bear scratched and chewed his way down the scaley bark by his long, curved claws until he stood once again beside the fox.

"I guess you have proved it once and for all-that your great strength is better than my cleverness."

"I have earned my meal, have I not," the bear p ro-claimed with a menacing snarl.

"Not yet," said the clever fox. "I have just one more test for you, and if you pass this one I will g i ve you the honor of being a better defender than I anu W e might even go out to dinner together."

"How generous of you, Brother Fox," said the bear, drooling with eagerness. But go on and tell roe. W hat is the test? I can take on any trial of my strength."

"Can you make yourself small like I am?"

"Small! Why should I want to do that?"

"Your physical power has no limits, "the fox a n-swered with grave care.

"You are right"

"Then come with me to my log,"

"Your log—la de da, grumph," the bear said with obvious amusemento The fox took him to the open end of a log hollowed out by storm, fire, termites and dry rot-and no small pawing and digging on his part. For it was his den logo.

"This is my-home."

"Crazy—fox! Your home! You go into that a t night?".

"Every night. Make yourself small with your great might and try it out. It is not too small. You will fit just nicely. Go on. Try it out."

The bear got down on all fours and scrunched himself into as amll a ball as he could and began to wedge himself into the end of the log. "I am strong," came the voice from the hollow interior.

"My wits cannot match your strength, Pokahunk. You see. It is dark in there. It smells. I am a blind fox. I am a dirty little canine. It is rank with old food. I am a bad housekeeper. And—it is unsafe."

At that final word, the fox rolled a dead limb in-. to notch in the log and stones on the ground, so t h a t the entrance behind the bear was solidly blocked.

"What is going on out there?"

"Make yourself at home, Big Time. When you come into my house, you better be prepared next time … Try the exit end." Brother Fox had never dug one; it was closed up.

"I can't get out!" Pokahunk pleaded with grunts.

"There is just one way, Smartass—as a rug," said the fox, and he loped off into the woods in search of a-nother log. The ants would have a big feed in a few weeks inside that old hollow log, plugged up solid by the strong, daring, courageous black bear.

The Coyote And The Crow Scout

A crow saw a coyote slinking along a dry gulch one day in search of meat. Its ribs showed in its flanks, its tongue was dry and caked for lack of water. Its pads were burnt and painful and it limped a little in the hot sand. The crow observed the misery of the coyote and came flying low, settled on a desert greasewood bush and watched as the brush wolf came closer.

"I see you are hungry, Mister Coyote." The crow always showed the coyote respect but contempt, too, because the wolf even when he is hungry does not have to sneak around like his shadow.

"You are hungry."

"You mock at me. You laugh at my misery. I have not eaten for days. While you can fly anywhere to find your food, I have to run in the hot sand to find mine. The man-animal feeds you. He hunts for me. That is why you do not starve""

"You do not respect the campgrounds of the Indi a n or the white man. You have no loyalty.""

"I have my pups to feed.'

"Come on, Mister Coyote. Your bitch does your hunting for you and your last litter is seven months old."

"I see you are smart, much smarter than I anu"

"Thank you, bold coyote. From you that is real praise."

"I will never trouble your spirit again if you will help me to find the man-presence. There I can find food."

"You are to be pitied, Mister Coyote. Where i s your nose, your instinct? You will not find a rabbit in this wash. Lizards make their homes in the cool of rocks, a great distance away. You are lost?"

"I am lost. Honestly, you are right. Have pity on me, Mister Crow."

"I see pity is what you really crave more than food. Maybe I can help. I will fly around high and see what is happening over by the mountains. There is a spring there."

"I will sing a song to your name on moonlit nights."

The crow had already flown away before he heard this feeble promise. Panting, the coyote made himself as comfortable as he could beneath the greasewood bush. In due time the crow returned to where the coyote lay as if lifeless and in desperate want of food and water. C a u g h t in the strong beak of the crow was a fat sausage. Th e coyote looked up at the crow and his mouth began to dri p with pangs of hunger.

"Where did you find that fat sausage?" the coy o te asked.

"Hanging on a pole many miles away."

"Oh, do not tempt me. Do not torture me, Mister Crow. I am starving and I shall die out here."

"Permit me to eat enough to satisfy my own hunger., Enjoy your self-pity. Then you shall have the rest o f my meal."

With energy the crow attacked the sausage wh i l e the coyote fixed his eyes upon the crow's feast wit h envy and drooling and anger. He waited for the crow to eat the entire sausage—but the bird did not. He dropped the fragment of skin and some of the meat onto the ground in front of the coyote.

"There is just a taste." The coyote bolted down the remnant of the sausage with lightning haste."More? "the crow asked in a taunting voice.

"Yes, yes, yes, yes!" said the coyote with passionate hunger. "I shall sing to your spirit if you will save roe—just this one time. On a night when the moon is high."

"Stow it, Mister Coyote. I have heard those promises before. But—there burns a spark of pity in roe yet-inside these black feathers—for the poor. Cawww.Cawww."

"Where is there more sausage?" the coyote asked.

"Keep your eyes upon me. Do not let a fresh track turn your spirit aside. A rabbit chase would kill you you are so weak and bony.'

The crow again flew off the greasewood limb.The coyote loped out of the wash and along the hot sands towa r d the distant mountains while he kept an eye on the crow circling above him.

"Cawww, cawww!"

The pair of them journeyed for some miles until a t last they came to the encampment of the mananimal. There the crow stopped and settled on the branch of a cottonwood beside the spring.

"I can promise that you will find food here, ' said the crow, "but not pity."

"I want only to eat, not to sing and dance, Mister Crow. And 1 thank you for taking me this far."

"Let your spirit mingle with the man-animal's. You have much in common you are like these creatures."

"I cannot thank you enough."

"Do not try. Now you may follow your." nose, Mister Coyote.

The coyote looked about him for the sausages that he expected to be hanging from a pole in the encampment. H e kept a wary eye on the inhabitants of the village. He sneaked about from tent to tent without arousing alarm, all within the square. But while food smells came to his nose he did not find the sausage.

"You have led me wrong," the coyote accused.

"Why would I do that? Here is the source of your food—the white man"s camp. That fat sausage came fro m the Indian camp."

"I do not care. I simply must eat or I shall die."

"You will survive. Your spirit will live as white man"s takes over your land."

"Do not play with me," the coyote pleaded. "Ah, what have we here? Food!" Under the flap of a tent the coyote sniffed some pork—and other good things. His mouth dripped with renewed appetite.

"Your spirit will live in captivity," screamed the crow. "Cawwwt Cawwwwt" he called.

A man-animal came around the corner when he hear d the crow cawing, for man does not find the crow an enemy. It is a spirit of good or evil. "Cawww! Cawww! Cawww I "the crow scolded again. The man-animal saw the dog tail under the flap. He jerked the tail hard and out came the coyote with a slab of bacon in its jaws and salivat ing like rain. The man-animal fired a bullet into the he a d of the hungry coyote as the crow flew away.

"You made one big mistake, coyote, coming in here. Never heard of bounty-hunters, I guess," the man said as he dropped the dead coyote into the sand and took the bacon from its lifeless jaws.

The Mouse And The Badger

"I have been wrongly accused of being too prolific/"complained the educated mouse to the badger.

"Do you not know? Have you not heard there is a way to cut down on litter size?"

"How? Tell me how. I have so many mouths to feed 1 can hardly find food for myself. And then—they up and leave the nest and I am alone again."

"Poor thing. Tragic/" the badger sympathized.

"Yes, I think so, too. After all, I have a name to preserve—small and insignificant. Mousey. Bedraggled looking. Mousey. Cheap and stingy. Mousey. Pitiable and timid."

"Mousey," said the badger. "I quite understand. You hardly have time to train your—offspring—and they are gone ..."

"Tradition, the mouse tradition."

"Poor thing. So sad," said the badger. "There must be something we could do to change the matter. A slogan: 'Fine for littering ...'"

"Never work. I'm too prolific they all say."

"No tears now, mouse. After all, you are at least eight months old and that is plenty old for a-mature mouse."

"Could not I—hide them—my progeny, I mean. until they learn the ways of mousey living? They run off, down the raceway and look so sleek and fat and contented. They have almost lost their desire to gnaw on the wood work, dig in the trash, and caution?—well, that's an o t h er world for them. Do you know, Mister Badger, they dart out in front of humans and never look right or left?"

"That so?"

"It is, it is. Why, when I was growing up, I always took a little peek at first to see if the coast was clear."

"And your many offspring?"

"Reckless. Reckless generations of house mice."

"Now. now, now, now." consoled Mister Badger as he saw tears beginning to well up in the pink eyes of Missus Mouse. "We must find a suitable way to—diminish the mouse population without. of course. creating havoc among the colony or alarm.,"

"How? How. Mister Badger?"

"Are there any—little ones at home just now?" the badger enquired.

"Eighteen of them."

"Eighteen! How horrible!"

"Yes, isn't it!"

"Poor thing. Tragic."

"You have said that before. What am I to do?"

"For one thing, I think you need more living space," said the badger. "To give you a feeling of—out-of-doors of abandonment, of loose and casual living—the relaxe d manner of—well, the badger burrow."

"Yes? That attic is rather cramped."

"Precisely," said the badger as he gnashed his gleaning teeth in the twilight. "The very fact that you are standing just outside the cellar window of the house tells me you yearn for more space. Burrowphobia."

"Oh, you are so intelligent!" said the mouse batting her lovely long eyelashes."

"Would you care to inspect my residence, just t o give you an idea?" asked the badger.

"Not at all. I should be most delighted," said the educated lady mouse. The badger turned on his paw and the two of them scampered to the mouth of the badger burrow.

"You won't have to duck this time. There is plenty of headroom. And—it is rather dark in here," said the badger as his voice echoed within the hollow interior of his burrow as in a drain pipe. He led the mouse furth e r inside. He obviously was proud of his pad and said so.

"Split level. You can train the little ones i n there. Now down the corridor a short ways, there is where you can stay if you so desire. Privacy, you know. Me? I will remain at the back of the burrow to guard t he rear exit.

"That dratted gardener has the uncomfortable habit of sometimes sticking his water hose into my home and trying to flood me out, drown me" He is difficult, but a t least I have got some secret passageways he knows nothing about."

The lady mouse was all acquiver with her tour o f the sly badger's burrow. She squeaked and she squea l e d with each new surprise. She had never seen anything s o magnificent in all her eight months of life. And—the r e was another litter on the way. Only the attic caretakers knew where the sire was—dead in a trap somewhere.He was another of the careless ones, ignorant, totally, of her circumstances, just as the caretakers were of—mou s e culture.

"So, let me extend to you my open invitation t o come—visit for a while and—enjoy."'

"I shall have to come alone for a while," said the mouse.

"Perfectly all right, "said the badger. "J u s.t remember, my home is yours."

"You are so generous, sir."

"Just my nature—unless a snake or a dachhund dares to enter."

"Snake! Dachshund! Oh, dear!"

"Do not fear, little one. 1 have the answer for tendering snakes." The gopher nipped the mouse in her little pink ear in affectionate reassurance.

The event occurred, as all of nature announced, fo r in the off-the-corridor room on the upper split-level, the lady mouse littered—fifteen little ones. She was e x-hausted in a very short time with dragging in old vegetables, a dead bird, some chewed corn cobs. She hop e d the badger would not say a word. She wanted to teach her progeny what mousey really meant. Keep the den smelly "Look bedraggled for a while at least. Filch food from the pantry so as to teach them what cheap and st i n g y means. These fine habits lady mouse was anxious to pas s along and did so in her motherly fashion. Meantime the badger did not say a word—until one night the gardener stuck his water hose into the back exitway of the badge r burrow and turned on the water at high pressure.

The mouse came dashing out, filled with grave alarm, her coat drenched and slick, the badger bobbed up at some distance through his secret escape hatch. He waved at her. She looked so forlorn; he had warned her. Everything had come to a sudden end for her.

"My little ones, my little ones!" she squeaked.

"Do not fret, dear mouse. They are perfectly safe where they are—in my split-level burrow."

"I hope so. I truly hope so. They have a great many things to learn." said the educated lady mouse.

"They have learned already how sweet it is to accept fate."

"Oh, you are so—tragic, so genuine, so tho u g h t-ful, so philosophical. If I were not a mouse—"

"Say no more, my lady. Now that my burrow is damp and muddy and will not dry out soon, why do you not run up to your place in the attic and dry off?"

"What a splendid idea, Mister Badger!" she cried and hurried away.

"While I return to my—den and enjoy my feast," the badger smiled through his needlesharp incisors.It appeared that he was happy the mouse wa s so prolific. Let there be shortages of old corn cobs but not of tender, fresh meat.

> I once dissected a rat and found nothing i n its figure or fa s hion to recommend it as hu-manoid. Yet how often are people compared to rats that smoke. go mad, incur horrible diseases and urinate with diabetic irregularityt

> It is strange that a domesticated dog can take up the ways of the timber wolf. Is this an example of symbiosis or of species adaptat ion? Is the feral animal an instinctual hybrid and why does domestication in som e species appear to dest r o y ancient instinctual ri t es and appetites? Or are they forever genetically dormant in the specimen animal?

Justice Is Slow Like An Ox

His heavy plodding hooves squished down deep into the fall mud. He sweat to a lather under his stained harness, that was held in place by tarnished rings and guides of Egyptian brass. The lead ring from his nose swung below frothing nostrils and mouth. Master Kadalish did not know that when he walked about in his muddy circle, blowing steam into the chill air and drooling at the sweet fragrance of the threshing-floor grain, he wished he were a n ox for keepirg by a different miller"

He was conscripted into the milling of grain—an ancient process that brought millstone and grinding stone together to crush wheat into flour. His slippery steps and that rumbling stone wheel mashing the wheat kernels were about the most ridiculous things in his circular lif e" Harness up, unharness at night, walk in a circle, e a t, sleep in a corner of the shed—his life made him wear y with boredom. Right now, this minute, his master a p-proached with a bushel basket filled with hay and a hand-. ful of oats. He pondered that the farmer would cheat him again. Things had not gone well on that score, and i t did not take a wild ass to figure that one out.

"I am here—where you saw me last, "said Ramu s the ox| putting a frown on his large, bony face.

"I could never get more work from another ox," said Master Kadalish, "only hurry up. Pick up the pace. You are so slow in walking around the circle."

"You want me to walk faster and grind up more wheat so that you can make more money for yourselfo"

"You are a very clever ox to see that," said R a-mus" master.

"Just wise in the ways of man. And—you know I will not receive any more food even if I do walk faster."

183

"Let us see if that is true," Kadalish replied. He brought out a thin olive switch from behind his back and he flicked the hind quarters of Ramus. The ox"s hide flinched.

"Crush my mush! But you sting me, 0 Masterl"

"FasterI FasterI Faster!" Kadalish began to lay on with the olive branch. Whewwwwwwww! It whipped through the air with a vicious sigh.

"Suppose—"He panted, his nostrils frothed, he snorted. "Suppose I fall to my knees. Then what will you do?" The ox was greatly disturbed by these ant i c s of his master.

"I will make you stand again, Ramus. And I will make you run instead of walk."

"How foolish you are! I cannot run. I am not a horse. I am useful because I am powerful. But r u n-like a deer?"

"I must get the most value from you."

"I can see it now—you are a greedy fellow." With this accusation Master Kadalish began to whip his ox until! instead of running faster, the animal 's stub b orn nature took over and be began once again to walk at his customary pace.

"Run, grind, pull, run, grind, pull—"sang out the owner of the ox, now furious that his beast de f i e d him. Without warning, however. Ramus suddenly threw all his strength into a wild … eyed tug on the harness. H e snapped the leather at the rivets, and he caused the huge upright stone to lie flat in the round tub of the concourse. The grinding vertical stone had snapped its spindle at the hub. Kadalish pulled angrily on his black beard. He called to his wife, Tesidim, She hastened out from among her clay pots and mending of skins and sewin g of new wineskins—labors for the woman of the household.

"What is it? What is it, Gazim?"

"This dumb ox has broken the spindle to my grinding stone| and now I cannot grind another shekel's worth o f flour until the carpenter comes to fashion another for me."

"What difference does it make if he grinds flour?He is an ox and must obey. It is his purpose to walk in the ring."

"But the wheel axle is broken, wife."

"We cannot endure a lazy ox under any circumstances. Get up, you-beast, Ox!" she said.

"I think you are right/" said Kadalish.

"Of course I am right. Maybe we ought to build a small fire under Ramus—precious beast." his wife proposed.

"An excellent idea. You are so smart—that is why I married you." Tesidim, the miller"s wife, ran and pulled some straw from a shock in a nearby field and presently returned with her wand. She dipped the ripe ends in some sheep tallow and then she waved this wand before the bloodshot eyes of Ramus. He was, it appeared. fast losing his sight from having to watch his slippery steps i n the mud for each everlasting day. Why should he care?

"Light it," Gazim Kadalish commanded. Rubbing her hard rough hands on her skirt, she struck fire from her fingertips and ignited the straw. Gazim's eyes blazed up with a bluegreen laughter he was so pleased.

"Now we will get the beast to walk or my name i s not Kadalish." The miller seized the burning straw from his wife's scorched fingertips and he let Ramus smell of the smouldering sparks and smoke. He then tossed the flaming bouquet of straw on the ground beneath Ramus.

"Blast me| you imbecile1 You are a thickheaded and stubborn man. You do not understand realities. You busted wineskin of farm dung! You vermin-brained sneeze i n life, you idiot without a gate into kindness. I can no t think of more things to call you I am so mad."

"But every ox must earn its keep."

"Your brains rattle in your skull like seeds in a dry gourd. You are heartless—and your smartsie-tartsie wife can go you no better."

"You are a very articulate ox when you are mad"

"I work for a living. What you need is a real com-. parison." Ramus blew loudly through his hoarse throa t. A jackal from a nearby farm, pawing over some chic k e Q scrapsı heard him and came running. He said so.

"What can I do to help you?" asked the jackal.

"You are obliging to come so fast." said Ramus.The miller and his wife backed off in fear. "You can howl so that this miller will know his money will not avail him against wolves."

The jackal howled loudly into the clouds, causing a nearby stream to bubble up with a loud noise. The o-range burning clump of hay almost went out. The miller, keeping a wary eye on the jackal, turned to his wife and said| "He howls, not because he is a wolf. He is a jackal and v e ry mean. You take care of Ramus while I go a n d check the flock. See that he does not wander. Meantime I shall call the carpenter to fix the wheel spindle. The miller's wife, however, retreated in fear.

While Kadalish was gone, the ox moved aside and with one puff blew out the straw brands. "Now all I want is to be paid for my labor."

"That is fine," said the jackal. "If you will walk about this circle—say— three times, by then I shall have stolen enough grain for you to satisfy your hunger."

While Ramus was performing his part of the bargain with the jackal, the carpenter, anticipating the need, brought along a spindle and deftly replaced the bro k e n one. There were few finer carpenters in the district.

Not being too wise in the ways of animals, Ramus complied with the jackal's instructions. He circled the ring three times. The jackal snatched the hay and oa t s from the bushel basket and dropped them under the nose of the famished ox, And Ramus ate of them greedily.

Returning at that exact moment, the miller's eyes lighted up when he saw the repaired wheel spindle, but then he observed the jackal at his back door.

"Did I not tell you to watch Ramus, wife!"

"This jackal has brought him food. Yet-husband, I am afraid of the jackal. I stayed inside the house. I merely watched."

"Watched! You ought to have thrown a stone a t the jackal and at least driven him away."

"I could find only mud, no stones."

"Well, we shall get some justice out of this matter regardless." Saying this, he loosened the ox from his fetters of harness, which Ramus had dragged around the ring during the repair of the wheel spindle. And with an a—bandon that was oblivious to injury—since he had purged his fear at the wineskin meantime—he harnessed up the jackal, an early instance of forceable domestication.

"Now pull!" commanded Kadalish. "Pull, curse you! Meddler! Ignorant trifieri Trespasser!" But the wild dog, for so were his ancestors or at best his kin, c o uld not move the heavy grinding stone.

"You see, Master," said Ramus, "you are so smart as to put this little beast in the harness. You did not appreciate my huge strength, my slow but steady pace, my patience in the harness. Now you must pay for your impatience as well as for your greed."

"No, Ramus, this is not true what I am seeing."

"Does life conflict with your—vision of justice, Master?"

"I will give you what you are worth."

"Ahhhhh, but you must learn this lesson. I will go out into the field tonight and when I return in the morning "» about the forenoon—I will inspect the mill to see how much grinding has been done. Then you will have a good way to observe how fortunate you are that I work for you."

The ox kicked over a bench, knocked down a few of the bricks from the circle wall, smashed a gate rail and kept on walking while the miller pulled on his tail. He ran to the head of the beast but could not catch the tether ring in Ramus" nose. It was a frantic scene. What is worse, Kadalish did not know what to say to his oxo He was totally put out and confounded by an animal that had outwitted him. Also, by this time his wife, sitting down on the broken wall, bawled great eves-dropping tears—kersplash, kersplash into the mud, for she saw the loss of their valuable ox and the end of their flour-mill business. She banged her husband over the head with a stick and then ran into the house to hi de her tears in her lambswool mattress.

Kadalish pulled hard on his fears, fixed as they were in the rock of his heart. He would let the ox g o for the night. Back at the mill and in great agitation he picked up the olive switch again and began this time to beat the jackal. The animal's guilty eyes and forlorn looks could not deter the miller. All the switching in the world could not force the jackal to lug the immense granite stone around in its millwheel trough.

Villagers claimed the jackal howled most of the night, after Kadalish had gone indoors. In the morning he arose early, as was his custom, and hastily went out to his mill. There he saw the jackal stretched out cold and dead in the mud. In his shed, Ramus was munching quietly on some dry straw and the last of the oats. Seeing his animal whom he had abused, the miller ran over to him and threw his arms around his ox—pretty much his only friend in that remote country—and h e whispered into Ramus" ear.

"Surely, Ramus, you are worth your pay in grain . I shall feed you plenty today if you will pull my wheel again. And I will not make you run around the r i ng "And you shall have all you can eat and be happy with us"

"Well, now," said Ramus in a confident manne r, "there is some justice in burning straw after all."

He continued to munch and to munch while Kadalish and his wife went to bury the frozen jackal.

> Is a dog's wagging of his tail learned or instinctual behavior?
> If learned who taught him? If instinctual, consider t h e wolf
> that never wags its tail.

Crocus, The Frog With A Passion

At about four o'clock I was sitting on a stone in a gurgling back-eddy of the Nile River. I was eyeb alling the scene around me. A boat cane down the river, a palace boat—I could tell by the crown and sword on the sail. On board were favorites of the pharoah out for an af t ernoon cruise. I was counting the slaves at the oars when I heard this awsome sound through the reeds on the riv e r bank. It was not like any sound I had ever heard before. It moaned. the tall reeds bent, and the voice splashed its tones up into the orange sun. I saw bubbles come fro m below the water, like the bubbles we frogs make, and out from those bubbles among the reeds the voice spoke.

"Get all your friends together, Crokus, and go together into the pharoah's palace."

"But. Sire, I do not know where all my friends are."

"Doyou ajrgue? You do not trust me."

"I will be honest with you." At that instant the rock I sat on turned into a thorny cactus. The river became an empty slough, the sky turned red hot and on fire. I almost died from the heat, let me tell you—because I go for the deep, cool watery places. Ribbet, ribbet.

"I'll do it then. Sire," I pleaded. Everything a s if by magic went back to wet and sunny again.

"I command you to go into the pharoah's palace-and enjoy yourself. Jump freely to your heart's content.Swim with wild abandon in the leisure pools. Invade the bath, the bedroom, the kitchen and pantry, the stables. Do anything you want. I give you total freedom because I, your Cotamander, make the laws around here."

"I will obey then," I said.

Immediately I called all my slippery friends, m y moist, chilly and slimey friends, my rock-hopping, flat-footed near friends, and those with puffy throats and fat bellies I'd just as soon wish dead—I called them all.

"Ribbet—ribbet," came from a million voices.

"Deoakkkk!"' I said, the sacred frog password. They then got the message. I said to them, the wandering, squirming and jumping millions along the river bank, "Tomorrow in the cool of the day we invade the pharoah's palace. Got that?'

Once more from the loyal multitude, "Ribbet1 R ib-bet! Ribbet!"

"Eat, get drunk, follow your slimey appetites t o the end!"

"Ribbet!" One great frog choir echoed assent.We are the master frogs!"

"When I say, 'Retreat,' 'Tribber! Tribberl. thatis what you do—retreat. Ro you ge t it, fellow frogs?"

"Ribbet1" came another swell of chorused agreement.

"We shall all croak together in this campaign," I said.

That night the pharoah came down to the river. H e looked worried. Presently a messenger rode up to him on a camel and delivered these words, words that spilled from him like h ot rain.

"Moses says you got to let his people go." That was the message.

"I told him already I refuse to liberate the Jewsl" That was the hot rain. The messenger shook the road dust from his tattered cloak. "Besides, they would starve i n the Egyptian desert. They would die of thirst without water—scorch and dry up."

"I could use a sip myself." The pharoah clapped his hands. A servant gave the messenger a slug from his goatskin bottle.

"You just trek back to that brick pile and tell that insolent old Moses that I do not want to hear any more of his freedom talk. And I am going to remove his hieroglyphic story completely from my next pyramid.

The voice from out among the reeds said in a deep rumble, like distant chariots, "Obey me—and the palace is yours" Disobey me and I will increase the heat of the sand seven times seven so that your flat feet and frog bellies will bake."

"Ribbet, ribbet, O Commander,"

In the light before the dawn, I heard this lov e ly music, like a million frogs kicking it up in new rain. At first I thought it came from the heavens, No, it floated from out of the Egyptian palace, clear over the desert sands. The pharoah was throwing a party.

"Friend/" I said to one of my close companions, "I think we ought to reconnoiter the situation. After all, if we go in there unprepared, raw that is, that might b e too dangerous and cost us lives,"

"I think you are right." said my fat friend, "W e are no longer tadpoles," I dispatched him to the palac e of the pharoah to check out the enemy's defenses. But I am ashamed to report that he was enticed into the pant r y and killed and cut up to go with a banquet of frog legs and river fish. Some delicacy! His demise came from his being too fat and gullible and too ready to leap into the frying pan.

Time was running out. Before dawn on the day of our invasion the reeds parted and there stood one of the guards of the palace,

"You make too much noise. My master says that h e cannot sleep. He has been partying all night and he can ... not fall asleep,"

"We are commanded to pay a visit to the pharoah soon. Tell him to take comfort and to just relax,"

"Why this—what did you say, .invasion"?"

"Because we love freedom. We are not the slaves you beat with your whips. We are going to show the pharoa h just how much all living things can enjoy their natu r al freedom,"

"I hope you joke with me,"

"I joke not, guard, Eibbet!" I replied in my loudest bullfrog voice.

The palace guard slogged and slipped and cursed i n the mud as he hit the foottrail back to the palace, W e frogs made outselves ready, I smeared mud on my big mouth to hide it from the enemy. All of us dabbed our green and warty, slimey bodies with muddy goop and bits of r i v er grasses. These preparations were for camouflage. It fell to me to give the inspiration speech for the invasi o n "This I did with frog pride, puffing up my body so that my head was hardly visible,

"Frog friends out there—I see you sergeants, you corporals of the frog pond—Major Warts of the Nile swamp-and Colonel de Grasse of the tall grasses all of your the pharoah cannot sleep!"

"Ribbet! Ribbet! What is that to us?" came the reply from a million devoted frog throats.

"We have assembled here together to begin a big, important mission— more vast than the destruction of the mosquito plague two years ago, more important than the c o n-quest of the West Bank of the Nile."

"Ribbet! Ribbet! Ribbet!" The omen of a big, black cloud appeared on the dawn horizon.

"We go—at the drip of the water, set your croaks-into all corners of the Great One's palace. We occupy. W e take over. We enjoy fun and games, total abandonment to our mystical, hippie hippity-hop spirit of play, given to us by the frog god. We search out every dark corner, we follow the fragrances of food, the perfumes of the bedroom, the musi c of the timbrels, harps, horns—yes, the murmurings of the harem ladies, the noisy curses of the eunuchs and guards. We shall occupy the palace and claim it as ours."

"Ribbet! Ribbet—ribbet!" The croaking sounds lasted long minutes. "Us—only us. Let the water drip, the grasses ooze, the swamp seep, the river swurgle, swurgle. We are ready!"

"Hear me! I am your leader, Crokus, the Gut. Ribbet! Ribbet! I am your inspired frog leader. Hear me, hear me!"

For more long minutes the frogs set up a deafening clamor of shrill voices.

"Listen to roe! Do whatever pleases you at the moment. We are given the liberty to be our true selves. Jump between the clean bedsheets in the harem quarters. Infest their love couches with your significant presences. Invade t he baths of all, swim in their pools. Jolly into the pharoah"s private quarters and discomposure him. Find delicious pastries, meats, jams, ambrosias in his pantry and on his table. Get drunk if you wish but keep your frog wits about you. Do not drown in the wine jug. At any time I could sound retreat— 'Tribber! Tribber! Tribber!' Are your orders clear? Are you ready to march— forward, gallant frogs?"

"Ribbet! Anything we want to do we can do?" A skeptic.

"Anything!" I promised them. Then we began our march. The sun was a rind of melon frost in the east. That b i g black cloud dropped some local showers on the hot sand t o make our way a little less burning to our web feet and ten-der bellies. All day we hopped, crawled and waddled our way across the hot dunes toward the palace. The afternoon was upon us, then dusk and nightfall. We were near to the LjOE-line of embarkation. I saw the cruelty of a brawny gu a r d with arms as big as cedar limbs when he squeezed a beggar to death. Our occupation would have cruel consequences. Some of us would pay with our lives.

Up the palace steps we hopped. The guard fled in—side to spread the alarm to the pharoah and all his r o yal kinsmen, his staff, his workers and his officials of the government. Since I was the frog chief I went at once into the big dining hall. The pharoah was having anot h er of his banquets. He saw me hopping on the floor toward his chair when he reached down to pick up his knife.

"A frog! A frogl May the gods of Osiris and all the god spirits of Egypt save usl A frog—and another! Is it my wine? Oziman—throw out this wine and bring me some fresh. They are into my wine, by the eye of Osiris, I swear it I"

"What is it, Master?"

"I am seeing things! Frogs—millions of them.Where are my barking friends? Dogs! Here Table Scraps! Here-bone! Waggon, here! Blood—

Chewell!" The pharoah called to his hounds that always cleaned up droppings from under the tables. But they were nowhere to be seen."

"It is not a cheap wine, Sire," said the wine-taster.

"Who gave you the right to come into my palace without my permission," the pharoah shouted at me. He trembled with fury. his face red with rage.

"A voice from out of the river reeds," I said. H e poured himself another cup of wine.

"Do you know what this is?" He raised a piece of meat before my frog face. This was once the fat leg of your advance scout." He laughed a laugh that brought down flakes of gold from the gilt ceiling and caused the candies, the ferns, the wine in the tumblers to quiver with his rolling laughter. It dried up instantly when he turned his blackbearded face and burning eyes down toward me, where on the cold stone floor I looked up at him.

"I shall do the same with you and all of those—beasts!" he stammered in his stupor. He meant the millio n s of my gallant invasion force.

"Do you know why I am here?" I asked.

"Because I do not let those cursed slaves go free."

"As a consequence, we are commanded to come here to make merry in your palace, O Great Pharoah."

"You will go! Leave at once!" threatened the brawny fellow, bronze rings dangling from his nose and ears, a loin cloth about him and a sheepskin over one shoulder.

"Absurd! Ribbet. Impossible! Ribbet, ribbet!" I croaked.

"I refuse to free the slaves. They serve me well. They make good bricks." The pharoah almost choked on a frog bone.

"We intend to occupy your hutch."

"Hutch! Hutch! My beautiful palace is a—hutch!"The pharoah again clapped his hands. A phalanx of over twenty black men in loin cloths appeared from out of the cracks in the stones. Their bodies were painted with rock and berry pigments and their faces were uglier thanafrog's on a dried pond bottom. They advanced toward us—with switch brooms made out of river reeds and grasses.

They swept and they swept and nothing happened. All my frog invasion comrades were arriving on the double-h o p and entering the palace. They hopped about on the stone floors and they scattered in every direction into the other rooms. We jumped up on the king's lap and onto h is dining table—some of us are pretty smart at jumping ten feet. His harem women screamed scared. We munched and nibbled and bit and ate and gorged and did all those go o d things with food. We jumped onto the plates of the palace guests. They fell over in pushing back from the table. They slid and slipped and fell over us and made such a shrieking noise that nobody could talk.

Ribbett Food was smeared everywhere. Robes dropped, gaudy reds, golds, purples—and white furs, all left behind. The pharoah was bleached white with wrath and fear and wonder now.

"Their god is a seer. My magicians can do all o f this. A curse upon their god!"

When the pharoah said that the harem ladies came a-bouncing through and they ran into the banquet table, tipping it over. Food was now in close, on the floor. One guard fell over the wine jug and got his foot stuck inside. The Great One stuck himself with his dagger when he stooped over to pick up his purse. The smell of smoke came into the hall.

"Master, Master, the torch has fellen from the wall in your bedroom and it has burned up all your fine cloa ks and linens."

"Oh, may you perish for your terrible news." The pharoah instantly killed the messenger with his sword.

"Master. Oh, Master, cried another servant. "T he frogs have eaten all that is in the pantry, and now w e shall starve." The pharoah thrust his sword through the second messenger for his bad news.

Yet still a third messenger, a servant to the pha-roan, stumbled in. "Master, Oh, Master. the wine set out for fermentation is filled with splashing frogs. The vats are ruined and we shall have only water to drink."For this horrible news, the pharoah pierced him also with his sword

Jeweled sword still in his hand, he thrashed about, and he killed a guard or two. He slew one of his guests. He struck down one of his hounds. He cut loose the cords by whith the drapes of royal purple festooned the hall, so that they fell into the clutter and chaos. He flung his sword upward and it struck into the cage of wild geese that hung suspended from the ceiling, killing a gander.He seized a pitch torch from the wall and was about to set fire to the whole mess when a guard restrained him.

"Master, Master—think what thou doest. The pharoah got control of himself and cooled down—likea hot iron from a hotter fire, from white to red.

"Tell that insolent fellow Moses at the brick yard that I will let his cursed slaves go—if he esteems t h em so highly—but get these frogs out of here!"

I heard this from a good friend who was down a t the brick yard that the guards laid down their whips and t h e slaves dropped their hods of bricks. They stopped mix ing the straw and mud and just stood there, worn out, their eyes like jug stoppers and their mouths hanging open.

"Get your stuff together and—go with your leader," one of the guards told the slaves.

Back at the palace were we having the time of our lives squirting and slipping and chewing and hopping on that nasty old pharoah's palace junkl

We ruined just about all the rugs in the place, all the grain in the barns—all the wine. Ribb-tt, burp. We spoiled the bath water, splashed around in pools like I never saw before. And we soiled all the Great One's fancy robes. Then—the fire in the c l o thes closet and—panic. Nothing but careless torch lighting. We were having the time of our frog lives!

I was in a passageway when the torches sputtered and died down low and a voice, like a shadow, moved across one dark stone wall, a voice like a l a m p in the night. It said:

"Crocus—is that you?"

"It is."

"Crokus, is that you?"

"It is." This fellow is hard of hearing, I thought.

"Pick up and leave."

"We are having a good time."

"Pick up and leave. This is your Commander."

"Bur, Sire—"

The torch came off the wall as if carried by a hidden hand. It swooped down over me on the floor and almost scorched me. I saw some of my comrades die from the heat.

"Go now—or I will destroy you."

"Now?" I said. "Ribbet."

"Not tomorrow morning. Do not show me a heart o f stone like the pharoah does. Now!"

"Comrades! Ribbet—reoak!" I echoed down the stone palace corridor. "Retreat—tebbir! Tebbir! Tebbir! Teb-bir!" sounded the command to the frog millions. Responsible frogs passed the message along, thr o ug o ut the palace's two hundred and fifty rooms. Subordinates led a well-disciplined rout march. We were all terribly disappointed as we started our trek back to the banks of the river. The same dark cloud we saw when we set out now spilled rain that dampened the sand for our cool return. Another day to c o m-plete the maneuver—and we once more took up our coll a—bode among the Nile's reeds and stones.

We had had our total freedom all right, our big chance, our anarchy to do what we wanted—it probably brought u s near to destruction. Still, we all of us obeyed the Commander. And we were glad to be back home. We planned to pool our <u>ribbets</u> into a letter to the pharoah and thank him fo r the hospitality of his palace. Of course a frog is pretty small when the Commander has big plans. But also we found out there is just a whole lot of enjoyment in hopping about to follow orders. You do not believe that because you are not a frog. Ribbet, ribbetl

Instinct is a form of intelligence, not cognative but purposeful. It is one of the paradoxes of the biological world that a creature of life can perform the most complex of movements| take the most subtle and exquisite o f directions and plan almost as if by foresight facts—reaching journeys and objectives—with the most elemental and rudimentary "intelligence."

—special to gladiator radio—

Interview With Daniel, Who Engaged The Lions And Escaped The Tower

What'd Dan.l say to them lions when he was thrown inter the den wit then? No, sir, you's wrong. He say, "What's the matter wich you, boys? Druther not have this here suit with you meal? I don't take it off to o-blige you. No, sir. Heh, heh, heh.

But I'm gettin ahead of my story. I was in the town of Babylon oncet and out of a job, when Sweet Father—that's Clemens Augustus "he come up to me. And he say, "Good t o see you come to our games, Brutus Piticus."

"Well, now I"ʙɪ mighty glad to be here, too," I says to him,

"You's looking for work, I spect."

"I am," I says to him wit a hungry look in my eye.

"Then I's got a tip—jest what you needs to fill in them wrinkles and provide you wit a good seat at the comin tractions."

"Corain tractions?"' I says to him.

"These here games is where Christians gets liminated. Dan'l, he a big shot in the govmint of this here govnor Darius. He got enemies| see. An they say he not bow down and worship Darius cordin to the law. Cause Dan'l he got his God to worship. They say they seed him at his winder high yonder, aworshippin. Well, Darius, he jes sign that law to make his-self god so he gotta keep his word to them BabyIons. He t h e govnor now. 01' Nebuchadned gone. Still he like Dan'l. Darius do, but he keep his word to folks. He gonna cast Dan" 1 inter the pit where Din Din and other ferocious lions is. And they mighty hungry cause Darius dont feed them. They r i b bones shows."

"How I help?" I asks Sweet Father.

"You go talk to Dan'lo Cause when they pitch him inter that pit like garbage. the Medee soldiers, they put the govnor's seal inter the stone. And that is that. Dan'l i s gone."

"Where is Dan'l now?"

"He at the jailhouse, Brutus. Jes right up the street there, where that big boulder is hanging by that string case you footsteps don please the govnor."

"This is a big event then?"

"Biggest e-vent of the year. These games. they.s special. Ain"t no doubt bout that. Persian king hear bout the re-sults. You can be sure of that."

"Wait. Sweet Father. That don sound like no e-ven t of any athletic portance to me."

"It ain't, Jes a little division." And Sweet Father, he laughed a terrible big laugh at his own joke. Any man knowed them lions would be mighty hungry. And the Christians what was sposed to be their meal wouldn" last no time-and Dan'l would drop in for desert, sure. Soldiers serve him u p in one piece and he go out in divided pieces—in the bellies of them lions."

Mighty funny, I thought. "What is yer propersition?" I says to Sweet Father.

"You is a radio caster, is you not?"

"It is."

"You like do a jailhouse interview with Dan'l? Keep you from stealing any mo of these here Babylon wineskins. An I heard tell these Babylon rich folks mighty fussy about wineskin robbers."

"Sounds fair nough," I says to him, warming up to this here ideee. "What I do?"

"You take this here ram"s horn and go interview Dan'l in his jailhouse cell. Unerstan? And then when you gets the information you desiraates it round town—jes like me, I is the Babylon crier—so's they all know what Dane's last words was fore he go inter them lions" cage to meet up with Din Din."

"And fer that I gets—?"

"You gets three free passes into the arena next game time. And a special pint of bull's blood blessed by the temple priest. And you gets eight hundred pounds of special prize camel meat for you deep freeze ice house."

"My, oh, my," I says to him. "I is a lucky man. But wait a minute. They aint no ice round here."

"It keep anyway—that's onery camel meat. Sides, hot and dry| it'll stay without turnin, jes like jerky."

"Or mummy flesh.'

"Is you game?" Sweet Father asks me for the las time, me who is representin the Gladiator Radio Station for the Ba-byIon Empireo

"I is." Wit that I sets off to my big signment-and I was carrying wit me the blessins of the gods of Medes and the Persians. Ise ready to con-duct a interview wit Dan"l fore he goes to them hungry lions.

"Dan"!!" I calls to him when I gets past the jailor, who were drunk on cheap wine. "0h, Dan"!!" He come over t o them heavy, black bars. He's tryin to get in a few winks of sleep fore his big ordeal. "Is you feard of them lions?"

"Me? Feared? Not tall," he says to me without blink-in so much as one eye. They wasnt no fear tall in that Dan.l.

"Why is you here in the first place? Ain't you one of them—commissioners or something "» got lots of satytraps t o look out for? Mighty pleased Darius was, I hert."

"He got spies. I got enemies. They seed me prayin."

"Then you is religious?"

"They is only one God—and He is external. Not Dar-ius. He dont last nother forty years, not that long if h e keep on eatin them rich finger foods."

"So he seed you?"

"His spies seed me. Jealous they is, of me. They got a law passed makes him god—to spring a trap for me. They seed me and tolt him and he got obey his own law that says—to them that don bow down death. Whisst! Like that."

"They rat on you. Thet's so. aint it, Dan'l?"

"That's so," he says.

"N so they get govnor's soldiers throw you in to Di n Din. Hert he's a big un, mighty big—over thousand pounds a lion flesh. You know he is gonna be mighty hungry," I says to him.

"So they is hungry. Ise gonna slide up to them there lions and look'm in their yeller eyes and long whiskers. And Ise gonna say, .Honey, is you perticlar bout you main dish?"

"An then, sposin, jes sposin they don answer, but they show you their big white teeth. You aint got much time to do no thinkin, you realize."

"I likes shap teeth—personally. I likes run m y hand ove r then edges. real careful like."

"An then they go crunch. crurapsh, chop, chop. gulp. And you hand is gone, down the hatch for the orders."I says.

"You jes wait an see. My God is good. He won let me down, no sir," says Dan'l.

"An those is you final words?"

"They is—I cain't take nothin back cause my God is more powerful. You'll see. You keep youself tuned in and, Baby, them folks of Babylon and that Darius—they got a real surprise in sto for them. yes sir." Dan'l turned round and went back to his corner where he layed hisself down and went right to sleep peaceful like.

That great day rived, sure nough. and Dan'l wit his chains adraggin on his feet and his hands still wit them handcuffs made of iron on them—he were dragged into vie w, close to where them cats was caged at one end of the ar e na. They was open doors wit bars on them so's all could see.

Crowd sends up a big roar.

"Why they not put Dan'l in the middle of thet arena?" Sweet Father aks me later on. when I finishes intervie tin wit Dan'l for Gladiator Radio. This is too hot to dr o p. "But why?" Sweet Father aks.

"He were special to Darius. I spect he liked Dan'l. But he were forced inter this. He don want make a big noise. He don want raise no sand. Jus put Dan'l way, seal t h at den and then rake out his bones—if they is any lef. I t were Darius' choice."

"Jus long's he foller the law?"

"That's right."

"An then them lions was waiting behind the bars." says Sweet Father.

"Dan'l. his voice was like God's—he commanded them cats sit up straight. long the wall o that den—like a circus trainer. Only he got no whip to crack."

"They obey him?"

"Course they do. What you think? They is obeyin God. that's what. Crowd cain't see much. atchually. Soldiers topside of thet den. they dragged this big man ho l e cover back over the hole and put some wax on the crack t o seal it shut tight. And that were that."

"Then what happen?"

"Well. Sweet Father. Ise standing down in front of them cage bars—I seed everything Dan'l, he calls the m lions by name and he says to them—he were workin down the line. mind you. six or eight of them cats—it were a big den—big waiting room—"cain't help it ifn I laugh-.Dan.l calls each of them animals. stinkin of raw-meat bad breath to the middle of that den. He says, .Open you mouf, big feller, big gal, so's I can see condition of you teef."And you know. Sweet Father, they done jes what he tell th e ra ter do. All this be goin out over the waves to the folks of Babylon when I gets back—specially to thet Govnor Darius.

"Dan'l grabs some grit from offn the floor. He take s a corner of his toga for a scrub brush an he scrubs t h e teef of them lions what needs cleanin. Dan'l shakes his head, "Pity that. You got a cavity or two. Bad food. I kin unerstan cause I turned down all that rich food n'self. Next!" Grit on thet den floor is his scrub toof powder. 'Next! If you ain't feard of ol. Dan'l."

"You needs one stracted, I can see that," Dan'l says to another lion, an" you pain is clear in you eyes. Yes sir."An to nother he say, "You chomp on some of the govnor"s ol throwed out candles—aint no good for nothin else. I per-scribes this. an that will sure nough bring down that swell-in in you jaw. How long this goin on?" Dan"l say to the t lady li o n? But it were too painful for her to talk. So Dan'l close her jaw an he patted her head so she start t o purr.

"Now nother lady lion"s got a toof come loose, so Dan'l wrap a piece of chain end round that toof and he yank real hard an it come out. He put it in his pocket.

"You will be feelin better real soon," Dan'l says t o her. An I spect all them was ver grateful cause I could see inter the dark inside through the bars of that de n-warnt no light in there much, they kept their distance from ol" Dan"l. Narry even a growl or a roar. Mighty kind man, Dan'l was. You see. he were a animal dentist. part from his ficial duties. He love them cats, yes sir. An this mo s folks don know.

"Well, he stay in there. He curl up gainst the war m sides them big cats an he slep off all the citement. A n they sure do treats Dan"l like a portant gues. But sfun ny, you know they was also somebod else in there gussiedup allin white. Caint rightly see who it were—his sistant mo s probly. Dan"l, he say, 'Glad to see you come. God." A n then thet ghost gone away. Well, Sweet Father, that's pretty much the way things happened. But I keeps you informed.

Next day, I, Brutus Piticus, radio caster is assi gne d by Gladiator Station to track down the res of the story. So I takes up my watch long the rena wall. The govnor, he gets out from his gold chariot—he don see me, course, but I can see everythin that go on—an he says to his soldiers, "Remove that big stone cover from over the lions den."They do what he say. Big racket, it made of heavy rock. A n "there, when the daylight come shinin into the pit, there stans Dan'l, lookin like he jes step out of his bathtub.

"Good Darius," say Dan"l. I don see nothing wrong with Dan"!. He all in one piece. "Good Darius, govnor of this here province, as you kin plain as day see, my God has took care of me."

"I don be-lieve my eyes," the govnor say. "Is you live down there, Dan'l?"

"I is."

"Come inter the sunlight so's I kin see you." This Dan"! done right off. "Well, I'll be the sneeze of a African parrot!" he say. "You truly is live. Fetch Dan'l out of there right this minute," Darius give the order. In a flash o f kingdom tine Dan'l were hauled up outa thet pit an set on his two feet. Praise th Lordl An he look fresh as a washed cook pot, he do. I takes a better position fer to see. He done saved from them lions, no doubt bout thet.

Now I, Brutus Piticus, tracks down the res of the story, case you who reads this wants ter record it all down. Soon's I gets back to Gladiator Radio Station I spreads it round, seminates it wide, like Sweet Father says, round the Empire o" Bab Ion folks. Next, I follows Dan.l up to the govnor . s big shack—his palace dey calls it. Werent no good let a hot story die. Seems like Dan.l, he gets freed of them cats and, right off, he rumbles up to this here palace in Darius"golden chariot—to drink some o" that prized wine and dine wit him, Baby. Course, Dan"! he still stick to his ve gie s an keep off all that rich food. But they gives him lots a music on the harps and th horns—an the dancin girls, they frisk round bout his chair.

Dan'l says to Govnor Darius, he say, "I"se got religion. You seed what my God kin do."

"I seed that rightly nough," the govnor say to Dan'l.

"So I cain't go in for this flashy kind a entertainment."

Darius were powerful upset fer a minute, an then he done a ver pe-culiar thing. He aks six men pick up ol Dan'l b y his toga tails and put him atop a big rug, an then they commence ter swing him trough the crowd an th smoke an the smoky incense of thet room. Then they puts him in a chariot an"seven more drivers for them chariots, they gang up round him. They is all outside now. The rumble of them hoi low chariot wheels was somthin t.hear, like thunder a ways off . They is rumble long that rocky street—I find me a farm cart fer a taxi. Them reins and harness jingle with bengles and clacking things—and them horses snort and blow foam from their moufs. All this jangle and noise fill the night air. It were sweet as hoe cakes, let me tell you who care listen.

"Where we go now?" Dan'l aks them. And he see the head of Darius hang over their heads. He stan back, next to der tall pillar o the palace, watchin goings on. He volved all right, but he don say nothin ceptin, "I bow down to your God. I worship your God—but you is still my servant leader."

"Then where is you takin me?"

"They is takin you for a small ride/" Darius say. He go back inter the palace an he leave Dan'l wit then seven chariot drivers arumblin trough the streets a the town—on th. big wheels a them hollow chariots. But they is not the same spies as got Darius to trow ol Dan"l to Din Din in firs' place. Darius, he feed them winderwatcher spies an their famblies to d'lions jes soon's he fetched Dan"! up out o f thet pit.

But the govnor, he is constabulated round with enemies. It's most like he believe Dan'l to bring him bad luck. He is suspicionin everythin" and everbody, cludin Dan"l. He tes t the prophet firs. Darius try to like the Jews, but he not aks them to build up their temple agin. Still, he don know .

"For trickin the govnor, we is goin ter take you up t o a high hill., an we is goin cast you out a high winder of thet high tower this time. We'uns goin make sure you don live. You is not a frien o the govnor. You is a enemy. You don bow down fore him."

"He say he worship my God."

"He jus say that. Don want no trouble from them Christians in BabIon— all seben of us. An we drive these here fine chariots jes to show folks in Bablon gold counts fer more in this here Roman kingdom than do your God."

Now Dan'l tolt me this hisself later on: while he wer e rumblin long on the streets to thet tower, he were thinkin. He say to hisself, "Maybe I kin bribe m"jailor. But I" s a hones man, so's I got get rid of that idee right off. May … be I can give him a gif and aks nothing back. That way,"Dan 'l is athinkin, and he fesses this to me—"that way I not beb'holden to nother man, only t"God. I got thet toof from th mouf o that lady lion in the den, where I was throwed fer over night."

While he was rockin" long he pulled that toof outer his pocket—plum fergot about it. That come to be part o his plan. Sides, Dan'l told me later on—he hert from his char. iot driver that thet tower jailor were a maker a songs. H e writ some jazz real mellow that spired by the roars a t h e m lions. Mebe, Dan"l thunk then an there, mebe he could give the song-maker jailor a gif o thet lady lion"s toof. Mebe also he could scribble a blues—"The Lion's Den Blues" "for Darius—bring in the bass, paw a mite at the drums.

I say to Dan"l when we stop—I get down outa my t a x i cart, "This report wich I got present when I gets back t o Gladiator Station, it ainU finish. You cain"t bribe the jailor. What you do then? How you get out a this mess o "the tower? Do I got to go wich you to you grave, Dan'l?"

"I got a real surprise for you, Mister—"

"Brutus Piticus, re-porter for the Gladiator Radio Station,"

"Mister Piticus—here."

Dan'l showed me down on th floboards o that chariot—when we come to a small ledge, —he show me what he pick up from the govnor's palace. "They is gifs from Govnor Darius hisself, Baby," Dan'l says to me. "Cain't do nothin about the law as"t stands. But he sure can come to m' rescue."He give me dese seben lions tails for the drivers one one lion mane—yeller and hairy—and a coat fer the drawbridge o-perator neath that tower. An lookee here—some teef from his wife's own Jewry collection. Darius, he say, 'Take all o them. They get you free. And when you come back here, we ee what we kin do. Mebe give you more satrapies to minister over."

"Wal, thet seem pretty fair to me," Dan'l say. An h e grin at me and give a kick to that stuff luggage on the floboards. "Course, mebe you can help me carry that mane i n to thet chain puller feller at the drawbridge. You te 1 1 s him I| Dan'l, got ter sleep on thet mane skintonight. Cold. But he kin keep it if he's a mind to and mebe gives a too t to Dan'l oncet a while. You know what I mean," Dan'l grins at me, an I grin right back. He some prophet all right.

Night come on fast like a shootinstar. An I done help Dan'l. We's down on the groun below. I seed him poke his head out top of thet tower, winder high up. I stan long-side m' studio chariot—m" taxi cart. Next thing I knows I seed that drawbridge come down crest the ditch. Dan's must've slipped that lady lion's toof to his jailor-or all the string of teef what belongs to Darius' wife. She got a big neck. Anyway. they was a jillion steps he come down an then, quick as a scootin' marmot, Dan'l come crost thet drawbridge. He pass out them tails to them seben chariot driver—and they fetched up to heaven, let me tell you, they was so serprized and stonedrunk happy wit them lion's tails. It were a fine stribution. Next thing Dan'l dumb into closest chariot and wit him leadin' the parade he set off back to the palace. I were trapsing and rumblin" long behind. It were turnin dawn now.

I got to re-port—at The Daily Scroll like at Gladi a—tor Radio Station. what news showed Dan'l's mirclous powers. News tells bout his prisonment an the lions that don eat him up. Course, most of this story I give out, like I sa y. I tells folks all 'bout his scape.

"Darius run a scribbled oath for genl 'stribution: "I give Dan'l, my former govnor of 26 satrapies. full par don for worship his God. He has a great God, and I tries t o worship him same's Dan'l. An I give back to my servant what he had fo his enemies seeched me throw him in wit the lions. Also, I give him nother sixteen trapies. Signed by Govnor Darius.'

Let me tell you, that do cock a few heads sidewise. DanM were no longer a crimnal—not even at large. Now Darius real ly do trust him. An he helt a feast in the govnor.s pal ac e jes for Dan'l.

I say to His Grace, the govnor, "I re-present the p *re&&*, you Grace."

"I knows that," says Darius.

"It be all right with you Grace ifn I sets up a cil i a ry bureau in the satrapies Dan'l looks after?"

"Why fo? Ain't the decrees from this palace good nuf?"

"They is, but the news go nighty slow. One chariot driver can desimate the news round so's all the folks know of you goodness, 0 Darius."

"Now that is a fine idee, a fine idee," say Darius. "A n Dan"! have ny full an whitewash authority to minister an watch after, see no flagration or killin or javelins or caterpaults wit stones crash into you headquarters, good citizen,"he say.

An so to this here day they is better covrage on the o f-ficial scroll cause of Da&'l faith in God. An he brung others long wit him, eluding myself. Amen.

Folks now really curious see this fellow, only man been captured who face a pack a hungry lio ns without getting nary a scratch on hisself. And, whasmore, he is so favorites wit Govnor Darius he got official rescue from enemies o the palace. We come mighty good friens, me an ol Dan.l. We break"d bread over the table in his fine house to celbrate occasn of his rescue from the den of lions an the tower o vengeance.

I tell you, frien, these things—an I tell them all t o Sweet Father, case you want to write them all down. Ise mak-in" good now, since he foun me this job as radio caster.

> Although animals in the wild forage and hunt for food, they are under man"s stewardship from God. Waste is an unacceptable methodology for control, and utility in times of plenty is subject to scrutiny .The question is not whether wild anima 1 s have rights, but rather does ma n have the right wantonly to destr oy what belongs to God. That is the only global attitude, the only international ethic worth consider a-tion. If decided in the affirmative then protective barriers for preservation must be established and guarded.

The Spirit Eagle And The Buffalo Herd

I had been reading about the decimation of sixteen million bison on the Plains of this country, when white man could travel into the Sioux territory on his new transcontinental railroad. They came in droves, the spoilers eager for the few paltry dollars rich eastern merchants paid for buffalo hides. Usually, however, the shooters lusted only for the power to kill aliving creature, an animal that roamed free compared to the puny conception of freedom distorted by white man's war p e d vision. They destroyed the buffalo often not even for meat, since the shooters left the carcasses to rot on the ground and the skins together with the flesh.

Just kill, shoot, shoot, kill. How often when a drunken, triggerhappy shooter brought down one of those magnificent beasts, loud huzzahs went up in the railroad car to signal the triumph of cruelty and the savage, gleeful slaughter of another buffalo. Often the animal died gushing blood, wounded, without the mercy o f a knife to its throat or an arrow of respect into its heart. These were the mindless shooters who marauded the new west for the pleasure of killing just to kill.

These pleasure-shooters were the predecessors to and the apostles of the approaching Manifest Destiny, philosophy designed to extinguish the Indians and all other forms of inconvenient life before its onrush o f power" The creed was said to be a divinely-inspi r e d appointment by God to extend the western boundary o f America to the Pacific Ocean. Instead, it was a blasphemous rehearsal for extinction that would wipe out all resistance by the Sioux, the Plains Indians, and consign them to another existence on barren reserv a-tions. This thrust of malevolence broke all treaties, all words of honor and trust, all oaths of protective rights, all pacts and signatures of mutuality and in-stead substituted the perfidity of dishonor, blood and conquest. The only final solution to Manifest Destiny was the removal of the Indians and the slaughter o f their herds.

The Indians derived food, shelter, tools, weapons, warmth, fire and inspiration from the buffalo. By destroying the buffalo the white man"s Government had decreed that the Plains Indians ought no longer to exist as a nation. When a Sioux brave brought down a buffalo, he felt a guilt for the sacrifice by the animal of life. The white man did not understand that humility and need in his parlor comfort.

And so, as I said, I had been reading about this destruction in blood, this annihilation of a whole culture, a people and their way of life at the heart of which was the wild, roaming buffalo. Such visual impressions in the imagination take peculiar forms i n dreams, especially when the sleep is light and rest—less. That very night my mind delivered to me this strange, exotic and almost incomprehensible dream.

A golden eagle wandered, searching, high overhead, its glossy wing feathers ashwhitened by the burning blue sun, its flight stilled by warm Plains a i r, hovering, voiceless above the buffalo grass quiveri n g in the summer's heat. The eagle sought shade, a rest, but only the mesquite here and there attracted its shifting black eyes. The eagle gathered to itself the icy hail and thunder clouds. It circled, flew onward, above the purple stretches below, livid with thunder bolts. Clouds like wind-driven ashes and dust formed around the eagle and tore at its feathers.

A voice called out—"Never downward. Seek the tree of rest in the sacred cove with the gray, peeling medicine bark,"

Between the eagle's wings, clutched in talons of iron that flashed and glinted in the somber light, there lay a clay vessel, like a bowl, fluted and beautiful with signs of trees and birds impressed by the Gre a t Spirit into its red clay. Inside the bowl there churned and stirred the blood of the blessing of the anim a 1 s from a Holy Creator, who gave them blood and flesh from out of the dust and breath from His eternal flame.

The eagle flew on, soaring in ever-lowering circles, flew down through the fury of the storm winds and thunder. Then it dropped the bowl. The fragile clay shattered across the land. Stretching into the distant black hills and down to the river, red blood from the broken bowl spread like a stream choked up with limbso It stretched away to the brass-colored rocks and cones that tinkled in the icy currents from t h e thunder clouds. The eagle had stained with blood th e reaches of the Plains earth and sand and rocks.

In a voice like a distant muted army of soldiers the eagle spoke. Its words had the erispness of brush scratching ancient rocks. Each touch. each fragment of speech was as distinct as the form of a brave a-gainst the sky or of a medicine chief's sand painting.

"Brother bison. Gather, spread—multiply and crop the lonely, the life-giving grass. It is as tough as you are tough. You are fashioned like the bowl o f blood by the Creator God.

A deep moaning like the wind bowing the pine tops arose in the east, low and sinewy and galloping in its measured haste like a thousand braves in their h e addresses and feathers.

"We are many of us. Who can kill us, we are so many?"

"Do not be confident of your lives," said the eagle.

"You contend with the mighty buffalo of the Plains," said the gathering voices, like cries of an i-Dials stricken by the knife and of sheep pierced with shafts of iron arrows, silent, falling—and the wailing of ten-thousand wolves.

The eagle was speaking to a mortal—to me, for I am a white man. "As for you—share death."

"I do not deceive you, brother bison. Prepare-prepare—prepare."

The eagle lifted off from the limb of a jun i per tree and flew in concentric circles, and as it did so, the bison sprang into renewed life and animation upon the cooling flash-thundered Plains. At first a few, then thousands, then millions. their vast numbers milling about in a boiling, pawing, bellowing mass of herd life, moving restless before the thunder and lightning. Stam-pede was imminent. They were frightened beasts, for they heard and understood the eagle. They rose up like a black cloud upon the horizon and ran until they could run n o more from exhaustion. Their hooves churned the sod into writing dust like vicious snakes, terror in their e y es, froth at their mouths and black tongues. The sound o f their flight deafened the skies like the roaring of a thousand storms in the tops of a forest.

Then from the east appeared a great black round rock, with flashing wheels of obsidion and quartz and jade and smoke rising from one end like that from the sacred rock of the pipe of peace, yet shaped out of black stone. This pipe gave off the scent of death and a blackness like roesquite smoke and the sounds of its wheels were as iron blades clashing and a fire beneath like the fire from an enemy's gun. It came on, not to be turned aside or stopped| its fire flashing so brightly the herd of bison stampeded to a distance, snorting, the calves bawling, heads bowed to stare at the enemy. They ran on and in confusion until their tongues rolled rich and thick and in. viting as delicacies for the humans who sat within the long and limber log—like a snake, it was, a caterpillar of overpowering might.

The white man's snake of death bore poison in it s sound and smoke and it slowed down. so that the buff a 1 o merely lifted their heavy, shaggy.

bearded heads to peer in wonder at the new beast just arrived onto their a n-cient lands. Few of the wild creatures felt the sharp sting of the fire rocks that sped to their hearts. They fell, tongues still holding wetly to the tufts of Plains grass, their eyes rolling upward to glimpse the final aura of the thunder-lighted purple heavens—and the eag 1 e that soared above in the mist and dust on the wind.

The giant beasts fell into the earth and lay still. warm and panting. throbbing, their blood rivers flowing onto the dying warm sands. First one and then another, the dark, heavy-furred masses. their humps and thei r horns pulsing. fell over into the dust. touched by t he death hand of the bearded strangers. they who in their fire log wielded fire rocks that struck like spears in t o the hearts of the grazing animals.

Shifting about uneasily, the herd moved off a ways, the fire leg diamonds in its wheels flashing eerily in the mournful light on the prairie. Their monster with its white clouds hissing moved the shooters ahead at a s 1 ow pace. the better to aim. Their piercing blows were t h e more deadly; the bead of their exultation was not bindered as a rider is hindered when he shoots from astride his horse. A crowd of people noises came from out of the small windows when a buffalo beast fell to the earth of its mother, its legs still walking in a sleep of death. Again—the cries of victory and jubilation. The f i re log did not stop and no man emerged from inside with his knife to cut off pieces of the meat for food or to pull off the skin for his own winter comfort when the snows fall.

"Other men will come when they find out," said the eagle.

"Are we not worthy—for the Indian?" cried out a voice from the herd.

"You are their offering for life—their lives/" the eagle said.

"We love to roam free."

"You stand in the way—"

"In the way—of what. great eagle?"

"Of destiny. They say this is the command from their divine god. It is evident."

"We have our destiny. We shall die of age."

"The Indians will no longer kill and prepare you for their food," said the eagle. "Your skins will adorn the floors of golden tepees in the east. Your great cloaks of fur for the prairie winter will adorn the backs o f the shooters—or else lie to rot without inheritance."

"We are sad, not afraid."

"You will be killed—all killed," said the eagle.

"We are dying, great eagle. We do not invite the carrion eaters."

"The prairie is a waste. The buffalo are a waste. The grass is a waste. The birds of prey have come."

Their rocks turned into pellets of gold and th e shooters" guns into flaming bows and arrows, as through the herd, scattering the great creatures, appeared fifteen horsemen, adorned in war paint and full headdres s, mounted on buckskin ponies. They stood in rank befo r e the window eyes of the snake of death. One of them spoke:

"Life to you is without worth—like the clay w e make our medicine from. All of life, all things living and not living have worth to us. You do not have wisdom, white man.

"We are wise, you are savage."

"We hunt out of need. You shoot for—laughter."

"These bison belong to us now."

"The buffalo belongs to all men—even to you. You d o not destroy what is good."

"For what—good for what," said the empty eyes.

"You do not understand the Indian's ways."

"Our father in Washington does. He tells us to kill the buffalos. Then you will go away."

"You will set free the spirit of evil over your land| our land. You will lose the roots of your 1i fe on the prairie. You kill the beast of the Plains. You make captives of free men. Free men—captives of free men—"

The Indian chief's voice faded into the thunder and wind. He and his fourteen horsemen wheeled as one and, turning their backs on the snake of death, rode off into the herd. The bison swallowed them up. as if they had fallen into the pit of blood or entered the mouth of mystical moaning cave. They were gone.

The fire rocks continued from the window eyes of the serpent like spitting fangs. As a buffalo fell into the prairie soil, the great eagle, circling, swooped down and lifted a firebrand—a fagot blazing with sul-pher fumes—from the belly of the great beast.It wa s the entrapped spirit of survival, of the agony of remaining alive in deep snows, of sacrifice with blo o d and flesh and fur for the Indians" life. The firebrand had entwined at one end a cluster of feathers that did not burn, and at the other a spirit-head of a b ison, transparent and bearing in its mouth a clutch of arrows and a bow. Prom the east rode one of the Indi-ans, the same who had spoken, and took the arrows and the bow from the mouth of the bison. The eagle then lifted the fiery, flaming branch with the entwi n e d feathers into the sky iand flung it up into the fire of a thunderbolt. It vanished in the flash of intense, purple light. The rich incense of the feast permeated the night, the feast of the Indian hunt.

Every time a shooter killed one of the buffa 1 o, even if two or three fell off to one side of the tracks of the death snake, the great eagle performed its rite. This act went on until all fifteen of the Sioux warriors had ridden from out of the midst of the herd and lifted the arrows and bow from the mouth of the ghostly bison head. The eagle, never tiring, at the deat h of the creature, seized the flame from its belly and cast it up into the livid skies made bright by flashes of lightning.

Fifteen times I watched this rite. Each time the shooters inside the snake of death cried their victory cry. Yet they did not see what happened when a beast fell into its grave, for they were blind before the life they wanted to kill without compassion. Then, as if lit by the hand of God, the great herd of mi l-lions changed into transparent ghosts of the Plains.

"Look! Look there!" a shooter called from out of his window. "They"re— my God! They are just melting away!"

The buffalo herd began to dissolve, as if cut rrom fractured floe ice, to last only until the heat of the sun should dissolve their lives. The dark and brooding death clouds moved away from the sun. Not a soli t a r y buffalo remained for the shooters. They closed their windows and poured for themselves heavy firewater. while across the lonely stretches of land and rising up in t o the shadowcarved mountains, the prairie was drenched not in blood but in the yellow of golden wheat that gre w thick and bending from out of the prairie soil of death. A light rain began to fall.

Counterpoint In The Wild

Antlers, the moose, wondered what in the world Elmira, the she-wolf, was doing sitting out under the moonlight and elevating her voice in an aria to the starry heavens.

And so Antlers cane close, as close as he dared, and said, "What in the world are you doing, wolf?"

"Elmira—K. Elmira. K stands for Katrina, y o u know. I'm a Russian wolf—a Russian wolf by pedegree."

"That so? Fancy that—way out here in the woods … from Russia. You got over here—?"

"Pretending I was a toy lap dog, stupid noose."

"Don.t get nasty with me, snappish bitch! I w a s just asking. You still have not told me what you are doing—elevating the noon just an inch or two?"

"Oowwwwwwwww! Naw—pushing the frost down another degre e or two. My voice carries better over the landscape when the night is cold."

"Personally, I get. better sound on a wet night."

"You would. That A—flat horn of yours would cal 1 up the weeping dead. You use that blast for a mat in g call?"

"I sure do—it's the purest sound around except for the sound of the Upland Spring."

"Let me tell you something, Mister Antlers, you keep that horny big head on you much longer you won't be calling anybody but a tree surgeon."

"Just you don't howl too long either, wise bitch, or the moon will fracture into cold ice and the dawn will turn into a hoar frost to freeze the sun. Don. tyou know you can't keep up a high B-sharp more than three minutes without putting out the stars?"

"Go on witcha," said Elmira. "You borrowed your sound from a cave somewhere. I ought to give up howling as a remedy for lonesomeness. That'd put an end to your bragging, moose. Only—I'm alone right now."

"It's a good thing, too—your howl is sharp e-nough to split timber." Antlers, the moose, moved off a short ways to crop some tufts of grass at the foot of a tree trunk. He kept a wary eye on Elmira though, and he listened to all the other sounds in the deep woods. He did not want a wolf pack to come unexpectedly in t o view around the bend in the trail. Instinct told him that if he started to run the wolf would give chase. That would be the end since the wolf could easily wear him down to exhaustion. Consequently he played coy and clever.

"Tell you what—you're such a wiseacre," said Antlers.

"Because the night is cold, it makes me snappy and sharp. I get all tingly inside for the taste o f moose blood on nights like this."

"Lets us do something smart for a change, you and me," said the moose.

"I'm witcha," said Elmira. "Got anything in mind?"

"I know that you are just killing time un t il the gang shows up."

"Killing is the right word, moose."

"Lets us dialogue together. You have your territory and I got mine. I see no sense in us getting all upset if one of us kind of strays over the line."

"Not at all. Besides, my trees are all marked by friends of mine."

"You got enemies, too?"

"I sure have. Man."

"Then lets us survive together," said Antlers, the moose.

"I'm witcha. Excuse me just a minute. I mus t limber up again. This cold gets to my windchimes.Arff." Elmira sounded a long, wailing howl. "It's mighty satisfactory when you can howl like that."

"I shouldn't wonder. Now, as to our dial ogue. Let us say you see a man approach—or two or three with guns in their hands. You take a high roost, somewher e up among those rocks and howl. Like this." The moose could not howl and so he bellowed instead.

"Oaf! Like this.'"The wolf rent the night with her wail.

"Exactly. I hear your howl and I answer it with this blast. The moose let out a loud, noisy bugle call that ended in a squeeky rasping sound. "Not my best-but it will do. You hear me, and you run in the other direction—that is, if I see the shooters first."

"We warn each other," said Elmira.

"You comprehend. A system of warning that leaves no scent, no tracks, no ruffling of the snow or the leaves or the air. What say?"

"Sounds instinctive."

"Good. Lets us try it out. Oh, and by the way, do tell your—pals first, please, so we get no mixups. Now—off to the rocks with you, Elraira, and—a test-run to work out the bugs—fleas."

"Can you hear me now?" the wolf asked as she sped off in the direction of a tumble of huge granite rocks.

"Just barely—but howl. Howl when you are ready, and I will send out my mating call."

The wolf disappeared and in another few min u tes, Antlers heard only the whining of the wolf's tremu 1 ou s voice. He knew well how agile, limber and adept the wolf would be at tracking him through the snow. H e did not dare to ruin the plan at this point, and so he gave forth with his heartiest blast—to which the wolf answered with a soul-shattering howl. The moon shifted i n the skies and drops of light and shadow tinkled onto the hoar frost atop the frozen new snow.

Again, moving off at a greater distance. Antlers. deep and booming voice, sonorous and beautiful as the mating call rose into the night air. And Elmira, the she wolf, answered with a prolonged howl that trembled on 1he air it was so fine and delicate and piercing.

Antlers entered the creek, almost covered with snow and slowly picked his way upstream. He called again. The wolf responded. Shortly, they were carrying on a duet. Call and response, call and response, howl and bugle, the sanguine howl and the thunderous boom of the weary moose. In time the moose heard the wolf.s call n o more and looked about him cautiously to see if the wolf had discovered the d 6 ception. But there were no telltale signs of a disturbance amid the foliage, or of the soft brush of snow falling from leaves to the ground.

The moose had forgotten one thing, though—not the wolf pack or the scent of the trail he was leaving or the ruse of walking in water. He had forgotten, in his efforts to save himself, that the roe had come on the scene. However| the wolf had not overlooked this detail. As nature designs such encounters the wolf pack, silent, deadly and swift, five in number yet hardly breaking the snow crust, showed up at about the same time as the roe picked up the scent of the bull and his tracks. They moved in for the kill. Terrified, panting, maimed, the female soon surrendered her life.

Antlers, the bull moose, never heard from the wolf Elmira again. Eagerly did he search long and wide for a mate for that season. Yet life sustained life through the blood of death. So it will always be. Hunger is the unfailing language of life.

> Man covets the power of the wild animal or h e would not try to pos "sess it by kill i ng. The talisman of the pri-mative impulses in ma n are his pelts, trophies, and captives. The In-dian understood the real and symbolic power in-herent in the beast.

The Vainglorious Hippo

Rising Moon was a hippopotamus. He lived in the Nile River not far from the Ethiopian palace of Addis Ababa" Rising Moon bobbed in the river's currents. He listened to chants of the river boatmen as they glided by him thr ough the still, hot African air.

His name meant "river horse ."' He wondered why th e Ethiopians never used him or his brothers to draw the funeral barges along. He splashed in the cool mud of the river bank and, by the hours, he watched the flatboats lade n with hides, clusters of dates, skins and brick, with stalks of wild sugar cane and mounds of grain, go floating pas t him. If he w as a horse, why not work as a horse instead of always playing at bathing in the mud and browsing on the river-bottom grasses? Rising Moon had an identity problem.

He was an enormous hulk. His mouth was shaped like a pink pot with an open lid. His hide was wrinkled from soaking in the water for years, and it would never stretch out smooth again. His big lip and peg teeth were good mostly for ripping weeds from off the bottom of the muddy river. His hulk floated; his small and dainty feet never got stuck in the mud.

Along the river banks other animals came tosh are the water, to drink and bathe and keep cool under the desert sun. A lion, known throughout the rocky places, lean and hungry always and roaring to feed on natives, goa ts and stray wild donkeys, came down to the river's edge one morning.

His name was Fabus, and he roared exceedingly well, He lapped up some water, gazed out into the river and saw Rising Moon.

"Do you come by this way often?" Fabus enquired.

"Very often. The forage under the water is particularly good right here."

"But you are out of place, hippo. I can see that at first glance." Fabus roared to accent his famous instincts.

"I know. I am a river horse, but I do not pull the barges."

"A shame. The boatmen do not understand you."

"I am much too big and round and fat."

"That is a tragedy—I could help you with your problem."

"I sometimes think I ought to be more handsome than I am."

"Vanity never hurt anybody. Just look at me." F a-bus roared. "What if my gorgeous mane were made of straw and my coat of goat leather and my yellow eyes dead stones? Would I not then be a horrible sight?"

"Oh, you would. You would."

"You know that you are—destined to be a hippopotamus—always."

"I wish it were not so."

"It does not have to be," said the lion. "Your friends and associates are so important."

"I have none that are glamorous, like you," said Rising Moon.

"Let me give you some advice. Come up here closer—to where we can talk confidentially." The hippo walked on the mud and came up out of the river. "Find yourse l f new friends like—say—the goats of the king."

"Oh, I could never …"

"Do not be so—pessimistic," said Fabus. "You need to attack yo ur identity problem. In the first place, you need to lose weight, trim down. You need to become like others—"

"Like the goats?"

"Exactly so. I would chew on the matter if I was you. You will have no— excuse the word—<u>bones</u> of con-tention with the goats. You will be—just plain, old gorgeous you."

"I will be like—another goat?"

"Exactly." Fabus roared. Rising Moon backed away ever so slightly. "Do not fear me, gentle one. I understand your problem very well. If you will go—and b e like them, perhaps even I can come and see how well you are getting along—and we can dine together. I give you my great encouragement. We can work together in this matter."

"But—they will fear you, king of the beasts."

"You will be like them and they will see how gentle you are and—they will accept me quickly."

"I certainly hope you are right. I need to ma k e some changes in my life."

"Just gnaw on what I have said and chew your grasses. You will find that I am right. Just remember who told you these things, too, old Faubus, king of the beasts."

"I shall never forget you. Faubus." He knew instinctively that the lean and hungry lion would not swim out to the middle of the river. He would stay where the snapping crocodiles flashed their scimitar tails. He and and his mates looked like bounders—rude and pushy beasts—in the middle of the river. They churned u p greatfoaming, splashing pools of water, always liftingup their pink mouths and big teeth as if yawning into the morning sun. Rising Moon was a proud hippopotamus" H e aspired to look trim. The lion was right. He looked toward the shore, but Faubus had gone elsewhere.

A bunch of Ehtiopian soldiers had stabbed their spears into the river sand. They were King Ababa's hunters and hersmen. They build a fire and they roas t e d a big bird and some fish when Rising Moon again came up out of the river. He had decided that he would follow the advice of Faubus. the lion.

"Good sirs, I come from the river.' The soldiers laughed heartily. They were surprised that a hippopotamus could talk. Rising Moon had learned Ethiopian just by listening to river boatmen. "I no longer wish to be near my clumsy river companions. When I herd with them, I am not distinguished in any way.'

"Is not camouflage better?" one of the hunters asked.

"Every leaf on the tree is the same. I want to be different. Is it possible that you can find a place for me among your goat herds?'

The king's soldiers split their sides with laughter, like wet logs on a hot fire. They could hardly stop hissing and laughing. Gales of mockery and ridicule rolled up from the morning's river silence.

"My herd brothers wonU have anything to do with me because I have grown fat and awkward. I think I can find better company among your goats."

The naked soldiers roared again. Here was a ri v er hippo begging to join a herd of the king's hillside goats. One of the herdsmen said, "Men this obviously is a v e ry smart hippopotamus. You will notice how sleek he has kept his hide—except in the wrinkled places. What a twinkle there is in his glassy eyes with the big eyelashes. S e e how pink his huge mouth is—how nimble his little f e et are—under such an immense hulk." The herdsmen grew silent. "What is your name, little one?"

"My name is Rising Moon."

"Oh, what a touch of poetry}" said the hunter. H e clapped his hands and they all laughed. "Rising Moon, eh?" The men rollicked all the more with this jesting. "Ithink, Rising Moon, that we ought to give it a try."

"Saddib, <u>sabbat rejuntalap isalwinonl</u>" they cried, which meant| "Let's do it right now. For sport."

"Oh, would you!"

"What do you say, comrades?" They all cons e n t e d to the proposal, laughing into their sandal thongs. I t was thus settled—and within a day—

arranged bet ween all the parties the goats, Rising Moon and the herdsmen—that the unhappy hippopotamus would join the goat herd. In a matter of two days, Rising Moon had become a big, big goat.

On his very first day out in King Ababa's pasture, Rising Moon had a hard time keeping up with the agile goats. Baaaaaaing, they scampered here and there among the rocks. They browsed daintily through their whiskers and sniffed the air constantly for enemies. They saw Rising Moon but paid no attention to him. Just as Faubus had said—no contention, no strife, no quarreling. Sweet peace. And such a feeling of relief to be among those who possessed wisdom, loved his beauty and appreciated his presence in the pasture. Rising Moon was proud of h is new place in life. He was now a working, eating mem be r of the king's goat herd. Just wait until that ordina r y gang of common lumps back in the river should learn o f this change.

Daily existence went along nicely, although Risin g Moon could not reach some of the more succulent shoots on the hillside because of the size of his mouth. He brib e d a goat to run up the slopes and snatch them from betwe e n the higher rocks and drop them into his big mouth. For this kind deed he gave the goat the privilege o f standing in his enormous shade on the hottest days. Since Rising Moon eould not climb and frolic like the other goats, he was content to watch them cropping on the rocky le d g e s above his head. He, instead, combed the low places i n smug and placid ease.

The great King Ababa soon found out about him from the herdsmen and, indeed, counted the hippo as one of his favorite goats. A herdsman shook a papyrus blossom i n his direction one day to bless his large frame with dainty mineral water from the king's bath. It was a rite of admiration. As for his small feet, the maker of sandals for the king came out into the field and carefully measured Rising Moon's hooves. He intended to fashion a pair of sandals just his exact size for the queen her s elf "Then the potter of the king paid still another visit one day to the palace's special goat and, in soft clay, h e took an impression of Rising Moon's big teeth. The mark was to emboss all the royal dining pottery. Truly Rising Moon was a favored goat. Naturally, too, the royal recognition was starting to go to his head. It taught him from real life about the jealousy of the other goats. He swelled with new pride, even larger than he was.

Faubus poked his huge maned head around a rock one day, quite unexpectedly, and asked, "Does it not go well with you, gentle one?"

"Oh, I am so happy!"

"Does it not thrill your heart to see that you are favored by the king?"

"It does. It does." When the goats in the field saw Rising Moon conversing with the lion, they scampered off to a safe distance.

"They are nervous. That is to be expected. Aft e r all, you do not meet their expectations."

"I don't?"

"No. You far surpass them. So that now they are envious."

"You give me great encouragement) Faubus."

"I could give you more if you would—introduce me to your friends."

"Would you like that?"

"Immensely. Immensely. To borrow the expression—bloody well right."

Rising Moon grunted. The goats kept on browsing, but they eyed the pair warily.

"They are shy around me, too," said Rising Moon.

"Timid—but, I shall have my fill. I just wanted to drop by and see how you are doing. It is—marvelous to see everything—close up. You'll excuse me, I ha ve a dinner on the rocks and must hurry off."

"Do come by again, Faubus." The lion had gone. "Such a wonderful friend!

The days passed in idyllic contentment for the hippo. Then one balmy afternoon, King Ababa, hirose 1 f, rode up on a camel to observe his fine, fattening goat herd. He saw Rising Moon and he said to his herdsma n, seated beside him on another camel, "What kind of a goat is that?"

The herdsman just laughed. The other goats dontinued to graze and frolic about while the king observed their hippo friend nibbling on remnants of grass beneath some nearby rocks. He was trimming down a little because he could not nibble like his brother goats did. So he pulled up a few delicious blades during the hea t of the day. He was frantic for food yet proud of his loss of weight.

The king spoke: "I see that this well-proportioned goat has gained favor with the rest of the herd. And I see that he has done well for himself in grazing over the spare land. He has put on a great many pounds t h e other goats do not have. He must be a beast of uncommonly good intelligence."

"He is, Sire, and he is also a lone forager."

"We can fix that, I'm sure. Now that the quee n has recovered from her long illness, I think it appropriate that we should hold a barbeque along the banks of the Nile River. Invite all the neighbor kings and governors over. What do you say, herdsman?"

The herdsman was ecstatic because the king had asked him for his opinion. Also, he saw a way of getting rid of this cumbersome, overgrown goat who gave him nothing but trouble. Rising Moon loved to scatter the herd to show his power. He stole favorite cropping places from senior goats. He apparently had made friends with a lion.

"That big goat is a nuisance, 0 King. He is too much trouble to watch."

"Splended! I.m so glad you agree with me. We'll then, it is settled. He will make a delicious and most excellent meal for my banquet out-of-doors. Distan t kings will catch his aroma—and my intimates will feoige themselves heartily." The king snapped his rope at the camel and rode away toward his palace.

It struck him with cold reality that he was to be the barbequed main dish for the king"s banquet feast. Rising Moon slept very little that night. If he stayed with the palace herd he would surely be slaughtered and cut up for the feast occasion. If he went back to the river and his old associates whispered his adventures a-round, they would laugh him to shame. During this p er-plexing moment, Faubus again appeared. He whined to reveal his presence to the hippo.

"I have not seen you for many days," said Faubus.

"No, and you will not see me again after tomorrow."

"I am sorry to hear that,"' said the lion. What i s the matter?"

"The king is going to slaughter me for his barbeque feed."

"Tragic! Nothing but that—tragic! Maybe I can help you again."

"How is that?"

"Stay—and let me sleep near you for I am afra i d of the night."

"You? A lion?"

"It is so hard to hunt alone—and no place to come back to,"

"I think I understand."

"In return for your gentle hospitality I shall drive off the slaughterers when they come to kill you and prepare you for the feast."

"Oh, would you? I should like that very much,"said Rising Moon. "I am almost prepared to retire right now."

"Marvelous, is it not, how everything works out?"

And so Rising Moon and the lion Faubus lay down together under the desert night sky and took their repose. Yet by now Rising Moon had learned how sly his friend was. While the old lion slept he arose, sniffed the sharp night air and the falling dew. He looked eastward and smelled the river water of the Nile. He ambled in the directi o n that his senses urged, leaving the lion alone, asleep and unattended.

I will not tell my brothers what has happened. I will say that I lost my bearings, that I wandered away.He grunted at these thoughts.

The night wore on. At last he reached the river bank. He felt a strange ecstasy inside. There were his old herdmates, backs glistening wetly under the full moon. They ignored him. The daylight would come and they would still ignore him. But amidst their delighted squeels and gutteral chompings of green river relish they would recognize him. And so it happened in this manner.

The dawn came and wildlife on the river began t o move and come alive. The hippo herd knew Rising Moon for what he was—a constant teller of lies. They did not believe him—even before he opened his mouth. He d o v e deep into the water, to the muddy bottom. His old browsing habits would help him to hide his mistake and his shame. Also, he was famished from nibbling with the goats. The cool water and oozy mud cheered him as he plucked clumps of weeds from the floor of the Nile. He swallowed these delicious and familiar greens once more, in the pain of his bad experiences. The king did not butcher him for his barbeque, but he, Rising Moon, heard bargemen several days afterward say that the royal pal ace hunters had speared a huge vagrant lion found amon g the king's goats. Poor Faubus!

To this day Rising Moon browses along the river bottom, rising from time to time only to catch his breath or sun himself in the fragrant mud of a late afternoon. He could hide from the mocking herdsmen and others who recognized him as the proud hippopotamus who wanted to cavort with the goats and become a goat. Yet deep down inside he knew he would never have learned to b 1 eat like a goat.

> A captive carnivore will lose weight and vitality if constantly fed an artificial diet concockted By reason rather than from observation. Why is it that such an ani m a 1 is so finely attuned t o its environment?

The Bear And The Fire Fish

In a wooded area above the roaring falls a coyote and a bear had gotten along together for a number of years"Neither had accused the other of trespassing upon his territory. But as time went on the coyote began to feel that the bear was hogging more than his share of small game for his meals. After all, he could fish the river above the falls, a venture totally beyond the skills of the coyote. Cons equently, he was bound to feel envious and put-upon, confined and squeezed within the perimeter of his hunting domain.

Massah, the coyote, was determined to do somethi n g about his sorry plight. He waited for the bear to fini s h his fishing expedition one afternoon and he accosted Clem, the bear, sharply when the beautiful brute sat down to gorge himself on the innards of a trout he had just caught.

"What say there, pardner?" the coyote hailed the bear, trying to sound jaunty and cool. All the while he kept his eyes and ears tuned into the bear's pawing and his chewing while Clem tore the fish apart. He had not heard. "What say there, pardner?" the coyote hailed a second time, only louder.

Clem looked up, growled a throaty growl but kept o n with his meal.

"Hungry is as hungry does/" said the coyote, this time trying hard to sound clever.

"What you bother me for?" Clem answered, sniffing the air to catch the scent of the coyote.

"I say, we got some sort of problem going on," said Massah.

"Problem? The problem is you, sharpsnout." The bear stood on his hind legs, his jaws dripping fish flesh and blood. The coyote backed off a ways.

"I—ah, I don't mean to cause you trouble, Mis ter Bear. But I got a thing or two I want to speak to you about.'

"Cause me trouble? You?" The bear dropped to all fours and had a short run at the coyote, who dashed into the brush near the embankment and watched warily. He emerged and announced his presence again.

"I want to ask you something, Mister Bear."

"You give me a pain in my belly, brush wolf."

"I say, can't we reach some kind of agreement as to where I hunt and you, your majesty hunt?"

"I hunts where I wants to, howler. You want to hunt where I hunt. That is your problem. I hunt where I can find food. You want to kill my food and drop it on my paws? No. You run away with my food. Coward!"

"But your majesty, I got to eat, too."

"Find your own hunting ground, sharpsnout." Clem the. bear went back to the fish, by this time almost consumed.

So much for that approach, the coyote thought. Some". how it had to be arranged that the bear would not take all the hunting ground for himself— leave a little for smaller creatures—such as his own clever self. He hit upon a plan, a brilliant bubble of inspiration.

"Mister Bear—"

"Now what's the matter witch you, noisy pokehole?"

"Did you know there's some fish in that river got fire in their tails?"

"Fire in—their tails? You silly sharpsnout.No fish has got fire in its tail, 'less it catches the sunlight just right."

"Real fire—ablazing fire—what starts camp fires and forest fires."

"I never heard of such a thing," said the bear.

"You catch another fish, you'll see." Of course, the bear doubted the word of the coyote. "I save you much pain and—bad burns and stomach distress."

"What's this—stomach distress, sharpsnout? I eat what I catch."

"Look there. I see them in the river now," sai d Massah, who looked down into an eddy where some firef i sh swam about. The bear looked, also, and his eyes and muzzle wrinkled in alarm. "Fire fish! Look there! Now you believe me? Go on—catch one. You'll see."

"I fish. I eat fish, fire and tail and all. I don't care." After delivering those heavy words, the black bear began to fish again. Meantime, the coyote ran to a campsite not far distant and deftly caught a brand from a blaze in a campfire and vanished with it smouldering bet ween his teeth. He ran back and placed it behind a big r o ck on the river bank. He then went over to the bear and began mocking him again.

"Look! You caught a fire fish, your majesty!"

"Aww, no, it's just a rainbow trout—they're call. ed."

"If you close your eyes it will catch on fire."

"Awww, no it won't."

"Go ahead. Close your eyes."

The bear did as he was told to do by the coyote, who quickly fetched up the fagot from behind the rock, puffe d on it to bring it to flame and put it to the pads of th e bear. The beast howled with pain and opened his eyes.

"You see—that fire fish set my stick on fire. Yo u believe me now?"

"Silly tramp cur, You don't fool me."

"If I were you, I'd leave that fire fish alone. G o find another that may not be burning like this one."

The bear turned back toward the river to quench the burning on his tender pads and to chomp another trout from the swift current. Meantime, the coyote tore off str i ps from the fish that Clem had caught in the river. He blew on the fagot to keep it alive and hid it once again b e-hind the rock while the bear's back was turned. In due time the bear caught another trout and placed it On the same spot.

"This is not fire fish. This is cool fish."

"You think so, eh? Close your eyes and it will turn into flame."

"Stupid brushwolf. You make fun of me. I show you it will inot burn."

"Trust me, your majesty. It is a fire fish t h at bursts into flame when it reaches the air." The bear once more shut his eyes. "Turn around or the fire fi s h can scorch the hair on your face."

The bear turned around. The coyote fetched up the smouldering stick and again blew on it to bring it to flame. He touched the heel pads of Clem, who instantaneously jumped off the ground and went loping into the woods. The re he sat down and watched from afar.

"Didn't I tell you? That fire fish has again set fire to my fire stick. They are not safe to catch and t o eat. I would not fish around here any longer. your majesty/" the coyote warned.

"If I thought you were trying to fool me—"

"Trust me, Mister Bear. You have great w i s do m, yourself. Now is it either smart or is it even safe t o fish for this kind of fish that burns your paws? It will burn out your insides like a tree in a forest fire if you try to eat one. See. The fire fish still smoulders."

The black bear edged closer, sniffed, waved his head from side to side, trying to catch a confirming look at what his poor eyes might tell him. Then he dared not come any closer.

"We have always been—friends, "said Clem.

"I know, I know. And how fortunate I have been to have such fine company. But believe me, your majesty, this is no place for a fine bear like yourself to be fishing. Up the river there are many cool fish, no fire fish. They will not burn your pads or give you stomach distress. Believe me."

"I find it hard to—still those cursed fish have burned my pads two times this very afternoon."

"Then let the nature of the fish and the life we share instruct you, 0 great bear."

"I see the sense in your words."

"Go then—and maybe I shall join you later. After all, you got to eat—and fire fish will madden you into starvation."

"I think that you speak wise words, coyote—though they are not my words."

"We are brothers in the woods, are we not, yeur majesty?"

"I go. Maybe you come later, huh?"

"Maybe. Sure, just maybe," said the coyote. Whe n Clem the black bear had ambled off into the deepening gloom of the woods, Massah the coyote gorged himself on the second of the fire fish. He quenched the smouldering fagot in a back-eddy at the water.s edge, then went about his chores for the night. This would be an especially f i ne night to howl, for it was a full moon and he could once again hunt in peace.

The Eagle's Revenge

Nimbus, the chick-eating snake, rolled his button eyes upward toward the sky where the eagle soared on the thermal updrafts. He was a very unusual snake, a snake with charm, a snake with venom to be sure, but, besides, a snake whose happiest moments he had spent in raiding the nests of birds along the river.In fact, Nimbus had once snatched the egg of a hatchling a 1-most right out from under the brood feathers of the mother eagle. She had screamed horribly in his ear-he could hear her still and sense her fury through his flickering tongue. He had a passion not yet unlocked, however, a yearning, deeply within, hotly, smouldering and driving with the pulsing throb of very life itself—a yearning to find karma, or fate, in some far off, distant bliss of peace and beautification—like that enjoyed by the eagle, for instance.

On this particular warm day, it was out of envy that the snake eyes the flight of the eagle. He knew that that great bird was the reincarnation of some lowly creature, bound to earth, like a lizard or a fox or even a badger. But having lived out its life within the orbit of its own nature, never trampling upon others, the great Spirit Force had brought it glorious transce n-dance, a meditation for the stars, a sweet somnolesc e n ce through death to the region of eternal bliss. It was while he watched the eagle gliding, soaring with effor t l e s s ease, tilting, shining its golden head in the aura of the noon sun, that he felt at one with the eagle and asp i red at that same instant to die yet to live and be reinca mated as the eagle.

The bird's sharp eyes spotted the snake below, a t the trunk of the tall lightning-shattered dead s n a g where she had built her nest, expecting that no creature could scale the slick cambrium of the dead tree and rob her of her eggs or her chicks. And yet it had happened, and as the fate of karms would have it the eagle and the snake were mutual participants locked in the tragedy of loss and the satisfaction of appetite. The eagle never forgave the snake; in her breast was created the lust for revenge. The snake never forgot the feast and the compulsion of his hunger and bloody devouring before the screeching alarm of the eagle at her empty nest.

In closer, closer, down, cuawafting of warm down current from the cool river and warm air, meeting in opposing drafts, the eagle settled into the shade. She at last came to rest on the limb of a Macabre Tree, some distance from the snake' but for each the other was clearly in view. It was the eagle who spoke first.

"I see you have returned, dread viper, cursed ven-emous thing, who devoured my young one."

"You took too much for granted, bold eagle. Yes, that was it. Up there, you thought you had security an d safety."

"You do not fool me. It was not to test my nest against marauders you ate ray little one—and just abou t to hatch. There is a dark sort of wisdom in your ambition, snake."

"You honor me, eagle—and in yours there is an air-y brightness that outshines the sun."

"Do not flatter me, accursed one. You kill-when you might have killed some other more—lowly creature."

"You kill, also, it appears to me."

"To survive, snake. That and that alone."

"Is it?"

"Do not enrage me again, snake. You are close e-nough right this moment that I could swoop down and d e-stroy you with one slice across your head."

"But you would not—or do not—because—

"It is my nature to kill for food and that alone," anguished the eagle.

"I hope so. I hope so." The casual manner of the snake was starting to infuriate the eagle, so that her head fell, she looked downward, eyeing her antagonist with the hatred of death's wish. She wanted to kill the snake, but her natural curiosity prevailed.

"Why do you come here again?" the eagle asked.

"Why?"

"That is what I said—why? To rob and kill and put to flight?"

"I come with a—purpose—no, no, not to kill, but one you can help me with, great eagle." The eagle was silent where she sat in the Macabre Tree. The snake uncoiled himself and lay outstretched on the warming ground. "Do you not see? Are your eyes so dull?" h e askedo

"Do not talk to me in riddles, snake.I have little patience with you. If you could only read m y heart you would understand the anger that burns like a forest fire within me."

"That is the matter—the—heart of the matter. You see—I have no heart."

"You have said it right that time, venemous, hateful snake. No heart—and may you never have one!"

"Hold, but hold a minute, eagle and hear me to the end. I wish to have a heart. Oh, I know i t appears impossible but then it is possible. The Great Spirit of fate, karma, the universal energy can give me a heart."

The eagle fluttered her wings. She could hardly believe what she was hearing. "A heart I You wish the spirit of life to give you a heart! Well, that is impossible. Since you are a snake and shall die a snake."

"Not—absolutely."

"What do you mean by that, snake—not absolutely?"

"I mean, if you will intercede for me, perhaps to the Great Spirit of universal life, you can arrange a karma for me."

"What blasphemy do you speak! What foolishnes s comes from your forked tongue! What pernicious hatred do you spew eut to despoil other creatures of life!"

"My yearning, 0, great eagle, is to attain to a karma of—of benevolence."

"Ingrate—destroyer! Do you mean to lie there and claim you have any right to improve upon your-your snake's existence in some better realm of life?"

"I mean all of that "and more too. I mean t o ammend this life of slithering toil and nightly rapine—though it was for food, I assure you—and in its place feel the throb of kindness for others."

"Trickster! Gargantuan, flinty, rapacious trickster with all your venom, scales and unmeasured strength! How you stretch out there on the earth. You are contemptuous of the nature spirit that creates the karma vision."

"You talk now like a raptor and not like a beau t e-ous soaring eagle."

"I talk out of wisdom, vicious snake."

"The nest—the old nest is empty. Perhaps if I could just go up there I could obtain the vision that would lift me into the world of beautiful things."

The eagle found this request quite curious a n d thought for a long moment. "How do you propose to bring about your—transmigration? You have no soul."

"Oh, but I do have a soul, an animal soul, and you shall see it fly into the heavens as the Great Spirit transmogrifics me—in the nest where, I will freely ad mi t, I made no allowance for kindness."

"Shall I grant your request then, snake?" In milence the eagle pierced the cold stare of her enemy. "Just this once—just this once." She gathered all her hatred into her breast as a fiery coal. "If the changeover fails, it will be your last chance,"

"I detect vengeance on your tongue. eagle."

"More than you know—my fury burns like a live ember within me even this moment."

"Then carry me above—up to the nest upon the to p of the snag."

"You would do well to earn your way up ". by era wling."

"It is late and—I am in dread need of satisfac—tion—of my vision of the karma."

"To become—?"

"A hawk."

"How is thatt A hawk!"

"To soar like you! To eat the small reptiles o f the earth as I once did but to share the skies with you."

"Stiffen yourself then, snake. for I am coming t o lift you into— nirvana."

The snake did as the eagle said and stiffened his form into a rod. And then the eagle snatched the viperat its midpoint and soared into the sky, up to the old ne s t atop the snag. There the snake went limp and fell into the heavy twigs and moss while the eagle perched on t he wall of her former home.

"Has the Great Spirit taken your soul now?" the e a-gle asked.

"Not yet. Not yet," the snake replied.

"Then I will hasten its capture of your life." The eagle seized the snake behind his head with her b eak, placing her great curved talons on the length of the viper. With one sharp blow she severed the head from the body. The length wiggled until it found the edge of the nest and plummeted to the ground. There it turned i n to a poisonous vine. The eagle then flung the head of t h e viper up into the heavens in her mother"s rage. And the head turned into a tarantula dragonfly, that grows its eggs in the live spider. From the soul of the snake came the life of the poisonous vine, climbing the snag andthe life of an insect that prays upon rock tarantulas.

"Let this be your karma, wicked viper!" the eagl e cried with screams of renewed rage as she heavily lif t ed off from the snag to fly into the sun.

> The capacity of animals to learn behavior i s the means for their a-daptation to new experiences and changes in the environment. Wha t mechanism establish e s the limits to that ca—pacity? Instinct, mimicry, necessity only? Or all of them in harmony.

Watch This

Saturday would be a big occasion in the village of Weedpatch, a day of carnival rides, popcorn and balloons, a time for a parade of horses and the village"s one marching band. Pie baking, spaghetti eating and beard grow—ing contests would garnish this cay townsfolk' called the "Day of the Hutch." Chicken farming was the breadwinner in Weedpatch, chickens and eggs—cockfighting was outlawed. When festivities did get under way on the appointed Saturday, an opening speech by the town's Mayor A 1-drin set the tone for the occasion: "Weedpatch is prosper ous because Weedpatch dares." There would be enough good fun to go around, with some left over for the five hu n-dred villagers who gathered between the sand dunes west of the village.

The town was located almost on the seachore. Its streets and open areas were gaudy with festooned bunt i ng and flags" The fairgrounds were to be the scene of a big event climaxing the day—an air show. The program ineluded a display of obsolete and modern aircraft and for true excitement—demonstration flights. B. B. C orney, the town"s notable buzzard, was entered in the compet i-tion. So, too, was Whistlin" Pin Feathers, the nickname for Personal Eagle—or The Bald One—who had lived in Weedpatch for many years.

There appeared on the list L.T., the Stork; Happenstance Barney, the wild turkey who had gone throu g h three wives already. And, finally, out of a sense of pride and honor and duty—Meriweather Ostrich was entered as a competitor extraordinary. He admitted privately that he had not flown in years and was a trifle rusty. An official source close to Meriweather had openly pointed out that pride egged on the big bird and had compelled him to enter in both the airflight show and aircraft display categories. His harshest critics in Weedpatch were, however, very quick to point out, when they learned of his desire, that he was dumb, o b-tuse, too blind to know his limitations, and that he was an aerial snob. But then in Weedpatch the demo c ratic spirit, parochial though it may be at times, was never snobbish.

These five Icarus-In-Flight competitors were instructed to assemble on the dunes and just stand there, behind their feathers, so that the villagers could a d-mire them in all their preened sleekness. Eagle, Turkey, Stork, Buzzard and Ostrich—the fivesome.

A balloonist by the name of Heathrow Brown woul d broadcast, in-flight, over the local radio stati on-KCCC Paduka, transmitting to Weedpatch listeners his observations from his hot-air balloon. He was to present vivid descriptions from the air of the parade route, the gathering of the villagers, the contestsgo-ing on at the fairgrounds—swooping in close for details. And, of course, he would announce the ongoing performances of the flight contest between the five aerialists.

For his demonstration flight Meriweather had s elected a stunning red scarf and conventional aviator's goggles to help him get into the role—he had forgotten to bring them.

He and the other birds now stood anxiously wai t-ing their turn to show off before the throng. The fabulous air show now lay in the hands of Adam Mahoney, a pink-cheeked Irishman whose straw hat, green ribbon down his chest and white gloves marked his official p l ac e at the starting end of the runway on the beach.

"You understand the rules of the contest?" The buzzard nodded sagely. The stork looked almost too composed. "Use the downwind strip for your takeoff"Become airborne for six minutes and then hit your soaring pattern. Glide into your landing north of here."

A general assent followed the instructions. "Remember," Barney barked, "loops and barrelrolls are out. Once you start your glide, you are not to flap your wings."Again, a general nod of assent. The eagle looked into the sun and the turkey preened his wing feathers. "FinallyiLand with your flaps up. Do not skid with your feet and avoid, avoid I say. the tricky stuff. I will score you onyour-natural grace. As for you, Ostrich, I shall have to scor e you on a pass or fail curve." Silence. "Are there any questions?" None. "Birds of flight—flex your wingst" Thisthey all did with vigor. The crowd applauded. "Step back, folks, please!"

"On my takeoff, sir, can I have a little more runway?" Ostrich asked.

"All will be treated the same." said Mahoney.

"I need more distance for my takeoff," Ostrich pro-testedo.

"There appears to be some discussion of the rules down on the starting line," Heathrow proclaimed from his balloon, as he set down his bucket near to the starting birds.

"Sir, sir—!"

"You put your money down to enter. We eannot chan g e the rules just for you," said Mahoney firmly.

"But, sir, I do not want to change the rules. I simply want more takeoff space."

"In fact. Mister Meriweather Ostrich, you should not be in this competition at all. You are not one of the Blue Angels.' Meriweather batted his eyelashes. "I just wanted you to know that."

"I can be just as spectacular,"

"What's more, you are not suited up for the flight. Where is your aviator cap and goggles?"

"I—I left them back at my hutch."

"And where are your assistants. Each of the others has helpers running last-minute errands. Well. look at th e m . A gargle of water, a quick shot of feather oil. s a n din g hair and feathers off the legs to cut wind resistance ". that sort of thing. You—you need—wing extenderstgor."

"Very funny. Okay. so I have no assistants"

"Then don't you have the brass to tell me your co a-plaints." said Mahoney, the rules enforcer.

"Gwauwkkk! Heathrow!" Meriweather called when Maho n-ey turned away to respond to the crowd. "You got a minut e to spare?"

"Can"t say as I do. I'm very busy—lots going on. I can't talk now "» I'm the only on-scene reporter." He turned down his burner flame. "What is it?"

"You wanna make a few easy bucks?"

"KCCC Paduka pays me enough. big bird—"

"I mean—big, big dolden eggs. Got one just for you."

"This broadcast is going out over the air right this minute. Don't bother me." He began to turn up his burner.

"Soon as you get about a hundred feet or so. give me a lift."

"Why you big-footed, rubberneck bag of bones. Y o u can't even get off the ground one foot."

"I can so get off the ground. Just you wait and see," said Meriweather.

"Don't talk about a hundred. Besides, there's n o such thing as a free ride."

"I'll fly up to one hundred feet and—I'll hitch a ride on your gondola."

"You silly bird! You do and I'll gut you! Hello, ladies and gentlemen. I.m talking to one of the contest-ants now. He has this crazy idea that he can fly." Han d over the microphone. "Look, Meriweather. Your idea i s not just unfair—it's illegal. The Communications and Flight Commission don't allow such things. Besides—I work alone."

"Give you a—hundred dollars if you do it."

"Want to get me fired—huh?" Heathrow looked a-round him and put one hand over his microphone. "I said-" The roar of the gas burner drowned out his voice.

"What—?" Ostrich asked.

"I said—I—think—over!" He turned up his jet and lifted off gentle into the air again.

The air show began. And—as everyone expected, Per-sonal Eagle, The Bald One. flew high in six minutes. H e soared another minute and eighteen seconds. Wings out … stretched to a full eight feet, he glided in to a perfect claw-foot landing.

"So dainty, that flier, he could"ve picked up a straw with his talons," Mahoney cooed over his crowd megaphone . Then B. B. Corney, the buzzard, matched the eagle 's high flight with blackwinged grace, his red gullet streaking ef-fortlessly through the afternoon sky.

"Some birdl A terror to any enemy," Mahoney cried over his megaphone.

L. T. Stork, though quaint and awkward, did quite well. He wobbled down the runway with his long, spindl y strides until the wind lifted under his magnificent white wings.

"That bird is a fast walker and that helps a whole lot it does," Mahoney commented. He awarded L. T. points for skimming, a special credit. "His wing action in retrofir e when he landed was phenomenal! Sure'n he can land in a chimney—and does in Europe," the official raved.

All this time the Weedpatch crowd was wild with their shouts and screams and applause and cries of "Go it, Bird! Go it, Bird!" The villagers had never before seen such a fantastic demonstration of bird flight and aerodynamic beauty. Gabbler Turkey, however, came in with low points, barely gliding to some oak trees on the far edge of the landing strip. Mahoney refused to disqualify him.

"Mister Gabbler is not used to heights. Ladies and gentlemen. He is more accustomed to the woodshed and the pot. So—we will keep him in the competition."

Great cheers greeted this decision. "He"ll get carried away in November," some wag shouted.

"I can do better than any of them birds!" said Meri-weather Ostrich, trying to sound tough.

"Yah, yah, yah,"' his critics taunted and waved their hats.

"You're real jealous because of my size," said Meri-weather to L. T. Story, who had just glided in to his perfect landing.

"Well soon see."

"Get going!" Mahoney prodded. He held his pencil poised in one hand, his bird-watcher glasses in the oth-er. "Take off!"

Meriweather flapped, ran and ran as fast as a horse. He continued to flap his stubby wings furiously, but for some reason—maybe that big meal of canned worms-he was unable to lift off the sand. Mahoney waved him ba c k to the starting line with his straw brimmer.

"What's the matter with you, dumb Bird. I thoug ht you said you could fly," Mahoney jabbed.

"I can. I can. You watch. That was just a try-out. This time it's for reali"

"Let's hope so—because the Eagle, the Buzzard and even L. T. Stork have thus far surpassed you. It'sa scandal you'll be wanting to start."

"I can fly, I can fly. I can fly. You are a cynic and a skeptic."

"I don't like liars. You fibbed to me about your qualifications. Meriweather Ostrich."

"You are not fair because you are so naive. You'd believe anything"

"I see what I see, Rubber Neck. And one thing appears clear—you can no more fly than a sack of dead bones at midnight."

"Oh, yes. I can, too. Give me clearance."

"One last chance. Hello, flight balloon. Is the runway clear?"

"It is, sir," said Heathrow, "clear and sandy,"came the bull horn from the skies.

"Meriweather Ostrich is taking off."

"Fly on, fly on!" came the voice of the balloonist in the sky."

"You hear that? Pull the foot chocks and get startr-ed," Mahoney ordered.

With a supreme effort of vigorous, wild flapping of his short wings, feathers flying into the air with every flap. Ostrich pulled out his throttle and started dow n the runway. However, run as fast as he could he could not get airborne. The crowd moaned, Mahoney shook his head in disbelief and disgust.

Then, as if intentionally, the KCCC Paduka ra d i o station balloon swept down across the path of the takeoff. Meriweather had reached zero point; there was no aborting the flight. He reached out his long neck and, as with plumber's pliers, he grabbed one of the ropes on the out-side of the gondola. Instantly the basket and the ba 1-loon, its hot air roaring, swept him off his feet. Cheers arose from the villagers down below in the bleachers, a t the starting line. They we re getting smaller and smaller. They were not aware of how he had achieved his marvelous takeoff. Meriweather held onto the rope for almost four full minutes e The balloon rose swiftly into the sky to a height of about three hundred feet.

Over the roar of the jet burner and the wind in his tiny ears, he heard the voice of Heathrow.

"You dumb bird. You don't know your own limit a-tions. Ladies and gentlemen of KCCC Paduka, good village listeners of Weedpatch. this reporter has to tell you that Meriweather Ostrich, the last contestant in to-days Flight of the Obsoletes, has just slipped his powerful bill into one of the side ropes of my gondola—a mooring rope—and he has hitched a ride with me and soare into the brilliant afternoon sky. He is tenacious. He is inventive. He has imagination, but he does not have understanding. This amazing animal—fowl is a beller word—flaps his short wings just outside my gondola. Listen. Maybe you can hear him.

"Is it cold out there, Meriweather?"

"Cawrkkkk!"

"He does not speak, radio listeners. We are over three hundred feet—would you like to let go, Meriweather?" Silence. "He does not answer, folks. You do not need to fly. Now you can soar." Meriweather 0 strich is silent. "Just let go, sir. Your courage, the speed, the absolute magnificence of it all and, yes, if we stretch our minds. folks—the dignity—"

At almost that precise moment, Meriweather did let go of the mooring rope. The balloon's roar floated away from him, and he was totally alone. He stretched his short wings, but he could feel no air-current uplift. This so astonished and alarmed him that he started running o n the air, mid-sky. But, of course, that action did not propel him as it did on the ground. He simply chu r n e d the air with his big feet while he flapped and flapped in furious panic. He then saw that he was plunging toward the ground.

"KCCC Paduka! Save me!"

He thought he heard Heathrow's mocking laughter come down from the sky. "Too late—too late. I cannot reach you, Meriweather!" The voice of the radio broadcaster faded into the afternoon blue. All that Meriweather could see was the approaching ground) the sanddunes coming up to blast him. Not even a graceful landing.

That was his last thought as, head and beak first, he plunged into the warm sand.

"Folks! Ladies and gentlemenI My bog of saints and all the holy relics preserve met We've just had a terrible accident out here on the sand dunes!" Mahoney screamed. "One of the contestants—Meriweather Ostrich—one of the competitors, the final entry, the Ostrich in today"s Flight of the Obsoletes has crashed to his death. Without mercy he plunged into the sand and to his death off to one side of the airstrip here at the show grounds.

"Cartain it was that he had tried to fool the crowd ly hanging onto the official hot-air balloon. He could not soar to safety. I saw it all through my glasses. He had to fall. He had to drop like a spent arrow into the sand.

"The crowd is rushing toward him. His leg s—I-I can't see right now—the crowd. Yes, his legs have stopped kicking. Oh, I'm afraid he is dead. His head plunged into the dune. Oh, this is horrible, horrible I A tragedy we've witnessed this afternoon. *A dark gloom has come over the festive crowd.* Without the smile of hope or the twinkle of a star to lighten it. Dead—he is gone!

"The animal medics are coming out. Sir, sir! Ther e was no flame or fire—just feathers and guts. Meriweather Ostrich tried without success to hitch a ride on the side of the official hot-air balloon—station KCCC Paduka saw it all. Ostrich let go at about three hundred feet and now he has plummeted to his death. Who knows how i t all might have been prevented? This is sad—sad. I'm afraid he is dead. I'm afraid he is dead. The brave flier scarcely knew his limitations.

"The cameramen are moving in close. This is a terrible, terrible tragedy—sure to go down in the annals o f aviation history as a disaster due to incompetence-and a big egg on the record books...."

The One That Got Away

"Poor fish!" I hear that dumb insult for so long the scales on my back are froze at D flat minor with age. And my tail fin is warped with swimming in shallows to beat the drifters—fishers who let their bait float downcurrent. What a fish consuming joke!

I now swim in the sea off-shore. I don't bang around inlets any longer or at the creeks of—mud! Too much poison bleeds from the rocks. I am a Galilean fish. The silver in my skin and fat on my ribs show I am not poor, not by a long cast.

To put the matter pure and simple, I am a mudsucker. I swim along the bottom and suck up what does not belong there in the first place—stuff like fish eggs, tadpoles in the shallow pools. dead pieces of flotsam, and once, just once, a loaf of bread some netter lost overboard.

Silly fellows! I follow the netters who cast nets for my cousins. I am also a scout and I keep a sharp watch for traps and broken nets. Not all fishers take time to mend their nets. They are lazy-or too busy with their wine flask. It is a chore for them. I know how to find the openings. I have not been caught yet. I have see pretty big fishers up through the water, throw their nets. They stand on giant legs with tiny heads and stare down at me through black eyes. They are not homunculus shadows. They try to c a t c h and kill me. I swim in the Galilee Sea a long time. I am not a fish fillet yet, or I would not be tell ing this fish life.

Let me spin this tail off and swim with it.A good rock fish put me onto their dumb joy—a sport the fishers call <u>casting</u>. Their sounds come down in the water. We hear them talk up there in their boats. They bang their oars. They shout. They slice and hack with their knifes to get us ready for market. They are crazy. I know, I know.

241

I got a friend—Blue Jazz he is a rockfin. He is eat good and his weight is close to fourteen. He always talk about the crazy fishers.

"Flash your mudsucker tail at them fishing boats. One of them will row to you with his flying net."

"Why do I want to do that—be caught, die, go to market and be eat by the giants?"

"You like to see fun?"

"I am a serious mudsucker," I say.

"Trust me—do like I say."

So I swum out from shore. A bearded fisher giant points to me. He makes big smoke with his noise and shouts. He flips his holy net into the water. It makes a hiss when it drops near me. His big arms gleam i n the sun when he leans over the side of his boat and stares down at me. His eyes are like net buoys, roun d and shiny like fish scales.

He hauls in the net.with other fishers. They catch a mudsucker or two, bluejacks, a school of scrawn-y perch, more rock fish. I get away. Those bul gi n g eyes!

"Casting is the name of their game," Blue Jazzssy to me.

"That all you want to show me?"

"Mudsucker—your life's a bore as it is.You gets joy in simple things of life. Un'erstand? Take risks! I try to lift up your fish spirits. We are all in this sea together. You got junk to learn, to joy in."

"You are one fast fish, Blue Jazz."

"Don't let the monsters scare you."

"Me? Scare? I am a mudsucker. I take on all their stuff and junk—'specting the sea floor."

I swim over to the shadow of a big rock and bang around a while. Then along comes another giant netter in his rocking boat bottom. He brings his stares from black eyes like buoys and his net that flies in the air. I see old friends destroyed by that monster. Goodbye, cousin, hello. fishfry. Off to the market in town t o dry in the sun and be salted for fisher food. It is a risky life—to be a fish. Here comes Blue Jazz.

"Trouble with you, Blue Jazz—you got no sense of responsibility."

"What you mean?" he burbles.

"You swim anywheres, any time. You eat only cripples and bugs. Your taste is all in your dorsals."

"You are choosey, mudsucker."

"At least I can tell a yellow lure from frog bait. All us mudsuckers can do that. We suck and spit, suck and spit."

"Cut it out, cleaning fish. You are a bore. A live fish is a responsible fish. Here I am, mudsucker-alive."

I cut a few curls and riffles in the water to show him I can still swim whirlppols around him.

"I "spect you can not tell a real live worm or a crawfish from a yellow lure that spins when the line drags,"' Blue Jazz insults.

"You say to me I do not know a lure in front o f my eyes."

"I am a much smarter fish than you are, mudsucker."

"See that fisher leaning on his pole. Why not go tug on his line, see what he does. I dare you." T h e rock fish obliges me ... The fisher pulls up his hook with a jerk. "You got away," say. "You truly are a smart fish."

"Wait a minute. I got away? You got that wrong, mudsucker. He got away. That's the way the sport i s played. He hooks you—you catches him! Understand?"

"No," I say.

"You catch a monster by his hook, he pulls you into his boat. You look him in the eye, gasp in his face, and he throws you back into the water."

"You are sure about that?" I burble.

"Bet my fish life on it. Just look at you. mudsucker. You are too big for a panfryer. You are too small for the marketplace. And you are too dirty for home cooking. You are a mudsucker"

"I needed that dirty hook, old friend," I says.

We swim and we swim, and around and around w e swim. I catches me a delicious wounded, wiggling min-now. Blue Jazz nudges me and stares with his eyeballs.

"What is the matter now?" I ask him.

"You really want to catch a monster?"

"I'm trying. I am looking," I say.

"Keep a sharp watch for a giant with arms like oar blades. He has a face like a hornet 's nest. His eyes will be like caves in the rocks."

"I will know him when I see him?"

"I hope so, mudsucker."

"Then just to prove that I am not a dumb fish, I will catch me a big fisher monster-and his eyes will look like caves in the rocks. He will be horrible."

"Cruise around. See that rocking boat bottom? Go try that. Act a little reckless—like you are not tending to his fishing business."

I do as I am told. This time the fisher throws a line into the water. *A* minnow dangles on it—anoth e r crippled minnow! I loves them. Just then I sees, this shiny thing on the bottom of the sea and, as you kn . w, the bottom is what gets my attention first.

"Go for it! Go for it. mudsucker! Time uou learned this lesson by heart 1" Blue Jazz i s thinking of the wounded minnow on the line. Figures I don't know what bait is all about. He swims in a tight circle to watch me get hooked—and go to market, salted.

I flash my tail and make a grab and a big gulp—not for the minnow bait but for that biny thing on the bottom.that is sparkly yellow. Blue Jazz is laugh in g through his bubbles. The line comes up with a jerk and goes whishing by me—just as that yellow thing that's too hard to spit out gets stuck in my mouth. What a trap! What a mash!

"You let that fisher monster get away," I hear Blue Jazz say. "The big fisher got away!"

But I.d got my troubles now. I could not spit out the yellow thing. It were really stuck in my mouth. Blue Jazz swims up close, eyeball to eyeball, to se e what the matter is.

"You poor fish!" There it is again, that dumb insult! "Where did you get that?"

"Bottom—" I burbled out. Talking was tough now.

"I do not believe what I see. Now whatcha goin g to do, mudsucker?"

I can not talk, so I swim around, reckless II ke to get rid of the yellow thing. The boat bottom gives a leap, and just then I feel strong currents that carry me into warm shore water, right into the sand y shallows. Blue Jazz is nowhere to be seen. I see all the old places on the bottom. I cannot eat because I can not close my mouth. Maybe I will die. I will b e belly.»up in a fish time. I see flotsam float by, crawly bits, a bug now and again. That fisher giant got away and I have only my—crippling to deal with. I am doomed.

I see a hand big as a rock dip into the water—almost breaks my ventral fins—grabs me, almost chokes me. I squirm. I thrash around. I gasp. Two homunculus fingers dig into my mouth and take out the yellow thing.What a relief 1 "Blue Jazz!" I burble out at last. He is gone somewhere—out where it is deep.

Me? I am still just a plain old mudsucker. I almost died from hunger—got a old yellow lure caught in m y mouth. You should have seen that horrible big fisher pon-ster that got away. Have to tell you about that some time—the whole story. I mean.

> The nature of an animal is keyed to its environment like a key fits into a lock. Change or remove artificially one indentation | one element| in the keyway of those natural surroundings, and the animal, like the key, becomes useless.Its kind will either die out or migrate. Rarely will it ever adapt beyond limitatations set by its species pattern. although that is proud man's obsession to justify his greed for self-accommodation. Man is so blind that he is to be pitied by a merciful God.

The Gopher And The Snake

"Dear snake, all is forgiven. Find your abode and your refuge from the great horned owl within." Having scribbled these words on a sign from an old picnic pie plate and stood it beside his burrow, the gopher ret i red to tunnel upper zero, zero—for he had numbered his tunnels—to await the passing of the snake who called himself Lothario.

Lothario was an inquisitive snake by nature. impetuous by temperament and rash by instinct. He had crossed the threshhold of Jimmy the Gopher's burrow at least twice already and had found its resident not at home. No pity for the snake, but Jimmy had smelled the presence of the obnoxious intruder and was not determined to rid himself of the viper. Jimmy was not devious, just h o n e s t with himself. He knew that Lothario would try once a—gain. With mating season just around the corner and the little ones to think about, Jimmy needed to be reassured that Lothario would not try to snatch away and des troy the babies for food. It was absolutely necessary that the snake be put out of commission, and a decapitation, if that was the means, could not come any too soon. All nature knows that he, Jimmy, had thrust this tidy morsel of thought before Igloo, the coldblooded horned owl that inhabited Mister Ramsey's old barn. But snakes are only cue dish out of many, and so Igloo had remained unmoved b y Jimmy's appeals for help. If it happened, all right, i f not—all right again.

Meantime, Jimmy the Gopher sat and peered into the morning sun. The dew arose wetly in steam from the fields of wild oats and grasse s. It was going on spring, and Lothario would need to satisfy his hunger after a rather cold winter. Always he was the hunter and the hunted. What especially irked Jimmy was that the snake did not try to find accommodations in the cheapest rentals a V round—the old barn—where rats and other varmints were plentiful. Why me? Why my burrow? The easy answer was food, squeeking little ones for the snake's famished appetite.

He thought he saw a movement in the wet grass.Sure enough) the rustle of the tall thin stalks, the distu rb-ance in the dew patterns that lay upon the leaves disclosed the presence of the snake called Lothario. H e would squirm, stop, squirm, stop. Stupid, dismal c o n-ceit, not at all deceptive. Who did he think he was fooling anyway? Jimmy pondered. The snake wove its sinuous way onward, either seeing the upended pie plate or smelling the presence of the gopher. Squirm and then stop—1 The pattern of the snake's movements marked a twisti n g swathe through the ground dew as he was obviously enjoying the morning's bath and thoughts of food and she 1 ter. About his own belly and his skin he was no dummy, the gopher mused. Presently Lothario lay quite still before the pie plate and read its lines, scratched with muddy claws, from side to side.

"Dear snake, all is forgiven," Lothario hissed as he spat out the words between his jaws and flickered his tongue to taste of their significance. Find your abode and yo ur refuge from the great horned owl within." The snake sensed a trap but, then again, he had always tried to give reassurances of his innocence, of his complete and total harmlessness. Hsssss. Why did any other animal doubt him? Was he not an honorable snake by his own measurement? He had never defrauded a soul—always h e played straight on. "Dear snake, all is forgiven".'-the words etched themselves into his snake cosciousness and sent a shiver down his length, quivering his tail and returning to his head like waves in a rope snapped in the wind.

"Such an eloquent invitation, too," he sneered, his most consuming sneer.

He moved closer, peered into the burrow"s blackness. Off at zero zero escape hatch the gopher smiled b e tween his shiny teeth and smacked his lips grandiosly. Af t er all. he was also something of a ham; he chuckled his gopher 's throaty chuckle. Two or more feet of the snake's full length eventually disappeared into the burrow b y fits and starts. A cautious snake, that one, the gopher grinned. He had taken the trouble to bait a particula r burrow tunnel with tufts of old baby-gopher.s fur, and it was the smell of that bait that was drawing Lothar i o into the burrow. Farther and farther in.

Jimmy put his ear down into the dirt and list e ned to the sounds coming through the ground, the scratching and sliding, the shoveling and slapping, as the snake in a burrow comfortably larger than itself moved eve r downward into the heart and interior of the burrow. H e kept his ear to the ground, the gopher did, a sounding device, a sure means for detecting any underground movement. He heard the watering system turn on at a distance. Lothario was moving more swiftly now. He to o k the turn at seven fork in the tunnel system and con t in-. ued on, deeper into the warming earth.

"What a deception," thought Jimmy the Gopher.

Then silence—Lothario had reached the end of the tunnel and the quest for food was ended. He had fo u n d the tufts of baby-gopher fur, was inspecting them w i th his tongue in the total blackness of the burrow, flickering, waving his head, trying the cracks and corners, the stones and grains of dirt for blood scent. But there was none. It was now Jimmy's time to act.

He hurried along the upper tunnel, his feet poun-ding on the dirt— Lothario heard him he was sure—u n-til he reached the end of the fast-lane tunnel, at the far end of the snake's body. He shoved dirt into the burrow tunnel and packed it against the walls for a t least one foot. There was absolutely no way the snake could retreat. The gopher then ran to the speak hole above the snake's head, where he knew a jar lay embedded in the ground. Peering down as he would at his babi e s, he saw the trapped snake waving his head in the act o f testing, searching for a way out.

"Smart slimy bunch of punk wood, aren't you!" i n-sulted the gopher above the snake's head. "No you don't." He shifted the glass jar over the hole to keep the snake from any sudden thrust of escape. "You came wanting t o eat my own flesh and blood, you skinny excuse for a beast, you sneaky squeeze of excrement in the home of J i mm y, the Gopher. It's your last foray, Snake. You believe everything you read. I know you. I don't forgive you nothing, Lothario, and may you rot for the worms!" Clatter, snap, the gopher screwed the lid down on the jar plug and sealed it into place with packed dirt, fixing the snake's doom. He could neither go backward nor forward, since the tunnel's dead-end had trapped him. Now he would lie forever encased like a mummy in the burrow o f Jimmy, the courageous gopher.

The little animal emerged from its burrow squeeking with laughter. He removed the sign from before his burrow and covered its message with a couple of backpitches of soft dirt. He then went to dig another for himself and his mate. who would share it with him in the spring. Too bad, he reflected, that Igloo would lose one good meal-but then that was life in the field.

> Learned behavior is the particular genius of the animal world. Instinct is its source, survival is its testing, experience is its confidence and transmission.

Interview With "Din Din" The Governor's Favorite Lion

Now this here is Brutus Piticus, taking a tip from my friend Clemens Auguste, that well-known Babylon crier. I do this scoop interview as a follow-up story o n Daniel's miraculous escape from the lions. That was one big miracle, I can tell you that! When Darius came and brought the spies, those who'd ratted on Dan'l for his praying at his window to God, when he came to the 1i on pit—the arens waiting room for the lions behind the bars—when he brought, dragged, them with their families to the pit and threw them in they were gone before they hit the bottom. So of course those lions were hungry, mighty fierce and hungry. No doubt about that.

So I come up to the bars from the arena cage d o or and I calls inside. "Din Din," are you in there?." He"s so fat and lazy from his family meal he's slow rising. But he came to the gate.

"The press wants a fuller story, 'Din Din'."

"Suits me just fine," says this favorite lion o f Gov'nor Darius. "Shoot the questions to me."

"Tell me tbis, 'Din Din, ' what were your first thoughts when you stand down here below the ground, just waiting for Dan'l to be thrown down into the pit?—the cover slides off and all them faces looking down inside? Held by his arms and legs, there was Dan'l."

"He.s sure going to be some messy baggage when he lands with all them togas wrapped "round him."

"Well, you got around that, didn't you?'

"Sure, sure," 'Din Din' said, "but I think them-a lion has got his pride of manners and his ways ab o ut him."

"Oh, that sure is true," I says to hinu "B u t what were your thoughts?"

"Well, like I say, one good bite is worth anoth-er." He laughs, .Din Din" does. "Besides, when Dan'l fall he hit Tilda on her back. She sure has got one sore back from that thump."

"Dan'l has just been tossed down like a bunch of old rags. What did you do to him them?"

"I sniff at him—and then I turns away from him."

"Turns away from him! Why is that?" I ask 'D in Din. is the gov.nor.s favorite lion.

He roars once and in a gruff voice he says to me, he says, one big favor is not same as another. What matters, he says, is taste.

I did not see through "Din Din"s' sense of humor right off. I knew for certain Dan'l never did traps e to the gov"nor.s table to eat all that rich food. He's not plump and fat like the gov"nor. Dan'l he likes his vegies, like all the other Jews the Medes capture for the palace. I don"t hit on the truth yet.

"Let me 'splain," says 'Din Din". "You see this here gov"nor, he keeps us half-starved. That's so"s he can have his fun with his emenies, at our 'spense."

"Your "spense, "Din Din"?"

"Sure, the fat of the calf"s more tasty than the skinny shins of his neighbors. They"s his emenies. You grab me?"

"Not exactly." I may.

"That Gov'nor Darius, he keeps us hungry sos we'll be a good garbage pit for His Grace when he wants to rid hisself of any emeny."

"And in this case—?"

"This case it were Dan'l." 'Din Din" let outa ferocious roar, woken the whole town and and seems mighty enough to shook stones loose in his cage.

"I see," I says. "So that's all you got t o recollect? I"m a reporter for the Gladiator Radio Station. and your words carry some bigggg weight, I can tell you that."

"Only that Dan'l didnH smell like no good meal—I tells you the truf, I couldnH touch him. Coul d n "t lay a paw on him." "Din Din" roars again. "He stunk so," says "Din Din".

"Fact that Dan"l was a dentist for the lions and other animals Gov'nor Darius keeps—he's a vet'narianthat had no .fluence on you?"

"Not at all," "Din Din" says. "He's going to push this fib off on a innocent public. But 'member that I's king of the beasts."

"Dan'l don't fib," I says. .Din Din" roar mighty loud.

"I's king of the beasts. What I says carry the weight of a king. Big king! You grab me?"

"Dan'l told it like it was—that God save him."

"Dan'l stunk so I couldn" open my mouf.'

"You see no angel in there?"

"Angel! Is you crazy, man? He stunk, that Dan. I did. There wasn't no angel in there atall. What's the matter wi f you?"

"I don't .spect you to believe me. And anyways, 1 un"erstand everything. Yes, you are king of the beasts." "Din Din. roar mighty loud again. "And you don't always tell the truth."

"Just maybe you don't write the truf. Even your hand shakes now."

"Anyway—1 got to go now. It is a pleasure talking to you, King of the Beasts. You got anything that I ought to say to Dan'l?"

"You jus" tell him he's mighty lucky he get off as good as he done— because he would be white bones if h e hadn't turn into a real nasty lump— here in my own den. You tell him that."

"I will—then he was repulsive?"

"He were mighty repulsive." With this closing statement 'Din Din" roared and he roared and then he moseyed away| back to his small, dark corner where he yawned. I heard him—then he settled down to a long nap.

I told the Babylon folks this story on Gladiator Radio, and I also ran it in "The Daily Scroll"—as it was a sensation, I can tell you that—a sensation!

The Animal Opera

Opera season was coining and in the village of Anni-mopolis the music lovers, the <u>grand dames</u>, the professors, singers, composers and just plain listeners—in fact, any-one who enjoyed watching opera, would have to select. Bmbers for the troupe that was to perform in the se a s oh" s productions. "The Greenroom Bla," a gaudy tabloid pres s sheet designed and printed in an afficionado's rhudabega storage basement, listed the works under considerati o n: "The Unfaithful Cat," a tragedy in one mad act carried over into the next night; "The Sheepshearer of Winnipeg,"an awsome piece said to represent the worst in imitative opera; "The Ring and the Wolves," a Germanic folk piece o f no consequence that harked back to the days of wolves i n Europe and that called for an ambitiously fat fern a 1 e howler to sing the lead role; finally. "Timmy and Tammy," a lovely romance about a spendthrift magician who was a heavy borrower from his god of stuff. These were d e-scribed as "all taxing roles" by the industry's Rhudebega Basement Press.

"Let us hope that it is the demands of the roles and not the patrons of the opera who are taxed by the performance," sighed the dank "Bla."

For the purpose of promoting the season's fare, a brief article also appeared in the village's "The Daily Nuance" summoning any with suitable talents in singing and acting to report for an audition. On the Friday night following. Sir Bat Wing, a furry flying beast who wrote clever criticism for the village paper, stood alongside o f Conductor Sir Cedrick J. Whipster. It was often said that he handled his baton like a French duelist.s rapier, d i s-patching the shouters and the screamers and disposing of the musically inept with his pointed musicological thrusts. The guests for the night at the Golden Barn theater in Ann i-mopolis came early, eagerly and with great impatience signed in on the alfalfa bales laid end to end at the door to the barn.

The kerosene lanterns were lit along the edge of the proscenium. Displays of photographs from past se a s o n s papered the walls of the exotic Golden Barn, converting its obvious purposes of storage into a thrilling spectacle o f shimmering beams and rafters and fluted columns of hay. All was in readiness, with villagers and the critics of animal opera assembled in a rich and lavish conclave of sweetly perfumed bodies and well-oiled fur coats, ready to flex their critical muscles and sensitivities. This promised to be a gala night.

First in line, standing impatiently in the wings amid dropped secrets and whispered condolences was Billy, the elephant. His enormous ivory tusks, suggesting carefully-d e-lineated piano keys—thanks to the makeup department-, impressed the surging audience and frightened the timid ones. They had the appearance of dully-flashing arpeggios in the wan and flickering light of the kerosene lante rns, Billy was ready. He pressed through the crowd in the wings, which had formerly housed rusting farm machinery, and amb l e d graciously to the front of the stage. Standing there b e-fore the wavering light, his corpulence promised to r e-gale the audience with a performance of immense music o l o-gical proportions.

For the audition he sang three bars of the trumpe t passage in "The Unfaithful Cat," where the feline is r e-turning to her lord's castle, in Act I, and is announc e d with a blast of alto trumpets. Billy could not quite hit alto, but his effort was remarkable. He gave forth with a mighty blast—a trumpet aria, as it were—from his trunk. In his impassioned performance he swung his elongated nose about so blandly that he knocked off Sir Whipster's toupe, and disarranged the village ladies of station—they who were lapping up the milk of human kindness in one corner of the barn. Sir Bat Wing managed, amidst the hustle, to convey to Director Whipster that Billy had "earned a 'C' for his performance. He was a tweezle too loud," Sir Wing i a said to have remarked, "and not altogether in key for the part."

"Yet he is capable of moving an audience," said Sir Whipster. "Those ivories are most impressive. I shall recommend—modulation—to his trainer—with a cold bath."

"A suitable, a very suitable proposal," said Sir Bat Wing. The conductor motioned for the next candidate to appear on-stage. The figure who emerged was none other, happily, than Monsieur Hyena from the Arpeggio Lyceum in Paris. Long bred to zoo life, he considered himself quite well trained. He had, in fact, taken singing lessons from a female hyena in the cage beyond his own wire screen. His was the—"carefully cultured voice," reported "The Daily Nuance" the following day. M. Le Hyena was prepared with a few measures adapted from "Ringamarole," the fantasia op-era from the Deadlands of Western America, a New World piece. Sir Whipster, it appeared, was quietly agitated by the contestant's .election of music. He would have preferred that the auditioners chose from the season's four productions. But—here he was.

All of his teeth showing with meaningful insouciance M. Le Hyena sang the chosen Aria of Conquest. He did so, Sir Wing commented later, with a light, frothy gaiety that titillated and amused his equally lighthearted audience of devotees. Heeehee, heeheeeheee! Up and down the scale he ran until Sir Whipster, fairly out of br eat h, thrust at him with his baton, catching M. Le Hyena sharply in the flanks. He then brought the butt of his baton, which concealed a lead weight, down upon the cedar stump that served as his podium. All devotees, patrons and mu-sic lovers within the enormous gilded interior of the Golden Barn, from the flickering kerosene lanterns on the apron to the enormous dancing shadows at the back—all were deathly still.

M. Le Hyena merely smiled. The ovation was turnu1-tuous. He beamed upon all the village females whose screems rose up b e fore him. He bowed deeply. He tro tted ami a-bly off the stage, his short back legs displaying the finest of bootery. He was a thrilling hopeful for the season and needed only fresh meat to quicken his rich voice "Sir Whipster and Sir Bat Wing exchanged excited whispers.

Almost unannounced came Mine. La Duck. Her shar p warning preceded her imminent waddling appearance—a true quackery. She needed but little tuning up. Acappello, with only chatter and jabber to furnish the background accompaniment, she sang the opening stanzas from "The Sheepshear-er of Winnipeg." However everyone with any taste and s a-voire faire in the opera knew from the first moment she o p ened her bill that she could not fit into any part with felicity and ease. The matter was not that she was-small with flat feet and made herself hard to under s tand. It was simply that Mme. La Duck had no voice at all. I f the good folks of Annimopolis village were to enjoy th e ir season of operas, they had to select—for their consummate enjoyment—only the most eloquent, the most lofty, soaring and silvery voices in the musical world. B u t this—!

Sir Whipster had forewarned and instructed her t o sing but five bars from "Wet Night," a drizzling opera by a Ge r in an composer. When she began her musical limitations were all too apparent. She sang the quack, quack and quack suitably well but missed the quarter notes and failed to stay on key. Mme. La Duck, also, was very angry and in consequence thereof she made out as if to bite the conductor and Sir Bat Wing amid a great scatter ing of her feathers in the air. The down of vengeance settled upon the backs of the gathered audience. Sir Whipster did not demolish her entirely.

"Mme. La Duck," he addressed her with an air o f elegant disdain, "I shall have to hold you in reserve."

"Quack—a thought to treasure."

"Yes—with Thanksgiving," he said under his breath.

A long and insinuating silence fell upon the crowd of notable critics and entrepreneurs of the musical world. The furor Mme. La Duck's performance had aroused did not dissipate at once. The silence was provocative, for i n that discreet interval onto the stage walked the stately and regal Ms. Winifred Over street. She had been much touted by the Rhudabega press and mentioned often in"The Daily Nuance." It was she pundits said who could hit a high "C". She was a giraffe, but nobody laughed her lovely voice so mesmerized her fans. Each note was agenuine pearl that rolled off her stained teeth and black tongue.

She took the stage as if she owned it—such pro-fessional patina, such stage arrogance! When the orchestra composed of squirre ls, toads and blue jays sounded the opening notes in "The Cat Opera," Mile Overstree t stripped a generous mouthful of leaves from the libre t-to, grinding her teeth in the low passages and m a k ing her dulcet voice bairly audible to the first row in the hay loft. Sir Whipster had cunningly placed his o w n musical scout up there, and bade him open the applause-which reached the intensity and volume of thunder.

"Magnifique!" the directorsaidand was soon joined b y all who were truly sensitive to French subtlety. H e clapped for the first violin, a country dog with a hind-leg fiddle. When the applause faded, the giraffe repeated the closing refrain of her selection. Sir Whipster bent forward, listening to the sinewy quality of Ms.Over-street's rhapsodic voice. For the encore, he took her into the flat stretches of "The Ring and the Wolves?!Act II, Scene i, —where the wolf fancier makes off with the mold possessed by the wicked buttonmaker. It was he, of course. who had fashioned the dazzling magic gold ring. Ms. Overstreet shed a perceptible tear in this passage, proving to Sir Whipster she could emote properly.

"Such poise! Such grace!" Sir Bat Wing whispered in the conductor's ear.

"Yes. Did you see her charmante, her elegance, her elan jolie as she moved her head among the rafters and rope s with rare great ease? She is so—natural."

Other singers appeared before the footlight lant e r n s and the stabled gathering. They performed, sang, emoted and comported themselves with greater or lesser skill and noise. The night was filled with the music of the anima ls. "The Daily Nuance" reported the event seemingly without the omission of a single program note or informed observation. A squib in the Rhudabega press stated that—"where music lovers are gathered together the whole world congregates." The editors included a few of its customary dank observations as incentives to village patrons.

However, there arrived those nights when all operas are cast in full. The entire village of Anniroapolis was i n-volved. Kindled enthusiasms flew skyward with the embers of bonfires and a lavishly festive atmosphere abetted by village decor and <u>expression</u>. The eager use of paint pots, the quixotic scenery construction, the rehearsals and oth e r tasks related to production went on for the next sever a 1 months.until, finally, the last night of rehearsals arrived. Naturally, the villagers and the cast of the opening production were on "pins and needles" a quote from the "Nuance."A palpable uneasiness hovered over the Golden Barn lest any one of the animals lose its temper, walk into the pastur e, and thereby scuttle the night's performance.

The exchange of confidences behind the scenes is al-ways in vogue. "The Daily Nuance" did, in fact. report one such encounte r, a scathing confrontation of temperament s, talent and jealousies. According to the reporter's story.before opening-night curtain, M. Tosca Lupin. the domesticated wolf, had gotten into a fight with Mme. Ullienne Hypomelita, whose voice is as rich. heavy and round as her figure. It seems, though. that M. Lupin made some cutting remarks about her figure and the innuendo struck a sensitive nerve in Mme. Hypomelita's generous being. At the very moment of open combat stage hands gathered around as did other members of the cast, a few outsiders among them, and so pre vented any blood from flowing. If Mme. Hypomelita had any hair on her head, Tosca would surely have pulled it in clenched teeth. W i t rout long ears, Tosco the wolf missed having his boxed b y Mme. Ullienne.s fat lip. She is justifiably proud of her voice, whether in or out of water. and it is too bad tha t M. Lupin could not restrain his artistic feelings.

After their exchange of verbal abuse, the crowd separated them and thereafter, on and off the set, the wolf sniffed with his nose and Mme. Hypomelita snubbed him with casual insolence. Such are the temperamental quirks of the divinely gifted.

Sir Bat Wing, critic <u>extraordinaire</u>, in fine f e ttle with his pen, reported the opera scene in "The Daily Nu-ance" with a consummate skill and enthusiasm. The cast looked gorgeous in their native costumes. The night was bright and gaudy and hypnotic to all. A circus retinue of leopards and other cats sat in the upper hay loft, havin g tendered general admission. The cultivated and train ed animals were entrenched in the pit, below the lanterns. A brief quote from the "Nuance" review might help to fill in certain details of the night.s fare.

> "You never heard such howling and yelping as when Mme. Hypomelita came on-stage in Act III, Scene i, of "The Ring and the Wolves". Her voice throbbing with emotion, she

sang until the rafters in the old Golden Barn echoed with her dulcet notes. Such a voic e will never be heard again. Of course the stage manager had been instructed to drench her with a tub of water, since she sang e-v e r so much more sweetly when dripping wet. Improvement on that impeccable voice is hard to envision.

Then M. Lupin, who had been finally cast, though with some open misgivings by t h e director, Sir Whipster. played the part o f the gay lothario with keen sensitivity. What his howl lacked he made up for in the frisky way that he danced around the urn maid … ens and bade the magician turn him into a handsome hero. Since he is only a common, ordinary. forest-variety timber wolf. and a rather scrawny one at that, such a met a-morphosis would have been hard to imagine. But then almost anything can be accompli shed with scenery, greasepot makeup a nd lights."

Of course with this quality of opening-night performance. the opera season in Annimapolis gave seductive promise of being a great success. The magic before the stabled throng had its rough places—pacing was slow. line pick-ups dragged—but in the main there was nothing of any great momen t to upset its sponsors, who are zoo specialists. We are forbidden to mention their names here. Newspapers elsewhere picked up on the story and carried glowing reports on the ingenuity. the extravagance, the informed imagination and brilliance of such masterful work. The Golden Barn opera season will be the rave of critics everywhere, it hereby predicted "The patrons had found in the performances of the animals much to praise and little to condemn.

Before departing from this brief accolade to the village opera theater at Annimapolis, this commentator draws attention to a program note o n t h e cultura lly-enriching evening. Appearing in "The Daily Nuance," next to an ad for Ready Hay and Tack, were these words:

"Who forgot and left the gate open? A pasture-full of cows walked into the Gold e n Barn on opening night, possibly thinki n g they were home at last. Behind them came the milking hands from the neighboring faxtn. Could it be that village opera attracts e-ven ordinary cows and the likeable denizens of the milking stool?"

Wild Dog's Last Hunt

"Look, Snapping Jaws, you want to stay in business you kick in with a part of your fresh meat kill." Yellow Hook, the bald eagle, was confronting the coyote from a safe distance, his talons clutched around a high limb i n a cottonwood tree.

"I don't need you, Balding One."

"Yellow Hook." The eagle demanded respect from the coyote.

"What I don't eat of my sheep kill the buzzards can have. They're you're smelly dead-meat cousins anyway."

"Smart—wild dog. Just heed my words, coyote.I. m working this here territory."

"There's plenty of sheep around. Go get your own. Isn't lamb your specialty dish?" With those hot words of disdain the coyote went dogging down the mountain trail.

A week later the same inciteful, cutting words broke out between the eagle and the coyote. This time the e a-gle sensed a weakness in the spirit of the coyote.

"Tell you what, Snapping Jaws."

"Oowwwwwwl What? My time"s worth a scent or two."

"Tell me," said the Eagle.

"Go chase a mouse," the coyote replied.

"How"d you like to become a warrior hero of the mountain?"

Come on, big bird, what's the trick? I haven't muzzled a good bloody meal in three days."

"Every time you haul down a lamb I'll make sure you count coup with Brown Feather, god of the eagle. After all you are a mighty hunter-warrior. I got nothing but admiration for you. Me? I pick at my food. Mice, gophers, small game.

"Sounds tempting but I smell a trap." However, the coyote strutted about for a moment showing off. "Still I don't need recognition from the gods. I need protection."'

"Who from?" the eagle asked, cocking her head to o n e side out of curiosity.

"From hunters and those wild-eyed city coots."

"Gh, well, you're going about things wrong. You think they're shooting at you. Intimidating—but you'll starve. You got to change your strategy."

"Like what?"

"Let'm shoot at you—most of them canU hit a mud puddle after a rain storm."

"They've already hung a rap on me for a killing spree," said the coyote.

"So—I'll be y o ur decoy. I finger a lamb, you snuff it out and we split the profits."

"You mean those wild-eyed coots won't blame me—farmers the same?"

"NooooOo You didn't know that?" The eagle pretended surprise as she dipped a sip from the creek. She hopp ed down to a lower limb in the cottonwood and became more confidential. "That boom-boom gang won't touch you."

"Say's you," said a dubious Snapping Jaws.

"They'll come looking into the sky for me. I'm th e thief of the sheep pen. Truth is, yo u're a warrior, Wild Dog. You clamp those mighty slobbering jaws down on the throat of one of those lambs and I heist it into the woods . It makes sense for you to be so secret—no blood or wool, no tracks. Fact is—come here. Let me tell you s o m e-thing, bright eyes. No, I think I'll save it."

"Tell me. Tell me," the coyote begged.

'You'll get your protection from the god Brown Feath-er, mighty warrior." Yellow Hook flew away, high into the cloudless sky. Snapping Jaws now quivered with eager curiosity. What did all this eagle talk mean? Maybe that bald bunch of feathers was up to some kind of trick.

That very night the coyote stole a lamb and butchered it with his jaws on the fringe of a nearby wood. He had cut its throat so that it could not bleat. The next morning the eagle took her portion, but warned Snapping Jaws to stick to the strategy—let her airlift the carcass. Yellow Hook prayed to the god of the eagle, Brown Feather, for help and mercy in war against the mighty Two-Leggeds. Circling high above her nest atop a cedar snag, she heard their thunder-. sticks.

"You will do this for me," the eagle spoke to the god in the sky. "Hang a dried sheepskin on the fence every time Snapping Jaws kills a lamb."

"I will do what you ask of me," said Brown Feather, the spirit god of the eagle clan.

"Stretch it and hang it on the barbed wire of the two-legged animals. I will do this to save you."

"For my hatchling—if it should fall. The jaws o f the coyote are always eager for blood."

"The chick, is it not small?" the god asked.

"Lambs are not always in the pasture, and when the wild dog goes hungry for days, any game flesh is tasty. I search wide and far, but I fly too high for the hunters."

"I will defend the eagle spirit by granting your request," said Chief Brown Feather.

Snapping Jaws once again made off with a suckling lamb and, severing its life with bloody teeth, gorged himse If. When the spirit god hung a stretched sheepskin on the w i re fence Yellow Hook thought that this time he would not scold the wild dog. Loud thunder from a distance told the eagle that the white farmer was shooting into the sky—perh a p s at a buzzard or at several buzzards that had come to devour the remains of the sheep's carcass. All was going 1 i k e smoothness in the air.

He spotted the coyote seated on a flat rock below and he glided in and settled on an adjacent rock. "You see all those sheepskins on the fence? That's real glory for you, warrior coyote. You have counted coup like the Indians do."

"I am contented with my kills."

"You have butchered a real cache of food, wild dog warrior. You have earned my respect and admiration," the eagle lauded.

"But why—" the coyote asked slyly.

"The Boom-Boom Coots will thunder at me with t h e ir fire sticks until the end of the world. Their hatred o f me is petrified. I cannot lift a lamb off the ground-t oo heavy. So gnaw and gorge, wild dog."

"Mighty kind of you, bald eagle."

The eagle was very shrewd and crafty. She knew that the coyote would not be hungry to touch her hatchlings i f he had a full belly. She had known that from the start and now it was time for flight lessons" She had diminished the odds against her.

This ruse went on for months until, finally, ten or fifteen sheepskins showed stretched out on the fences of the white farmer" The spread of sheepskins looked to Yellow Hook like the work of an act of vengeance, yet he knew that it was the spirit god of the eagle, Chief Brown Feather | who was posting those skins on the wire fence. Brown Feather was keeping his promise. And Yellow Hook was contented with his trick on the coyote" The danger was a 1-most passed. Snapping Jaws never tired of gorging him-self, growing sleek and fat, while the eagle continued to play the decoy in the sky.

Then one night an incident occurred that brought sadness to the eagle. Confident of his skill, Snapping Jaws was no longer ready for battle when he entered the pa s-ture. He searched for his next food. Yellow Beak had failed to show him where to attack. He had become tood e-pendent upon the great bird in the sky.

In the distance he heard running paws, then he hear d panting sounds. Two huge sheep, the sire and the ewe, were loping toward him as if to defend their lamb. The coyote at once abandoned the hunt and ran to a corner of the pas-ture. But the big sheep ran very fast. They ran even faster than he did and they cornered him at one end of the field.

They did not look like sheep when they came up closa. His eyesight was poor. Their legs had claws and their jaws were sharp muzzles, not the blunt noses of sheep. They also had tails. His nose now identified the kindred c a-nines.

"We gotcha now, you cursed thief. Our master has sent us out here to kill you for killing his lambs."

"No. no, no—you got the wrong evildoer."

"We can smell sheep all over you."

"You are—dogs—in the clothing of sheep. I—I did not put those skins on the fence." Of course Snappi n g Jaws did not know that Chief Brown Feather. the e a g l e spirit, had done this.

"We will put yours on the fence." Those were the last words that the coyote heard. They mauled him, cut his throat with their sharp fangs, and between them they dragged the coyote's carcass to the white man's hogan.

"You have done well, my slave dogs," he praised th enu "I shall keep all those sheepskins for my own use.At least that greedy wild dog will not have his total victory.I suspected the eagle for this crime when all the time the coyote was the marauder."

Just then Yellow Hook settled on a wooden rail out-side the hogan door. "When I fly high it will not be to escape your firestick, Foolish One. I see better from a great distance."

The bald eagle took off in his heavy, slow way and soon was soaring high over the hills. The two-legged animal spat fire at him and missed. That night Chief Brown Feather had his helper-spirits remove all the sheepskins stretched over the farmer's fences. He was possessed of wisdom and kindness and was able to grieve over any loss of life| even when it was for food.

> Among most animals there is an apparent hierach y of "values|" as it were. First comes the ere a-ture's own survival, then the offspring, fina 1 ly, loyalty to humans. N a-ture has given her creatures the instinct to acquire for survival, not for pride. The order can vary.

The Hard-shell Tortoise And The Soft-back Toad

"As a conservative, sir, I'd like to make my position clear."

"The Hard-shell Tortoise from Sandy Rock has the floor."

"As you all well know, we have fought a downhill fight to recover the green grasses of the scorched land and r e-plant the once-flourishing pine trees. And we will continue to fight for legislation that protects the wilderness."

Shouts of "there! there!" and "huzzah! buzzah!" filled the hall of Congress.

"Here, here!" came the voice from the speaker's podium and the gavel rapped loudly.

"I propose, as a Hard-shell tortoise, that we make it an offense for anyone to pick up a pine cone from the floor of the forest."

"There goes your gnawings, Squirrley," a voice clamored.

"What has that to do with conservation. Congressman Tortoise?" Congressman Chipmunk squeeked. "Pinecones are useless by and large."

"Make them profitable and they will be worth gold, Congressman Monk. Gold! Gold! Gold!" boomed a conservative.

"A delectable idea," said Rep. Tortoise, sticking out his tongue to nibble at some asparagus shoots. "It has lots to do with a cautious, scrutinizing, flat-bellied, slow-moving conservation of nature that curbs colossal waste and and wanton neglect" "Cries of approval again flooded the hall. "It is fine if a camper wishes to start a fire.His smoke can be seen for miles. There is no deception there, but to pocket a pine cone—now there is a crime that deserves jail."

263

The gallery crowd noises and shouts now rose up to the plaster flowers in the ceiling. "Here! Here!" Chairman Squirrel knocked again, gnawing like a buzz saw on a ripe pinecone at his desk.

"I challenge your new bill, Congressman Tortoise, "decried the hoarse voice of Representative Toad from a-cross the aisle. Cautiously, lazily he closed his eyes and opened them again, looking self-satisfied. He hopped about on his big feet, scanning the bill of legislation. "I find—ribbet, ribbet—that water is a more pressing matter. Liquid assets. gentlemen."

"Oh, I understand well. Congressman Toad, but i s that not your personal preference?" Rep. Tortoise cajoled. "After all, where would you be without water?"

"Where would any of us be without water, Congressman Tortoise? Furthermore—and I see this as a weakness in other bills you have introduced, a weakness that shrouds foresight like a boat in the water without a bottom— a weakness, I say. Harrumpf—where was I?"

"Verily, you we re on the point of a weakness, sir," Chairman Squirrel piped up.

"Yes, well—you are so slow to come to anywise conclusion," Mister Tortoise.

"Whereas you hop to conclusions based solely on your feelings."

"At least I have feelings," responded Congre ssman Toad.

"Yes, cold and slimy—" They arose to do combat, Rep. Toad spit and Tortoise hissed softly.

"Gentlemen, gentlemen, we are getting nowhere,"said Chairman Squirrel, who now sat munching upon pine seeds and filling his cheeks with bagged acorns. "We must get something useful passed."

"Then I propose, Chairman Squirrel, that we try our skills in the water." Representative Tortoise was speaking. "We are both adept in it. We shall go to the Pond of Endless Caucus, nearby to the Capital, and there w e shall hold a contest, fair and open for all to see."

"You ought to try your skills in the wash tub, Congressman Toad— scrub them clean of corruption." H e looked pleased with his wit. "You are incapable of originating good laws."

"Whilest your hard shell re sists all reasonable honesty," Toad spat out in his fury.

"Does it now?" Tortoise cried.

"Here, here!" scolded Chairman Squirrel in a shrill and chattering voice.

"Then let's get on with it. I challenge you to a duel to see who can go under the water and make it from one end of the Caucus pool to the other and back," Rep. Tortoise wheezed. "I shall swim under the water—my true forte.

"Chose your means, gourd-brain. Under water—what a catastrophic, silly notion!" said Toad.

"You know very well, sir, that I can disappear and not show up for days."

"Yes—I've seen your performance on important bills in the House—like a clock tower for the White house—at nine, a bourbon with the Southern delegation, music and tea at three and for the mid-afternoon a safety net at the Circus Room for the caucus jitters. All done with the consumate skill of your absentee vote. You do have the capacity to submerge indefinitely, Representative Tortoise."

"Let me make one thing perfectly clear. Mister Toad: I pay my dues. You, however, on the bill that would outlaw de-flagillating flat leaves, you reneged. On the bill to sequester gophers until summer you backed down, changed your vote. On the powerful legislation to help poor gardeners with cutworm eradication, you played possum. Quite frankly, sir, I don't believe a thing you say."

After that exchanged barrage of angry accusat i ons, all of which Mister Owl, the Congressional reporter scribbled down assiduously, Representative Toad hopped upon the back of Tortoise and they ambled around the room for a brief time—until Chairman Squirrel called a halt t o their antics.

"You don't dare to try that the other way around,"Toad flung at Tortoise,

"No, I might crush you with my weighty argument if I did," the hard-shell politician replied.

"Then we have it settled. Tomorrow, gentlemen, Congressmen-it is a day for labor. And so we shall a d-journ to the Pond of Endless Caucus and there hold a contest of endurance, stamina, strength and—speed."

Great huzzahs erupted from the other Congressmen . Their wild clamor and competitive fervor over the duel to come shimmered the cut-glass chandeliers and vibrated the window draperies. It was a scene of pandemonium, underlain by an issue of the most profound seriousness. Re-solved, that either pine cone theft or water conservation shall occupy the minds of the House in the months to come.

"Now you understand the rules of the contest?" said House Leader Squirrel when the other Congressmen had assembled on the bank of the Pool of Endless Caucus. "The test is not to see who can stay under the longest but who can reach the other bank and return the quickest. Bank is the buzz word. Do both of you fine specimens understand?"

"Whoever wins this contest of physical guts and ruthless stamina wins for his legislation?" the Torto i se affirmed.

"Precisely," Chairman Squirrel whistled through his fine little teeth as he popped another nut shell. Some pretty tortoises. waving their "STATUS QUO, WO" leaf banners smiled from the pond bank and quietly cropped on the lawn grass. Nearby, a whole mess of liberal toads hopped about with great glee, holding their caucus out of earshot.

"We understand," said Rep Toad at length. "Hibbet I Ribbetf Ribbetl" he bellied, with throat tremblings a nd wheezes of pleasure, toward his supporters.

Both contestants, with a waddle, drag and a hop, drew up to the edge of the pond. It was plain that hardshell Tortoise and soft-back Toad were well matched for this official marathon and duel over pinecone theft versus water conservation. It had been a difficult matter to decide upon.

Rep. Toad and Rep. Tortoise plunged in, distorting the reflection of Congressional bunting in the water.Each Representative cut fine, circular patterns in the still pond water as they struck out for the opposite shore. Yet Tortoise was much more adept at hiding what he was up to . Long practice at this had evolved his shell—a million years in the House, if that could be imagined. He was tough, a prehistoric vanguard. He chose, therefore, t o swim under the water's surface. Congressman Toad, known for his broad, fine, distinguished strokes of wisdom, chose the surface of the pond. His beady eyes and streamlined forehead cut a swathe. From long use he knew the value of oleaginous and frictionless effort.

Both swam until they were almost out of sight fro m the starting bank. Of course every stroke was costi n g the taxpayers money, but let ambition measure its heroes. They swam and turned around and entered on the return lap.

"Go! Go! Go!" came the cries from the crowd of rooting Toads and shuffling tortoises on the shore. When-look sharp—a deathly silence fell upon the assembla ge. Had he drowned? Would the Congress have to drag his lifeless body from the Caucus Pond? The Honorable Tortoi s e was not in sight, not by a ripple or shadow or the t i ck .» ing clock. He was an underwater representative, but what of that. Many mystery fish swam beneath the surface in Congress. Clever, clever fellow—the astute Congressman that he was, he had simply refused to show any emotion, an-y clue or hint or giveaway as to where his real sentiments and efforts lay. He was—was he gone? Would the obituary columns in the dailies carry the banner story that Representative H. Tortoise from Sandy Rock died yesterday in the Caucus Pond?

Unknown to any party on the shore, the hard-s hell had engaged the services of a Conveyer—a cheap, shoddy device| the well-known lobbyist who called himself a Blue Gill—after the stock he peddled on the Hill. It was he who had said to Rep. Tortoise, "Grab onto my tail with your horny beak and I'll skid you through the water." None of us learned this until long afterward.

"Will not this cost me something?" he had as k e d Blue Gill, sleek and powerful.

"It surely will—but we"ll settle on that when you win. Return the favor, as it were." The old contingency play, a lawyer.s trick. Folks called this type a lobbyist—he was so unctuous and cooperative and desirous that Congressman Tortoise win the race. As a matter of fact, that is exactly what did happen. When Rep. Tortoise had almost reached the home shore again, he let go of the tail of the Blue Gill and swam to the surface of the pond. Deafening shouts of commendation, of applause and tearful rejoicing greeted him. J. BraxtonMid-dleton Owl, Congressional scribe, with his pen in hand, flew in to interview him and to write the story for the Congressional Record. It had all happened with such-breathtaking slowness and giddy surprise.

"You won! You won! Honorable Tortoise," Mister Owl exclaimed. Just abo ut then Rep. Toad came swimming in, his bulging eyes and fine head, his powerful brea s t strokes visible to the crowd. He was puffing might ily. His cheeks were swollen with intense exertion. H e was about to collapse on the bank of Caucus Pond.

"You cheated! You cheated!" Rep. Toad wheezed accompanied by loud ribbet! ribbet! ribbet!. He spat at Rep. Tortoise.

"I played fair and honest," Tortoise proclaimed.

"You couldnH have been that fast. Some t h ing smells rotten in the Caucus Pond.

"Let me see if I am right," said Owl, the reporter. "Representative Toad alleges that you cheated, but I saw the whole contest by myself and so I am qualified to write about it. Official sources will say you could not cheat. Is it not true, Representative Tortoise, that mud a nd weeds and murky water blocked your way?"

"They did. They did. You may quote this well-informed official that, .The Toad does not have a leg to stand on."

"Ribbet! Ribbet! Ribbet!" Rep. Toad expired, still out of breath.

"I shall sue Congressman Toad—as a private entity if he makes one more false accusation."

"Gentlemen, let us not be reckless in our assumptions. It is clear to all— except our esteemed Congressional r e-porter Owl—that the Honorable Toad has won. Water will be the issue in the next Congress" Pine cone legislation must go to Fiscal for a review. Is that clear, Mister Tortoise, Mister Toad?" chairman Squirrel chittered with solemn voice and pontifical look about him.

"Whatever my opponent says is a bunch of slimy lies," Representative Tortoise hissed in shrill puffs of prehistoric anger.

"You phoney hard-shell bigot, you lummox, you slot-witted representative of the dinosaur age. You do us all an injustice. You are about as enlightened as—as your attic," croaked Toad.

"Get off my back!" While the assembly of toads w a s hopping mad, the bevy of tortoises pulled in their necks and legs and turned into paving stones, able Representatives o f the Lower House.

"Ribbet, ribbet," said Congressman Toad, gather ing strength again. "We shall deal with water. You always did show a wicked mind. Mister Tortoise. Devious in the caucus, belligerant on the floor, recessive in your alliances."

"Why you intellectual rock-hopping grotesqueriej You splay-legged aspirant to tree flight/ You spendthrift of the well-lilypadded bankers!" Tortoise could not find words adequate to express his contempt.

"I still don't see how you came up first—unless there was skullduggery," Rep. Toad said quietly as his frien d s gathered around him to share their slime.

"Yes, and I heard about your vast h oldings," the tortoise said, his voice calm once again.

"Better my vegetation than your sandhills, Represen-tative Tortoise. After all, who can build a gambling casin o in a swamp? I am disqualifying you, Congressman Tortoi s e, ex _officio_."

"Why?"

"Because I have watched you pull off other stunts while I've been in the House. Your reputation follows you about, sir—follows you about. Out under the hot sun is whe r e you can show your best aptitudes—for concealment—not in the House of Representatives."

"Sir—sir, are you forgetting that I am an endangered species? Huh? Answer me that."

"YouI Endangere d!" xroaked Toad with a spit a yard long. "Your kind's so numerous we could turn the for est floor into parquet tiles with your backs and still have t o o many left over."

"Insulting insolence!"

"Gentlemen, gentlemen! We shall have to wait for the voters to decide the real outcome, no matter what this contest shows, no matter what our personal feelings are." Chairman Squirrel parked his nut bag in the crotch of a n e ar by tree and scampered down again. He scolded the due lists roundly for their vituperative words.

"Don't you fellows know that caution is the best a p-proach to the handout? But his wisdom was lost upon th e m. "You will—I hope—return to your desks in the morning."

"I have been cheated. Cheated, do you not understand," Toad gasped. "Ribbet, ribbet, ribbet!"

"He who is losing the worst complains the loudest,"the Tortoise hissed.

"Dismissed!" cried Chairman Squirrley as he cracked an acorn with a loud snap. "Back to the old sawmill—ahheee," he laughed.

The crowd began to disperse. Some of them hopped a-longside of Congressman Toad with exclamations of surpr i s e and wonder, encouragement and congratulations. Repor t e r Owl among them continued to pop questions as fast as he could scribble them down with journalistic wisdom and ambigu i t y.

"You allege that Congressman Tortoise did something—well, ah, strange, odd, out of context, not at all a classical maneuver of politics?"

"That's just the point. His—cunning was so classi-cal it was obvious—fishgill alliances, Blue Gill mon ey. Un'erstand me?"

"I think I see, Congressman. But he is your opponent, in the next House race," proffered Owl.

"He lacks funds, sir—lacks support on the iss ues, lacks credibility. Dragging himself along? Do you thi n k that sort of conservatism represents the American way o f life?"

"Our editors will respond to that, sir. But, yes—I can see that—all those—female tortoises. Would it hurt your chances in the House next year if he were to be found-let us say—to be a turtleizer?"

"A what?"

"A tortoise philanderer?"

"That would depend upon his bedfellow. I cannot say. Let the record stay moot on that point, Mister Owl."

"Here is our official photographer from the paper, Mister Tanglefilm. Would you care to pose?"

"Yes, I would. Let Representative Tortoise do the posing. I shall stand forth in open honesty. Shoot, s i r. Shoot."

Chairman Squirrley scampered away to the Hill, leaving behind chewed grass, nut shalls, suspicions and broken reputations.

As he hopped back to his waiting lily pad, the Honorable Toad promised, "Let me say it this way, Chester—he was talking to Owl. "I will never run from defeat, but what the press don't know they will find out."

"Ohwoooooooo! No flap is ever totally silenced," the owl replied.

> Most people enjoy going to the zoo because they see reflections of themselves in the behavior of the animals.
>
> —A. Sage

The Sale Of The Split-level Burrow

Al Cleverturn, a gopher who owned—or had dug—numerous burrows in the old baseball field, had just about had his fill of the ground squirrels. They were so fancy wit h their plumed tails, their dainty little feet, their quizzical and sparkling eyes, and their egos—always wantin g handouts. Now he was ready to move. He would have to put his burrow up for sale.

He had dug a nice one, with seven tunnels, two secret exits in case of malicious entrapment by the gardener's water hose. He had a parlor where he stored fruits and nuts-he would leave some of those there for the next tennant.

He had dug, at great expense, soreness of paws and struggle through tree roots above the ground—he had dug a cavern for a den, bedroom and rumpus room. In fact, his mate—who had mysteriously disappeared—had birthed sixteen little ones. And they, too, were gone. So, he sighed, the burrow's tunnels were filled with sad gopher memories—and darkness. Once he had wanted to dig a skylight, but his mate, Aletia Cleverturn, had said, "Yes, and when t h e heavy rain comes, we will be washed out." She had made him fill it in. The darkness was unbroken by any light.

Now his manor burrow was up for sale. He posted a sign outside that said: FINE SEVEN-CORRIDOR GOPHER BURROW FOR SALE. AFFORDABLE HOUSING. GOOD STARTER. And he waited for results of his efforts, sleeping off and on throughout the day, since he no longer had hungry mouths to feed. He was alone.

His first caller was a jackrabbit. who poked h is sniveling. tweeky. little quivering nose into the front-hole door and enquired. "Is the owner of this residence at home?"

"Yes, I am at home," said A. Cleverturn. "Are you interested in buying my burrow. perhapschance?"

"It will be chancey. since there is no light i n-side for me to inspect things by, but is there runn ing water?"

"Is there ever running waterl" said Cleverturn. "Just wait until the first November rains come and you'll find out. Why, do you know. Mister Rabbit—pardon.I didn't catch your name—"

"Jack Z. Zag. Of course. no pun intended."

"NO, course not."

"Well, Mister Zag is my name. and I.m in need of a place to settle down. But—" The rabbit looked all around him. at the roof, the walls, at the size of t h e entranceway."It is—a little small. I mean—I can hardly get my head in through the door."

"0h, that can be taken care of easily enough just a little interior modernization! updating) and all t h at sort of thing."

"It'll take more than modernizing. Mister C1everturn. It's just too— small for my needs."

"Then let me suggest D. J. Terroy. who digs fo r varmints. I happen to know—"

"He's—?"

"He's a little terrier dog. lives other side of the ball field. Old man keeps him to flush rats out fro m under the house. Now he's not in the business, but h e knows about pawing holes out to get himself a better looksee—you understand."

"Not entirely." said Mister Zag. "I need a custom fit. and I want to be able to sit and stand up in my burrow, not lie down all the time."

"In that case—"

"How much do you think Mister Terry would char g € to enlarge your burrow tunnels?"

"Probably somewhere in the neighborhood of—let us say—eight bones and some chicken scraps."

"Pretty high expensive, I'd say. Well, let m e go home and think about it. I need to get closer to my work. I'm a insurance-policy chaser. I chase varmints like field mice and, in particular! those not caught up in their policy payments. Sometimes I have to chase them a long ways. But seems most of my business is close. by nowadays, what with all the human building 'sbeen going on—field mice have become pretty independent a nd irresponsible."

"I quite understand. Of course, you know you'll have squirrels., lots of squirrels, for neighbors."

"I can deal with that," said Mister Zag. "I hate acorns and acacia seeds and things like that, and I don.t run up the trunks of trees. So we got no competition on those scores."

"And the price will be cash."

"I have the lettuce."

"Then a pleasant day to you, Mister Zag," said Cleverturn, and he pulled down some tufts of grass t o shut the door.

"Pleasant enough fellow," thought Clever turn, "but he requires a total-new concept in housing—bigness is everything t o Mister Zag." On this thought, Clever turn fell asleep at the door to his burrow.

He did not know how long he had slept, but h e heard a frantic chittering outside his grass-thatch doorway. He opened his sleepy gopher eyes only to see-wouldn't he know itj-one of those fool ground squirrels, grey and so happy with life it made you want t o vomit.

"May I help you?" Mister Cleverturn said, trying to sound as civil as possible.

"I couldn"t help but notice your sign outside as I was running past."

I couldn"t help but notice your sign outside as I was running past, Cleverturn mimicked to himself.

"Yes, it is a good sign, is it not? And it gives the important—the really important information."

"Let us hope so," said the squirrel .

"How smug and egotistical this fellow is{"thought Cleverturn, "just like all of his kind."

"Allow me to introduce myself."

"You are allowed," said Cleverturn.

"My name is Barney, Barney Nibble. I'm a ground squirrel—live not too far away—but I want to move in close to the ball park. Peanuts, dropped popcorn, handouts—junk food, you know. Good resource mat er-ial."

"I quite understand," said Cleverturn dryly. H e waited. "Well, this fellow just sits and looks. Something the matter with his tongue?"

"I'm—I"m looking for a place I can dive into in a hurry. You understand."

"Oh, yes, a sort of emergency entrance. Lots of headroom and dark."

"That's it exactly. I hope you don't have modern light ing in your burrow."

"Oh, no. Modern darkness is more like it. I abho r light—except outside the burrow. And, by the way, I got seven tunnels, nicely designed and dug, with a big den and a separate storage area."

"Sounds great, just great," said Mister Nibble. "But-well, It'll have to—"

"Stoop? You can make some changes, I'm sure, to ac—commodate yourself. You got a family, of course."

"Not just now, but in another month or two. S e v e n tunnels, huh?"

"Yeah, split level in case it rains real hard."

"Flooding, no doubt?"

"Only minimally—bottom two levels."

"Running water?" Mister Nibble asked.

Cleverturn paused. "The last potential buyer asked the same question, Mister Nibble. It runs when it storms out-. side. In fact it drips in several places in one of the tunnels. Then again, if that gardener forgets to turn off his sprinkler system, well—you just have to make the best o f it, that's all."

"Oh, I think I *can* handle that one," said the squirrel. "But tell me—that gardener—he never puts his hose i nto the burrow hole, does he?"

"Did once to a friend of mine. She lost her e n tire home—got flooded out desperately, she did."

"A regular practice of his?"

"Just for fun, I suspect," said Cleverturn. And he led the grey squirrel further into his burrow, showed him th r ee to p tunnels and then one of the two panic exits, secret o f course, just in case he had to make a fast getaway.

"I'll think .about it. It is interesting, the layout, I mean. Unexpected running water, modern darkness, a storage area, just the things I've been looking for. But, uh, one more thing."

"Yes? What is that?" asked Cleverturn.

"What kind of security protection you got—a l arms, locks and all that?"

"Glad you asked. Lemme show you. Follow me." They made several tortu o us bends and arrived at the overhangi n g fillaments of an outside acacia tree root. "This is the best thing since the invention of the acorn. An alarm system. If you got an intruder, he gets caught, trapped between the roots, can't get his head out. He squeals. That's the a-larm. He can't get his body pa st-roots spring into place-snappo! Just like that."

"Clever, but how do I get by?"

"Simple. Press this nodule and there—the entire root apparatus springs up out of the way."

"Amazing!"

"Yes, isn't it! And—something you may have overlooked. Come." Cleverturn led his potential buyer into another tunnel. "Here—this is my all-season comfort a-rea. See? Feel that water pipe. Go ahead, just feel it." Mister Nibble did. "That is a water pipe that runs cold water the year round. Now if you store food down here, pack it against that pipe. If the day is too infernally hot. just lay your little head against that pipe. If you need to sharpen your teeth somewhat, just gnaw on that pipe. If you want to know the presence of the gardener in the vicinity, just flatten your little ear against that pipe. Simple. Cost effective, and comes with the burrow."

"I think you"ve almost sold me|" said the squirrel, Mister Nibble. "But I will have to go and talk it over with my mate first."

"That's okay," said Cleverturn. "I understand. But-you be the man of the family, Mister Nibble. This ought to be your decision. And it's just right for you, I can tell that by the excitement in your voice." He led his visitor to the back exit of the burrow. "This is the fastK est escape dig hereabouts. Trust me," said Cleverturn.

"Until—later." He popped out onto the playing field.

"Until—then," said Cleverturn. He had given h is best that time. And he retreated into his burrow only to hear a strange sound at the other end through his keen ears.

"Hello, hello, hello, hello," said a squeeky voice. "I am a field mouse outdoorsperson, and I seen your sign, .Up for Sale."

"Look Mouse, I hate to have to tell you this, but this just ain't your style of pad. It"s too big, it's too clever for your small brain and—it just ainH safe from-cats."

"Cats! Oh, dear, oh, dear, oh, dear."

"And tell your friends," shouted Cleverturn afte r the retreating scamper of the field mouse. "The nerve o f him," he mumbled. "Why, he don't know a hole in the wall from a burrow in the ground."

Things were certainly going better than he had anticipated. But then again, this was a popular are a and the amenities of the ball field on a Saturday afternoon were worth the extra outlay of effort and services.

Time brought the next enquiry, but a risky one. Just as Cleverturn was about to shut out the night, he heard a rustle at the opening to his burrow. There, there wit h all of its flickering, pestilent, dangerous nuisance was a water snake.

"I hate snakes. My house is not for sale to snakes of any description," said Cleverturn before the snake had even pushed its head through the door.

"Ahhhhh, I see you have a mighty clevah pit here."

"Not for you, Snake," said Cleverturn.

"You are partial to—your buyers?"

"I match the buyer to the residence if I can. And you certainly ain't what I'd call a likely purchaser."

"No, but ah can just—pass through and get a quick impression, can I not?"

"You can not. And, furthermore, I got this here poin-ted stick I'll shove into your flat face if you make one more squirm to get inside."

"Your words are mighty unfriendly. Mister Gopher. Ah'm truly sorry for that as—as the gardener is my friend, and he likes to see things done with—equality. You know how it is these days."

"Well, you"re not equal to me anytime, anyplace. You're a snake and I'm a gopher and I know something about m y kin would raise the scales on your back a full octave. I got blood relations'd make canned steaks out of your innerds, and booties out of your skin."

"Wall, now, there don't appeah to be a reason for you to get all snappish and upset," said Snake. "I saw yo u r sign as I squiggled past, read every word carefully, forwards and backwards, side to side. You understand."

"I do, but this is no place for you to lay your eggs."

"My mate—"

"Your mate! Now would you please withdraw your head from the opening of my burrow, or I shall be forced to punch out your eyes with this here sharp stick."

"Xhm agoing. But—I shall re-port you to the garden-ah and he will deal with you—with justice."

"Do it—if that's what you think you ought to do."

"C. Oil S. Quiggley is my name. Mighty glad to hav e met you—even if the conversation was—laced with poison."

"The poison is yours, Mister Quiggley. Goodbye!" That was the last of their dialogue as the snake wiggled off into the dusk. It certainly seemed to Cleverturn that he had had enough visitors, but nobody with good taste yet—and yet with all sorts of personal demands.

He heard the sprinklers start up, the throb of the w a-ter through that pipe back in the burrow. But they would be on only a short time. Then the most amazing thing happened: one of his own kind, Miss K. Lass Plainiew, swept into the opening of his burrow—he had met her informally at a house-wrecking party when a neighboring field was ploughed. Of course, she had to ask the usual questions. Of course.

"You do live here alone, naturally. I mean—the layout, the design of the tunnels, is for one person only?"

"Oh, no," said Cleverturn, "another adult and, well just a whole family—with some improvements and enlargements could live quite comfortably in my burrow."

"Is that so!" said Miss Plainview. "How nicel How-"

"Yes, isn't it."

"Would you—ah, would you mind if I had a look around?"

"Not at all, my dear. In fact, this may be just what you are looking for."

"Really," she said, using a low voice that was music t o his ears.

"I—uhhh," he stuttered. "I have modern darkness as a feature—running water, expecially in the winter months when the gardener forgets his job. I have cooling comfort duri n g heat waves with my—my water pipe. And a most clever and effective passageway barrier against intruders."

"You have just about everything," said the Miss quietly.

"Yeah, just about—only—here, let me show you." They walked on a ways, entered a lower tunnel.

"You were going to say—just about everything.But what-Mister Cleverturn? I saw your name on the sign Or then-perhaps I—remember you from somewhere."

"You are right—the name is Cleverturn—Al. And I have everything except—company."

"You mean—permanent company?"

"I mean permanent company," he said, and they touch e d whiskers.

Needless to say, the sale was completed without any cash changing hands, since the prospective buyer, Miss K.Lass Plain-view, became Missus Al Cleverturn and he did not have to get rid of his fine burrow after all. Still. by opening |iis heart to others he had certainly learned a great deal about some o f his neighbors. It seemed to him that all but one wanted-convenience without doing any of the work. Work was a drag and a trap.

How I Escaped From Vanity One Crocodile's True Story

I get consarned tired of hearing folks use my name in vain—a "crock" of this and a "crock.of that. Don . t they know I got a image to pertect? Course, a crocodile ain't the prettiest of critters, but then again he ain't the ugliest either" I can think of a whole lot worse-looking, like—well, like a dog trying to bit a flea inside a hind leg. There's one I seen out hunting one day, and—that thing that never flies but looks like it . d like to—strich—ostrich? There's a crazy bird if there ever was one. It'don't look like either a animal, bird, cartainly ain't no fish and would drop like a rock in the river if it fell out of a tree.

My image. That's what's important, make no mistake about that. Oh, I could tell you plenty about painful chomps and thrashings and mud-slinging about my image. Like, take for instance, them hunters that come out onto the river nights with their lanterns. They're after m y skin for shoes and bag s, belts and coats and the like-and meat dishes for their wicked appetites. But, seems like they come gunning for me many a time.

I seen the lantern oncet, I dove, come up under the wooden row boat, bumped it hard like a rock with my stoney head and dumped the hunter into the river" I dove. Wouldn't touch him. Stunk with booze. Friend of mine got dizzy one night from just such a drunken dinner. Lantern burned a long time on the seat of his boat. But no hunter.

Then there was the time I come up with a piece of river fruit—growed along the banks—sinks when's ripe—like a gourd it was. This time it were a rat give me away. They was shafts and spears and gunblasting all round me, but I swum out of that river, churning just in time. It's awful to be so gorgeous.

Oncet some feller tried to ride me. I swum half way across that river till he dropped off. Cousin of mine took him inside permanent for his dinner. Wild. Ever seen torches flicker over the water? Like witchery things the y is. Cause me to riz up one night from the frog bank, just fo r curiosity. This here feller slips a noose over my lovely long jaws. Then I drug him into the water and took off with twenty meters of hemp rops trailing my tail. Took a couple of close friends to gnaw me loose. That's just a few of the things"s happened—all cause of my lovely image.

Fact of the matter is, I once was so attractive to hunters, long, knotty, slender, the skin of perfection and white teeth like bleached rocks, they was, I couldn't stand myself. 1 guess the best proof of all was when I played a extra in a movie of the jungle river they was making out where I hang around. That was a real blast for my vanity, I'll tell you.

Let me go on. A nice calm pond now stood near b y, where the river had loaded up a sinkhole. Nothing ruffl ed the water except the breeze through the thick forest trees. I could go there and gaze at my reflection for long prehis-tories at a time—in that smooth, calm, slick and unruffled pool of water. It was fun, and how I love myself I can't see the end.

I lay there in the mud, the squishy, cool, ploppy, o-oze of mud. The grass and rive r reeds rattled pleas a nt-like and my eyes filled up with the mists of the loveliness of it all. Twickham, the Crock Bird, fluttered down and perched on my long rows of chalky sharp teeth and commenced to picking them. Course I let him—Twickham. I got the nicest double-row sets of choppers from that bird's flickering around me like that—keeping my chewing tools clean. I keeps them sharp on bones, of course. He and me, we get a … long real nice together. And do you know, my image of njyself kind of growed on me, so that I got to dividing up my time between hunting and admiring myself. It's hard for a gorgeous crocodile like me to give up food, but I can if I want to.

I got to stop now and tell you about this dread ful thing that happened to me one day. As I squoozed along in the mud to find a cool spot, slimey enough for a quick launch into the river after a dog, but deep enough to peer at m y-self through my bulby round-the-world eyes—all direction s at oncet, I noticed a trickle of water at the lower end of my Admiration Pool … Something, maybe a river snake—wo u l d be just like that viper—had sluced a notch and the pond w a ter was running out. In a prehistoric flash, it would be all gone. I felt a sudden desperation seize my short, fat legs and m y powerful tail. The river was too ruffled, too rippled a nd gushing for me to enjoy myself like I did in the pond. My reflection was disappearing, draining away. I grunted. No response. I roared. Most often, I am a long, silent one.

Then a good friend, a female neighbor, slid into my mud slop. Her name was <u>Bagitta</u>, which means little bag, since that's what hunters hunted her for.

"What's your problem?" Bagitta asked. I didn't like her accusing tone of voice.

"My Admiration Pool is going dry and I won't be able to look at myself any longer.

"What a shame that is! You will lose your image and your pride, won.t you?"

"Confidence—what about that? I mean, my Admir ati o n Pool gave me a powerful, snappish, leg up on confidence. I never knowed till I began watching my lovely reflectio n that my tail was so long and my teeth so white."

"Not until you admired your gorgeous image?"

"That's it. Big, gen'rous mouth, tail to match."

Bagitto yawned. "So you lacked confidence! Don't make me laugh, lazy bones. Last time you slid out into the river after, them hunting dogs you got there first …"

"Had nothing to do with my confidence in my beauty. I was just—hungry."

"ArenH you the one thouch, Crock! You even rode one of them dogs on your back—just to show off."

"That's different, Bagitto. What I mean is, if I don . t keep in touch with my good looks, I might just forget who I am."

"Give us a big smile, Crocodile." She laughed and snapped her teeth shut and clapped her fine tail down int o the mud. "Cut it out, Crocky. You? You got a identity problem? With that bumpy hide—like a sack full of rocks."

"If I don't keep telling myself how good looking I am with all these white teeth Twickham picks for me, I might—I might just go into a real depression."

"That can happen any time. Mud's deep enough aroun d here after the monsoon."

"You know what I mean. Look there—I'm losing my mir-ror hole, my Admiration Pool."

"Too bad about your mirror hole—and you out there in the sun asleep like you wuz drugged. Not much to catch alongside that riverh ole, is there?"

"My reflection—that's the most important ghing."

"All right, I see it now. You're so in love with yourself it stinks." Bagitto yawned, clapped gobs of mid into Crock"s face, scraped her iron skin against his a s a sign of closeness. "I got something better'n your old Admiration Pool, Crocky."

"You have? What's better than my image of myself?"

"A full jaws-to-tail image of yourself, not just your magnificent chewing tools, bulby eyes and Twickh a m the dentist.".

"Full image! Are you—are you asking me to-that we, well—you know."

"DonH be silly. All them white teeth of you rn don't impress me one bite. What I mean is—if you"l 1 come take a short swim with me down to the river outpost, I can fix you up with something that's better than your ol' waterhole."

"What's that, Bagitto?'

"Admiration Pool don't need a rainstorm to depend on. Use it anywheres—river, forest, mud, rocks. You name it."

"What is it?"

"It's a looking glass. glass.'

"Glass?"

"Frozen water, like ice—dead-winter stuff. You ain't seen it, but I sure have. The man-animal admires hisself in this—frozen water, his glass. Just like you. You got one—you're just as good as he is."

"You're sure nice—but I donH like the way you said "dead …""

"You want to check out your image the year round, donH you? Not have to wait for the old soaking hole to fill up with rain?'

"I guess so."

"Then we're goin' to steal that looking glass-sits out there on the dock—at the river bend. Always looking in it, the man-animal is. You'll see."

"Let's go," I said.

We cruised down the river, snorkeling, eyes above the water| powerful tails pushing us along. In prehistoric seconds we were there.A sign said: CROCKODILE HUNTING, GUIDE AVAILABLE. SKINS PURCHASED AT PREMIUM PRICES.

"See there. The man-animal's got your numbe r—you got a skin's worth big bucks, Crocky."

"Yeah, but I want to keep mine." A man-ani m a 1 standing on the dock seen us at oncet. He went into his shack and come out with a stick that spit flame and death and blood. He splashed up the water near toy head—just missed me.

"You see it there—the ice glass to look at yourself in?"

"We got to rip it out by the roots, Bagitto, Then hour"re we going to carry it?"

"No sweat. On our backs. We swim together."

Another slap on the water and flame from the fir e stick and a sting on my nose forced me to dive. When I come back up Bagitto was laughing at me. "He's trying—it looks like he wants to kill us. Big game. Skins for his trade."

"Don't worry, Crocky. You are vain and handsome and everlasting."

"I sure hope so"

"If that hunter.s goin" to hurt you then that hunt-er's goin" to hurt you, only—he will ruin your gorgeous skin with a flame rock."

"But I don't want to look nice—on the feet of human animals. I want to go back to my Admiration Pool."

"Full jaws-to-tail image, Crocky. Think about i tt Right there on the dock. Just reach up and grab it. One chance, Crocky."

"You fooled me, Bagitto. I'll never forgive you. You did not give a snap about flame rocks and death ."

"If you want to look gorgeous, you've got to f a ce death."

"I—I don"t think I want to look that gorgeous—more than life."

"You'll squeek when you're new, Crocky."

"I don't care if that old Admiration Pool dries up, "I don.t love myself more than I love life. I got to live. I'm going, I'm going,"

"Down, then. Dive down, Crocky." These were her last words she said with a big grin that showed all her sparkling rows of teeth. Then she went under, belly up, floating darn the river like a dead log and all the blood going out ofher. Horrible! Awful! Tragic I Sad! The flame rocks got her instead of me, ol" Crocky. I never looked back.

As quick as I could, I swum the three kilometers up-river fast as my tail could thrash me. I busted like a water-logged tree into my circle of crocodiles. I sung out with a grunt and a roar. I flashed my tail, popped my eyes and splashed up great beads of silver river water. What a-what a close escape! Bagitto would make the shoes and bags-poor thing.

As fast as I could I went to my hole, but it was not completely a mud slop. Still—no reflection any longer.It wuz much, much better to be a living crocodile and dug into the mud of Admiration Pool sump. When night come, I w a s ever so glad. I wouldnH mess with them hunters in the river boats, ever again any more, or smart around their lanterns at night. Now I could see myself as a gorgeous crocodile all right, maybe to be admired for my rocky hide, b u t best of all a survivor in life.

"You know," I chomped with fatigue and ennui, "I think she wanted to get me killed out of—jealousy." I squiggled down deeper into the mud for security. After all. the rains would come again and fill my Admiration Pool. But even i f they didn't life was sweet to chew on just being humble me.

The Narrow Trail

Rolling Red Rock, son of High Butte of the Hopi tribe, fixed the rope across the nuzzle of his horse Bitter Tre e and leapt astride his black roan. He was not old enough to participate in the Sun Dance. He had only watched his father ride out from the mesa, across the desert floor, t o look for the magic tree on the bottomland of the creek. He fed Bitter Tree a handfull of corn grown in his own patch, beside the east rock face where rain moisture and dew fall filtered down to the foot of the precipice.

Rolling Red Rock had observed from a distance W h i te men currying their horses. He took just as good care of Bitter Tree, maybe better. He rode his animal to grass up the gully to the north. He had brushed the pony's mane and fetlocks and haunches affectionately with his hands and a clutch of tumbleweed—and always watered him at a sha d e d spring up the same gully, four miles distant. This day, a-way from the Indian Bureau school, he would ride Bitte r Tree for the pleasure of the wind in his face and the hot sun casting up waves of life-giving strength from the sands. He wound his way down the back trail from the mesa.

He gave Bitter Tree slack rein, and he stopped now and then to let the animal crop tufts of bunch grass that grew from cracks in the rocks beside the mesa wall. He listened to the caw of the crow high above through the morning s i-lence. Looking back, he counted the mesa hogans from a distance. He was sharply aware of the irregular fall o f the hooves of his roan, kicking up stones. He watched the trail dust scatter like pollen into the coves of the rock shade"

The trail moved straight as an arrow to a low crest on the plateau. From there Rolling Red Rock gazed out over the mesa into the desert glare, toward where his friends lived on the Navajo reservation. Alone and motionless,

rider and horse were painted into the glazed blue sky and ripp ling hot sands"
The boy was on the hunt for a tortoise that he could use in the Butterfly
Ceremony.

He let out the reins. Bitter Tree exploded like acy-clone in the path,
whirling. flinging his mane high i n the windstorm, amid sounds of hooves
thundering over rocky out-croppings, the gritty blows to the earth, and the
clatter of stones pummeled aside. Tears flooded Rolling Red Rock's eyes. He
had thought that some day he might run his horse to the front entrance to
his father's hogan, spring to the roof and leap, as over a ravine, to the roof of
his friend's hogan. He and his horse shared a sense of power without a hobble
or a rope halter.

The creek bridge sprang like a fish from the surface of the sand-sea ahead.
An Anglo rancher had constructed it with no more reason that he had shown
when he built a fence two miles distant that started and ended and enclosed
nothing. It was not a circle corral but just a line of rotting posts. Indians had
stolen the barbed wire for their own use long ago.

He heard the hollow drumming of Bitter Tree's unshod hooves on the
rotting planks. Before he realized it the pony had fallen through to the
bottom of the flood-eroded defile. Only the embankment had broken the
animal's hard plunge. Rolling Red Rock, having half-jumped, was thrown
clear, onto the embankment. His head narrowly missed some rocks.

The pony whinnied and lay quite still on his back, down in the narrow
cut. The animal was caught like a wed g e driven into a split log, his feet in the
air and pawing aimlessly. Rolling Red Rock got his breath back and scrambled
over to quiet his horse, whose eyes were wild with fright "Horse and rider
were four miles from the mesa. In the heat of the desert the animal might die
by the time Rolling Red Rock walked back to the mesa and returned with
help. The exposed belly of his roan would lie unprotected under the baking
heat of the sun.

Rolling Red Rock began to pray to the god of the animals for the life
of Bitter Tree—and for help from the Spirit of life. This was the creek
where, above, he had watered the roan many times before. He dug into tne
embankment and found damp sand and, removing his head kerchief, allowed
the dampness, with his own sweat, to impregnate t he cloth. He returned to
Bitter Tree and moistened his muzzle with the kerchief. He prayed harder.

The worst of all possible calamities occurred. An enemy armed with a
Winchester rifle appeared over the rim of the defile. When Rolling Red Rock
looked up, Sant/had his gun leveled at him.

"If you help me to save my horse, you can have him, Sante."

"You are too clever for me, little one, stunted plant."

"I do not mean harm. I mean truth/" Rolling Red Rock called up to the other Indian, he who was older like a brother but filled with venom like the scorpion.

The one called Sante'dropped the reins of his horse, brought out a lariat from under his saddle blanket and, his horse's halter in hand, picked his way down the embankment.He looped the lariat behind the roan's forelegs, high up, a . gainst the heavy chest muscles. He led his buckskin along the bottom of the gully until the draw was taut. Chirping to his mount he then dragged the fallen roan ahead to a place where the eroded defile widened. The roan instinctively realized he could struggle to his feet and quickly did so with much snorting and blowing and bobbing his head. Sante picked u p each leg and released the rawhide loop.

"Now I have a fine horse, "said Sant.

"You give me ride—back to the mesa?"'Rolling Red Ro c k asked.

"You will trick me at the mesa. You will sh o o t out my honor." He laughed a devil's laugh. He shot into the ground in front of Rolling Red Rock. "You do not try to get your horse again."

"It is far to walk."

"The spirits will take you there. Just pray to the whirlwind," said Sant/, mockery in his voice. He and Bitter Tree disappeared from the edge of the gully—and now came loneliness. Rolling Red Rock would have to walk back to the mesa—very far without water. The heat burned like coals in the hearth of day. Then he would have to explain how he had lost the fine animal his father had presented to him for the ancient ceremonial hunt, a token of his initiation into tribal life. He had depended on White Man's bridge. The pain of this guilt would serve him right.

He started out on the hot walk toward the mesa. T h e soles of his feet at once blistered on the whiteheat shimmering sand. He looked behind him when he thought he had distinctly heard the whinny of Bitter Tree. The pony was a half mile away but he had heard the voice of the horse on the wind, and he saw him rear up, pawing with his forehooves as if fighting aff a bear or spooked by a rattlesnake. He thought h e saw Sante fall from his horse to the ground when the rearing and plunging captive animal struck him. Sante did not get up from the sand where he lay.

Running wild, the roan galloped in the direction of Rolling Red Rock, Dust flew up in boiling plumes beneath t h e explosions of the pounding hooves. The roan, his black shape growing larger, dropped from sight at the rim of the flood-eroded gully, then bobbed up on the near side and, not slackening its gait, ran up to the side of his rider. The boy was overjoyed, while the horse snorted, flinging it s head and dragging his halter rope about. The distant black escrescence of Sante" and his own mount remained fixed e n the desert sand. Rolling Red Rock flung himself on the back of his treasured horse and sped off in the direction of the mesa. He would make a gift of Bitter Tree to the spirit god at the next Sun Dance ceremony, as a sacrifice. Then h e would not need to worry about his enemy. or any thief, stealing his horse. The spirit of life would protect Bit ter Tree.

Pity, The Government Agent

"Busy, busy! I can't talk now!" the beaver said when the toad croaked on top of the dam. "Besides, you're trespassing," said the beaver. "That means I got the right t o slap you with my tail right off this dam, right this very exact, miniscule minute. You dig me, Toad?"

"Don"t understand a word you"re saying. Ribbet! Rib-bet!"

"Don't mess with me, Mister Toad. I got work to do. I built this dam across the creek. It's got no door for you or anybody else. I got more work to do on my residence.Bus-y, busy." The Beaver slapped the water with his tail. H e made a big splash just to show his power and his author i ty and his right of possession. "I own territory, see. Now don't mess with me."

The Toad hopped down into the water. He thought he would just do some inspecting on his own. After all, h e had not told Mister Beaver that he was the General Domiciled Inspector of the Bureau of Declaimation hereabouts—for dams, bridges, houses and structures of all types. Yet he wanted to see what the river beaver had built and if he had done the construction work right.

Al Toad, GDI, gulped in a full lung of air and dove down to the bottom of the creek. Above him in the shadows of the swiftly-moving water was the beaver's dam-house. He swam up close. caught a glimpse of Missus Beaver going a-bout her chores, up inside the dry part of the residence of sticks. Everything looked all right from the bottom foundation side.

"Excuse me, ma"m," croaked Toad at the underwater entrance to the beaver's dwellings

"What do you want? Can't you see I'm making flapjacks out of bark curls and old leaves—they"re delicious/' Silence followed. "I would invite you to stay, only I know you don't like old leaves and bark bits. Too common for you snoopers. Besides, I.m busy."

"Ma'ra—ma'm, I just wanted to come in and take a look around, if I might. Government regulations say you got to have just two rooms, no more, to a suitable dam."

"I don't see that law gnawed into any tree what says that."

"No-, it's all right here in my head. Ribbet, ribbet."

"My husband's topside now. Maybe you ought to talk to him first."

"This won't take but just a minute. Twigs, branches got to be wove together just right, right as can be. And tight—"The government Toad swam up to the entrance.

"If you insist, but I'm really very busy."

"This won't take but just a minute. Ribbet. Forks in the branches carry main load of the current—ver t ical posts set well into the base of the dam, —plenty of fine stuff woven in just right. Hmmmmmm. Ribbet. Your husba nd put in a lot of work on this dam."

"He sure did, Mister Government Toad."

"One thing's wrong."

"What's that?"

"Section eight, subsection five, any number, small "i" indent four, paragraph thirty-seven, flapdoodle line eighty-five, last year's ruling: branches wove too tight—like they was solid. Water pressure.11 tear out the whole foundation if it's not changed. Rule Yakety-Yak."

"Oh, oh, I better go tell my husband." fluttered Missus Beaver.

"Won't be necessary, ma'rn. I'll just swim up ther e and tell him myself. And—I know you got things to do. So good day." Toad dropped through the underwater entra n c e and swam out of the beaver's dam. Topside, sure enough, he found Willows Beaver busy, busy at work. Ribbet1 Ribbet.

"What is it now? Confound you, Toad! Can't you see I'm busy?"

"Your wife said the very same thing."

"What! You've been talking to her?"

"You gotta make some changes, sir—in the structure of your dam."

"Who are you to tell me? Just who do you think you are?" said Beaver swelling up with pride and standing at op a small log on his dainty hind feet. His pride in his building expertise agitated his whiskers and fired his eyes. That someone like Government Toad, who knows nothing at all about constructing a dam, should paddle by and question his skill!

"I won't have it!"

"You'll get into a peck of trouble with the Establish-ment," said Toad with an ominous, bloated puff from his quivering throat.

"Damn the Establishment!" squeaked Beaver" "I build my dam the way I want and not the way somebody else wants!"

"The law is the law," Toad replied.

"If you"re so careful and cautious and concerned a-bout the law, how come you grow your tadpoles in folk s' drinking water?"

"I've never done such a thing—not in all my life."

"Nobody's perfect—nobody," smiled Mister Beaver, displaying his shiny incisors. "Now if you'll let me get on with my work—"

"One condition," Toad said,

"What"s that? I'm half-gnawed through this here tree and if you don't hurry up I'll gnaw it so's it will fall plumb right on top of you—or close by."

"You got to build a causeway into your dam so spill water can go on down the creek."

"What! You tell me how I am to engineer my dam! Impertinent bull! What insolence! What arrogance! What a n imposter! From now on I'll make sure you and your kind *never* enter my domicile again. I'll ring it round with thorns and sharp sticks and rocks that cut."

"The law is the law," said Toad,

"I'll slap holes in the mud with my iron tail—trap s where you can croak in the mud all you want. You're too-slimy and noisy to 'preciate my engineering."

"If your dam gives way it will wash out an entire village of squirrels down the creek. They have dug into the embankment. Ground squirrels have their rights, too."

"Don't you talk to me about rights—unless you talk to me about responsibilities. Low-water nit pickers! You come by here in your highhanded way and want to change e-verything."

"I got my duty to perform," said Toad.

"And I got mine. You're tresspassing, so get off my dam this very minute. If you show your face around here, a—gain, why I shall drop a tree upon your skull and crush it flat and you will float down the creek like a dead leaf. Is that clear, meddler?"

"I shall report you to the Consternation Co mm itte e and let them handle the matter from there."

"Crara your old Consternation Committee! I got my development project to finish." With that salvo Willows Beaver gnawed the final fibres of a tall aspen and it flew crashing down into the water, narrowly missing the Inspector Toad—who swam away downstream on the current "It alwa ys did seem to W. Beaver that Al Toad took the easy way to get things done—not the hard way like himself. Besides, n o toad ever built a dam—wouldn't know how. Just paddles a-round gulping down insects. and criticizing other folks" hard work.

What! Another Writer's Conference!

He read that dreary old elm-bark post card again. "Hit You are cordially invited to the Elysian Conference of Newspaper Writers and Editors—at Just Plain Loaf Mountain, California. Please bring your best thoughts and your quill pen."

"Humpf. Stupid twaddle, that," Porcus thought. "Why should they want to invite a rodent to their party anyway?"

He pitched the card onto the floor of his log den and sighed. "Oh, well, I might as well polish up my pens all at once and go to the dratted affair. At least I will have some company in misery."

So Porcus walked through one end of his log den several times to polish his pens. He ambled down to the creek, took a sip of water, scoured off by shaking his quills and went back to repeat his procedure. He wanted his bristles to shine. And they would. He had sharp things to say in matters of confrontation.

On the day of the occasion, the Chaircritter and overseer to the event| a ground hog, invited him into their conclave with a cheery, "Good morning, Porcus. I see you've come to join us."

"What a stupid thing to say!" Porcus thought" He wouldn't be there if he hadn't come to join them.

"We are—most of us—arrived," said G.H. in his superior way, looking about him with a stretched neck as if peering from his hole in the ground.

Ground Hog rapped on a plank with a length of tree root. The gathering of about forty journalists all grew quiet at once. They looked mightily

293

important to Porcus, but then—humpf! what were looks? He was just glad he had put a real shine on his coat of quills.

"We have gathered here together to resolve a change in the ethical standards of journalistic writing. Be it resolved: that a rock is a rock, gravity is gravity, and that a prevarication is a prevarication."

Silence. Then applause and huzzahs from the island of attendees took place. Just Plain Loaf Mountain floated in the mists of doubt, ignorance and pale platitudes of e-vasion. It appeared to Porcus they were all in tune with the message. Had they not labored for years to write and to print and to edit the truth and nothing but the truth-so help them Bacchus? Yet they must improve in another way-no more editorializing! no more personal opinion insert e d between the lines of facts in hard-news stories. That had to come to an end, without censorship.

"Mister Games T. Otter. The Hole recognizes your pam"

"Sir, when I swim and see a fish, do I call it something else? No. I call it a fish."

"Meaning—?" replied G.H.

"Meaning that we have got to get back to the old school of calling a fish a fish-and not something else of metaphorical elegance just to impress our readers."

"You have spoken well," said the Chaircritter, Ground Hog. "Yes, Mister Beaver? You have a comment?"

"I have. Mister Hog."

"Proceed with your comment then."

"As a hardworking beaver I have seen many trees topple into the river for my dam. I have labored long and hard for the verity of perfection. But why, why sir, I ask this august and well-informed group of journalists—why cannot others in our craft cut and hew and trim and fell as carefully as I do? I address the editors." A great outcry o f pain broke forth from tne editors. Waves of super he ate d froth swept toward the podium and momentarily obscured Chair-critter Hog.

Me C. "Chicken Coop" Weasel from Easy County. Califoinia."

"Mister Chaircritter, I have never heard such absolute squawking. Beaver from the county of Dam Upstream ca nn ot possibly know what true freedom means."

"Sir—sir—!" Great commotion. "Sir—!" More rapping by Chaircritter from his Hole. "The ends of free speech—as the irresponsible segments of the press de fine it—is anarchy. The total absence of responsibility."

As the room erupted with wild fur in the air, spitting and clawing and rabid denunciations of their accuser, the chaircritter sought to restore order. Finally—some calm and peace.

"What would you have us to do then, Beaver?" We a sel asked, gnashing his small teeth, acid in his voice. "Freedom of expression is just that—freedom of expression. As Mister Otter says, let us call a fish a fish."

"No matter what, no matter how?"

"Are you insulting our intellects, Mister Beaver. We, too, work hard for a living."

The assaults on Avery Beaver continued without let up. He banged his flat tail on the podium in agitation. "Do you mean to say we have no morals?" the journalists confr onted Beaver,

"I mean to say that your brand of freedom of expression is anarchy, and anarchy is evil."

"Moralist! Insane moralist. Blatant piety! Religionist garbage," the room burst forth in wild denunciation o f Beaver's stand. Chaircritter Hog let the storm subside o f its own accord this time. He simply watched in dismay a s these respectable and articulate creatures gave vent to their dissident fury.

At last Chaircritter Hog saw calm. "Mister Be a v e r has his right to speak. Is that all, sir?" Hog asked.

"Control is not censorship. Selection and choice are not censorship, riddance of the hurtful is not censorship."

"What then? What! What! What!" the cries sprang u p from among the journalists.

"Censorship is the silence of a voice, totally-as in death. And even the more—lecherous members—have had their trick at the wheel of the ship."

"Hear! Hear!" cried Weasel. "No more of this. Mister Chaircritter, we are ready—you"ll pardon the expression-to slash the neck of the issue. We are—"

Pounding with the tree root for a full two minutes, until an absolute calm ruled. "We have heard from you, Wea—sel, and take cognizance of your—wants."

"The Chair recognizes Mister Basset Hound."

"Beaver," the City Editor of <u>The Daily Bark</u> entoned, "have you ever seen the amount of copy goes through . u r hands in a day? Huh? Have you? Huh?"

"Where is your reason, A.B.?" Weasel asked.

"Have you ever visited a newspaper office?" Basset continued with dripping sarcasm. "We wear our p e nci 1 s down to the nub, the nub I say, our paws to the bone to get it right. Accuracy is our motto. Accuracy, sir.And let nobody argue with that."

"I am not talking about accuracy, "said Avery Beaver. "But that is involved. I am addressing the issue of moral responsibility."

"Sit down, flapmouth!" came the surly challenge in the form of a roar from A. Crocadile, who had drifted in with the current at the last moment. He had lain quite still in the mud that had been flung about by critic s and editors.

Beaver spotted him back there, a non-welcome personality known widely for eating up critics of his tooth-y yellow press.

"You sound just like a bunch of copyrats again, "said Beaver. "We.ve got to get back to the basics o f careful editing—no more, no less . Keep opinion out of the news and, for the most part, news out of opinion. If that's censorship. then make the most of it."

"We could never sell newspapers if we tried that," disgruntled A. Crocadile roared. "After all it's sensation that sells, not humility. You, yourselves. kn ow what one good bite does to the competition."

"I agree! Bravo! Correctamente! It is the same . Takes guts to slash and stab and—hack—"

"Hack! Hack! Hackl Don't ever say that word a-gain." cried Weasel. Words of similar fervor, meaning and toothy bluntness arose from the pack of paw f o o t ed journalists. Poreus, a quiet observor up to this point, looked out over the crowd and saw that he was the o nly one invited from his ilk.

"May it please the Hole, I have a suggestion!" Pop. cus began.

"Please proceed," Chaircritter Hog responded. H e rapped once again with the tree root on the plank to quiet dissension, for the whole assembly was still put out b y the matter of ethical selection disguised as freedom o r censorship. It was a hot trail all right, and Porous saw some shiny, polished incisors still showing in the crowd. The hackles of the furry guests had not yet lain dow n.

Weasel had just sat down in a cooling puddle."Well, speak, sir, or forever hold your quiverings," he said, This remark seemed to amuse the Chaircritter, but Porcus did not retaliate.

"I think it is appropriate that the matter of ethical nonsense be decided by one creature, so that all get it straight at once." He rolled his beady, black eyes over their heads and saw some shaking. "Ethics come from character and not from circumstances."

"Here, here!'"some shouted, blood in their eyes, their lips flecked with the froth of anger.

"Rubbish!" cried another. "Times have changed!"

"Are you the lawgiver around here, Mister Porcus? Why you"re just a rodent!"

"Are you the idol of morality, Porcus?" Reporter Catnip of The Elevator Sneeze challenged. "We-I cannot help what goes on in elevators," the scribbler from The Sneeze said.

"I shall make it perfectly plain that when you smash against another party ethically. that ought to be to yo u r damage and not to his."

"You babble in riddles," said Grey Fox. "Only one log makes a home. One principal makes a case. But the next log is different—totally different! And—so, t he principle ought to change with the scene."

"You pontificate so beautifully. Mister Fox, but you will be trapped by a clever snare. You will not know danger when you see it," said Porcus.

"I will know it if it hurts. Principles cannot protect me then."

"You tire me out. You—all of you. Do you hear what Mister Fox is saying—that principles can change a s expedience demands. Why be stuck in the mud? he is asking you.

"Huzzah! Huzzah! <u>Freeshanapolism cart esuanva mag-</u>situewonl" they cried as one voice

"Fresh metaphor, that!" Porcus decried.

"We follow the crowd. We please. How else can w e sell our stuff and our names to the readers?" Chomp-chomp! Guest Crocadile reduced the assemblage by one by hastily devouring Muskrat| who had strayed too near to the sensationalist fringe of the gathering. Chaircritter Hog had to rap his root on the plank to restore order. The guests moved off a short distance from the yellow press.

"You are impossible! One source, one principle, one ethic—honesty!" Porcus screamed.

"Wrong! You defame us! Rebel, radical! Liberal! A revolutionary religionist! Tyrant over our minds!" These shouts and accusations flew up like fiery darts from the conclave. Porcus bowed his little head and beady eyes majestically to Chaircritter Hog and muttered, "They will learn." He turned and addressed the convention. "So that you will all know that honesty has one source, learn from me. It will sting to write and edit for the truth. b u t-well, what more can I say? Have some souvenir pens fro m me." He turned his back and scattered quills all over the hall. "Take that—and that—and that!"

With that final gesture of defiance and indifference Porcus waddled out of the meadow hall of Just Plain Loaf Mountain. To this day, writers in the press who attended that conference respect that supreme gesture, on the part of honesty, by one of their touchy and a-little-dangerous colleagues. Whenever they write with honesty, the quill in their paws quivers its message: <u>Verite est sumroa.</u>

Tamarack, The Coyote And Horatio, The Buzzard

A huge male coyote called Tamarack was loping past an acacia tree one day and his eye caught sight of a buzzard, rednecked, its giant wings folded, that sat like a silent shadow up in the branches. watching every move that Tamarack had made within the last half hour. The buzzard held his complaint inside. He wanted all or none of the rabbit that ran before the coyote, injured by the brush wolf's fangs on first confrontation. But the jack h ad gotten away and ran crazy for his life—across the land, no holes, no abandoned burrow, no empty tree killed by dry-rot or lightning. Nothing. Away at a distance he had stopped, panting hard, in his eyes a terror of the big carnivorous beast"

"Say, what you chase that little animal for," the buzzard said at last. The coyote did not answer, for he, too, panted under the blazing, arid sun. He stopped when the buzzard spoke and coughed with the dust of the run, his lolling tongue running a torrent of saliva. He was fagged out. The buzzard saw this. It could be that the dog would g o first| the buzzard thought—for all the countryside around knew that he was a devilish fowl that did not take to life but to death, and flesh was flesh in his gizzard. Besides, like all buzzards. he would settle down for his feast alone, and invite none of his cousins to the mealo

He watched with big, black, g entle eyes, shifting a little on his branch to obtain a better view of the partpants. "You kill'm, I eat'm," said Horatio, the buzzard ' s moniker.

"You eat him, I kill you," said the coyote. It a p-peared there was no way to unite their appetites, one for the warm and bleeding, the other for the

299

dead and smelling.—that is, not until the buzzard, with great forethought, announced to the coyote:

"Let me kill that little beast for you. You take a rest under the acacia tree. I can handle the little vagabond in no time."

"You will eat the rabbit, that's what you want."

"Ain't you got any symbiotic sympathies?" the buzzard chided.

"I got only one sympathy now—with my stomach."

"Gotta trust me. Now come over here—foot of this tree there.s shade. Course, you'll have to shift around some as the sun goes down."

"I never knew a buzzard had any sympathy with the living."

"Oh, you just don't know. Try me. You'll find I.m a delight and a comfort to be with. And I can help you—be your sky spotter—help you shag down the little beastie s, and now and then share in your sumptuous repast."

Tamarack was truly a very tired coyote after his l o ng chase of the rabbit." he needed the sympathy of the buzzard-and so he gave in to the giant bird's plea. The coyote picked a place at the foot of the tree and decided to wai t, anguished as he was for a lap or two of cool water-but patient.

"How long I got to wait?" the coyote asked.

"Only until I bring this little rabbit down to earth. Mighty tender morsel—and worth waiting for. Besides, I can wait for ray portion—this first time—if that is your desire, coyote."

"Just bring me the rabbit. That is all. It is too infernally hot to do any running today, and I have not eate n for almost a week."

"I can see them rib bones starting to show through," the buzzard sympathized. "And when rib bones show through that's when I starts to take an interest."

"I can see that," said the coyote.

"Besides, I like loyalty. Stick with me," the buzzard encouraged. The coyote curled up for a nap as the buzzard flew off in the direction he had last seen the rabbit run in. Since Horatio was a very crafty buzzard, as most of his kind are, he knew that while he and coyote were engaged in palaber the jack had absconded. No need to fret. Horatio flew high and wide but found not a trace of the little creature. I n-stead, he found a lost pet dog that was abandoned to die, and he made a feast for the night from its carcass. He soared back toward the acacia tree and there lay the coyote, asleep in the morning dew. One thing he admired was the brush wolf's loyalty. When he said he would stay, he stayed.

Horatio soared away and found his next meal in a small ground squirrel that had been killed by traffic on the roa d-way. He picked up the scene of a farmhouse death where h e found, on the following day, at a distance from the dwelling, a sheep that had died out in the pasture. The disassembly of this particular animal took him a long morning; he had some help from his cousins. The sheep was his kind of food and filled him with zing and stamina. No need to pander to th a t coyote, the buzzard mused.

Yet, buzzards are creatures with curiosity, and so he soared toward the acacia tree, miles away. When he circ 1 e d above the spot where he had left the coyote, he found tha t the brush wolf was gone. He gained some altitude and foun d what looked like a flat rock in the cry creek bed below. The drought had long ago dried up any hint of water, but there stretched out beside a sink hole was the coyote. Tamar ac k had died going for waterJiad he stayed under the tree, Horatio felt he might have led his ally to water, but now it was too late.

No mere buzzard could ever train a wild coyote to follow, for this ancestor of the dog was independent, wary and cautious escept for one now and then that accepted h e Ip from another wild creature. The big black bird, the rednecked turkey buzzard, enjoyed fresh coyote meat for his evenin g meal, consumed by the buzzard's sympathy for his plight.

The Teakwood Brave

Umquat had run out of buffalo jerky. The buffalo-skin robe on his back was tattering with split seams and ba 1 d spots. He rode his skinny mare into Broken Arrow one day.He had decided that with the onset of winter.s first snows, h e would have to buckle down to some sort of work in town. I t was a hard choice. His mountainside potato patch was barren. A stray horse had foraged in his corn and the wild yams were dead. Umquat, the plains Indian, was terribly hungry. If he was to lash his soul and teakwood body together he certainly must eat.

The little Indian dismounted from his bony horse, Hardtack, dropped his reins over a railing and walked into the town drugstore to find a job. A sign in the window r ead: "Wanted—One Good Indian—under six feet "of good character—patient as a block of wood. Inquire within. Ubber-meyer, Druggist and Tobaccoist." Maybe he find his spirit in Umquat, he thought.

Mister Ubbermeyerls round, pink cheeks shone, his eyes sparkled behind the thin frames of his glasses as he looked across his bench at the latest applicant for the job of Sentry.

"Me Umquat—need work. No like whiskey. Like smoke pipe. See big sign in street. Work much."

"I see. You look capable, sturdy, strong."

"Strong—like tree, not rotting tree."

"You ever—done this sort of work before?" Umqu at did not understand. Mister Ubbermeyer squinted closely at the weather-splits in Umquat's arms, the weatherstreaks o n the buffaloskin robe, the nicks and dents in the carved arms and chest, life's batterings. The tobaccoist saw that the colors were good, the paint had not flaked off. His face brightened. He appeared well pleased,

303

as if Umquat were just the sort of Indian to stand Sentry outside in front of his tobacco emporium. He hired Umquat right away.

The two of them went to a back room where Mister U b-bermeyer filled a big oak tub with hot water.

Umquat protested. "Hot water bad for Indian. Get warped in hot water—lose paint, spirit looks."

"I see. In that case, some cold—"

"No, no—wood split. I no good for work."

"Oh, all right then. Wash towel?"

"That good," said Umquat as the tobaccoist wip e d street dust from the Indian"s face. The feet did not matter ""Feel good—like in creek," he said. Ubbermeyer then touched up the old buffalo robe with shoe polish and hu n g some blue-glass girl's beads around Umquat"s neck. He wound some copper electrical wire around the Indian's head and stuck a plastic feather under the strands.

"Work of art," the proprietor exclaimed. He carried the teakwood Indian out to the front of his shop and stood him in front, on the sidewalk. Umquat was exultant. He had found the job he needed and without a search. The god o f plenty was good to him.

He had hardly taken up his new post when an elega n t, painted farm wagon rolled up to the board sidewalk. Umquat sensed an attack. He could not run and stood fixed to one spot. The wagon sported white wheel rims and polished brass side lamps. "BBQ RANCH" read letters on the shiny gre en sideboard. A powerful grey that pulled the wagon was twice Hardtack" s size. Two men jumped out, grabbed him. lifted him off the ground and laid him down carefully on the wagon bed in back. They bucked away. The wagon clattered an d hammered over the chuckholes.

It sped down the main street of Broken Arrow in almost reckless haste. Umquat feared he might split and be hurt as he smacked against the sideboards inside the wagon. The driver turned around and said, "I guess you know wh er e we"re taking you."

"Kidnappers-they hang," said the Indian. "Dry out-like jerky." The men up on the wagon seat did not hear him.

"Big feed t'other side of town. Buckskin boys and the and the woodcutters is holding a jamboree"

"White man call Indian. That good."

Just as he was thinking this he heard one of the men say to the other, "that Indian'll burn all right." Umquat almost died when he heard this.

"Spect so," came the answer back.

"Make good coals for the ribs," said the first man.

"At least. At least/" said his companion. They were planning to burn him for firewood. Didn't they know he was a sacred relic, to himself anyway?

Other things were in store for Umquat. The buckboard pulled to a stop. Strong hands seized him, threw him ov er a shoulder and trudged him into a nearby woods. He heard grumbling and argument. His handlers propped him against a tree.

"Cool like water—in forest," Umquat thought. The White man had not tied the Indian's feet and hands w i th rope or thongs. They did not fear his running away, back to Broken Arrow, and they did not hear his heart beating fast. He remembered poor Hardtack. Mister Ubbermeyer, he would be cruel if he did not feed the pony.

For the time, he was lost. He would wait until read-y to burn, then talk ransom to his robbers in front of their White faces.

Leaning up against the juniper tree, he watched a long line of villagers begin to form. Their cooking camp fire blazed up} their knives flashed when they cut the meat. Their axes glinted when they chopped on the oak logs. Firelight glowed on their faces and on the red sand. H e was observing these things when he heard his name suddenly called out from the darkness of the woods.

"Umquat—" A wood owl hooted, its wings brushed the air.

"What you want?"

"I ride my horse. I save you from roasting-take you back to Broken Arrow. You make promise let Hardtack go free. You also give back money you steal."

"Who speaks to Umquat from the trees?" No answer. Umquat thought that only he knew he had kept coins t h e townsmen put into his wooden hands. They respect Indian spirit like superstition when in front of store. His ter Ubbermeyer would drag him inside for the night, but Umquat had kept hidden in one arm band a few silver coins. Umquat thought much—then made a treaty with the bird spirit o f his rescuer. "Hardtack a good horse. I find another, a better horse, stronger, swift like the wind."

He again found himself lifted into the air and lashed across the rump of a waiting mount, behind the saddle. They flew away at a gallop through the trees, past the White man's campfire and out onto the open road. He had escaped the burning for a feast of cow steaks.

That night Umquat slept standing in barn—or a place to store bones and rattles and relics and weapons. White man"s keeping-place did not smell like the earth. He could not see the night stars. He slept as if drugged on the berries of the visions. He did not awaken until he heard wierd noises around him, banging, clanging, clashing a nd bellowing like wild steers. His surroundings were tota 1 ly strange to him. He rode up into the darkness without stars and then slid along as if on lake ice. When his motion had stopped he stood upright a s a rock.

A bunch of prairie chicken feathers on a stick tickled his face and nose so that he sneezed.

"Did you hear that?" said an enemy, who was dressed like his tormentors at the feast of the cow steaks.

"Hear what?" another enemy asked.

"That sneeze—that wooden Indian sneezed. I swear to old bones he did."

"Come on! You" re spooked. Let's get out of here. Curator will look him over in the morning." The en e m y went out of the big room. He now had a worth, but he did not know why. He sensed only that he would have to stand idly among musty bones and relics, carvings and many gla ss boxes all night long.

A tear ran down Umquat's cheek. He was so far away from his own tepe village and his Indian friends. And he was starving. Mister Ubbermeyer had not paid him a pe n ny for standing out in front of his tobacco shop. The mother world was falling to pieces around his ears. Umquat yearned for wide-open lands and big sky, to be astride hie Hardtack.

"Me lost," he said aloud in despair.

"You iddiot. You noww a rrrelliicc. Inddian."

"Who speaks? You trick Umquat."

"I amm a dinnosauurrr—wwayyyyyy back heerrre, "said the voice.

Umquat di m ly saw, by the light through a window, the jointed bones of dead animals and, closeby, pottery jars that Indians like himself had made. The peculiar moaning voice said. "Dooo not bee affraid, Inndiann braave."

"Me no can see"

"II amm Sppiney—that's wwhaat I cccall mysself-Spi-ney. I amm a dinnousauur—on mmy own platteau. Do no t look arroundd. Cccann you hearr meee?"'

"Me hear you good."

"II wouldd likke to escappee. Lett uss get out o f herre—togethher."

"How?" Umquat asked the dinosaur.

"Wee go to oppen countrry. I amm Spinnneyyy—old bonnnesss. Swaamp skelleton. II will takke youu to riv-errr. Flooat orr swiram like a tree thatt floats, II-I retturnnn to marssh lannnd on the hiigh platteau meadow. landds—wherre I wass foundd byy sorrane diggers."

"Me like sand painting—go north, south, east, west."

Creek, screech, conkkk, clackk. "Doo nott fearr.My bones squeek andd clitterr, claackker wheenn I walkk. I ccannot help itt. Theey need grease, butt therre isss none arroundd. Mmmy jointts arre all driedd up."

"That bad. You get in water. You be all right."

Life on the streets outside the museum was quiet.A clock in the corner of the big exhibit hall ticked o n. Umquat heard a screech, thump, clumping and rattle and crassh and grind, like wet thongs that stretch tight i n the hot sun. Spiney was coming down from off his platform and stomping across the floor to the little Indian. Through Umquat's mind flashed the hope he would see his reservation soon—where all his friends were safe from woodpeckers and robbers and barbeque roasts and—the deep winter snows. And where buffalo was like the grass, every way over the earth. Wild Horse that spirited him away from his people was now gone. Dinosaur make good Indian brave, Umquat thought.

A nightwatchman came early in the morning. He poked his light through the aisles in search of trouble. Spiney froze. He left and turned the key in the lock behind him. Umquat and Spiney were again alone.

A steamboat whistle blew in the distance. Umquat knew by instinct that he and his skeleton friend did not have far to walk to reach the river. A splitting clatter of hollow bones and sounds like squeeking dry t i m-ber shook the silence like a dead thing. Swinging his head from side to side, the dinosaur reached down t o where Umquat stood. He picked up the wooden Indian i n his rocky jaws like an immense clothespin. He moved with his burden toward the doors. The dinosaur knocked a-gainst them with his bony nose and shattered the hea v y wood at the hinges. Spiney bashed a hole in one wall of an outer corridor. He set Umquat down on the ground in the blackness of the night. The dinosaur stepp e d from the building out onto the dirt, picked up his friend and they headed for the river.

They lumbered along, squish and squuk through new mud. The giant dinosaur carried Umquat lightly aloft in his strong jaws. He towered above the houses they passed. Spiney"s feet were as big as clay jugs; he left prim itive tracks along the road. Umquat's eyes searched for the river. Then the smell of fresh river water came up to his nostrils. No villager had screamed at the frightful sight of a giant dinosaur skeleton clomping among the houses with an Indian clamped in its jaws. No citizen cried alarm.

The escaped relics reached the riverbank. Umquat saw a raft| complete with pole, tied up to a tree on the embankment.

"Fishhhroen huunt rivver liffe from rafft, "said the dinosaur. He put Umquat down in the mud. He could not talk much with his mouth full.

"Me like you. You save my life," Umquat said.

"Noooo!" the giant skeleton howled into the r i ver night. "Greeatt sspiritt of yourr ancesstors lead y o uuu heree."

"They not take me to tepee."

"Askk yourr Inddian brotherrs, chomp, chomp." T h e dinosaur ground his huge teeth and he screamed a bloodcurdling howl. He puffed and grunted his satisfaction. Umquat drifted into midstream on his borrowed raft. He watched Spiney, the dinosaur, lumber into the starlit night, head. ing toward the high-mountain meadows.

Umquat listened to the gurgle of the river water a s he floated down the current. Black shapes in the night were the cliffs, the high plateaus, the trees. They glided mysteriously before his eyes. A lantern appeared on the shore and then was gone through the trees.

At dawn Umquat arrived back at the reservation. H e could see his friends" tepees and curls of smoke coming out of the smoke holes. Squaws cooked the morning's corn mush and buffalo stew. The village chief came to the shore. He greeted his lost brother. He embraced his friend and warrior kinsman. He lashed the raft to a rock for Umquat and they climbed the embankment to the village.

All the inhabitants—the braves, the squaws, the children—were glad to see Umquat return home. I na special ceremony that night in which everyone danced and ate and took part, Chief Hail Rocks made all the braves take an oath never to stand as wooden Indians in front of any store, even if it sold tobacco and whiskey. That was an humiliation. Better to go hungry when gone into strange land. Eat buffalo when come back.

"Never, never, never give up," said Chief Hail Rocks. Umquat had blown fresh air into the village's tepees. His disappearance from in front of Lobermeyer's shop was honest freedom—like when he had ridden to the plains in 1879.

When the reunion ceremony was finished, Chief Hai 1 Rocks walked behind his buffalo-skin tepee. He returned into the firelight| leading Hardtack.

"Him walk back to camp," said Chief Hail Rocks. Um-quat wanted to throw his arms around the neck of his pony.

"Brave man rescue me at White man's camp. Me ready to burn. Only scorched."'

Chief Hail Rocks handed the brave a knife with a bone handle. "Here. I cut thongs on feet and hands. I rescue you. You foolish to run away and wait like village d o g for wampum."

"Spirit of Wild Horse take me."

"Hardtack not wild horse." The Chief handed Uraquat the few coins the teakwood brave had tried to hide from Ub-bermeyer. "He does not pay you. I pay you," said the Chief. "You work for White man?"

"Me work three days, Chief Hail Rocks."

"He pay you?"

"No wampum—make promise."

"Then you keep silver. It is just," said the chief. Umquat led Hardtack away from the chief's tepee and disappeared into the ring of darkness around the campfire.

A Woodcutter Gets His Scam

"You ever noticed one ting about d'apwood?" the woodpecker asked the woodcutter.

"Whatzat?" The woodcutter stopped splitting short logs-

"D'sapwood's the hardest. Me? I like'ra dead, real dead. Cam't bore m"hole for m'acorn not unless bark—whole tree for that matter's dead."

"Heya, I didn't know you have problems."

"You wouldn't believe'm. Now you—you just pick a firewood limb and start chopping."

"It's not so easy as you think." said the woodcutter. "You want to try it?"

"You mean—work that there axe?"

"Sure."

"Little heavy for me."

"Go ahead. Try it." So the woodpecker tried to lift up the axe with his strong bill but of course he could not.

"Got a proposition for youse, "said the woodpecker.

"Whatzat? Hope it won't take too long. I got a lot a wood to cut."

"You climb up that tree wit me and while I drill out d'holes you pop in d'acorn. Get it?"

"That's dumb. That.s your job."

"Jes fill your pockets. nit wit. Simple as that."

"Why.d I want to do a thing like that?" the woo d-cutter asked.

"Labor exchange. You helps me, I helps you."

"Gowan with you. You got no labor I need."

The woodpecker stopped and thought a moment. "You know, you jes said one of the most truthful things I ever hert of. Da trees that are drying out are the easies" to cut, numbskull. I jus make my test bor and—there, that's the one you chops on. Get it?"

"If I cut down the tree there goes your pantry."

"We codpt see. Dis tree stays—dat tree goes. Everybody 's happy then—including d"forest danger."

"One for me—one for you."

"Dat's right."

The woodcutter thought long and hard, then gather e d some acorns, about two dozen of them, and stuffed them into a pocket of his coat. He embraced the tree the woodpecker was hammering on. Scooting up the trunk inch by inch, he began to work his way up the pine. They were like a pair of lumberjacks.

"Not so easy as you thot at first," said the woo d-pecker.

"Yeah, but I got no claws to hang on with. This is hard work."

"Just tink of the time you's saving, treeclimber."

"Hanging on while you drill that hole is the hardest."

"Takes woik, I'll admit it, boss. But—dere's a i-ways rewards."

"I hope I donH fall,"

"Watch me. While I drill. I clamps my claws into the ridges of the bark. You try it." The woodcutter, some distance off the forest floor, seized the trunk by his fingers and gripped hard. "Good going. You got d'hang o f it."

"How much—farther—?"

"How many more nuts you got in yer pocket?" the woodpecker asked.

"Can't count them now. My hands are busy. What are you doing?"

"I'm scouting round the tree. Some good soft spots higher up. Lota dead junk right over yer head. Not much farter to go—say—eight feet."

"Eight feet! I'll fall."

"Preciate claws now, don't you?"

"Yes, yes, yes."

"Notice how d'tree trunk gets smaller'n smaller?"

Panting. "I think so,"

"It does. Take my woid for it. Dat should giv e youse real courage" Rattatatteytat. Rattattattateta. "The woodpecker went on drilling and the woodcutter popped acorns into the drilled holes with his teeth. He bumped them in snug with his shin. "You got d' real system dere, pal."

"Takes—system—organization," said the woodcutter.

"Dere's one ting wrong wit yer technique though," said the woodpecker. "You got courage—without d"convincing woids."

"No time for jabbering and yak."

"Hot them acorns wit yer whole poisonality—with d'chin. Smacko!"

"Like this?"

"Like dat."

The woodcutter, clinging to the sugar pine with all his might, arms and legs wrapped around the bark, looked down at the ground far below.

"Pay no attention to the distance, pal. On the job training. Yer catching on. A little harder. "Member, you got a whole forest to chop up and I'm yer pal. W e splits the deadwood."

"I'll—I'll—try to—remember."

"Den—nail it home—we'll get to yer job. The woodcutter slammed his chin into the tree—hard enough to make the acorn disappear but in doing so he knocked himself out, and he fell all the way to the ground, passing two or three large limbs on the way. He lay there below the tree, stretched out and as still as death.

"You know something, pal," said the woodpecker. He flew down and lit on the woodcutter's forehead. "I got to .preciate the woik you done for me. Keeping dead trees around ain't easy by a long shot. But popping a-corns into holes is the toughest part of logging. Dere" s no shortcuts, nitwit."

The woodpecker flew back up into the tree to finish his winter preparations.

On The Margin Of Time

I have a sense of gathering doom as I scratch this pictograph with my claws in the clay of the bog where I live. I will miss their wild screams of alarm and fear and triumph between bestial neighbors. I can still hear their wet snor tings, their clumsy, grunt ing, tromping crashes through the splintered forests.

We are all cast from the same iron mould, we giant creatures of prehistory. I possess a delicate, green head armored with scales and feathers, and a spiny back joi ne d to firestump legs. Finding forage for just a day is getting harder and harder. Many of the plants and shrubs and herbs and vines, especially the juice-filled trees, are dying. I weigh three tons, six thousand pounds, and almost half of that bulk I consume in foliage. The struggle for fodder keeps me thumping and crashing about. It rains less than it did eight hundred years ago and springs—many of them—have turned sour and muddy. A close friend of mine, J, Theodosius Cougar, lost his life the other day in what looked to him like a good watering hole. It turns out the stuff was tar | deadly, sucking tar. Imagine that—like coal turned to water!

What denizen of my forest has never heard that seri o-dosius, earsplitting, consternating screamthat shatters the echo of night in here? It comes not from Triceratops. It does not roar from the nostrils of Brontosaurus; no, I would scorch the earth if I shrieked like that; may the good earth receive my carcass. That horrid scream emanates not from that hawkbeaked bat with the silly putty face, Pterodactyl, that fans the air with his pointed wings. That scream is wierd, eerie. It echoes through t h e forest darkness. It is ghostly. Inquisitive, sniffing, blowing sticks and tree needles from the trail one day, I followed the sound, expecting to encounter a distant cousin. But I heard only myself. Strange—my scream pursues me like a trail of wildfire smoke. That's

313

because the world is slowing down and I catch up with my scream—sounds never die, prisoners of time.

But what has that got to do with survival? The slowdown of a spinning world means more heat—ice turning to water, rotting trees into sticky tar. The fact is, one day I slipped and fell into a tar pit, but pulled myself out just in time by snatching a tree limb in m y rocky teeth. Not every prehistoric hulk is so fated to survive. So much for the predicaments of myself, I ricerotops.

"One of these days that scream of yours is going to get you into deep trouble," warned D. D. Dinosaurus, Doctor of Dining. "It's too much like the real you."

"You got no cause to attack me," I said.

"Big racket you are."

"You're a glutton—primitive first cause of a dying forest. Look at billions of little treetops you've stripped. How long do you think the woods'll last with you fattening your useless tail on new growth?"

"Never you mind about my tail—just as long as you can scream for a prehistoric rating."

"You're a silly beast. Lookatcha! Head the size of a dust lizard and body size of a mountain.," I taunted,

"You listen to me, thistlehead. The forest is dying mostly because the world is slowing down, not b e-cause of my foraging habits."

"Alibi," I cried.

"Fangs. Ever see the co ugar's fangs? You'll die like me because there'll be just meateaters left. Besides, right now, you're in my territory."

"I'm not afraid of you one bit," I said. "I.m a Brontosaurus, and I can wiggle my dorsal bones like the spine of a fish."

"Hooplala and howdeedee, I'm a Dinosaur. See that little bush? Whhsssss! It's flat, stomping flat on the ground. Try that."

You give me a pain. Go chew on tree tops." With my angry words of insult in his ears, D.D. Dinosaurus slapped his treetrunk tail into the mud beside me.

"I mean business, relic. Get lost!" he screamed.

"Beating up a storm in a tar pit, that's all you do."

My pride was wounded. "Your tree domain will turn into a desert."

"Go scream into space!" roared D. D. He returned t o munching succulent big leaves.

I'd like to stomp on him. I could hear his thrashing and cracking about two miles away. Still I was worried a-bout food shortages. I like forest salad au <u>saurus</u> same as the next Brontosaurus. But—maybe I ought to call on The Iceman, find out what was causing the temperature changes if the world wasn't slowing down, and if it was maybe our big menagerie had made it lopsided, or the tangle of the tr e es and roots was scraping o n the skies at night. Anyway you looked at it my scream always caught up with me.

The Iceman lived in a retreating glacier miles aw a y. I.d just pack up there and we'd gnaw and chomp a while, find out about fanulities, the constabulations and fixities with their fluxalities. The meridial sujunctions were terri b ly important. Maybe they were in awful shape and the ea r th had a hidden strategy in store for all of us.

With much arduous labor over granular and microsm i e rocks of broken durasis, sharp and nee dly through my hide, around concastinating precipices of frightening obnexions, they were so high, I made the trip. Cold, mighty cold without fur—but I snuggled beneath my tough hide to keep myself warm.

Crack "crack—schlussss! I sounded with ray small head against the ice laminations. . No answer forth cane from the icy door to the glacial chamber. I turned about and whamsmacked the ice with my grotesquous tail, knocking off chunks and flakes from the pulverized ice wall.

"Whatkall the pounding about/" moaned The Iceman. H e was the Master Don of the ice cap.s ice cave—retreating from the forest. Igor Rant, woodsy dwellers used to call him or—today, the Master Don. That's Polarese for The. Real-God-of-the-Ice-Cap.

"Come inl Come ini" he boomed. "Don't just stan d out there in the cold." He threw some big boulders of ice aside. I stepped into his chamber and the blue and green crystal light blinded my eyes for a second. The ice glistened beneath the sun far above the ice. I blinked.

"Find a chunk of ice and sit," The Iceman invited, and I did it. "We don't stand on protocol—because this whole situation is in a slow melt. What bothers you, Brontosau-rus?"

"Rains've almost stopped. Forest is drying up. Weather is turning dry and hot. Bare spots like rubbing places on the tree bark are starting to show up in the forest. Frankly, I tin worried."

"Ahhhhooooo," laughed the Master Don and clacked his huge tusks together with great precision. "Have I got one for you! You see, the world's temperatures are shifting. I have to keep moving my stuff further and further north "Leaves a lot of rocks and lakes and junk behind, but there just isn.t any other way."

"I can't change my diet. Raw meat sets my teeth on edge."

"You vegetarians, you and your kind are going to have to draw tree shoots—see who stays around the longest."

"Top leaves of the trees are going first."

"That'll knock out old D. D. Dinosaur."

"There's still lots to eat for the noble carcass.Cougar and Flying Bat can handle that all right. Low branches shrubs'll die out last. That leaves you. You ever tried thick, juicy yams with your salad?"

"Wild pigs is another curse."

"Oh, I know, I know. Come with me, Brontosaurus, Let me show you something." He led me, slippery, icy, fee t skidding every step up a long inner passage and into an e-normous cave. I heard the steady dripping of water from many sources. The air of the room was chill and its walls cast off a silvery blue light. But I saw no source of the light; it shone from everywhere inside the ice cave. Huge icicles hung like tiger's fangs from the ceiling of this cavern. Our voices boomed, echoes rebounding from the ice walls, and faded into ripples of sound down the nearby corridors.

"My laboratory," said the Master Don. "And my bench."With his great ivories he pushed an immense slab of ice before my eyes while I stood shivering in the frigid air. He adjusted the ice lens, a flake of frozen water. "Cock your head and cast your eye down on that."

I did so, and a strange, new world arose from the brain of the creature below the ice. "That little animal carries the plan of the future in its head. Today it is big, bigger than me. In a light year or so its vision of destiny will shrink down to match its size, b e com e small and shrunken—matching its diet. Do you—can you even guess what your own fate is?"

"I will also shrivel down—to that—my destiny, too?"

"Keep your disgust to yourself. When I pass int o Icenervalia for all Master Dons—and scientists—I had forgotten. Humanoid shapes will speculate. I will be their entombed standard. Devolution, I call it."

"Scientists—humanoid? You are too far beyond roe.I simply want to know what will happen to the world—and what I ought to do. Isn't there any way to speed up the world, make it rain more—?"

"No way—the world .s off its axle—creaks a n d grinds. You hear that— sounds of dripping water? The scrunch and crunch—that's melting ice and the retrofit of the heavy ice walls." The same light as I first d e-tected glistened now even more brilliantly from all a-round me, like diamonds and emeralds that would put o ut my eyes. Master Don saw my wonder. "Pretty, is it not? But it won.t last."

"We are doomed then—me and my kind."

"Fraid so—unless you can beat the heat. Here. Let me show you how." He rapped with enormous tusks on a block of ice, and there flew out a bird from its hollow-tree tomb in the ice. As it shrieked and cawed the ice caked around it shattered and melted. "Waves of so u n d give off heat—but in doing so they dissolve the g 1 a-cier's freeze," Master Don told me.

"That was a batbird," I murmured. The Brontosau-rus for eons of time has murmured. Master Don was impatient. He clacked his tusks again on the glacial ice. A Musk Ox appeared from one of the corridors and sh o o k its frozen, hoary coat.

"Caught for all time in this—sanctuary," Master Don explained.

"You called for me, Mammoth One?"

"Dumb Ox—since that is your first and your only name. You got an assignment. Show Brontosaurus to the outer ice door. Then lead this fine animal and his kind to safety—to clear water and to wet climate."

"But I am too dumb to know such things."

"Come on now, Ox. You lasted all froze up in that huge slab of ice this long. Shake the wrinkles out o f your hide, comb your hair and go with Mister Brontosa u-rus here. You can come back."

"I got to show them how to survive?"

"Tha's the plan."

"What if I lose my way—or—or die from heat prostration in all this fur?"

"Take my gimlet-simulator. The trees that c o n-tain water are the trees that lead north. You also blaze the bark for your return."

"Like the sign of the moss—or the screech of the batbird?"

Master Don nodded his great head. "North side. Be careful. If you stick your proboscus into the wron g tree, it will die," he bellowed.

"Me or the tree?"

"Both. Now, Mister Brontosaurus, just follow him. He will lead you to climate that's more soothing to your thick hide—more mud slops sprouting tons of chewable green stuff."

"I got to have somebody to thank. After all the gift of a longer life like mine does not come free."

"It does if your believe in me, the Master Don."

"How can I not believe?"

"Some do." Master Don pushed me out the entrance to his ice caverns, and he brought down a roaring ava-lanche of snow. He cracked some huge blocks of ice t o cover the entrance—and he was gone.

"This way," said the Dumb Ox.

"I shall not call you "dumb. but—Musk."

We journeyed many days southward until once again, we arrived at my kind of environment. "Now you fol 1 ow me. We travel in a northeast direction—where the rain falls and the weather is steamy and not dry. I now bore into this tree—that tree." He did so. The gimlet-simulator Master Don had given him drew water from two trees.

I screamed aloud at the top of my voice. I heard screams of reply, then to my astonishment found a long string of ancient animals tromping behind me … How splendiferous! I screamed again.

The Musk Ox was boring his way with the gimlet-simulator as we crashed on ahead.

"Where are you taking us?" I shouted to the Ox.

"To se renity, peace, tranquility and—extinction or—as Master Don would say—a metamorphosis. Don" t know what it means but sounds big and icy and dangerous."

Oh, may the bowels of heaven suck down his blac k visage| I murmured aloud to myself. We were being led to our doom by a demon from the darkest regions.

"Pterodactyl! Fly ahead and see where we are going," I shrieked, my head uplifted into the skies. I slapped my tail and wiggled my dorsal bones. He winged his way leagues ahead and then returned.

"You are journeying into the inland seas, into the muck and the wasteland, the trapping ooze and the slime."

"Then we are lost," I said to Pterodactyl. To witless, to wisdom—mauwwww—you followed the false promise of survival. The giant bird cawed and screeched i n predatory hunger, soon vanishing in the rising groun d mists.

"The Master Don has given us a false helper. He has led us astray. I, Brontosaurus, have guided my k i nd wrong. The deception passes along down the line. The cord of the vine is never cut by the teeth or the claw. Its bronze can never be severed. I am tricked, as ar e the dwellers of the steaming rain forest. I had forgoten this sort of thing happens because the world is slowing down.

"We will all be lost. We will all be lost," I cried.

"Except me—with my gimlet-simulator and my directions from Master Don," said Musk Ox.

"Oh, help us to return to our forest," I begged him.

"You get what you wanted—change in your environment by what you call—'dominion.' You are your own dominion . Scream, thrash your tails, stomp hither and yon. Some of you this very instant are sinking into the boggy muck between the tundra and the soft floor of the ancient jungle. You are creatures of the meridian, of the margin, of the inexhausta-ble, impenetrable, unsupportable—and changing—marginal land of the earth. Suffer and die."

"So cruel! Glub. I cannot believe I could be misled by kind words, by helpful advice. I did not look into the inside of the Master Don. His ice cave was so magnificent, and it sparkled in the sun and its beauty blinded me."

"You will be found out," groaned the wild Ox.

"You are the screaming voice of trickery," D. D. Dinosaur taunted from the bleak, misty distance.

"You led us away from—survival," Tricerotops charged.

"I meant only good for all of you," I begged. But it was too late. I could see that. Glub, blub, glub.

"Perish for your arrogance," were the last words from the Musk Ox that I heard, and I sank down into a pit of smelly darkness.